Praise for Suchen Christine Lim's writing

Rice Bowl

… powerful writing … showing how history can be retrieved and changed to release creative energies

— Peter Nazareth, University of Iowa, USA

… a vital example of the beginning of [Singapore's] post-war fiction … important insight into a turbulent and yet often forgotten part of the history and culture of Southeast Asia

— Tamara S. Wagner, NTU, Singapore

Fistful of Colours

… difficult to put down once you start reading … the story of the forefathers of Singapore around the turn of the century, the ordinary people responsible for the shaping of Singapore

— *Tenggara, Journal of Southeast Asian Literature,*
Malaysia

…. from the contemporaneous to the past, Lim delineates the entanglements of ordinary lives with the historical and political life of their countries

— *World Literature Today,* USA

A Bit of Earth

… An astonishing tour de force … on issues of political import

— Peter Marroni, poet, Scotland

… a literary masterwork … it also has the virtue of being un-put-downable

— Wong Phui Nam, poet, Malaysia

The River's Song

… prose that's subtle, clear-eyed and lyrical, linking a city's rise with the emotional travails of its inhabitants. A fine, deeply felt saga of lives caught up in progress that's as heartbreaking as it is hopeful.

— *Kirkus Reviews,* USA

SUCHEN CHRISTINE LIM

DEAREST

INTIMATE

Marshall Cavendish
Editions

Supported by

NATIONAL ARTS COUNCIL
SINGAPORE

Published by Marshall Cavendish Editions
An imprint of Marshall Cavendish International

A member of the
Times Publishing Group

Other Marshall Cavendish Offices:
Marshall Cavendish Corporation, 800 Westchester Ave, Suite N-641, Rye Brook, NY
10573, USA • Marshall Cavendish International (Thailand) Co Ltd, 253 Asoke, 16th
Floor, Sukhumvit 21 Road, Klongtoey Nua, Wattana, Bangkok 10110, Thailand • Marshall
Cavendish (Malaysia) Sdn Bhd, Times Subang, Lot 46, Subang Hi-Tech Industrial Park,
Batu Tiga, 40000 Shah Alam, Selangor Darul Ehsan, Malaysia

Marshall Cavendish is a registered trademark of Times Publishing Limited

National Library Board, Singapore Cataloguing-in-Publication Data

Name(s): Lim, Suchen Christine.
Title: Dearest Intimate / Suchen Christine Lim.
Description: Singapore : Marshall Cavendish Editions, [2022]
Identifier(s): ISBN 978-981-5044-34-8 (paperback)
Subject(s): LCSH: Friendship--Fiction. | Grandparent and child--Fiction. | Marriage--Fiction.
Classification: DDC S823--dc23

Printed in Singapore

For

Lim Teck Yong

and

the Cantonese Opera fraternity
keeping the art alive in Singapore

ACKNOWLEDGEMENTS

A big thank you to the Writers Immersion and Cultural Exchange (WrICE), RMIT University for inviting me to the Vietnam residency in 2015. It was in the ancient Vietnamese city of Hoi An that the genesis of this novel came to me in a dream at 4 a.m. one dark morning. In my dream I saw a pair of mandarin ducks and two Chinese sentences embroidered on a cream-coloured pillow. I woke up and jotted down the words that became the first two sentences of this novel. And thank you to my readers, Shirley Soh, Melissa De Villiers and Meira Chand, for your insightful comments and encouragement, and to my editor, Lee Mei Lin, for your meticulous copyediting.

The Cantonese operas cited in the novel, *Madam White Snake, Butterfly's Shadow on Red Pear Blossom* by Hong Kong librettist Tong Dik-sang (1917–1959) and *Forty Years of Cherished Love* by China's librettist Chen Guanqing (1920–2003) have been re-imagined by the author based on performances she had watched. *Forty Years of Cherished Love* was last performed by Opera Works at the Gateway Theatre in Singapore in August 2019. Though the story incorporates these operas, and actual historical places and events, this is a work of fiction. Any resemblance to persons living or dead is entirely coincidental.

PART 1

Intimacy lets itself out and lets the other in.
It makes all love possible,
and yet it also reveals our utter incapacity
to love back as the other deserves.
– *Fr Richard Rohr, Franciscan friar*

Dearest Intimate,
Before I lay down my head upon the pillow with the pair of
mandarin ducks so lovingly embroidered by you, let my lips send
my spirit flying to you. Tonight I am writing down our night
thoughts and our heart's yearnings lest our eyes grow dim and
our hearts change, lest our memories fail us in our dotage.
Then, oh then, at least we have these few grains to feed our
starving souls.

Though hills and mountains, rivers and plains separate us,
nothing can separate our thoughts and dreams.
Though a thousand li separate our bodies, no mountains nor
rivers, not even the Four Mighty Oceans can separate our hearts.
If you were a damselfly, I would be a dragonfly.
If you were a water lily, I would be the willow
Bending down to caress your petals.
If you were snow, I would be ice, same yet different.
Till spring we melt and flow into the wide yellow Yangtze.

I couldn't believe these words were my grandmother's. Por Por wouldn't
have addressed my grandfather as a damselfly or water lily. A cripple and an
erhu musician, Grandfather was not an effeminate man. Por Por must have
copied the words from one of her opera scripts.

I imagined her as a young girl with hair braided in two plaits, writing
on a hushed cold winter night in her rural home in the village of Saam Hor,
far from the city of Canton. Her face innocent and unlined, her eyes dark
and earnest she bent over her desk in the flickering light of an oil lamp.
As she wrote shadows danced behind her following the movements of her
brush on the page.

The undated mottled pages were sewn together with a red string. Just
like the books we imported from China long ago. Several pages had come
loose and were stuffed in between the other pages. Vertical rows of Chinese
characters written with brushstrokes as fine as a sparrow's footprint covered
each page. The traditional Chinese script had complex brushstrokes like
those still used in Hong Kong and Taiwan. Quite unlike the simplified

script used in China today. What looked like two different characters to me was actually the same word. For example, take the character *loong* or dragon. With its complex curves and strokes, *loong* (龍) in the traditional script looked strong and majestic. The *loong* (龙) in its simplified script had lost its majestic vitality. It looked more like a serpent than a dragon to me. Schooled in English, I had difficulty reading Por Por's traditional Chinese script.

My heart is broken. My soul has fled.
The whole village knows you are betrothed to the goldsmith's son, and I to the pig farmer's son. How are we to live from now on? My tears are blinding me. I can't hold up my brush…

Oh blasted rain.
Lash me.
Whip me.
Slash me.
Kill me.
Drown me!
Why don't you gods kill me?
Why not let thunder and lightning strike me?
If you didn't want us to be together, why let our hearts come together?
The storm raged all night.

1

It was very late when the phone call came. Robert had been in one of his foul tempers. If he had ripped the phone line off the wall a minute earlier, I would have missed the call. I rushed to the Mount Alvernia Hospice praying that Por Por would hold on till I arrived.

When I reached the hospice, the nurses were trying to place an oxygen mask over her face. Coughing and sputtering, she pulled off the mask and struggled to speak. I put my ear close to her mouth. But Por Por's sunken eyes were staring straight past me at someone in the doorway. I turned to see who it was. No one was there. When I turned back to her, I thought I heard her cursing the person in the doorway. But the wretched hum of the air-conditioner was so loud I couldn't catch what she said. Her breath was growing more and more ragged. She started to thrash about the bed, flailing her arms. Alarmed, I called for the doctor. The shot he gave her gradually eased her pain, and after a while her thrashing ceased. Her white head sank into the white pillow and her eyes closed. I drew a chair up to her bed and sat next to her, holding her bony hand.

Her breathing was hard and irregular. Her loud, raspy breaths filled the room as the clock ticked. It was almost one by then. There was still no sign of Robert despite the messages I had sent. I told myself it was futile to expect him at this hour, but a part of me, insistent and stubborn, couldn't stop hoping that he would somehow pull himself together and come to the hospice.

I dozed off for a while. At about two, I woke up and wetted Por Por's parched lips, and wiped her hot dry face with a damp towel. Her skin, darkened by the cancer and drugs, felt like parchment. Holding her stick of a hand in mine, I heard a soft mewling cry coming from my throat. *Por Por! Por Por!* As though my cries could stop the inevitable. Then I dozed off again.

Sometime towards morning, I was startled awake by the thick silence in the room. The air had grown very cold and still, and the rasping had stopped. I put my arms around Por Por and rested my head on her chest. *Not yet. Not yet.* I was crying, no, I could not let her go yet.

A Malay nurse came in. Gently, she ushered me out of the room as other nurses arrived, and then the door closed. I waited in the deserted corridor pacing up and down till the same Malay nurse came out and handed me a bundle of pages tied with a red string. By then the grey dawn had started to drizzle, tiny silver drops falling and gathering into rivulets flowing down the windowpane. The lightness of the pages in my hands was adding to the weight of my loss as I stood in the corridor watching the rain.

I was the lone family member at her wake. The only one holding three joss sticks behind the two Taoist priests circling her coffin chanting prayers to guide her soul to the nether world. The wake was held on the ground floor of the apartment block in Jin Swee Estate where she had lived the better part of her life.

Robert was sulking in a corner. He had wanted the wake to be held in an air-conditioned funeral parlour instead of this void deck in an HDB estate with the coffin under a white tent. After the priests had left, I sat next to Por Por's casket surrounded by wreaths on wooden stands, and the white plastic tables and chairs set up by the undertaker.

Throughout the day neighbours and strangers came by to pay their respects to the former Cantonese opera actress and *xiu sung* singer, who had sung and acted as a man on stage. When night fell, a large group of elderly men and women arrived. I recognised some of them. They were the former actors and singers in my grandparents' Cantonese opera troupe. They glanced at Robert in the corner as they sat down at the white tables. Led by a spry silver-haired lady who introduced herself as Madam Mei Lai, they offered their condolences in beautifully enunciated Cantonese.

'May your grandmother's soul rest in peace in the Pear Garden in heaven,' Madam Mei Lai said in accented Hong Kong Cantonese. 'Your grandfather, Wah Jai, may he too rest in peace. He was the more fortunate of the two. You don't remember me, do you, Xiu Yin?'

Taken aback by her forthrightness, I shook my head. The other women chuckled. 'Don't you know her? Madam Mei Lai knew you when you were just a little mite.'

'She's the former *fah dan* in your grandparents' opera troupe, and sang with your Por Por,' one of the men said.

Elegant in her dark blue cheongsam, the opera diva suddenly looked frail as though mention of the past had overwhelmed her. Her dark eyes gazed at me.

'Aye...' she sighed. 'When your grandfather passed away the entire opera troupe and orchestra were at his wake to mourn his passing. We were there with your Por Por and you, and his great granddaughter. Where is his little great granddaughter tonight?'

The group looked across the hall at Robert again as though they hoped he might answer them. But Robert did not look up from his cell phone. I knew he was deliberately ignoring the elderly visitors. Punishing me, no doubt, for not following his instructions to hold the wake in a funeral parlour. Hiding my embarrassment, I turned to the visitors and smiled.

'My daughter Janice is no longer little. She's a young woman now studying in Vancouver, Canada. She's in the midst of her exams so I told her not to fly back. Por Por's spirit will understand. My grandfather if he were alive will understand.'

I sounded defensive.

'Quite true, quite true,' Madam Mei Lai soothed me. 'Kam Foong's spirit will understand.'

The others nodded. They glanced at Robert once again.

'That's your husband, isn't it? Did he perform the rituals with you?' one of the old men finally asked.

'No, no, Old Uncle. His family goes to church. He can't participate.' I smiled.

'Those three large wreaths sent by his family are beautiful,' a woman with a husky voice said.

I nodded and gave her a grateful smile for changing the subject. But my smiling was getting rather painful. I told myself to stop it. Besides, I could see the old folks were not fooled. They were just being polite.

'Such beautiful wreaths,' they murmured, and started to eat the dim sum I was serving them with cups of hot jasmine tea.

There were more than twenty wreaths placed near the casket, many of them from her fans. I looked across the tent to the three largest wreaths.

Ugly and ostentatious with large fronds of ferns and palm leaves with the green painted a bright silver, and the large expensive white lilies and white orchids stuck out like white clenched fists. Sent by Robert's parents and siblings, the three silver white wreaths dominated the smaller wreaths of chrysanthemums and roses sent by members of the opera troupe and Por Por's opera fans and students.

'The Palmerstons are not coming to the wake,' I told the group of elderly actors and singers who were like my relatives at this moment. 'If you remember, my in-laws also did not attend my grandfather's wake and funeral.'

'But your grandfather and Por Por would have gone to their wake if it's the other way round,' Madam Mei Lai huffed.

I took a sip of tea and decided not to tell them how I had tried to explain to Robert yesterday that attendance at my grandmother's wake wasn't praying to a different god. But he had growled.

Don't be a fool. It's a Taoist wake. Not an interfaith event.

My elderly visitors got up. We went before Por Por's casket and stood still for a few minutes as a huge wave of memories rose and engulfed us, the rumbling of drums, and cymbals barking commands like crockery shattering, and my young grandmother resplendent in her judge's robe, red silk shimmering, swept out to the stage. The audience shouted, *Marry her!* The young judge tore off his red robe and black hat. *My elder sister!* His sorrowful voice rang out singing the most painful aria of regret in opera, voice brimming against the theatre's ceiling, he cried out for the woman who was eighteen years older than him, the woman his parents had matched him with when he was still a babe, the wife who had brought him up after his parents had died but still, still he could not love her as his wife, so she had thrown herself into the raging river. *My wife!* he cried too late

'This was one of your Por Por's most memorable roles'. Madam Mei Lai rested her head on the casket and wept.

'It was their last performance together,' one of the women said. 'Poor dear. She's been crying since she received the news of your Por Por's passing.'

'Both of them were so close. Like a pair of chopsticks,' another woman said.

We waited for Madam Mei Lai to stop weeping.

'We should leave soon. It's very late. I'll go and get the car.'

One of the men went off.

'Mei Lai. Come, dear, we have to leave.'

The women had to pull her away from the casket several times before she would let go, still weeping on the arm of one of the women.

'There, there, it's a mercy. Kam Foong was in so much pain, it's a mercy she went quickly.'

'Take care of yourself, Xiu Yin. Come and see us sometimes especially Madam Mei Lai.'

'I will, old aunties and uncles. Thank you all for coming.'

After the group had left, Robert walked up to me.

'That was a very melodramatic scene. But I've got to go back to Sea Cove now. I need a good night's sleep. I've several meetings tomorrow.'

'Why didn't you take leave?'

'Now don't be impossible. If you had followed my instructions and booked a funeral parlour, we could lock up now and go home.'

'No. I can't leave my grandmother alone in a cold funeral parlour. How can I do this to her? I just can't.' My eyes started to well.

'For god's sake! Stop crying. You chose to stay up all night here. Fine! I didn't. I need my sleep. I've got to work tomorrow!'

The day after the funeral, I returned to the crematorium to collect Por Por's ashes. Robert did not come with me, and I didn't expect him to. Madam Mei Lai and the group of elderly men and women who came to the wake were already there, waiting for me, as though they were my elderly relatives.

'Thank you for coming, thank you.' A wave of gratitude washed over me.

'We can't let you pick your grandmother's bones alone.'

Madam Mei Lai went into the small room with me. The man inside bowed and handed us each a pair of rubber gloves. We put them on. Then the man went out and returned with a tray covered with a saffron satin cloth and the jade green jar I had selected earlier. With great reverence he placed the tray on the table in front of us, lifted the cloth, and withdrew.

A boat sailing in the calm and storm,
Blithely you came, blithely you left.
Till we meet again, my dearest, till we meet again.

Madam Mei Lai wept as she sang under her breath and picked up one of the pale grey bones and placed it into the green jar.

Tears welling, I said a silent farewell to my grandmother and gingerly picked a bone too. Was this what old people meant when they spoke of loving and hating someone to the bone?

That night I waited for Robert to fall asleep. Then I left the room and went to Janice's room. I sat down and began to read Por Por's journal with the help of an online dictionary.

2

1930 – the year of the Horse carried you away.

A disastrous spring did not stop you.

Saam Hor was devastated. Our village was not spared.

The storm blew down part of our roof. The pig farmer's son came over to help Father and Elder Brother re-thatch it.

'The boy did a good job,' Father said later. 'He will make a good husband for you, Kam Foong.'

Nah! I didn't even bother to waste a single glance on him. Did you look at the goldsmith's son? Did you steal a look at him? My heart is shrivelled up tonight as I write. Steeped in vinegar and jealousy when I think of you betrothed to him. I was so grateful to Heaven for the flood. There would be no wedding, I thought. The flood had ruined every family in the county. Let there be more floods! More rain! More storms! Flood the village! Drown the pigs! Let there be no wedding!

☙ — ❧

My prayers were not heard. The flood did not stop your betrothal to the goldsmith's son. Your parents were so happy when they sent over those hideous pink, green and yellow marrying-off-our-daughter cakes to my parents.

How could I eat them? How could I? Those cakes were like daggers glinting pink and green on the bamboo tray. Yet I swallowed one for your sake. It sliced my throat. My heart bled. How can I go on living now? How am I to live when you are gone from our village? Yet I wore a brave sisterly smile and shed a few sisterly tears like all the other village girls during your hair combing ceremony. I smiled when all I wanted was to throw myself into the village well. I walked to the river last night but someone followed me. I don't know who it was. Bitter tears had blinded me. She brought me home and put me to bed and told everyone I had caught a cold. Did you send that girl?

℘ — ℭ

One month and twenty-nine days since your wedding.

A cold wind had blown through my hollow heart on your wedding day. On the morning you left our village, I hid in the bamboo grove and watched your red sedan swaying past on the shoulders of the men, heaving and shouting. The band was playing the Good Fortune Bride Song. My eyes followed your wedding procession till it disappeared over the hills.

When will we see each other again? Aged fourteen, you are already a bride. Soon I will be one too. How long do we have to wait before we see each other? When can you come home to visit your parents? What are you doing in your new home now? Do they treat you well? I see your face in every lotus. I hear your voice in the bamboo grove and babbling brook. Each morning, I take the longer route home through the bamboo grove just to pass by your parents' house. To breathe in the air you left behind. Last night I dreamt of lotus buds again. As I bent down to kiss them, the early morning mist wrapped its veil around us. Deep inside the bamboo grove we lay on the patchwork quilt you had brought to the river to wash. How fragrant was your hair, how sweet your face in the morning light. I knew it was a dream. I didn't want to wake up.

℘ — ℭ

Two months since I last wrote. Already it feels like a year has passed. Betrothed at fourteen, married at fifteen, I am already a woman. As a daughter-in-law my duty is to obey my mother-in-law and do things her way. There is no other way. Only her way. Do the laundry her way. Wash the rice grains and cook the rice her way. Brew and serve tea her way. Everything her way except in the toilet when it is my way. Ha ha ha! It makes me want to run home. Some days I pray that she will die soon. When will you visit our village to see your parents? Every night I wear the gold hairpin you sent me hidden in the box of threads that Uncle Oxcart brought last month. The tiny scoop gleams like a little gold dot in my hair. I plan to use it if the pig farmer's son comes near me on Mid-Autumn night. May he be too drunk on that night! Let this night remain ours. Heaven, please grant my wish. It was on Mid-Autumn night that I gave you my heart, and you gave me yours. This night will never change, you said. This is our memory. Our history. Like that heroine in the opera that came to our village, you said I am yours, and you are mine. Do you remember how the actress taught us to sing? Aye, ages ago when we were carefree girls and the best singers in our village. The troupe master even offered to take us with them and train us. But our mothers, aye, our mothers said we were already betrothed. Both of us should have run away with the opera troupe.

℘ — ℭ

Rain. Lashing rain. Heartless rain.
Wash me. Cleanse me.
His pig's stench clings to my flesh.
Last night I had to give in to him.
How he smelt of pork and pigs.
I had to close my eyes and think of you.
Why have you not sent me anything?
A single word from your writing brush will revive this shrivelled heart.

℘ — ℭ

The willows have shed their leaves. Soon winter will be upon us. The days are turning dry as bones. The pigs are growing thin. There is no rain and no word from you. Have you forsaken me? Have you grown heartless?

The winter solstice came and went. Though we ate sweet *tang yuen*, the little pink dumplings brought no joy. Two of the family's pigs died yesterday. The pig farmer's son and his father cried. My mother-in-law wailed, but my eyes were dry. My heart is parched as the land. There will be drought this coming summer, the fortune-teller said. May Heaven have mercy on us!

℘ — ℭ

It is the season of flying sleet, the season of howling winds
and muffled crying under the thatch.
Muffled voices, and muffled hunger in the village.
The winter of icy winds, head lice and thin rice gruel is upon us.
I have to write sparingly, secretly.
Soon I will have no more coins to buy paper and ink.

3

Dearest Intimate,

I cried when I read your letter. I am writing you a reply straightaway. I thank the gods, it's spring. I can bribe Uncle Oxcart to take a fan with my reply tucked between its folds to you. Please do not leave the goldsmith's son. What you intend to do speaks so deeply of what is in your heart that I can only shed futile tears. But no! You cannot leave your husband. You must not. You should not leave him. I cannot accept your sacrifice. This ill-fated worm here does not have the *fook* or good fortune to receive your sacrifice. The thought that you are well provided as the wife of the goldsmith's son is my only comfort in this mud pit of squealing pigs. I am the wife of the pig farmer's son in the village. You are the wife of the goldsmith's son in town. So Heaven has decreed.

ᔒ — ᘓ

Oh Dearest Intimate, what is this I hear? Is it fire or is it smoke? Barely a month has passed since you tried to run away, and now there is more bad news. The villagers said you tried to run away. Tried to run back to our village again. At first I was elated. Then I was afraid. I fell on my knees and prayed. I begged Goddess of Mercy to protect you. Your husband's family will beat you. They will hammer you. Even kill you. You have made them lose face. I fell on my knees in the pigsty and begged Lord Buddha to keep you safe. I will find an excuse to visit you. Uncle Oxcart said the family has locked you in the woodshed. I pray they are not starving you. Oh my Dearest Intimate!

ᔒ — ᘓ

I have taken in some extra sewing. I am also washing clothes for Old Madam Chan's family. I am saving the money I earn. Once I have saved enough to pay for a ride on the ox cart, I will visit you. Patience. Patience. Sew and save, I tell myself. Mother-in-law is pleased. She thinks I am sewing clothes for the family. The lychee tree we planted is fruiting. I will bring you some lychees. No, I will bring your mother-in-law some lychees to sweeten her foul mouth. Patience. I pray for patience every day.

℘ — ℭ

This is what I remember of my visit.

A bowl of thin rice gruel seasoned with tears you served me. Sallow as a reed in late summer, your eyes were bright with longing.

When you opened your mouth to speak, your mother-in-law's shadow fell between your lips. Her hawk's eyes trained on you.

You swallowed your words and bowed your head.

But your eyes had said what your mouth could not.

I bowed to your mother-in-law and sat beside her.

I drank up the bowl of thin rice gruel you served me and took my leave.

Do not despair, my heart. We saw each other.

Think of the song our mothers used to sing while washing clothes in the river.

...*Living a thousand li apart,*

still gazing upon the same moon...

We were splashing water as our mothers sang. We didn't understand the words then. We were so happy, you and I, listening to your mother and mine singing.

The opera troupe came to the village again that year, and we sang with them. It would be heaven if only we did not have to marry, we said. Laughing our mothers sang: *Foxes have lairs; birds have nests. Women must have families.*

℘ — ℭ

The season has changed.

At the river, flowers bloom; grass sings.

But having no one to enjoy them with, I sing alone.

Up in the hills alone, I sing the songs we used to sing.
May the summer winds bring you the songs I sing!

Yesterday I was at the river earlier than usual. No one was there. Your shadow and mine were humming a song in the soft grey mist. On the water a pair of mandarin ducks swam on the jade green sky. Swimming together day after day, who would think of sorrow if one were a mandarin duck? But not being one, I miss you, my sister, my friend, my love. As long as mountains rise and rivers flow, as long as sun and moon shine and wane in the sky, may fidelity live on in our soul. I try, I try my utmost to live in the family I married into.

℘ — ℭ

You must have heard misfortune has struck our village. Not once but twice. That is why I have not written.

Spring fever killed most of our pigs in the village. Then bandits came and took the rest. My mother-in-law cursed my dried-up womb. Blamed me for bringing misfortune into the family. The pig farmer's son tried but he could not protect me from his mother's blows. In anger he left to look for work in the city.

The next day, his mother sold my labour to the farmer next door. Now I hoe the earth with the men. Chop wood and cart water from the river to the fields like the men. At noon I rest under a tree and tell my sorrows to the sky. At night I look at the moon and write in the chicken shed where I hide my papers and ink.

Last night I thought of what our mothers told us when we were little girls. On the day of the Mid-Autumn Festival, they took us to the temple and tied a red string on each of our wrists. They told us we were closer than sisters. They had betrothed us to each other when we were in their womb. If I had been born a boy, you would have been my wife. But I was born a girl. So they told us we are closer than sisters. We have to take care of each other, learn to eat the sweet with the bitter, the salty with the sour. But they forgot to tell us that sometimes, aye, sometimes we have to eat the chaff and grit when the harvest is poor. There has been no rain for weeks. Our well has dried up. My mother-in-law curses my barren womb and beat me every day.

Will the rains never come?

I hope the goldsmith shop is doing well and you have rice to eat.

℘ — ℭ

I am tired. Dead tired.

I carted rocks all day.

The men are digging wells.

I am running out of paper. But I need to write to you. When I write to you, I feel you are near. Your presence though imagined helps me to get through the days. I have a dear friend to talk to and address my thoughts to. How else do I live?

℘ — ℭ

Dearest Intimate, what is happening to you? I heard you tried to run away again. I heard what happened to your hair. Then I heard how you hid in the bamboo grove. But the men in your husband's village found you and dragged you home. Our village head told us your mother-in-law, that old bitch, had ordered your husband to cut off your hair, shave off your lovely long strands and whip you while she watched. All his brothers and their wives were ordered to watch too. What humiliation for you and for him. What terrible shame! What hurt! What pain! We heard your husband wept as he whipped you. He must be a good man. And an obedient son!

Oh core of my heart! Why did you do it? Why did you run away? I know I shouldn't ask. Don't I know your heart? Your heart is my heart. I would have done the same if I were in your place. But I fear for you. Third Aunt said that your husband is the fifth son. He is not his parents' favourite son. And you are not the favoured daughter-in-law. Please, oh please, I pray that Goddess of Mercy protects you.

℘ — ℭ

No news today. No news from Third Aunt. I dare not ask anyone. Your relatives and neighbours are wondering what draws you home. What made you run away from a family that gave you a gold bangle for your wrist? They questioned your parents. Asked if there was a man in your heart before you married the goldsmith's son. Your family is worried. Your mother is so ill with fear and worry, she has taken to her bed. Neighbours say your mother is ill with shame. Your father has grown silent as a rock. Dearest, I fear for your safety if you were to return. The village elders are unforgiving. Our village laws are strict.

℘ — ℞

Cruel! Cruel! Cruel! How could the old bitch punish you like this? Was it not enough that your hair was cut? Not enough that you were whipped and locked up? Yet when your mother was ill, your mother-in-law would not let you come home to care for her. And now that your mother has passed on, you cannot even come back for her funeral? It is too cruel. Too severe a punishment! A scandal! A shame! Unheard of! Everyone in our village is on your side now. All our village sisters are grieving for your mother and you. Beneath my outer garment, I am wearing white and a piece of hemp cloth to mourn your mother for you.

Three kowtows and three libations to the gods.

I pour three cups of rice wine into the earth on your behalf. May Heaven have pity on you and protect you from that old witch. Your mother-in-law is more unreasonable than mine. I have to slog in the sun with the buffaloes and men. But you, you are left to wither in the log shed.

℘ — ℞

Oh thank the gods! At last! At last! After months of silence some news of you at last! News that stabs me in the heart! Tell me it's not true! You are not leaving us. You are coming home to bid us farewell, the elders say. Third Uncle said that the goldsmith's son had pleaded with his mother to let you return one last time to our village before he takes you to the Nanyang. The elders are pleased that you are leaving with your husband for a new land, pleased that you are leaving your vicious mother-in-law. Yet how can I bear it? How can I bear to see him take you so far across the South China Sea? You are leaving our homeland. We will never see each other again. We will never meet again. I cannot bear to think of it. Are we never to meet again in this life? O Heaven, I beg you. O Gracious Heavenly Majesty, Almighty Jade Emperor of Heaven and Earth, show us some pity!

℘ — ℃

Yesterday I went to the temple to make an offering. I prayed for you to remain forever bald. Yes, forever bald. May your hair never grow long again! May the goldsmith's son on seeing how bald and ugly you are, not take you with him. He will leave you here, and you will have to stay behind with that wretched witch mother-in-law of yours. Then we will be able to see each other at least twice a year. First, when you come back to greet your father on the second day of the New Year. Second, when I visit Third Aunt who lives next door to your in-laws. Twice a year was not enough before this terrible news, but now, even twice a year is a fading dream. You are leaving China. We will never see each other again in this life. These eyes of mine will never behold my Dearest Intimate again. The thought is unbearable.

℘ — ℃

Forty-nine days.

Forty-nine days after your mother's passing at the end of your family's deep mourning, you came home. Your head was covered with a blue scarf. Your eyes were bright with unshed tears. Inside your parent's house, you tore off your scarf and stood before your mother's memorial tablet on the altar. Your once beautiful long hair stood up like tufts of grass and weeds. And your eyes, your tear-filled eyes, were glinting like the sword of Hua Mulan, hard and brilliant as steel. You knelt in front of your mother's altar and sang a daughter's farewell song. Keening your pain, the cadence of your voice rose and fell. Grief choked, your voice started to falter. All the village sisters who grew up with you started to keen to give strength to your grief-drained voice.

Oh, how we sang our sorrow. We knew it was the last song we would sing together with you.

I stood stiffly, pressing my hands tight against my side to prevent them from reaching out to you. I was yearning to hold your hand. Then I caught your glance, and it fell on me like a raindrop refreshing a withered plant. Our eyes, brimming with tears, met above the heads of our seated elders. Boldly you walked over to stand beside me. Our long sleeves touching hid our hands. I felt your icy cold fingers press something hard into my palm. You squeezed my trembling hand so hard I had to bite my lips. We uttered no words. We shed no tears. And thus we parted.

I watched you walk away with the goldsmith's son as we, your village sisters, who had grown up with you, washed clothes in the river with you, cooked and sewed with you, sang you our farewell song. You turned back once to look at us. Then you looked at me. And bowed low.

You knelt on the soft earth and made a deep heartfelt kowtow to your father, and another to the village elders. Your stern father's sun-browned face cracked like the dried earth. Tears watered his proud and sorrowful smile. The whole village was happy for you. How very blessed, the old aunts said. Her husband takes her with him to the Nanyang. He does not leave her behind like other husbands. So fortunate, the sisters sighed, their hearts missing the husbands who had left them and sailed overseas.

When I could no longer see your tiny figure on the dusty road, I slipped away. Inside the darkness of the outhouse, I opened my fist. Unwrapped the bit of paper in my palm. I could not believe my eyes. In my hand was your golden token of love. I hid the gold ring in the folds of my samfoo jacket and read the eight words you wrote on the bit of paper.

Eight words in your feathery brushstroke.

Eight words to sustain me in the lonely days ahead.

Eight words. I screwed up the paper and threw it into the dung hole.

4

My wedding anniversary came and went. I let it pass. I sat at the small table in the balcony trying to decipher Por Por's bird-like brush strokes with the help of the online Chinese-English dictionary.

'Yin!'

'Here.'

'Hiding in the balcony again? What the heck are you reading?' Robert yelled from the living room where he was watching a football match on the telly.

'A paper I've to read before my meeting at the National Archives tomorrow.'

'Finish it quickly and come in.'

'I will.'

My voice sounded cheerful but I looked out at the sea with a heavy heart. The night was very warm. I would have preferred to read in the study or Janice's room with the air-conditioner on. But Robert always wanted me to sit where he could see me, and it was best not to argue. He could be very sweet if I simply obeyed him, and often I did. No point in arguing over little things like where one should sit, was there? Yet a small part of my mind disagreed. For years a keen sense of resentment and injustice had niggled me as if some undeserved damage had been inflicted on my sense of self and freedom. A petty hurt as inconsequential as a mosquito bite that had grown larger and more intense over the years till here, I was pressed by this huge resentment that had been sitting on me hard as a rock.

I gave the pot of bamboo a kick and looked up at the dark sky. The few stars above the ships beyond the lagoon were feeble and faint. From fifteen storeys up here I looked down at the expressway. Aggressive streaks of red and orange from the taillights of traffic were whizzing past Sea Cove towards the city.

When we first moved out here to the east coast there was hardly any traffic on the newly built expressway. No hawker centres, car parks,

tennis courts, or skating rink, or MacDonald's along the beach. The East
Coast beach was just a vast expanse of white sand, wild grasses and rows
upon rows of swaying casuarina trees. And Sea Cove was a quiet little
condominium built on reclaimed land, its apartments sold to civil servants
at a low price. Not many people had wanted to live on reclaimed land for
fear the apartment blocks might sink over the years. Jokes about flooding
and fishing from one's window were bandied around. But the apartments
were spacious, and a young couple expecting a baby needed space. Janice
and her school friends had loved the beach but now that she had grown and
left us to carve out a new life for herself in Canada, the apartment felt large
and empty. Every December when the sea winds howled through gaps in
the creaky windows at night, it could be cold and lonely.

I glanced into the living room. Robert was still engrossed with his
football match, a drink in his hand as was his habit. His eyes were glued
to the screen. I studied his ruddy profile. More than twenty years with this
man, I thought. How did I get through them? And there are more years to
come. With the advance of medicine, we could both live possibly up to a
hundred. A dreadful thought, and my spirits sank. For better or for worse.
More than twenty years of my life. How could I just get up and walk away?
I had stopped counting the years I had stopped loving. When we were
young it was easy enough to plunge into love's fire. Easy to fall passionately
and deeply in love. And then live together thereafter blind to the slow dying
glow of love's embers till one morning we awoke on a bed of cold grey ash.

My sweet, sweet darling, he had whispered in crowded Trafalgar Square
on the night of our honeymoon. An arm around my waist, his fingers
sending thrills down my spine, he'd whispered, 'If ever we're separated by
war, darling, if ever Southeast Asian nations fall like dominoes, promise me,
promise you'll make your way back here. London will be safe. No matter
what happens I'll come here to look for you unless… unless I'm dead.'

'*Choy! Choy! Choy!* Don't say such inauspicious words.'

'Honey, I didn't know you're so superstitious,' he had laughed and
kissed me.

He was in the Ministry of Defence working on some secret project
for our vulnerable island nation. Anything could happen, he said. No! I
wrapped my arms around his handsome muscular frame clinging to him

as though war was imminent that very minute, the solidity of our intimacy was threatened that very instant and our lives would evaporate. I sobbed. How deeply, how intensely, how permanently I felt our love to be then. How passionate his kisses that night. How oblivious we were of the jostling, pushing crowd. And the roar of the red double-deckers trundling past us that beautiful summer night. I thought we were the first couple to kiss in Trafalgar Square. How very naïve, vulgar and clichéd that memory seemed to me now. It pained me to think of it.

I heard the click of the telly.

Then the *flap-flap-flap* of his slippers going from the living room to the kitchen. I heard the opening of the fridge door. The sound of the icebox and the clink of ice cubes against glass. Then a pause. The brief silence as he inhaled what he called his '*whisky's bouquet of fragrances*'.

He had never tried to hide his drinking from me. *No reason to. I'm not a pathetic drunk.*

I stuffed the pages of Por Por's journal into my office bag when he padded out to the balcony, a drink in his hand.

'Look at those ships out there tonight. It'll be a good year for us. The more ships, the better the economy. The better the economy, the bigger the bonus for us, the government's eyes and brains. It's a no-brainer, isn't it? I tell you no other country pays its civil servants as well as Singapore. Not even the US.' Chortling, he raised his glass to the ships and finished his drink in two gulps. Then stuck the glass into one of my flowerpots and patted my bottom.

'To bed with you now! Go, go!'

I wasn't ready to go to bed but immediate compliance was the only way to ensure me a peaceful night.

In the bedroom I put away Por Por's papers and changed. Then I got into bed and switched off the lights.

Minutes later, I heard him fumbling with the doorknob of the bathroom muttering as he groped his way to the toilet.

'Shit!'

He had kicked his toe against the closet under the sink again. The bathroom light came on. The door was left ajar. A habit of happier times. We used to leave the door open when we showered or sat on the bowl.

There was so much to share, so much to tell each other, our talk flowing like water while we soaped each other under the shower then. Through the gap of light, I saw him fumbling with his trousers' zip. Heard the hiss of his pee hitting the side of the toilet bowl, then sounds of the flush. The tap was turned on full as he washed his hands, gargled with water and brushed his teeth. Then the lights were switched off. And near the bed the swish of fabric as he pulled off his shirt and dropped his pants. A creak of the mattress as he sat down on his side of the bed and pulled off his brief. Eyes shut, I held my breath. Another creak as he turned around and then he was on top of me. Our bed shook and squeaked. When the shaking and squeaking finally stopped, he rolled off and fell asleep.

I got out of bed. Went into the bathroom and washed myself. When I came out, he was snoring. I took my office bag with Por Por's journal in it and opened the door. I went into Janice's room and turned the lock.

5

Cold grey days.

No bird sings.

Water drips from the eaves.

At the river I saw your shadow. I see you everywhere. Your face is smiling in the bamboo grove. At night your shadow drifts beneath the pale moon.

Are you still at sea? Have you reached the Nanyang yet?

Daily I pray to Mazu, Goddess of the Sea.

I beg Lady Mazu to send the Heavenly Guardians, Thousand Li Eye and Smooth Wind Ear to keep your ship safe from storms and lightning. Safe from giant waves. Safe from the anger of the Dragon King.

ଽୠ — ଓଃ

My day to day living in the house.

I cook. Eat. Wash. Iron. Sew.

In the field. I hoe. Dig. Rake. Plant.

This is how I live my days.

Feet sunk deep in mud, I plough the earth, and plant the rice seedlings.

Feed the pigs. Wash the pigsty.

Feed the chickens and ducks. Collect their eggs.

Plant the vegetables. Harvest the vegetables.

Cook the meals. Eat the meals.

Wash everyone's clothes at dawn's light.

Mend everyone's clothes by candlelight.

Yet work cannot fill the hollowness of my days.

If I do not write I will grow mad.

ଽୠ — ଓଃ

This morning I stood in the rain-soaked bamboo grove in the spot where we used to wait for each other. I closed my eyes and whispered aloud the eight words you pressed into my hand. Eight words that lifted the heavy grey log pressing my heart.

℘ — ℂℛ

Twenty-one days have gone past. New Year is here. There is still no news of you. How I detest the sound of firecrackers. I run to the hills and call out your name. Alone I sing the songs we used to sing in these hills. Not a single echo of your voice answered me.

℘ — ℂℛ

Two weeks after New Year, the spring rains arrived dripping from the eaves. Inside the house, we cook, eat, wash, iron and sew. I feed the pigs. Wash the sty. I am back to my life among the pigs. At night the winds rattle the bamboo rafters threatening to snuff out the oil lamps in the house. There are days and nights of torrential blinding rain. I run out into the storm. The rains wash away my tears and pelt my face. The river is rising high. The fields are already flooded. Soon the houses will be flooded. And still I wait for news of you.

℘ — ℂℛ

At last Heaven takes mercy on us. The sun has come out. The floods have receded. Last night the pig farmer's son returned from the city. He brought some joy to his parents when he gave them the money he had earned. Then as he sat down to dinner, he told us about a new China that is rising in the cities. A great man called Dr Sun Yat-sen will build a new China, he said. And he spoke about the youth he had met in the city. The girls are going to school like the boys to read and write, he said.

Chieh! Those girls have no shame, his mother scoffed. The idea of young girls leaving home to sit with young men in school! Unheard of! It's unacceptable!

His father, brother and sister shook their heads. The youth in the city are turning wild, his brother and sister laughed.

When he came to bed that night, I kicked him when he tried to touch me. But in the end, oh my heart, in the end, in the darkness of night I gave in. I had to do a wife's duty. Now no rain will ever wash away his stench in me.

∽ — ∾

Spring rain, where have you gone? Trees, when did you change?
Seated by the riverbank I sing our mothers' song.
Rivers flow downhill to the sea, the sea.
Water never flows up to the hills, the hills.
Daughters will marry and leave the family.
Sons will marry and bring a daughter into the family.
This has always been. This will always be.

I folded a paper boat and let it float down the river. May it flow down the hills and out to the sea. I am here in Saam Hor, and you are out there over the sea and far away, in the land they call the Nanyang or South Seas.

∽ — ∾

Dearest Intimate,
I turned fifteen last month but I was too sad to write. What is there to write? Village life is always the same. Seasons come and seasons go. In summer the sun shines down on the rice plants and lychee trees. My mouth is parched, and my prayers sound hollow. But I continue to pray for you and the goldsmith's son. I pray that both of you will reach land safely!

Merciful Mazu, Goddess of the Sea, let no storm toss their ship. Let them step ashore soon.

On a red string I wear your gold ring next to my heart under my inner garment. Each night I think of the eight words you wrote on that piece of paper, and wonder how I could do what you ask. I have to find a way. Heaven, help me.

ℰ—ℭ

Summer has slipped away with the autumn winds. The rice harvest is over. The pigs have grown plump. The sows have new piglets. Last night my mother-in-law suddenly said there is a law in our village. If a wife is barren for five years, the husband can take a second wife.

It's not five years yet, Mother, the pig farmer's son replied.

Surprised, my father-in-law lit his pipe and looked at his son. No man in the village had said no to taking a second wife before. That night the pig farmer's son came to me, urgent and needy. In the dark, we did our fervent duty.

ℰ—ℭ

I am still barren.
Goddess of Mercy, change me into a bird.
Let me fly to her in the Nanyang.
I am running out of ink.

6

The next night I made sure Robert was in deep slumber before I slipped out of bed and went into Janice's room again. When the door lock clicked, I stood and waited till the distant hum of traffic on the expressway grew reassuring. Then I sat down at Janice's desk and switched on her computer. Accessed the online Chinese-English dictionary again and took out Por Por's journal from the drawer.

Eagerly I flipped through the pages, to get some idea of what this journal was about. The more I read into the night the more amazed I grew. My hands shook. I looked out of the window at the slice of moon above the ships at sea, Por Por's journal lying on my lap, my thoughts going back to the years of my childhood, growing up with grandparents who hardly spoke with each other.

I missed them. Their absence left a dark cavern in my heart. Do not cling Buddha taught, but how not to cling to those who had loved us since our birth? How could I read Por Por's journal and not be moved by the courageous young girl in those pages? As grandchildren we never think of our grandparents as young men and women once upon a time. What lay on my lap was a young woman's private journal about a way of life and time in rural China, and later in wartime Singapore. A rare document. Few women of my grandmother's generation who immigrated to Southeast Asia in the early 1900s had left traces of themselves in written records. Thousands of women came to the Nanyang in their youth because of war, natural disaster or poverty in China, none of them were literate like Por Por who came to the Nanyang because of love.

Young, strong, good looking or plain, thousands of these Chinese women had worked in tin mines, gold mines, construction sites, vegetable farms, and pleasure houses in Singapore and elsewhere. Unable to read and write, upon their death, they might leave an anecdote or two, a hand-sewn quilt or a few faded photographs for their children who might pass them to their children or grandchildren. But these objects kept in an old rusty tin or battered suitcase would soon be lost or forgotten. And the great grandchildren were more likely to know and remember what their great grandfathers had done. Rarely what their great grandmothers had accomplished, except perhaps for a recipe or two for a soup or rice dumpling passed by word of mouth from daughter to granddaughter.

Yet not all our great grandparents' stories were simple immigrant narratives of from rags to riches, the common theme of the great grandfathers' stories found in our history books and biographies. The more uncommon tales of our grandmothers and great grandmothers were always left untold. Stories of love unexpressed and inexpressible, of love stunted or twisted, or love beaten, slapped and kicked into hate. Or a love so deep, it was etched in the hard lines on the faces of the women who sat with their old men on the benches on the ground floors of HDB blocks, and in the hawkers' centres, old people who spoke a language of silence or a dialect that few of the younger generation could understand these days.

I realised the tattered pages I was holding in my hand were very precious not only to me but also to Singapore. My grandmother's journal was a cultural treasure.

7

Dearest Intimate,

I have reached the Nanyang. What a strange country! Other than my clansmen I don't understand what other people are saying. They speak such strange tongues. This island called Sing-ga-pore is full of gwai lo. Some look so pale; others are dark and brown. I understand not a word they say. Scared and confused, I huddle close to the man who brought me here.

Ten thousand li I had sailed to find you. Eight words on a piece of rice paper you had pressed into my hand. '*Sell ring. Buy passage. Come to Nan Yang*' you wrote.

Those eight words had sent me hurtling, tossing, vomiting and aching on the vast South China Sea till I reached this strange island of 'Sing-ga-pore'.

The man brought me to this clan house. He told me to stay here and wait for him to return. I dare not leave the clan house on my own. It took me a long time before I could obtain some paper. Luckily I had brought my brush and ink stone. Paper, brush and ink are my only consolations now. What else can console me on this strange island of a thousand tongues? Foreign devils speaking strange tongues are everywhere.

When I asked the old man in charge of the clan house how big is the Nanyang, he laughed, put down his pipe, and looked at me. 'Young lad, the Nanyang or South Seas is bigger than a thousand villages. The area stretches from the country of the Siamese and Burmese in the north to Singapore here in the south, and west to Sumatra and Java, and east to Borneo Island and many thousands of islands that I haven't even heard about.'

I thanked him and turned away. I didn't want him to see the desperate tears in my eyes. I did not know the Nanyang is so huge. You too must have thought the Nanyang was like your town when you handed me the piece of rice paper with the eight words. But this foreign land is so huge. How am I going to find you? Oh, I am a fool. Goddess of Mercy, please do not forsake me. Help me to find her. The only one who can help me is the one who brought me.

ℰ — ℛ

I am still staying in the clan house waiting for the man to return. The days float slowly away like leaves under the bridge while I wait. And wait, trying hard not to cry each day. I have floated ten thousand li away from the green fields we once ploughed, ten thousand li from the green hills we once climbed. Far from the river where we once washed our clothes, far from the home I grew up in, far from the house I married into. I have left them all behind because you had asked me to come to the Nanyang.

I am here! I am here! But where are you?

Day and night I search the faces of strangers on the streets. Three months have gone past. I am three months older. Three months more wretched. Three months more desperate.

Three months ago I had followed the man who brought your father the news of your safe arrival in Sing-ga-pore. To him I foolishly gave the gold ring you gave me. I asked him to take my brother to Sing-ga-pore to look for you.

The next night, I stole out of the house and followed the man out of our village. I had cut off my long hair and dressed in a man's loose jacket and pants. With my flat chest, big feet and height no one suspected I am a woman. We travelled all night and day by cart and riverboat to Hong Kong where we boarded a large ship. Countless days of wind and rain followed. The ship was tossed like a leaf on the ocean. Below deck, the floor was slippery with the vomit of sick passengers. The stench was worse than an unwashed pigsty. I cannot remember how long we were cooped up in that dark foul hold before we were allowed to come up to bright sunlight. We were told the ship had reached land. But this land had turned out to be a land of lost hopes. I have been waiting in this clan house for the man to bring me news of you. Where are you, oh dearest? Where are you?

ℰ — ℛ

Scoundrel! Villain with the heart of a wolf! Blackguard with the lungs of a dog! I wanted to kill him! He had lied to me! He doesn't know where you live. After weeks of waiting and searching, he has returned without you.

'Your sister is not in Singapore,' he grinned. 'She has moved with her husband up north. Most likely to the island of Penang. I am taking my opera troupe up north. Work for me. I will take you there.'

Do I have any choice? Do I? I know no one in this strange country. I have no family here. I have to follow him. Is he lying? How can I tell? I have no one to turn to. I curse my foolishness. O kind gods in Heaven help me! Protect me.

Every night I kneel and beg Heaven for help but of late Heaven has turned a deaf ear to my pleas. Oh dearest Sister. Oh dearest Intimate. Where are you?

₧—₨

The world is a cold hard place. Relationships are paper-thin. If you work you get to eat. If you don't work you starve. People shrug and shake their heads when I ask about you. The scoundrel has set me to work in his Cantonese opera troupe. Everyone calls him Big Boss. He calls me Young Dog.

'Don't you worry, Young Dog. My troupe travels from town to town. We put up shows from Singapore to Penang. Find your sister we will someday.'

I have to believe him. What else can I do? My hope is seeping through wet sleeves. My pillow is soaked every night. My heart cries out to Heaven but Heaven is deaf.

I am the youngest and the lowest in the troupe. Knocked and ordered about by actors and crew. I cannot complain to Big Boss for I can neither sing nor act nor somersault. So I cook and wash for the ten men in the troupe, and sometimes more, when other men join the troupe. All the actors and singers are men. They are scoundrels, gamblers and drunks. How low have I sunk! There are no women in opera troupes, I was told.

'Women bring trouble and bad luck. The only all-women Cantonese opera troupe is an upstart troupe in Macau. Nothing but trouble they are.'

'But they're good for a massage and a cuddle, Boss.'

'*Chieh!* For a fuck, you mean!'

I join in the laughter to hide my fear. Each night I pray no one smells a rat. Everyone thinks I am a quiet lad. They yell for me to run errands.

When they are in a good mood after winning a game of mah-jong, they treat me like their young brother, and throw me a few coins to spend. If they gamble and lose, their mood turns foul. Then they cuff me like a dog. Knock and knuckle my head. Accuse me of forgetting their orders. The day before a performance I slave from dawn to past midnight to air their costumes, heat the brass iron on the coal stove and iron the main actors' outfits. On performance nights I help backstage. I carry props. I have learnt to change props, handle the pulleys, raise the curtains and change the sets. After each performance, I serve tea and bring hot towels to the veteran actors and singers. I run errands, buy opium for their pipes, and serve them their suppers, and bring them endless cups of steaming tea. Then the next morning I cook porridge for their breakfast, empty their spittoons and chamber pots. Wash their foot basins and clothes. Some nights I am so tired, I just want to lie down and die.

Where are you, my sister, my friend, my dearest?

Only the moon knows.

શ — ૦૨

A month! I have not written for a month. I was too tired to hold my brush. Many were the nights when I just wanted to lie down and die. But the gods saved me. My life changed all of a sudden when Big Boss caught me reading one of the actors' scripts. He roared and hit my head when he found out that I could read. Then he laughed like a madman.

'You fool! You fool!' he yelled, wagging his finger at me. 'Early, early, why didn't you tell me you could read?' He laughed again and again calling the actors to gather round. 'Listen all of you! Our Young Dog here can read! He will be your prompter from now on.'

So now I have a new duty. I must learn to read the scripts. It is hard work but I am willing to learn. Glad to learn. Grateful to learn. O Heaven, I love learning how to read those new words from the actors. Every day I learn to read more than what we had learnt a whole year from Old Teacher in our village school. My life now is a thousand times better although I still have to cook and wash. Empty spittoons and get knocked on the head. But I do not have to carry heavy props. And Big Boss gives me some money each time after several performances. I save the money to buy paper, brush and ink stick. I am very careful. I hide these inside my tin trunk. Writing is the oil that fuels my life. It is my solace and consolation. May Heaven let me find you soon!

Do you remember how we stole learning from our brothers? Like stealing fire from the gods. Do you remember our indignation? The boys could go to school but we could not. They were taught to read but we were not. They could write and we could not. Daughters must stay home to help their mothers. Sons must go to school and out into the world to earn a living, our parents said.

Every morning when our brothers went to Old Teacher's school we went to the river to wash clothes and fetch water. Do you remember the day we walked past the village school, and you, jealous and angry, said, 'Stop here. Let's listen to what Old Teacher is teaching our brothers.'

The two of us crept under the window and listened. We watched Old Teacher write the words on the blackboard as he read aloud from the Three Character Classic. The next day we stopped again and stayed longer. We copied the words that Old Teacher wrote on the board, writing in the earth with a bamboo stick. Each day we did this. Each day we memorised the strokes of one word. We taught each other our word. Two other girls joined us. So every day we learnt four new words. Quiet as mice we sat under the window. Later each girl managed to learn two new words and taught the others. So then we learnt eight new words each day.

One day your elder brother found out our secret. He was very stern but very kind. He didn't tell our parents. He taught you to read, and you taught me. That autumn, you had another brilliant idea. The trees were shedding their leaves. You asked Old Teacher to let us sweep the schoolyard. Every day slow as snails we swept the schoolyard, and kept our eyes and ears open. When Old Teacher was teaching our brothers, we stopped sweeping and caught some of their learning. If Old Teacher knew what we were doing, he did not say so. He did not stop us. That stolen learning was our secret. Who could have known then that the stolen learning and your brother's teaching would prepare me for my work as a prompter in this Cantonese opera troupe in faraway Singapore? You will laugh if only you can see me now in my loose men's jacket and pants. Do you know where I got them?

I stole them from the pig farmer's son. I can hear you laughing. Oh how I long to hear your laughter.

ℰ — ℛ

We have left Sing-ga-pore. Town after town after town after town we travelled. I am so tired. We have been travelling all over this strange new land, full of foreign ghosts. The trees here are always green. How can I tell the passing of time? There are no seasons in Malaya. The days are always hot and dry or hot and wet. Day after day the season is the same. At night the moon is dull. There are no rivers where I can sit and think of you. No bamboo grove or willow trees to hear my cries. Each night I sleep under the stage among the chests of actors' robes and props, and know not where my heart is gone. A storm is brewing tonight above the grey roofs of this nameless town. Thunder God rumbles above me. Merciful Guan Yin, Compassionate Goddess of Mercy, please keep her safe. Let her not forget me.

ℰ — ℛ

Another month has passed. Or is it another year? I am so busy I have lost count of the days. The monsoon rains have come and gone. And my life has changed again. Last week when one of the actors fell ill, Big Boss ordered me to take his place. I had to act as the young servant of the scholar in *Leung San Pak Chuk Ying Toi*. Fortunately, since I was the prompter, I knew all the lines in *The Butterfly Lovers* opera, and the lines of the boy servant were few.

Before I could go on stage, the troupe held a special ceremony. They had to inform the Patron Gods of Opera and initiate me. First, Master Wu, the most senior actor of the troupe, taught me how to paint my face. After everyone had painted their faces and done their hair, the entire troupe gathered in the backstage before the altar of the Patron Gods.

'Young Dog, stand in the centre. Remember this day of your initiation. You are presented to the Tang Dynasty Emperor Xuanzong. The most important of the heavenly opera deities, and founder of Pear Garden, the training ground of opera singers and actors,' Master Wu said.

The entire troupe lit joss sticks of incense, knelt before the altar and prayed.

'Heavenly gods of the Pear Garden, bless our night's performance. This here is Young Dog, our new actor. Bless and protect him while he's on stage,' Master Wu intoned.

I kowtowed three times, poured a libation of rice wine, and asked for the gods' blessings and the confidence to act my part. When the ceremony was over, the actors slapped me on the back.

'Have no fear. Tonight when you step through the *Fu Doh Muen*, you will become the servant boy.'

'Where is the *Fu Doh Muen*?' I looked around for the doorway.

'Fool! Worked here for so long and you don't know where's the *Fu Doh Muen*?' They roared and pointed. 'There! Look over there! There! There!'

The men pointed in various directions, and I looked all around the backstage. That made them roar even louder. 'There! There!'

Master Wu ordered them to stop teasing me. 'Young Dog, listen,' he said. '*Fu Doh Muen* is an invisible doorway that separates ordinary real life from the dramatic life on stage. Once the gods have accepted you, you will step through the *Fu Doh Muen* when you go on stage each night. The moment you go through that magical doorway and enter the acting area, you will become the character the audience sees. So! Tonight you will be Ah Mung, the boy servant.'

I thought the drums sounded louder than usual. The music of the erhus floated higher than usual. And my heart was beating faster than usual. Silently I said a prayer to the patron gods. Then I went on stage, trudging behind the young scholar acted by Master Wu, and a strange feeling came over me. I was walking as Ah Mung, talking as Ah Mung. Throughout the entire show, I was Ah Mung the boy servant, sharing my young master's joys and sorrows. I do not know how to describe it. It was magical. The moment I stepped on stage and entered the opera of *The Butterfly Lovers*, I was transformed. There I was, Young Dog, a woman acting as a boy servant. And there he was – the male actor singing and acting as Miss Ying Toi, the girl who disguised herself as a young man to study in school with other young men for the imperial examinations. Everyone on stage that night was not what he was in real life.

In *The Butterfly Lovers*, girls were not allowed to leave home and go to school to study for the imperial exams. In the theatre, women were not allowed to go on stage and act with the men. Yet there I was, a young woman, acting with all the men, and no one knew. Not one of the men knew that I was a girl! That night I laughed. At the end of the show, the actors slapped me on the back. 'Well done, Young Dog!' The troupe didn't know. Big Boss didn't know. The audience didn't know. I had fooled them all. Only the gods and I knew that I was a woman striding across the stage with all the men as Ah Mung, the boy servant. That night was the first night I went to bed and did not cry.

8

I am so blessed! Master Wu is going to be my Sifu, my Mentor!

I thank Heaven. I thank the patron Gods of Opera. Thirdly, I thank Master Wu, my Sifu. Heaven has blessed me, dearest intimate. Do you remember how we used to sing up in the hills while looking for mushrooms? How we learnt new opera songs whenever an opera troupe came to our village? Who would have known then that singing in the hills would prepare me for this day? We were so good that sometimes an actor would teach us how to sing. We should have run away together to join the opera troupe instead of obeying our parents and marry.

This is what happened after Master Wu heard me singing that night in *The Butterfly Lovers*. He told Big Boss that I have a good voice. He wanted to take me under his wing. And Big Boss agreed! Master Wu is the troupe's best singer and actor.

Yesterday I went through the ceremony of discipleship. I knelt before Master Wu and kowtowed while the whole troupe watched. Then with both hands I served him a cup of tea and called him 'Sifu'. From now on, Sifu is both father and mother to me. Under the rules of discipleship, I must obey and serve him.

I serve him his meals, bring him his tea, empty his spittoon, and massage his feet and back each night before he sleeps. I buy him his opium and prepare his bamboo pipe. Opium helps him to relax. Each morning I do his laundry separate from that of the troupe. I make his bed and take care of his costumes. I help him to dress during each performance.

'Breathe!' Master Wu shouts. 'From here!' His palm slaps the area around my navel. 'It is important that you learn how to breathe from your diaphragm. Control your breath in your singing. Like this. Understand?'

'Yes, Sifu.'

I hope to sing on stage again some day. But first, I have to learn how to walk across the stage and practise voice control. I am extremely fortunate to have a teacher. Though I am still the troupe's drudge, I am a drudge with a future now. Someday I will sing a full aria on stage. And you will come and watch me.

ဨ — ଔ

'You cheat! Show your hand!'

'Fuck off!'

A fight breaks out among the mah-jong players.

Lately tempers have been flaring up in the troupe like wildfires. Quarrels and fights erupt especially after an all-night gambling session.

The weather is flaming hot. There have been no rain and no engagements. Everyone is in a foul mood, especially Big Boss. Money is running short. Yesterday Master Wu slapped me more than twenty times.

'Fool! Who can hear you? Squeaking like a mouse! Open your mouth! When you sing, let your voice rise from your belly! Send your notes over the rooftops! Louder! Louder!'

He was furious about some other thing but he took it out on me.

'From tomorrow get up at four to practise! Do you hear?' He pulled my ear. 'Whoa! What's this? Your ears are pierced like a girl's.' He fixed his eyes on me.

My heart dropped to my toes. 'Sifu,' I squeaked. 'My… my mother thought I was going to… to die. A priest in the temple told her to… to pierce my ears so the demons would think I'm a girl and leave me alone.'

'Hahaha! Aaah so! Your mother pierced your ears to fool the devil, eh? I've heard of such a practice,' he laughed.

It was close. Very close. I almost wetted my pants.

ဨ — ଔ

Dearest Intimate,

I have had no time to write these past weeks. Where are you? Will we ever meet? Some nights I lose hope, and doubts assail me. Who knows when you are able to read these words? Yet I continue to wield this brush in hope and write. I imagine these words calling out to you, and you will sense my presence just as I feel your presence somewhere out there when I am writing.

Then, oh, then I don't feel so alone. This brush and ink are my only hope that some day we will meet, and you will read these pages and know what I have gone through in coming to the Nanyang because of your gold ring and eight words. Should I depart this world before you do, I hope these pages will find their way to you. On grey rainy nights like this my hope fades when I sit alone in the backstage among these costumes and props.

$\wp$ — $\wp$

The days have flown away like leaves in the monsoon winds. Tired to the bones, I have lost count of the days. I have been travelling with the troupe from town to town. Every few weeks we are performing in a different town. When we stop at each town, I have to practise my singing. Sleeping at past midnight after the show, I am up at four each morning. Master Wu is relentless, demanding and cruel in his training. One wrong note. And his thin cane stings my back. When the troupe is not performing, I have to practise even harder while the others rest. Yet he is not satisfied.

'You call this singing? Ha! Were you whining? Or wailing like a widow?'

He sneered. He scorned. He mocked. He smacked and caned. My back is covered with red streaks. The other day when no one was around, I wept. One of the older actors saw me.

'Young Dog, why are you crying?' he asked.

I told him about Master Wu's frequent caning and showed him the cane marks on my arms. He threw me a stern and scornful glare.

'Who are you to complain? You were nothing before Master Wu took you as his disciple. You should be grateful that he slaps you so hard. It means he sees something in you. The harder he canes, the better you learn. Look around. Does he cane the others? Does he scold them when they sing badly? If you have no talent, he will not even look at you. Much less cane you.'

I hung my head in shame. The old actor was right.

$\wp$ — $\wp$

Practise. Practise. Practise.

Day and night I practise. Up at five, I gargle and clear my throat. Then I practise holding the notes for as long as I can. Ah...ah...ahhhhhh...

I practise letting my voice rise from my belly up to the dawn sky. If there is a lake or a river nearby, I go there to practise sending my voice across to the other side. I try. I try a hundred thousand times but my voice, my stubborn voice, remains at my side. It will not go over. Do not despair, I tell myself. Try again.

If there is no river or lake, I sing to the wall. Master Wu makes me train my voice on an empty stomach facing the wall, and I do just that. I sing when I can, wherever I can. Sometimes in a village or town if the stage or theatre is near a river, I practise near the river singing my scales. When I practise sending my voice across the dark glimmering waters at dawn, I close my eyes and pretend I am back in our village, Saam Hor, standing at the river, calling out to you on the other side. Sometimes when the sun rises, I end my practice by singing our village's mountain songs. Women washing clothes by the river would join in and sing with me. How I miss home. I miss you. I even miss the pig farmer's son sometimes.

℘ — ℜ

Alas, it is useless. Useless. Useless.

I am but a tortoise training to be a dragon. I will never be able to fly as a dragon or roar like one. My voice is still so weak. I am still squeaking like a mouse. It is useless. I have no talent, no skill, no family, no friends in this world. Master Wu has made a mistake. I cannot go on.

℘ — ℜ

We are in the town of Kampar resting for a few days. Master Wu suddenly asks me to meet him at three the next morning. He does not say why we have to wake at that ghostly hour, and I dare not ask. The next morning when I am up at three, he is already up, and waiting with the training cane in one hand and a basket in the other. Without a word, he hands me the basket with a flask and two bowls inside. Then he starts to walk. I follow a few steps behind him. There is no moon. The road is pitch dark. We walk in silence out of the town, past the dark brick houses and shops, past the stream, the thatched huts and vegetable farms, and still we walk on till there are no more huts, and only wild grasses and jungle grow at the side of the narrow road. I am growing more and more puzzled. But I dare not ask him. The sky is peppered with faint stars when we reach the cemetery. A white mist floating over thick grasses and gravestones. Clouds of thick mist rising from the tall grasses and dark clumps of bamboo and trees. Something slithers in the grass. Then a sudden fluttering of unseen wings is followed by a night bird's eerie cry.

Master Wu stops under a dark rain tree.

'Put the basket down. Do your singing practice here.'

A sudden shiver slithers down my back. The air is so cold, damp and misty.

'*Aaarrgh*,' I begin, my voice thick and shaky.

Whack! His cane lands on my shoulder and I straighten my back.

'Louder. How can the Honourables hear you?' He points to the vast acres of mist-covered gravestones all around. 'Those ancestors farthest away, over there, want to hear you too,' he growls, his figure disappearing into the mist.

I am left alone among the gravestones and wild lallang grasses. The sharp blades, covered with tiny hairs invisible to the naked eye, can slice my skin like a knife. A chill flows down my back. I catch a glimpse of light among the dark clumps of bamboo trees swaying in the distance before a thick mist obscures my sight. Thoughts of the thousands of immigrants buried here in the cold earth, their ghostly presences hovering in this graveyard far from home and family in China troubles me. Alone these ghosts had come, alone they had died. Had any kin come to say a prayer? I want to cry.

'*Aaaaaah!*' I begin. My plaintive notes quivering like a whining calf.

'The Honourables can't hear you!'

I jump at the voice that came out from the mist. Where is he?

'*Aahhh...aah!*' I sing louder, singing my scales to the silent witnesses of my fear. '*Ah-ah-ahhhhhhh!*' Aiming my notes at every tombstone, headstone and gravestone, '*Ah-ah-ahhhhhhh!*' I sent my notes out.

After my scales I sing the aria I have been learning, imagining the vast cemetery as a vast theatre, and the rows of gravestones are the audience listening to me, the faces of the Honourables are those of the villagers in Saam Hor. Not fearsome ghosts, no, no, not ghosts, I comfort myself, not ghosts, but honoured ancestors and I sing to each and every one of these villagers till the air beneath the rain tree turns warm, and the thinning white mist rise in wisps from the tall dew-wet grasses, and grey clouds sail across the sky as the light slowly turns a slate grey. As I go on singing, colour returns to the dark clumps of bamboo, and pink streaks the slate grey sky.

'Young Dog!' Master Wu calls from under his tree. 'Come over here. You can stop now.'

When I reach him, he opens his flask, pours out a clear steaming hot liquid into a bowl, and hands the bowl to me.

'Drink up. It's imperial bird's nest soup.'

Shocked, I hold the warm bowl of translucent jelly with great reverence in both my hands and bring it to my lips. I have never tasted such heavenly sweet soup. Made from the swallows' spit that the birds use to build their nests in limestone caves high up in the mountains, and harvested by poor men risking life and limb climbing the rock faces. Slow cooked for hours over a small charcoal fire and flavoured with honey rock sugar, imperial bird's nest soup is a delicacy that only the rich could afford.

'This soup will nourish and strengthen your lungs.'

I slurp up every drop and wipe away a grateful tear.

'Sifu...'

'Don't thank me, Young Dog. Words are no use. Practise your singing like this morning every day. Singing in a cemetery improves performance. Now pack up. Let's go home.'

  

It's four in the morning. I am awake, and at the river sending out my notes to the honourable ancestors in that cemetery in Kampar Town.

At every town we stop in I practise sending my plaintive notes above the rooftops. This is to make sure that my voice will grow loud enough so that a person in the last row of the theatre can hear me.

'And yet, you must not strain your vocal chords,' Master Wu said.

When the sky turns pink, I stop my practice and go into the kitchen to light the wood stove and cook a big pot of rice congee for the troupe's breakfast. Then I bring Master Wu a basin of water to wash his face and serve him his breakfast. While he eats, I make his bed and empty and clean his chamber pot. After my own breakfast, I see to the laundry of the troupe. I have two boys to help me now. I give instructions and they do all the washing and take over my chores when I join the others to practise for the night's performance.

'Eyes front! Head point to heaven! Feet firm on earth! Knees wide apart like riding a horse! Clench fists! Now punch! Jab! Right! Left! Right! Kick! Twist and somersault! Again!' Master Teng yells.

We practise these moves again and again till we get them right.

My last chore of the day is to prepare Master Wu's opium pipe. While he smokes, I give him a foot massage. The pipe and the foot massage help him to relax before the night's performance. In the cool shadow of his room with the windows shuttered, he often falls into a reverie and tells stories of his own training.

'To be able to sing and act, an opera actor must have heart and principles. Be diligent in studying all the skills of the craft. Learn from every actor, even the person on the street has something to teach us. Study the scripts, and understand the emotions, the heart of the opera. Heart is passion, Young Dog. Heart is gratitude towards the Gods of Opera and the craft, and gratitude towards our audience. Sing and act with heart. Talent without heart leads to hollow art.'

Wreathed in the smoky fragrance of opium, Master Wu's voice changes into that of an ancient philosopher on those cool rainy afternoons when no woman comes into his room. But when he had had a quarrel with one of his women the night before, he foregoes his massage, and barks at me.

'Young Dog! Where are your eyes? Use your bloody eyes and ears! Listen! Listen and sing! The same note! Every word must be heard! Look. Copy. Mimic. Imitate. Watch my movements tonight!'

Today he is in a good mood. He shows me a gesture and a look. So simple yet it conveys such feelings I am amazed. Then with a flip of his long water sleeves, he controls their length and folds them back like a gentleman. So simple to the eye so difficult to perform. To get him to teach me this move, I save what money I have to buy him more opium. A smoke or two keeps his voice strong, he tells me.

He acts all the scholar's roles in the operas. And I act as his servant boy these days. The boy servant is a walk-on role. Most of the time I do not sing or speak. Sometimes in his women-drunken moments, he would train me to sing the scholar's songs.

Arh-arh-arhhhhh! Listening, imitating, aria after aria I sing after him. Immersed in the singing I am the scholar, the judge, the poet, the young farmer in love with the king's daughter, the prime minister.

'Every word must be heard. Learn to drag and hold the note. You're not a hawker selling your wares. If you shout when you sing, you ruin your voice. You are not the martial type. I'm training you to be a *xiu sung*. Your role is that of the young gentleman scholar who holds a brush, not a rake. Well-bred and gentle, your voice should rise naturally from your belly. No stress. No struggle. Each word is clear. High or low, your singing should flow like water. Control your breath. If you work hard, very hard, someday you will sing as a *xiu sung*. The seed in you will blossom.'

His words crack my heart. Crack it open like a walnut.

'I will give my life to this art, Sifu.'

Master Wu laughs. 'I should have had you when you were a little boy. But no matter. Life is destiny, Young Dog. Stand up. Stand tall. Head point to heaven, feet rest firmly on the earth. Sing not just the words. Sing your heart. Sing your emotions. Sing not like the kitchen drudge. Sing like the scholar and poet in love or in pain. Do you understand?'

I no longer care that he knocks my head every day. I am learning so much from him. I can read a lot more words now than before. I can stride across the stage like a man. And mime entering a house or a room, or up the stairs in the male actor's robes and wooden boots. He is teaching me how to use the long water sleeves of a scholar's robe, how to fold them back elegantly as though all my life I have never lifted anything heavier than a writing brush. There is so much to learn and watch in opera. So much to learn from Master Wu and the other singers and actors. My heart knows I am just a tortoise yearning to fly like a dragon. But if it is Heaven's will, this tortoise will fly like a dragon someday.

ℰ — ℛ

Dearest Intimate, how I wish you were here! I tell myself, 'Some day, some day we will meet.' So many 'some days' have gone past since. When I close my eyes, I try to remember your face, your long hair shimmering in the sunlight when we washed in the river. On your last visit home your hair had looked like tufts of weeds under your blue scarf. Your hair must have grown longer now. Does your husband treat you well? Where are you? When will I find you? When will you come to see me at the opera?

Guan Yin, Goddess of Compassion, I will donate a thousand lotuses and free a thousand tortoises if I find her. Then in my next life if I were reborn a dung fly, I will be content.

9

Today the God of Change strikes yet again!

'Young Dog, you must take on bigger roles.'

'He is not ready!' Master Wu declares.

'He should be ready!'

'Not ready!' Master Wu yells at Big Boss.

And he yells at me. 'Rice bin! Be ready to sing on stage. Or else return to the kitchen. Empty the spittoons! Move the props.'

So here I am. I have to take on a bigger role on stage. I have to sing more. I am scared. But if I take on bigger roles on stage, I will get a small allowance. Then I can buy paper, brush and ink. Don't worry, I tell myself. Be very careful. Always write under the stage among the chests and boxes in the hot humid afternoons when all the actors are napping. No one comes down here. I am the sole caretaker of the props here. I pretend I am studying scripts. No one knows when I write. No one knows I can write. I lock up my papers in my tin trunk and hide my trunk among the props. The veteran actors can read. They box my ears when they teach me to read the scripts but it is worth it. I am learning more words. More poetry from the opera scripts.

Yet what is the use? What *is* the use? The poetry in my heart has dried up. The Seven Sisters' Festival is drawing near. My heart is sore. How am I going to celebrate it without you by my side? In my dreams, I see the heavenly Weaver Maid floating towards me across the Magpies' Bridge. Light as a breeze, lovely as a cloud. I am the Cowherd. You are the Weaver Maid. Such hopeless dreams I have.

∞ — ∞

Dearest Intimate, I have not dipped my brush into ink for months. I am so tired. The troupe has been travelling and performing in town after town, village after village. How long has it been since I left our village? Since

I joined this floating world of shadows? I am already seventeen. Like a boat without an anchor, I have become a piece of flotsam tossing in the sea. I have not written home. The family thinks I am dead. Disowned and despised, a nameless hungry ghost, that's what I will be when I die.

I dare not think about the pig farmer's son. I have cut off his nose and his family's face. He will kill me if he finds me. His family must have cursed my father, mother and brothers. Cursed all our ancestors for giving them such an unfilial, unfaithful, ungrateful wretch as their daughter-in-law. Oh why did I run away to look for you? I was foolish. Very foolish. Yet if a goatherd could search for days for his lost goat, how could I not look for my lost heart? How could I not leave when my heart had left our village? How could I stay after you had thrust your precious gold ring and eight words into my hand?

'Sell ring. Buy passage. Come to Nan Yang.'

These eight words in your feathery brushstrokes changed my life. But Heaven is punishing me for leaving the pig farmer's son. The gods will not listen to my pleas. The ancestral spirits will not bless me. I am alone. Alone I will die. A lonely wandering spirit I will be. Dearest Intimate, where are you?

ℰ—ℛ

'Young Dog, let a woman love you,' Master Wu tells me. 'Else you will be very lonely.'

Tonight we are in Ipoh. The past months the troupe had performed in Penang, Taiping, Kuala Kangsar, Teluk Anson, Kuala Lumpur, Muar, Batu Pahat and Johore Bahru. I am learning the names of towns. An opera actor's life is an itinerant life. We never stay more than a few months sometimes a few weeks in any one place. The men have mistresses or a wife in every town. Master Wu has a woman in Ipoh, another in Kuala Lumpur and another in Singapore. And they adore him.

Today his woman in Ipoh has brought him special herbal drink and soup to nourish his lungs and throat.

'Here Young Dog, have some!'

I am fortunate. As his disciple, I get to eat with him.

'My woman here is pregnant. I will marry her if she bears me a son.'

'What if it's a girl?'

'Then she remains my woman!'

I wanted to box his ears. He is just like our fathers.

I thank Heaven that no one suspects I am a woman. I do not want to bear a son. With two hands and two feet, I will earn my keep with my voice and skills. Master Wu is giving me a solid foundation in the four skills and five methods that an opera performer must master. Singing, speaking, acting and movement skills. How to use my hands, eyes, body, feet and hair to express my emotions and my station in life, and a host of others like how to *lai saan* or 'pull mountains' and perform *wan sau* or 'cloud hands'. Pulling mountains and performing cloud hands are two of the most important basic movements in opera besides walking across the stage in boots with high wooden heels. As a male character, I must take big strides. It's fortunate I am tall, and my legs are long. The male actor who sings the female roles is short. He has to take small mincing steps like a woman with bound feet. I am grateful that my feet were not bound like the girls in rich families.

$\text{\textbuilt}\text{\textbackslash}$ ℘ — ℛ

Tonight I am alone. The temple is empty, dark and silent. The festival is over. The worshippers have gone home. Master Wu and the actors and singers have gone to a feast. The temple that engaged us for their festival likes our operas. The temple's donors, the town's rich merchants and their wives, have invited Big Boss and the troupe to a grand dinner. As usual, I do not join them. As the youngest and lowliest of the actors, I have to stay back to guard our props and things. I pretend to grumble but I like it. Alone I loosen the cloths that bind my breasts. My two buns are flat as pancakes. I check the temple grounds. Except for the gods and spirits, no one is around. I give myself a good wash in the bathroom, and I wash my underwear, especially the cloths I use when the red aunty visits me each month. I am very careful every month. I wear black pants so that if there is a leak, the red is not visible. Then I light two oil lamps. With the help of a mirror I give myself a haircut. I dare not go to a barber. Those men are sharp as their scissors. They will smell a rat when their hands touch my head. The other actors laugh that my hair looks like tufts of grass sticking up. But I don't care. The uglier the better. And I save money. Money that I can use to buy paper.

⁊ﾟ— ੦ੜ

Singapore. We are back in Singapore.

And I stole learning last night. I was at the grand Majestic Theatre watching the Hong Kong master actor performing, paying attention to how he sang a tragic aria with such clarity, heaviness and mellifluousness of voice, how he held a note, or folded a water sleeve in new ways. Most of the stagehands were either catching up on sleep or gambling. Master Wu was away with his woman, and the other performers were out with their female admirers or visiting their favourite prostitute. Whenever I could I stole away to the Majestic to watch the troupes from Macau and Hong Kong. Watching these Hong Kong masters helps me to improve. I dream of singing like a *xiu sung* someday. Then you will come and watch me perform at the Majestic.

Sighhhh! It's a far-off dream, I know, I know. It's three in the morning and I am still wide awake watching the dewdrops shimmering dully on the grass under the street lamps. I have been training harder. Master Wu has taken such pains to train me I want him to be proud of me. Each night I pray some day you will come and see me on stage. Every night I look out for you. Every night you are not in the theatre. You are never in the audience. Never in the streets. Never in the squares and temples. Never in the towns where our troupe performs. No matter how many candles and joss sticks I light, you are not in the towns we stay in. I have made countless enquiries and performed countless kowtows to the gods. But Heaven is deaf to my pleas. But I will not despair. Buddha is ever compassionate, ever merciful. Someday my prayers will be heard. As the ancients said, if it is your destiny you will meet even if a thousand li apart. I will not despair. I must not lose heart. I must go on hoping. So here I am. Back on the island of Singapore where I first landed. Three? Four years ago? And still no sign of you. I feel old.

10

Tonight is the opening night of our opera season in Singapore. There is shouting and cursing in the backstage. Lu Tang who sings and acts in the minor roles is drunk again. Just hours away before the performance, he's dead to the world. Big Boss is furious.

'Young Dog! Take over!'

My soul flies out of my body at his words.

'Look at him! The pale shivering puppy!' the men around me guffaw.

'No, no, please. My Sifu trained me to sing the young scholar's roles. Not the martial roles. I... I can't be the palace guard.'

'Damn you! Have I not been fucking kind to you? Have I not been generous? It's only for tonight! You don't even have to fight! Just stand there and sing a few lines! A short aria! Is that too much to ask? Old Wu! What's wrong with your disciple?'

Master Wu pulls me aside.

'Do as Big Boss says,' he hisses in my ear. 'He's giving you the chance of your life. Show your skills. Go!'

Scared stiff. I sit up still as a corpse while Master Wu paints my face. What if the audience finds out I am a woman when I sing? No! Don't think of that. Have courage. Be resolute. Your first singing role. Sing with your heart! You know that aria.

I don the costume of a palace guard. I am going to sing an aria for the first time on stage. In front of a large paying audience. Cold sweat runs down my neck as I wait in the wings. I pray to Lord Wah Kong, patron saint of opera singers. When the erhu and drums sound, Big Boss taps me on the shoulder. Out I stride onto the stage and take up my position on the table that serves as the palace wall. The erhus play a doleful tune as the imprisoned imperial concubine enters with her four-stringed lute. Her soulful song serenading the lonely moon brings tears as I sing my reply.

The audience applauds.

'Young Dog, you caught the spirit of *The Imperial Concubine's Lament to the Lonely Moon*,' Master Wu smiles.

'Well sung, you rascal! Much better than that drunk! The role is yours from now on. Be ready for the next performance tomorrow,' Big Boss grins.

'Waah! Great opportunity, Young Dog!' Everyone congratulates me. The men thump me on the back. 'Well done! Good singing and acting!'

But the moon knew I was not acting. I was thinking of the one I missed when I sang. Where are you tonight, Intimate? Are we gazing at the same moon tonight? Are you thinking of me tonight? Besides this writing with my brush and ink, the theatre is my only solace. In the theatre, loved ones are found. On stage, justice is done. Some mornings I stand on the empty stage and send my voice soaring up to the rooftops to you. Wherever you are, may my songs find you.

Every morning I train with the actors. Each afternoon I memorise my lines and practise my movements. I keep busy every day. Only my brush knows the loneliness in my heart. I miss our home. I miss our village and our years together, playing with our village sisters. I try hard not to think of my mother and father, my brothers and sisters, or the pig farmer's son. His mother must be cursing me tonight. Should she lay her hands on me, she will strip me and whip me. Just like your mother-in-law.

₧—⁗

I cannot write!

I cannot bear to write.

Yet I *have* to write.

I want to write.

I will grow mad if I don't write this down! When I am dead and gone, I hope these pages reach you. Then you will know how this wretch has suffered for you.

No, no, I do not blame you. I do not blame Heaven. I do not blame Earth. I blame my life. My Fate. My miserable Fate!

It is Fate when instead of you the pig farmer's son came to the opera the night I sang in the Lai Chun Yuen Opera House, the grandest theatre for Cantonese operas in Singapore. The pig farmer's son found me! Even though he did not cross the ocean to look for me. Destiny led him to Sing-ga-pore and to our troupe's opera on the night I sang in the grand opera house!

That pig farmer's son and his gang turned it into my night of shame! The very night I sang and acted as a young scholar for the first time, the pig farmer's son was in the audience. Is that not Destiny?

Ever since I sung that short aria in *The Imperial Concubine's Lament to the Lonely Moon*, Big Boss and Master Wu had assigned me more parts to sing. Master Wu was training me to sing the parts for young male characters. And I was happy! I felt blessed! Then cruel Fate struck me down with a sledgehammer on the night we were playing to a full house. I had to sing a short aria of five lines in the scene. Only five lines! And that was enough for the pig farmer's son to recognise me.

After the show he rushed to the backstage with several of his clansmen.

'My wife! My wife!' he bellowed like a raging bull.

'Who the hell are you? What wife?' Big Boss roared.

'That young scholar! She's my wife!'

WHAT??? A huge uproar arose.

'Young Dog is your wife? Young Dog is a woman? A woman in MY troupe? And I don't know?' Big Boss roared like a wounded lion.

'Blackguard! Scoundrel! Traitor!'

Names and curses rained on me. The actors grabbed me and threw me out. But this is NOT the reason. NOT the reason, I want to end my miserable life.

෨ — ඥ

I screamed. I yelled. I wailed. I swore. I cursed him and his kind. I kicked and bit him. Scratched and clawed him. Several times I tried to run away from his room. He chained my leg to his bed and locked the door whenever he left.

I refused to speak to him. I would not speak with a pig. I refused to touch the food he placed in front of me. I would not eat or wash for days till I smelt like a sick pig sitting in its own filth. He didn't know what to do. He begged and pleaded and apologised again and again. Finally he asked what

I wanted. I told him I wanted to find you, my dearest sister and friend from our village. He was surprised but he promised to look for you if I promised not to run away after he had found you. I agreed at once.

'Then kneel and swear before Heaven. Repeat after me. May Thunder God strike me dead if I run away!'

'May Thunder God strike me dead if I run away,' I swore.

'Will you eat some rice now?'

I shook my head. 'Find her first.'

Without another word, he took away the chamber pot in which I had deposited a dump. 'Let me do it,' I said. He pointed to my chain and shook his head. I felt very sorry for him then.

'Look at the fool. No man should do what the fool is doing. Washing his wife's chamber pot. *Chieh!*' I heard the other lodgers, all men, jeering when he went out. 'His wife ran away, and he empties her shit pot! Why not kill her, Wah Jai? Dump her corpse in the sea. If we don't tell, who will know? The foreign devil police wouldn't know! If you're scared, we'll help you.'

Like the opera troupe, his lodging house had only men. I was the sole female. Before he left for work each morning, he placed a flask of water and a cup of watery rice gruel next to me. All day long my body struggled against itself. Desire and will fought. Will and hunger wrestled over the cup till I took a tiny sip. Just enough to wet my lips. Then my body curled into a ball, eyes shut against the nourishing cup all day. Heavenly gods, where is she? Please let him find her. This is my prayer. My refrain. My supplication.

A few days later he tried another tactic. Before he went to work each morning, he left a cup of tea and a bowl of rice porridge on the table. He moved the table within my reach. Then he left the room and locked the door. When he returned in the evening, he lit the oil lamp, removed the untouched porridge, and emptied the chamber pot. After several days, there was just urine. I had drunk only water. I lay curled like a prawn on the wooden floor, too weak to sit up.

Time moved like a thousand-year-old tortoise. No news. Each night he muttered the same words. No news. When he lit the oil lamp in the room, I knew another day had passed, and another long night awaited me. My hope withered. I had left home and family for nothing. Chained to his bed, dry sobs wracked my breast. On the plank bed above me, he was fast asleep.

Last night, all of a sudden, he asked, 'Are you going to starve to death? Is this how you repay your mother? For the ten months she had nurtured you in her womb? For the pain she had suffered at your birth? For the pain your father had suffered to put rice in your mouth?'

I did not answer him. I had not written to my family. I do not know if my parents are still on this earth. I wish I were dead. This unfilial one deserves to die.

The next night I asked him, 'Are my parents and your parents still in this world?'

He went on chewing his rice and fish. He ate in front of me every evening, trying to tempt me with fragrant fried fish and tofu. My belly itched and ached with hot craving when he ate. And he ate with relish, chewing slowly, smacking his lips, enjoying his morsel of freshly fried fish. I hated him. His chewing made my mouth salivate. My lips and tongue burned with such desire. But as the days passed and I grew weaker, all desires for food were drained out of me.

He cleared the dinner things and put them away. Then he blew out the oil lamp. I heard him get into bed as I lay curled on the floor too weak to move. After a long while his impassive voice, utterly devoid of feelings, came out of the darkness.

'Kam Foong,' he said my name for the first time. 'I don't know where to begin. So many things had happened after you left our village. For days the whole village went out to search for you in the wooded hills and valleys. The men and I searched the hills for several days until we had to give you up for dead. Some said a tiger had eaten you. Others thought you had drowned in the river and floodwaters had carried your corpse downstream. We thought you were dead. I did not travel ten thousand li to come to the Nanyang to look for you. Our village had suffered great disasters. War, drought, flood. One after another. Heaven was in great anger. The stars had clashed. A strange sickness had killed all the pigs in the county. Our village was not spared. After that, a drought had killed all the crops. The villagers including my father had to beg and borrow from the landlords. With the borrowed money, we bought piglets. We bought seed rice and started our farms again the following year. After two good harvests when we thought life was normal again, civil war broke out in the provinces. The warlords' armies fought and ruined our rice fields. Like locusts their armies ate up our food. Their soldiers took away our pigs and rice. My two brothers died fighting the thugs. My sister was raped. One night she jumped into the river. Her bloated body was found days later. My mother was so heartbroken she followed my sister not long after. There were just the two of us left. Father and I struggled on. After he died in the great flood that summer, I could not repay the loan and the landlord took our farm. With no land, no farm, no wife, no family, no one, I left our village, sold my labour for a passage on a ship and came here. The entire village and county were devastated. I don't know if your parents are still alive.'

I lay on the floor chained to his bed. The dark silence pressed against my chest, thick and oppressive. I could scarcely breathe. All night I kept thinking of what he'd said and could not sleep. On the bed above me, he too was awake but we did not speak again. What was there left to say?

The next morning before he left for work, I asked, 'Why didn't you die?'

He did not reply. He opened the door and left the room.

In the evening when he returned from whatever work he was doing, he ate his dinner in silence and did not try to engage me in conversation. After he had blown out the oil lamp for the night, I lay under his bed, feeling more and more contrite.

'I was rude this morning. I am sorry.'

No reply. The silence above me thickened. I began to regret my apology, and my apology turned to anger when I heard him snoring above me.

The next morning, he set a cup of very thin rice gruel next to me.

'I am the only descendant left in my family,' he said. 'My ancestors will grieve if I die. It is my duty to stay alive and carry on the family's name. You are my wife, my only family left. Drink this up. Please do not die.'

Before I could reply, he opened the door and was gone.

℘ — ℞

At last! At long last! After countless days Heaven heard my prayers. Thank you, Lord Buddha. Thank you, Goddess of Mercy. His clansman has found you.

'She's a widow,' he told me.

A widow? I sat up. That means you are free. You can leave your in-laws. We can live together. These thoughts were tumbling over each other inside my head as the pig farmer's son went on.

'Her husband owns a goldsmith shop. The shop is in…'

I didn't catch the rest of his words. I was trying to kneel and kowtow, tugging at my chain. I wanted to thank him.

'No need, no need', he laughed. It was the first time I've seen him laugh. 'Thank the Jade Emperor in Heaven. Remember your oath.'

He brought me a bowl of watery porridge seasoned with salt.

'Sit up and eat,' he said.

But I was too excited to eat. After days of not eating, I could not eat. I drank some of the rice gruel and watched him eat. I couldn't stop smiling at him. I was so grateful. So very grateful. I would have kissed his feet if he would let me.

After dinner, he brought a large basin of warm water and a towel into the room. He unchained me and left the room. That surprised me. He was so polite and considerate. After I had washed my face and wiped my body I ran a comb through my matted hair. The water in the basin was grey.

That night, unchained, I fell into a deep sleep.

꧁—꧂

The next morning voices of the other lodgers woke me. After the men had left for work, he took me to the bathroom next to the kitchen. There was a large Shanghai jar filled with tap water inside. He closed the door and left. And I took my first bath in weeks. What sweet joy! My whole body tingled with pleasure as I poured mugs of the cool clean water over my head. I washed my hair, and I scrubbed and washed every nook and crevice of my body. Then I dried myself with the thin cotton towel he'd given me and changed into the suit of samfoo he had found in my trunk. I felt awkward. It had been such a long time, years since I wore a woman's clothes.

When I returned to our room, there were two bowls of rice porridge seasoned with salted egg on the table. He and I sat down, and we ate together for the first time like a couple. His face was wreathed in smiles. When he had finished, he said, 'I have to go.'

Left alone, I sat in his room, unchained, the door unlocked. He trusts me, I thought. And an expansive feeling of freedom flooded me. I was free to walk out of his room. But he trusts me, I thought. He trusts me.

In the afternoon I ate the food he had left me and slept. When I woke up it was evening. Waiting for someone to come home had never been so happy. When he came home that night he told me in great detail how his clansmen had found you. His tale steeped my heart in honey so sweet, I cried. I was so overjoyed, so excited and so tired that I fell asleep after dinner.

Sometime in the night I woke up and felt him sleeping on the floor close to me. I did not push him away. My heart was so filled with gratitude that I let him do what he wanted in the dark of night. He had found you. That was all that mattered. He had found you and he was going to take me to you. I clung to him and fell asleep.

The next morning he said, 'You are a strange one, aren't you? Why suffer so much for a village sister? Why not for the husband you married?'

When I did not answer, a rueful smile shadowed his face. He sighed.

'Deep as the ocean is our heart indeed. Too deep to fathom.'

He scratched his head and looked at me.

'The men say I am strange. My wife ran away. By the laws of our village, I should whip her. And I am not obliged to look after her. Yet here I am, looking after you. Am I not strange like you?'

Before I could reply, he was gone.

ℰ—ℭ

You! I do not know what to call you!
Traitor or Heartbreaker or Devoted Mother?
By the time you read these words, I will be dead.
But I will remember. How could I forget the day we met?
Not till I die will I forget the widow in mourning black.

A white flower in your hair. A look of utter joy in your eyes. And tears streaming down your face when you hugged me. How could I ever forget all that? How could I forget the puzzled frowns of the men watching us as we hugged each other again and again, and yet again, laughing and sobbing in each other's arms, hugging so long and hard that the pig farmer's son had to pull us apart. How could I forget the looks of your stone-faced in-laws in the goldsmith shop? Those men's faces were like vultures waiting to tear our flesh.

'She's my sworn sister,' you told them.

Silent, they looked me up and down. But you took my hand and pulled me up the stairs. The pig farmer's son was left to sit with the gravel-faced men in the shop, lined with trays of glittering gold ornaments.

Running up the stairs I felt I was on the cusp of paradise. You took my hand and pulled me towards you. My eyes are tearing again at the memory. Brush poised above the page unable to move, my hand trembles. Blots smudge the words. Outside my window, the trees and houses are swimming in the harsh sunlight.

Upstairs in your bedroom our hearts, oh our two intimate hearts, were too filled to speak. We sat on your bed, our eyes swimming as we gazed at each other, drinking in all the years we had missed. Time had cut off our tongues. Light danced in our watery eyes. I should have listened to the whisperings of the breeze then. Delirious with joy, I held you close. Your head rested on my pounding heart, so full that I feared it would burst.

'Come away with me,' I whispered, happiness streaking down my cheeks.

Just as your lips were about to caress my cheek, there came a soft mewling cry. You sprang back at once and brushed away a hair from your eyes.

'Wait here,' you whispered.

I was so drunk with joy I didn't catch the rest of your words. How shocked I was when you returned with the mewling bundle in your arms. And your eyes were bright with joy fighting with sorrow. 'My son,' you whispered, your eyes glittering with a mother's pride.

Staring at the bundle in your arms, my head emptied of thoughts, I felt the room shifting and turning. A sudden dizziness seized me. The light outside the window had suddenly dimmed. The world was devoid of sound. Everything had grown quiet as though my ears had grown deaf. Unable to think, I didn't say a word.

'His father died the day our boy was born.'

You looked at me, your eyes expectant, waiting for me to say something. Congratulations. Was that it? I couldn't utter the word.

'If my baby were a girl, the family would have strangled her at birth. The family said my baby son had caused his father's death. But my husband had been ill. He had a sudden seizure after his son was born. He was holding his son in his arms when he collapsed. My poor, poor baby. They accused him of causing his father's death. Harbinger of ill fortune! The boy had killed his father, my in-laws wept. My husband was his mother's least favoured son. His standing in the family was low. Now that he has passed on, my son's standing will be even lower without his father to protect him. My baby needs me. Don't you see?' Your voice choked up as you struggled to speak. 'If… if I were to die or remarry and leave my husband's family, my poor boy, my poor child, my bereft baby will be an outcast. His standing in the family will be lower than even the roadside grass. He will lose all that his father had worked so hard for. All that his father had built. This shop. This business will go to his uncles… those men sitting downstairs. They're waiting to take over my husband's shop and this… this gold business, which he and I have so painstakingly built these several years… I… I can't let it happen to my son and my husband's legacy. He… he…,' you choked out his name, '… Weng Onn was a good husband. He treated me well. We came out here together, suffered together, worked hard together. We were never a day apart. He took me with him everywhere. Everywhere.' You were sobbing so hard.

'We… we even went into the jungle together to buy rubies and gold from the tribal people. We built up this gold business. He was so kind to me. He taught me how to count, and how to read the accounts. He taught me so many… ' The bundle in your arms wailed. You patted it. Keeping your eyes on the bundle, you went on. 'I owe it to my son's father, do you understand? I owe it to Weng Onn to bring up his son and stay in this family to safeguard his legacy for our boy.'

The air in the room had grown stifling. Dust motes were floating in the beam of sunlight from the window. The bundle in your arms let out another wail. Your eyes swimming with tears, you unbuttoned your blouse and offered him your breast. Tenderly you let him suckle the nightingale egg I had once held in my hand. I wrapped my arms around you as you fed the baby. You placed a finger on my lips when I tried to put my lips on yours. Gently you pushed me away.

'I am a mother now,' you whispered.

I didn't know where to place my feelings then. All I remembered thinking was not on your face. Not on your face. So I forced my tight lips to smile. And you too smiled. Tears streaming down our cheeks, we kept smiling at each other like two idiots sitting on that blasted bed, smiling and smiling in the beam of sunlight as the baby suckled at your breast. And all the while I was thinking of the little white boat we used to row out on Lotus Lake. Loaded with the lotus roots we had harvested and the fish we had caught, we rowed our little white boat and sang to the sky.

Hai, hai, ho! Hai, hai, ho!

Carefree as little sparrows. We were so happy. Where is that little white boat now? Where is that smiling sun? And that blue sky? And the girl who sang beside me?

'Hoi! Up there! When are you coming down?' A man called up the stairs.

'Coming soon!' Eyes reddening, you turned to me. 'That's Eldest Brother-in-Law. We have to go down now.'

You buttoned up your collar and stood up with the baby in your arms.

Mute, I followed you down the stairs as though a vast grey ocean had swept in. All of a sudden the two of us were on different shores. So much was left unsaid. So little had been said.

I left the goldsmith shop with the pig farmer's son. You stood beside those stone-faced men in the shop, holding your son in your arms and watched me depart. Not a word did you say. Not a single word.

11

Disappointment with those we love is normal.

This was what I was thinking as I stole a glance at Robert. It was my birthday. We were having a simple dinner at home. Spaghetti and beef bolognaise that I had cooked.

He pushed away his plate and got up. Walked over to the sideboard to refill his glass. His second or third or fourth. He had started drinking when I was cooking.

'Remember Yvette Goh? Daughter of the Health Minister.' His voice beginning to slur. 'Met her for lunch today. Forgot to tell you. She's back to see her ailing father.'

'I don't remember meeting her.'

'Arrogant bitch! How can you not remember Yvette Goh? So smart and vivacious. Mom had hoped I would marry her. Not you. Even after I met you, she didn't stop trying to get Yvette and I back together. Especially after that time when I took you home. Ho, ho! What a melodrama that night after you'd left!'

Chuckling, he refilled his glass.

'It's so long ago,' I said under my breath.

'Ha! Heard you. Memories rise up here.' Giggling, he tapped his forehead. He was in a good mood tonight. 'Memories have a way of sneaking up on us middle-agers, you know. And this one slipped in when Yvette phoned me this afternoon. Intelligent girl. Correction. Woman. A Master's in economics from Yale no less, and a PhD in sociology under her belt. Both my parents were very keen on her. But they weren't the one marrying her, I said. So don't you forget, my girl, I gave up a cabinet minister's daughter for you. What a laugh!' Sputtered and choked on his drink.

I cleared the table and brought our plates and cutlery to the sink.

'Should've listened to my mom, don't you think? Yvette is head of an economic research institute in Canberra now. Well known, well dressed and well groomed. Very elegant. Her Aussie husband is an MP in the Conservative Party. Can't remember which state though.'

He went to the fridge for some ice cubes while I wiped the table clean, turned on the tap and started on the dishes as he went on telling me how important Yvette had become in political circles in Australia, and how when he looked at me standing at the sink washing the dishes, he couldn't help thinking what if he had chosen Yvette back then. Could've changed his fate. He could be working in Canberra right now instead of being stuck here in Singapore under lousy bosses.

'Always listen to mother, I tell the young ones now.'

I said nothing. No point getting jealous on my birthday. It was just talk to make me feel small. I was used to it. I dumped the leftovers into the bin and washed off the remnants of our dinner in the sink. He was tipsy but he still loved me despite his disappointment with me. I glanced at him, sprawled on the couch in front of the tv, and sighed. Tipsy speech. Petty to hold it against him. And yet as I scrubbed the grease off the frying pan, his words gnawed at me. And the gnawing was still there when I was getting ready for bed. A familiar experience, one of countless over the years, especially after Janice had left us. But I was feeling weary tonight. Tired of being reminded yet again that I had failed to measure up. I knew I had failed him. I had grown too quiet. Too mousy. Even at work in the National Archives I had not quite measured up to the directors' earlier expectations.

I brushed my teeth, changed and went to bed.

Next evening Yvette's name came up again when we were in the balcony.

'Yvette paid a visit to my parents yesterday. She and my sister Ruth were in the same school, belonged to the same smart set. They're planning to go skiing in the Swiss Alps. Ruth called me from London. We're invited, she said. But I declined, and you know why. I guess I don't have to tell you.'

He turned away and went to the fridge. When he came back, he let out a big theatrical sigh.

'I'll tell you why I declined. I don't want to see my wife in a ski outfit struggling on the slope. Making a fool of herself.'

I went on watering the plants. The ferns had shrivelled up and needed watering.

'So quiet? Can't laugh at yourself? Can't take a joke?'

I looked up and smiled.

'Lots of fun you're! God! You've become so damn boring.'

He went in and switched on the tv.

I went on watering the plants. I refused to be baited. I was used to his little cruelties. Whenever he was tipsy after a hard day in the office, he was like one of those little boys who deliberately pulled off a wing from a moth or a feeler from an ant just to see how the poor insect suffered.

I changed and went to bed with feelings suppressed. With little hurts niggling at my heart. Tonight they were hard enough to affect some small recalibrations. Night after night like this over the years, like the slow calcification of seashells, some small perceptions, small shifts in attitudes or responses, though nothing big, or unusual taken on its own, each shift or change being so minuscule it was hardly noticeable at the time. But ignored and overlooked these small hurts and offences, these small put downs, resentments and disappointments, these reluctances to admit what had wounded the heart, these words and gestures that had bruised and cut the flesh, these minute alterations over time to my views and perceptions I had refused to give a thought to, had pushed aside pain, suppressed wounds and distracted myself by turning away, refusing to look or listen had thickened the interior silence inside me till like grey mildew plastering the lungs I couldn't breathe, couldn't take in air at times. On which day then was my love choked and withered, and unhappiness began?

I took in a deep breath and breathing out slowly, looked out at the faint slice of moon as I lay in bed, and thought of my marriage, and the man I had married for more than twenty years.

12

'These bombs were designed to maim, not kill.' I stopped.

I was a history student in the University of Singapore showing slides of the bombs used by the American Armed Forces at the height of the Vietnam War. The young man, who had interrupted my speech, took a seat in the back row.

'Please introduce yourself,' Marianne Singam said.

'Robert Palmerston, graduate student in the political science department.'

The group laughed. Actually everyone already knew who he was even before he had opened his mouth. Marianne smiled.

'This is a private meeting of the SCMP, Student Christian Movement for Peace. It's not open to the press, Mr Palmerston.'

'Please call me Robert. I'm not here to file a report.' A broad smile spreading over his sun-browned face.

'Aren't you stringing for *The Asian Reporter*, Robert?'

'I am... eh?'

'Marianne. Marianne Singam, president of the SCMP.'

'Glad to meet you, Marianne. I'm not writing a report tonight. This attendance is purely personal. I'm a history buff. And I'm interested in meeting the only history and political science student group on campus still speaking out against chemical warfare.'

'And using Southeast Asian countries like Singapore and the Philippines as their soldiers' R&R during the Vietnam War,' I added, annoyed at the interruption of my presentation.

'Wait,' he held up both hands. Still smiling he said, 'Let's not fight. You guys are known to be very critical of our historical past. Like the government's detention of the Marxist group. Be careful. The authorities keep an eye on groups like yours.'

'So what's new? This is not the first time we've been warned that we're being watched. We're not doing anything wrong. Discussion isn't a crime.

Neither is the dissemination of historical facts. The chemical bombing of Laos and Vietnam in the 1960s is a fact. So were the types of bombs used. Chemical bombing did not stop with the Vietnam War. Look at what's happening in Iraq, Iran and Syria now. The Geneva Protocol had banned chemical weapons. But during the Iraq-Iran conflict, the US secretly supported the Iraqi military's use of chemical weapons. We should be concerned. When contemporary events become history it's too late. So what's wrong with discussion of chemical warfare when the US have secret torture camps?'

My tone had bordered on the hostile, but his smile was disarming as he turned to the group. 'She's right, you know. Discussion isn't a crime. Singapore is a democratic country.'

'You're welcome, Robert.' Marianne gave me a wink and turned to the group. 'Tonight we're fortunate to have a journalist in our midst. Shall we ask him why the Americans bombed to maim, and not to kill during the Vietnam War?'

'Yeah!'

'Hey,' he grinned. 'I'm not a military strategist. But if you look at the bombing from the military's point of view, maiming is more effective in weakening the enemy's side than killing. Maiming soldiers and civilians will drain more of the enemy's resources. The injured need medical care, medicine, doctors, nurses, ambulances and infrastructures like hospitals and roads. The dead need nothing.'

The group applauded him. We had to admit that we hadn't thought of that angle. He asked if we had discussed the Cold War and the Domino Theory.

'What would have happened to Singapore back then if our government hadn't cracked down hard on the Communists?'

His question sparked such a lively discussion that Marianne invited him back for future meetings. And he did come back and brought others with him.

During these meetings I was conscious of his light brown eyes looking in my direction. Whenever I looked up our eyes met and he smiled, as if pleased that he had succeeded in willing me to look at him. The attention was both irritating and flattering. It added another dimension to the SCMP meetings. I found myself looking forward to the meetings although I would never have admitted that it was because of him. He was our senior, and much admired. And the fact that he was stringing for a regional newspaper added to his glamour. His contributions during our discussions were often thoughtful, well informed and thought provoking. For example, if you were a committed Christian and soldier, what would you do if your army uses chemical weapons secretly, despite the Geneva Protocol?

Marianne, Duncan and the rest of the SCMP committee thought highly of him. One night he thrust a book into my hands.

'For you.' His manner was gruff and abrupt, and without his usual smile.

I read the title of the paperback. It was Noam Chomsky's latest book, which I would have bought if I had the money to spare.

'A gift. Take it.'

'I… I… how can I thank you?'

'Have supper with me? I haven't had dinner.'

Noam Chomsky's book was the first of many books that he lent or gave me that year. Books on subjects ranging from war and the military-industrial complex to theology and social justice. Under his guidance and encouragement, I started to read books like Paul Tillich's *The Shaking of the Foundations*, Paulo Freire's *Pedagogy of the Oppressed* and Martin Luther King's *The Trumpet of Conscience*. Books that had moved earlier generations of university students in the west to fight for justice and equality, he said.

'But not us in Singapore,' I said.

'Not true. What about LKY and his group?' he asked, ready to play tutor.

Over late-night suppers of roti prata with mutton curry and cups of piping hot coffee and teh tarik at the hawker stalls in Adam Road we argued endlessly. After supper, he walked me back to my hostel each night, often taking long detours around the Bukit Timah campus. I had never felt so alive, so engaged and involved with the world of ideas before.

Back in our hostel, Marianne sang, 'Oh dear dear me! Our ice maiden is melting.'

'Who cares?' I laughed. 'Which girl wouldn't fall for a man who respects her intellect and gives her books instead of flowers?'

I was walking on air. We were a couple.

Two months later a new report by the world body of the SCMP on the devastating effects of chemical warfare was published in several American major newspapers. It stirred anew controversies and discussions on warfare and weaponry in the SCMP.

'In the 1960s and 70s American military forces had mass sprayed tons of lethal chemical defoliants like Agent Orange into Laos and Vietnam. Hundreds of thousands of acres once covered by rich crops and forests were devastated. The land looked as if an atomic bomb had fallen on it. Pictures of children maimed and crippled, without legs or arms, with skins burned and singed by the chemicals, horrified us. The world organisation of the Student Christian Movement for Peace condemned chemical warfare. In Singapore our group distributed photocopies of the report. To lukewarm interest! I'm so cheesed off! We have to do more than photocopying.'

'Hey, cool down. Supper?'

'I can't. Our group is meeting tonight. We're planning a candlelit sit-in to protest against chemical warfare.'

On the morning of the protest, before the protest could take place in the evening, Robert's article was splashed on the front page of *The Asian*: "Students To Hold Anti-War Protest In Staid Singapore!"

It was a scoop for Robert.

The university announced an immediate clamp-down. Marianne and other SCMP office holders were called into the Vice-Chancellor's office. Faced with the threat of immediate expulsion, the protest was called off. The event was postponed and the venue changed to a nearby church. Instead of a protest, it became a *Prayer for Peace*. The students were frightened off, and the turnout was small.

Back in the hostel I moped in my room. I blamed myself. I refused to take Robert's phone calls. In the hostel, we had to use the phone in the students' lounge.

'Xiu Yin! Phone!'

My name was called several times each evening. But I refused to take his calls.

'C'mon girl! It's not your fault!' Marianne said. 'He's a reporter. Sooner or later, he would've nosed it out.'

'We were talking over supper! It was supposed to be personal.'

'So? He made a mistake. It's not end of the world. This is the fifth night. He's not giving up. C'mon!'

When I finally took his call, a huge quarrel erupted between us.

'Where are your principles and ethics of journalism? You mix private and public! I thought I was talking to my boyfriend! Not the bloody *Asian's* reporter!'

I slammed down the phone.

The whole hostel knew about the altercation. Yet like a thick-skinned penitent, he came to the hostel each night. Marianne pleaded his case. Even Duncan chipped in. After two weeks of his nightly visits, I finally relented. We went for a long walk in the Botanic Gardens trudging down the maze of tree-lined paths, our heated arguments interspersed with long periods of angry silence as we strode into the dark and mysterious moving shadows. Few people were around. For hours the two of us wandered down these paths arguing, arguing, arguing until, all of a sudden, he pulled me into the thick shadows of foliage, knelt down and kissed my knees, and wouldn't let go till I forgave him.

13

Just before my graduation, he drove me home to meet his parents.

'Oh, Rob,' a gasp escaped me as his car turned into the sprawling grounds of the two-storey bungalow shielded by luscious greenery and a row of majestic rain trees.

'You didn't tell me you're living in this district of the rich.'

'Would you have come if I'd told you?'

He squeezed my waist as we walked up the tree-lined path.

'Don't worry. My parents won't bite you.' He took my hand.

'I've never been to such a mansion.'

His parents were seated by the swimming pool where several armchairs were arranged around a low table set for tea.

'My father, Judge Magnus Palmerston.'

'Sir,' I squeaked at the august presence, heads taller than me.

Judge Magnus gave a nod, sat down and closed his eyes. The light of the setting sun seemed too strong for him.

'And this is my mother, Aileng Soo-Palmerston, chief inspector of schools.' Robert was gleeful as a schoolboy.

I was totally unprepared and bewildered. For a girl who grew up in Chinatown with a Cantonese opera troupe, making polite conversation with a judge and his wife was an ordeal. And drinking English tea with cold milk poured out of a delicate white porcelain jug into delicate white cups edged with silver. It unnerved me. I wished Robert had prepared me.

'Robbie told me your grandparents are Chinese wayang performers. Are they still going on the road?'

'Er… no, no, not anymore. They're teaching Cantonese opera in the community centre. My grandmother is a… a Cantonese opera singer.'

'Oh, is that so? I didn't know that the community centres teach Chinese wayang. Did you know, Magnus?'

The judge grunted from behind the papers he was reading.

'It must be so tiring performing and travelling in the back of lorries on those ghastly Malaysian roads. Moving from town to town. Living out of a trunk. Such a hard life.'

I wanted very badly but lacked the confidence to tell the Chief Inspector of Schools that Cantonese opera was no longer a 'wayang' performed in the streets. It was a full-scale opera performed in the theatre. Much like operas in the west.

'And yet…,' she smiled at me. 'Your grandparents have done well. They managed to send you to school and university.'

I shifted in my seat under her beaming smile, suddenly self-conscious and ashamed of my white blouse with eyelet frills down the front, and my black and pink floral skirt with the white elasticised belt that I had bought from a stall in Chinatown's night market. Mrs Palmerston's smile and tone though kindly meant had made everything I wore look cheap. I looked out at the swimming pool, and the white clouds floating in its waters in the waning evening light. Her rich sea green silk blouse was shimmering as she poured tea into one of her beautiful white teacups. She looked very elegant.

'What instrument does your grandfather play, Xiu Yin?'

'He plays the erhu.'

'Oh dear me, I must confess my ignorance of Chinese music. What's an erhu?'

'It's a two-stringed instrument held upright in the lap like this, and played with a bow. An essential instrument in Chinese opera.'

'I'm afraid the music in Chinese opera does sound like so much noise to me. All that *tuk-tuk-cheng* gives me a headache.'

A soft chuckle came from the judge as he sat up and accepted the cup of tea from his wife.

'But we're not an unmusical family. Robbie and his brother have had violin lessons. My daughter Ruth and I play the piano.'

I followed her glance into the spacious living room. A young woman was seated at the highly polished Steinway by the open French windows, softly tinkling the keys. Beyond the French windows stretched the large green lawn and rose bushes, and pots of white and pink bougainvillea and ferns.

'Ruth darling, do play one of Mozart's light pieces for us.'

'Oh Mummy, must I perform?'

'Don't be rude, darling. Xiu Yin is our guest. Do you know Mozart's music?' She turned to me.

I shook my head and caught myself thinking of Grandfather's prized two-stringed erhu at home. Carved by one of Canton's greatest erhu makers in the seventeenth century, it was a gift from Master Loke, his mentor. The precious heritage instrument was kept in a worn leather case, and sat on our kitchen table covered with a green oilcloth. Suddenly I wanted to shield my grandparents and our dingy three-room Housing Board flat from Mrs Palmerston's solicitous gaze.

Robert reached over to squeeze my hand. Seated on the cool tiled floor, he was lolling between his mother's armchair and mine munching on a curry puff and letting the crumbs fall onto his white shirtfront. Looking at him I wished I had his ease. The same ease and self-confidence I had seen often in my classmates in ACS who expected to ace their exams and study overseas. And if their grades were low, an overseas education was still attainable for they were from well-to-do, English educated families who enjoyed a quality of material comfort and a cultural life that many in my neighbourhood could only dream of. But it wasn't just their family's wealth that gave them that ease and confidence, they had that extra something, which sociologists termed 'social capital' – that knowledge of the world that gave them the confidence to speak with ease in august company, that careless grace and elan seen in those who grew up in families with doctors, lawyers and judges in their midst. Like these Palmerstons. Would I be as elegant as Mrs Aileng Soo-Palmerston when I am her age if I married Robert, I wondered.

'You must take Judge Magnus and I to watch your grandparents perform some day, Xiu Yin.'

I nodded. But I couldn't be sure that I was absolutely right in the way I saw things that evening. I was so busy trying to make sure that the crumbs of my pastry didn't fall onto the floor. Aileng Soo's words had sounded kindly enough and her smile was gracious. But the Judge's silence unnerved me. I felt very vulnerable and exposed. I murmured that I would take them to watch Por Por, but I never did.

Later that evening Robert told them we were getting married. Several minutes passed before Judge Magnus coughed and congratulated me. Very politely.

'When?' Mrs Palmerston turned to me.

Both of them were icily polite. Neither of them spoke to their son. Robert stood resolutely by my side holding my hand throughout those awkward minutes. Minutes that had felt as though the air had solidified, and no one could speak or move naturally except Robert who kept my hand in his and would not let go. I was so moved by his resolute gesture. I let myself lean towards him till shoulders touching we were standing shoulder to shoulder before his parents.

Now years later, when I thought of those difficult moments, and him standing so resolutely beside me as we faced the judge and his wife, my heart could not leave him. I simply could not.

14

But as they say people change. The first time it happened there was no witness. Janice had already left home. I fell onto the floor, cut my lips on the wooden arm of the sofa, and the front door shut with a bang!

I lay on the floor till I could pull myself up. The fall had knocked the breath out of me. After the third attempt I got up and limped into the kitchen. I had hurt my right hip when I fell. Already rehearsing what I would say to the doctor if I needed to go. I turned on the tap, cupped my hands and splashed water on my face. His work was getting to him. It was my fault. I shouldn't have read Marianne Singam's book at home. The moment he walked in through the front door, his glance had fallen on the book.

'Another bloody memoir!' he'd growled. 'Every detainee has a story to sell! And gullible fools like you will buy! Throw it away!'

He stalked off to the kitchen. I heard him pull open the fridge door. Heard the hard clink of bottle against glass as he poured himself a drink. I should have put away the book then. But Marianne was my closest friend in varsity. We had lost touch after she was detained for her involvement in a Catholic group helping migrant workers. I could not put the book down. I was halfway through the chapter on her interrogation. I was so engrossed I didn't hear Robert coming out of the kitchen until he snatched the book out of my hands and flung it across the room.

'Your name is in here! How could you?'

The words were out before I could stop myself. 'You're in ISD, Home Affairs. But you told me you're in SID, Ministry of Defence. I couldn't have misheard all these years. Could I?'

His palm slammed into my cheek so hard I lost my balance and fell.

'That's for calling your spouse a liar.' He turned and left.

I had almost blacked out when I fell against the wooden arm of the sofa.

A hostile silence descended on our apartment the following day. His glowering eyes followed me wherever I went. I ate alone at the dining table under his watchful eyes. He refused to eat with me. The office was my only escape.

'What happened to you?' Mavis asked.

'I was helping my grandfather out of his wheelchair.'

'You need to get a helper. Did you apply?'

'My grandparents don't want a helper.'

'Old people can be so difficult. Can I visit? Can I help?'

'No, no, no! It will make things worse. But thanks, thanks for the kind offer. You can buy me lunch today. Take me to a nice quiet place.'

Back home, Robert's suppressed fury heated the air at night like a volcano's red-hot lava. I lost my appetite. I couldn't sit or eat in peace. His glowering silence held a threat, especially after he had had a drink or two. His eyes followed me. Even when I showered, he insisted the bathroom door be kept open.

'Like before!' he growled.

I sat in the balcony under the bamboo plants, fearful of going into our bedroom until he had drunk himself to sleep.

The days passed. I regretted reading the book. Perhaps he did tell me he was working in ISD, and I heard SID. Internal Security Department, not Security and Intelligence Division, Ministry of Defence. I blamed the government's frequent use of abbreviations that confused the public. I began to think it was my fault. After two weeks, I was convinced it was indeed my fault. I had started this war, but we couldn't go on living at war. Someone had to initiate the peace process. That night I wrote him an apology. Just a few lines. No response. Days passed.

One evening he brought dinner home and we had dinner together again.

'Drink? White? Only 13 per cent alcohol.'

I was so relieved, and grateful for the return of peace, I drank. Two glasses. And we went to bed together. But I dared not hope it would last.

On Sunday morning we went to church as usual. My hope rose. After church and breakfast, we went out and bought three more potted plants for the balcony. Two ferns and a jade green bamboo. And I thanked God for the peaceful day.

On the night of the Mid-Autumn Festival, I was doing our laundry, stuffing a load into the washing machine. Robert was at the kitchen sink doing the washing up after our dinner. Before I pressed the switch I heard him singing softly as he soaped the plates, *'God of mercy and compassion, Look with pity upon me...'*

I recognised the words of the moving hymn and stopped to listen.

'I went to church this morning. Asked God for forgiveness. Hope you forgive too,' he muttered, his back towards me.

'Oh, Robbie.'

I hugged his back. He patted my hand and moved away, and we continued with our household chores.

Gratitude filled me as I sat in the balcony, enjoying a cup of tea. The full moon was bright as a silver disc. I wished Janice were here tonight. I wished she could see her father now cutting me a slice of the moon cake and pouring me a fresh cup of Chinese tea. My little girl used to hold a butterfly lantern on Mid-Autumn Festival night. A young woman now, she was making her way in the world on the other side of the globe as far away from home as she could get. And my heart swelled with pain and maternal pride. *There's such courage in my daughter.*

'I'm going in. It's Arsenal versus Liverpool tonight.'

'Thanks Rob, I'll come in soon.'

I looked up at the full moon again. The Lady in the Moon was raining her benevolent rays upon the earth. I got up and watered my plants. Glanced into the living room where Robert was watching his football club play a winning match, shouting on the phone to his friends. An evening such as this was rare, and I was savouring it.

To be fair, we did have good times. Not everything was bad. In the early years, he used to mop the floor and do the laundry every Saturday morning. His mother was shocked when she visited.

'No helper? You've a little child.'

'We don't want a stranger in our home, Mom. Yin and I would rather that Janice goes to day care where she can play with other kids.'

He was firm with his mother, proudly showing her the plaque that I had made for him. *Father, Commander-in-Chief & Laundryman.* Considered an up-and-coming young officer, he put in long hours in the office, sometimes on weekends too. He was keen to prove to his father that he was as good as his elder brother, the head of neurosurgery in one of New York's top hospitals.

He kept Saturday mornings for the two of us. Waking up when the sky was still dark, his arm would reach out and pull me towards him. Later, after a shower together, we woke up Janice. Walking to the market with our little girl between us, holding our hand, the three of us sang, '*To market, to market to buy a fat pig!*' I was a happy wife and mother on those pink dawns twenty years ago when the air was fresh and clean, and the trees were dripping with the night's dew, and Robert was laughing at something I had said when we reached the sweet bean curd stall in the market.

'Good morning, Mr Tan! Three bowls, please! My *wifey* here will pay.'

On Sundays, he woke up Janice.

'Up! Up! Sleepy head! Mummy is getting breakfast ready. After church, we'll go tooooo…?'

It was the same question every Sunday, and his darling girl loved the game.

'Waffles and ice cream, Papa!' she squealed as Robert swung her out of bed.

When I looked back on those times, my heart softened despite the bruises on my arms. For better or for worse, the church had taught us.

'Our fingers… some are long; some are short. No one's perfect,' Grandfather used to say.

15

'Dearest Intimate' never crossed my lips again.

Never again would I use those two words.

Never again would my shadow darken her goldsmith shop.

I returned to my brush and ink like a drunk to his drink.

Who else can I turn to? I am like a bird without a sky to fly, wings beating in the dark void. Daily I long for a glimpse of home. For the village, and green hills and rice fields I had left. But I had burned all my bridges.

Honourable Father and Mother.

I don't deserve to be your daughter. I don't deserve to be my brothers' sister. My sister and relatives will have nothing to do with me. And rightly so!

I am dead. I am like a nameless ghost. I want to kill myself. Jump into the river or sea. Or hang from a rope. But I am a coward. I don't deserve pity. Yet this foolish bloke, this foolish Butcher Bloke, he pities me.

To think I gave her my heart. I trusted her. Believed the eight words she thrust into my hand. What did I get in return? A widow's loyalty to the dead. A mother's love for her son. Should I hate her son? I should kill myself first. But the pig farmer's son saw me eyeing his meat knife the other night. The next morning, all the knives were gone.

Jade Emperor in Heaven, here is my solemn vow.

From today I, Wong Kam Foong, will keep an honest record of a life endured on earth. If I should fail, let me wander forever a nameless hungry ghost when I leave this earth. But if I should succeed in keeping a faithful record, may it please Your Majesty, Jade Emperor of Heaven, and my Ancestors in the Other World to forgive me. May my parents and parents-in-law, brothers and sisters forgive me. Forgive this wretched worm and take me back into your fold. If not, I will die a wandering nameless ghost. Condemned for eternity. I have broken the laws. Ignored the proprieties.

Forsook my duties. Forsook my parents. Disobeyed my in-laws. Left my husband and homeland to embark on a thousand li journey across the vast seas. To what end?

To naught!

It is my punishment.

Heaven has decreed I am to remain the wife of the pig farmer's son. A fate I cannot escape. A fate I accepted when I left her goldsmith shop in Singapore and took the train with him to come here to Ipoh. Never again will my shadow darken the doorway of her golden shop.

Never! Never! Never!

℘ — ℭ

Ipoh.

We have settled in the town built by Cantonese and Hakka tin miners and traders. The two-storey shophouses and temples make me homesick. The houses remind me of the towns back home. Each time I think of Saam Hor I feel compelled to kneel and beg for my parents' forgiveness again and again. Each morning when I wake up, each night before I sleep, I kneel before the window of our tiny bedroom. I look up at the sky and pray: Father, Mother and Honoured Ancestors. I have done wrong. Please forgive your wretched daughter.

℘ — ℭ

My young and bitter face leans out of the window above the tailor's shop. The tailoring shop is a two-storey townhouse where the pig farmer's son has rented the front room that looks down on the street. I am looking out for him. There he is! Cycling up the road, a straw hat clapped on his head, and a large box strapped to the back of his bicycle. The road is sizzling in the afternoon heat. The town is a furnace. And I am burning in the heat.

'Chee Yok Lo! Butcher Bloke!' I screech.

An airplane streaks across the sky drowning out my words just as he cycles past below my window. His sun-browned face looks up and breaks into a smile. I scowl at him. His skin is thick as cowhide. No matter how often I insult him and call him *Chee Yok Lo,* the Butcher Bloke smiles at me from his bicycle like an idiot cycling in the sun. His good humour riles me. When I scold him for smiling, his reply is always the same.

'Why shouldn't I smile? I have a wife. Two is family,' he grins.

Four years older, he looks younger. My face in the mirror looks like a sun-dried bittergourd. His is smooth as a watermelon. His customers adore him. Young housewives address him respectfully as Uncle Butcher. Older women treat him as though he is their younger son, calling him *Jai* or Sonny. They call out to him with such affection as though he really is their youngest and dearest boy. They even give him food to bring home. They have heard his wife does not treat him well. He just smiles and shakes his head. Named Chan Tuck Wah when he was born, no one had called him by that formal name. His parents and the villagers back home had always called him by his diminutive and affectionate pet name, Wah Jai.

'But you are my wife. You can call me anything. Pig Farmer's Son. Chee Yok Lo or Butcher Bloke. Chan Tuck Wah or Wah Jai. I will answer to any name you choose. My head is full of names.'

'Full of shit you mean.'

'Full of shit here at your service.' He bows.

Oh Heaven! What crime did I commit in my past life to deserve such a clown? When I push him down, he bounces back with a smile. Like one of those clown dolls.

'Butcher Bloke!' I shout again from my window. 'Bring home some liver for dinner tonight!'

'Aye, aye! I hear you, Wife!'

'Listen to our Wah Jai answering his imperial consort.'

The old women tease him.

He smiles and rings his bell. From my upstairs window I see more women coming out of their houses to crowd around him. Like flies around dung, I told him once. He smiled. His good humour infuriates me. I am a sea of liquid flames every day. My temper flares up easily. I blame him for what had happened when I should blame you. And myself.

Memories of that day in the goldsmith shop plague my sleep. I have nightmares. I cry every day. Some days I have no will to live. Some days I want to wield a chopper and kill those grey men in your shop. Regret gnaws at my heart. Everything had been too much and too rushed that day. I was too overwhelmed. Too happy, too unseeing, too impetuous, too insensitive, too hasty, and too judgemental. And you? Too timid, too quiet, too respectful, too dutiful, and too obedient. Too submissive to your in-laws and elders. Your silence stabbed me right here in the core of my heart. Twisted the knife in when your relatives insulted Wah Jai and I. When your brother-in-law insinuated that we were a pair of leeches come to suck your family's gold, not a word did you say in my defence! Not a whisper! How could you? How could you remain so tight-lipped? Respectfully you held your tongue. Demurely you cast down your eyes. Dutifully you sealed your lips. I admit I am poor. I was shabbily dressed that day. But was I a rat trying to burrow into your family's rice bin? A leech out to suck your blood and make off with your gold? Enough! Enough! It is as the ancients said. Easier to hoard a ton of gold than keep a trusted intimate friend.

We were so young when we were betrothed to our men. Fourteen. And now you are the mother of a son, and widow of the man who brought you to the Nanyang, taught you how to do accounts and run a goldsmith shop. And I? I am the butcher's wife. As our mothers used to sing, umbrellas have different handles; people have different lives. I rage in my heart but life goes on. I will not waste another tear on you. Not another drop! I weep for myself. For the fool that trusted you.

$$\mathcal{E}\!\!\!O - \mathcal{O}\!\!\!R$$

Heaven, help me! His kindness is killing me. He works so hard yet he does not complain. He cleans and dusts. He cooks and scrubs. And he washes our clothes while I wander in the land of the half-dead. I sit in our rented room all day and have no heart to do anything. Yet he does not say a word. A quiet man. A patient man. Why should he tolerate a wife like me? How could his patience last so long? Is he really so kind? He has not asked about you nor talked about what happened that day. For that I am eternally grateful. I am grateful too that he continues to sleep on the floor and lets me sleep on the bed. He does not try to touch me. If he does, I will kill myself. Perhaps he knows it.

Guilt sits on me like a rock. It presses on my heart when I think of my parents and the village I have abandoned. I think of his parents and the family he has lost. The grief he is holding in his heart. The grief he is hiding behind that smiling Buddha face. I have not forgotten the oath I swore though not once did he mention it again. I had sworn a vow never to leave him if he helped me to find you. And he did find you. That it came to nothing is no fault of his. What am I to do now? What am I to do?

I am chained to him. First, by marriage; second, by oath; third, by kindness!

Oh Heaven, help!

₲—ℱ

Two nights ago, I saw a new side of him. His music drew me to the stairs. I didn't know he could play the two-string erhu so well. This pig farmer's son I was forced to marry is not just an itinerant butcher. His father and elder brother were the pig farmers and butchers. He, being the youngest, was sent to school and studied up to Middle School.

'If the world had been at peace, if the warlords had not turned China upside down, I would have been our village teacher. I would have taken over from Old Teacher in the village school,' he said.

I was silent. I have been around men in the theatre long enough to know that they boast and tell big lies to their women. But he is not an actor or singer but an erhu player. And a very good one too.

His erhu sings the longing in my heart, the sad notes teasing out forgotten memories. When he bows his erhu strings, I hear the cries of the swifts and sparrows roosting in the hills at sunset, the bleating of goats under the lychee trees as Mother combs my hair. I hear the breeze sighing in the bamboo groves, and my brother coming home with his catch of fish. Visions of green hills and fields of spring rice jade green in the sunlight float before my watery eyes. How can these eyes not weep for the home I had left because of you? I remember a moonlit night by the river with our village sisters when you and I sang *Thoughts On A Quiet Night,* Li Bai's poem, which we had stolen from our brothers' learning.

Before my bed the bright moon shone,
Frost glittering on the ground.

Lift my head to gaze at the moon
And lowered it yearning for the village home.

℘ — ℭ

Every evening after dinner, he plays his erhu in the covered walkway outside the tailor's shop. Some nights, his melodies stirring my memories, I long for the return of those days in the opera troupe when I was singing and practising with Master Wu and the men. Life was simple then.

The beat of drums.

The clashing of cymbals and sighing strings.

Painted faces in the evening.

Cooking porridge in the morning.

Emptying Master Wu's chamber pot and lighting his opium pipe at night.

How I miss those chores, and the excitement in the backstage each night.

I miss the troupe, and the laughter and teasing of the men. I miss their yells and cuffs on my head. And Master Wu's teaching stick striking my back. Life was hard then. But my heart was burning with hope. That fire has burned out now. I am naught but a scorched worm.

I creep down the stairs to join the neighbours on the covered walkway. He is playing his erhu and narrating a story in a voice I have not heard before. It is the voice of the storytellers in our village, half singing and half speaking in the lilt characteristic of Saam Hor Cantonese. To hear him narrate his story as he draws out a long plaintive tune on his erhu, his arrival as an illegal immigrant sneaking into Malaya was the start of Life's greatest adventure. Like the others, I listen spellbound. Bowing his erhu, he half-sings and half-speaks in the manner of the traditional village storytellers.

'*Yan hoi mong mong...* alone in a sea of strangers tossing in the ocean wide, floating hither and thither among ten thousand leaves suddenly flung by waves onto a strange new shore. A stranger among strange faces. With no family and no friend. I looked up to heaven and saw no stairway. Looked down at earth and saw no path. I called out to heaven but heaven made no reply. Called out to earth, earth did not answer me. Hungry and desperate,

I begged. Aah, aah, aah, I croaked, and begged for my first bowl of rice in this foreign land, and took whatever came, and accepted the first thing that Life thrust at me. And that was to slaughter pigs! Ahhh! That was the hour I met my destiny in this new land. Whatever life I had dreamt of in the motherland, whatever deeds I had done in my past, all melted into the mists. For the present, my destiny, oh my new destiny is to be, is to be your wandering butcher, my friends.'

'Ho-yeah! Ho-yeah! Encore! Encore!' His audience laugh and clap.

His eyes light up when he sees me. His erhu strikes up a lively tune. In that same instant six military planes roar across the night sky. Children scream! Babies wail! Mothers cling to their small ones and cover their ears. Our anxious eyes look up at the sky and turn to each other.

'War is coming. We have to leave. Ipoh is not safe.' He packs up his erhu.

℘ — ℀

On the evening before the horrendous happens, we follow our neighbours and push through the crowd inside the tailor's shop to listen to his radio.

'The Japanese have landed in Kota Bahru. The war has reached Malaya.'

The grave voice on the radio shakes us. All of a sudden life has quickened. Women rush home. Mothers shout for their children. Men shove and argue with one another in loud angry voices.

'The Japs won't reach us.'

'You're a fool if you think that!'

'The Brits will defeat them!'

'So bloody sure, are you?'

The men's voices shoot through the air like bullets. Many are undecided. Leave or stay in Ipoh? And if they leave, where to go? These are anxious trying days of indecision. The sunlight takes on a different pallor. Hot dry air stings our skin.

'Kam Foong, pack! Now! Hurry!' Wah Jai shouts. 'We're leaving. We'll go south to Singapore. The British have a large army there. They will protect us.'

Thousands have the same thought.

The train station is a sea of shoving bodies, flailing arms and crying children clinging to their parents who are fighting their way into the train. He yanks me on board just as the train pulls out. We squeeze into the overcrowded coach with our bags. Every seat, every bit of floor space jammed with bodies, bags and bundles! Children with frightened eyes crouch between our legs. All night shoulder to shoulder we stand with nervous betel nut chewing Indians, surly Malays and quarrelsome Hakkas and Teochews clutching their frightened children in their arms as warplanes streak overhead. The sound of explosions follows our train as it thunders into the night. I was half asleep, head on his shoulder when a sudden explosion rocks our coach and plunges it into darkness. His grip on my arm tightens.

'Hold on to me!' He shouts above the noise just before another explosion drowns out his voice.

'Fire!' A man yells.

A huge blast rips through the coach.

'*Chee Yok Lo!*' I yell for him in the exploding darkness.

A huge brilliance swallows my cry. Everything goes dark.

When I open my eyes a brown smoky pall hangs under the grey sky. I sit up, my arms and face bleeding. Dazed men and women calling out to each other. Wailing children covered in blood wandering around crying, 'Mama! Papa!' Dazed and unsteady, I stand up.

'*Chee Yok Lo!* Butcher Bloke! Chan Tuck Wah!' I shout his various names. 'Wah Jai! Answer me! Wah Jai!'

Shouting his names, I push through the crowd milling around the overturned coaches. The thought that I have lost him makes me scream out his names louder and louder. Wailing and howling I rail at the heartless dark sky that has covered him. Where is he? O gods in heaven, where is he? I have lost everything since coming to the Nanyang. Don't let me lose him.

'Wah Jaiiiii!' I run towards the burning coaches. What if he's trapped inside one of them? 'Wah Jaiiiii!'

'Bomb! Bomb!'

An Indian man pulls me away from the fires. What is he saying? I can't understand his jabbering. He pushes me away from the burning wreck.

'Bomb!'

'Wah Jaiiiii!' I screech like a mad woman, racing down the wooded slope running from group to group, asking everyone if they have seen a man in a dark blue tunic and black trousers. Gunshots and small explosions peppering the grey dawn as I run from bush to tree, and tree to bush calling, yelling, howling till the sun is high above the wreckage of humanity, its merciless rays raining on the wounded and the dead. My throat is hoarse and dry. My arms and legs are bleeding.

'Don't die, *Chee Yok Lo*! Please don't die. Wah Jaiiiii! Where are you? Don't leave me. Wah Jaiiiii!'

The sky turns dark again. Sinking into despair I sleep on the ground like others lying down not far from the train wreck in case he comes to look for me.

The next day a group of Malay men lead us to the Seremban Hospital where hundreds lie groaning in the corridors of the overcrowded wards. I rush from ward to ward and find him on the floor in one of the wards.

Face ashen and twisted in pain he is curled on a blood-soaked blanket. He has a high fever and barely recognises me. A large piece of metal shrapnel sticks out of his right thigh, just above the knee. Holding a blood-soaked shirt, he had tried to stave off the bleeding. There are cuts on his head and face. Glass fragments are embedded in his arms and knees. I search the wards for a doctor and find a nurse, an Eurasian who can speak a little Chinese. Kneeling before her, knocking my head on the floor again and again, I beg her to come with me.

Thank Heaven for her kind heart, she attends to Wah Jai. While I sit on him and hold him down, she pours some liquid on his wound and cuts out the metal shrapnel stuck deep in his knee. Wah Jai passes out. The nurse pours iodine on the gaping wound, bandages it and hurries away.

May Heaven bless her and all her descendants! I spend hours pulling out the other bits of shrapnel stuck in him.

That same night, I found out a lorry is leaving for Singapore. I take out the gold bracelet hidden with the rolled-up pages of my journal sewn into the lining of my samfoo jacket. I offer the gold bracelet to the lorry driver and keep my pages in the cloth belt. I had bought the bracelet with savings from my opera days. Gold will make the devil push your cart, my mother always said. The lorry driver agrees to take us. But Wah Jai is feverish and very weak. Fear and will gives me strength. Using the blood-soaked blanket, I haul and pull him out of the ward. Then heaving and panting, I carry him out of the hospital on my back and onto the back of the lorry. He is in such pain, he's barely conscious. His fever is very high. I cradle his burning body under the tarpaulin of the lorry and pray. All night I hold him close and sponge him with a wet towel.

'Wah Jai, Wah Jai, don't die. Don't leave me. I am your wife. I will never leave you. You must live,' I keep whispering in his ear over and over again. A single night together is the same as a hundred days as husband and wife, our elders had taught us. We have been together for more than a hundred nights. He has looked after me. Fed and clothed me. I am destined to be his wife. I wet his lips and forehead and hug him close to my breast as explosions rock our lorry and warplanes roar overhead. The world is on fire. The gates of Hell have opened. But the pig farmer's son and I are together alive. Thank you, Mother, who taught me how to save. I thank Father who sent me to the well and river to fetch water. Those trips gave me strong limbs to carry Wah Jai to the lorry. Oh gods in heaven, please let him live.

'Here. Let him drink,' a woman hands me a bottle of water.

Hiding under the tarpaulin among the sacks of rice in the lorry, the Teochew family of five can speak Cantonese. As the explosions grow louder we pray together, calling on the gods in heaven and our ancestors to protect us.

§ — ☙

The war and bombs followed us to Singapore. Barely two weeks after we have settled under the stairs of a shophouse in Chinatown, bombs fall in the small hours of the night. Air raid sirens screaming, we rush out of the lodging house. Wah Jai is limping beside me. We run out to the brightly lit streets. Red lanterns everywhere because of New Year. The gwai lo are such fools! The government did not order a blackout of the city. Do they not care? Have they forgotten the danger of light at night? With no blackout in the city every enemy plane flying low can see us. Scurrying like mice! There's a shrill whistling. My heart freezes. The whole sky explodes in brilliant orange. We are flung against pillars and walls. Incandescent columns of boiling black smoke rise to heaven. Clouds of fiery sparks light up the night sky. A white brilliance blinds the eyes. There's a colossal deafening roar. I feel the road heave. I skid uncontrollably sliding away from Wah Jai as one thunderous explosion after another rock the streets. My head hits a lorry.

'Kam Foong!!!' I hear him yell my name. But with grit in my mouth and ash in my eyes, I couldn't answer him.

A great stillness descends. It's as if I have gone deaf. As if the bombed streets are traumatised, the buildings hold their breath. The world is silent. Slowly my ears start to hum. The humming fills my ears. I ease myself onto my hands and knees. My head is bleeding. Blood is seeping into my eyes. I sit up, my back against the wheel of the lorry. As the black smoke clears, I see his dust-covered body.

'Wah Jaiiiiiiiii!'

PART 2

16

'Great Grandmama, once more please! I've got to perform this aria next Sunday. Please…'

'Just look at our Miss Shameless! Just look at her,' Por Por laughed.

Seated in her old cane chair, she turned to me her eyes brimming with pleasure. How could she refuse her great granddaughter? When Janice was a toddler she used to carry her and sing to her whenever I visited. And now Janice was so keen to learn the skills of Cantonese opera aria singing.

'All right, girl. One more time. Stand up straight. Now breathe from your diaphragm. Open your mouth wide and sing. Hold the note as long as you can.'

'Aaaaaaaaaaaah…!' Janice collapsed, out of breath giggling.

'Up! Up! Get up! Where's my cane? In the old days, your back would be covered with red streaks by now. That was how my Sifu, Master Wu, taught me. I wasn't so lucky like you. I didn't go to an opera institute. There were no opera schools in those days. Listening, watching, imitating, and practising hard. Very hard. That was how we learnt.'

'Things have changed, Grandmama! We're more professional now. But I still want to practise hard like you. Sing as good as you. Now please sing that aria one more time. *Pleeeease, my Sifu,*' Janice sang.

Her heart softening, Por Por got up from her chair. Threw down her walking stick and stood up straight once more like the scholar-poet on stage years ago. Once more she was the great poet Su Dong-po in the Song Dynasty, singing the aria based on one of his popular poems.

'A clear bright moon when will that be?
With cup of wine in hand let me ask the sky…'

Her voice though not as powerful as in her youth was still strong and clear, each word flowing like a brook as she sang the aria, showing Janice at the same time the operatic gestures that went with each line of the exiled poet's longing for home, longing for a brother he had not seen for years.

I stood by the doorway watching the pair of them rehearse. Following each gesture of her great grandmother's Janice sang parts of the aria again and again, trying hard to match her youthful energetic voice to Por Por's slower, mature confident rendition of the aria. And my heart filled with love and jealousy as I watched the pair of them. Janice was so at ease with Por Por. Cajoling and teasing her great grandmother in the way she used to with her father, at times leaning into Por Por's breast like a kitten seeking a mother's warmth, at times pulling away laughing at herself when she missed a note in the aria. She was such a far cry from the cold and distant teenager at home.

In Sea Cove, the chasm between her and I was a dark silence I could not fathom. Most days she stayed in her room after school.

'Janice. What're you doing in your room the whole afternoon?'

Her door opened.

'Nothing, mom.'

Her door closed.

She rarely sat in my company, and when she did sit, we had nothing to talk about. Dark and moody, she was worse when Robert was at home. During dinner, she was silent throughout the meal, and left as soon as she finished. Questions were met with monosyllabic answers. Talk at the table was usually a monologue from Robert or a stilted conversation between the two of us so that over time our meals became mostly silent affairs. And in the silence at the dinner table we ate quickly and the table was cleared quickly. I didn't know how to engage my daughter other than visit Por Por's flat every Saturday. There I could see the lighter side of my child. See how light and happy she could be when she practised her opera singing and learnt from her great grandmother the specific gestures and stage movements of a *xiu sung*, the role of a young male in Cantonese opera.

When they had finished rehearsing for the day, I made tea, and the three of us sat around the table in the kitchen and ate the dim sum I had brought.

'Oh, oh, oh, such stories you tell! True or not?' Por Por laughed.

'It's true! I have a classmate like this! And he strokes his pretend beard and wags his finger at us like this.'

Janice was regaling us with stories about her classes at the opera institute and junior college.

'Yin, your daughter is like her great grandfather. A born storyteller. Listen to her. Just listen to her. I can hear your grandfather in her voice. Monkey she is! And she does a good imitation too. Sometimes when I'm alone I laugh when I think about them.'

After my grandfather's death, Por Por was living alone, and she looked forward to every Saturday with Janice. Watching Janice laughing with her, I grew relaxed and laughed too.

'Great Grandmama. Tell us again how your opera troupe trained you.'

'My troupe used to call me Young Dog. When I was in training I had to serve them tea, fetch them their hot towels and even empty and clean their chamber pots every morning.'

'Ughh! You emptied the men's pee pots?' Janice bit into the treacly egg tart.

'Aye, I wasn't trained in an opera institute like a princess. I was part of the crew learning as I worked. Dressed as a lad. The troupe thought I was a boy. And treated me like one. My Sifu even forced me to sing in the dark till dawn in the middle of a cemetery.'

'That's so cruel!'

'No, no! Not cruel. My Sifu, bless his soul, was a very sharp and meticulous teacher. He knew he had to force a timid voice to emerge and sing out loud with confidence.'

'That's hard to believe.' Janice scoffed with the scepticism of the teenage young and reached for another egg tart. 'These are so delicious.'

'Listen, if I could overcome fear and sing loud enough to wake the dead in the cemetery then I could sing with confidence to the critical living. Master Wu used an extreme method. How else to force a timid disciple like me to overcome her fear?'

'Great Grandmama, then will you please ask Mom to drive me to the Bukit Brown cemetery at four tomorrow morning?' Janice turned to me and winked.

Surprised, I smiled but said nothing. These Saturday conversations about Cantonese opera were between her and her great grandmother. I was usually not included. But once in a while my cool distant daughter would show by a turn of her head or a look in my direction that the conversation included me.

'My dear girl, if your poor mother has to drive you to the cemetery at four in the morning, that will scare the wits out of her!'

And the two of them laughed and laughed as though they saw something in me I didn't know.

'Hey, I'm not that timid.'

'You aren't? Here, brave mother of mine, have a *char siew bao*. The bun is full of sweet barbecued pork.'

Those Saturday afternoons seemed so long ago now. They were my happiest moments with Janice and Por Por before one left home, and the other passed away.

I went on sitting in the balcony, watching the traffic flowing below, streaming past Sea Cove like a river of headlights ferrying people towards the future. After Janice had left home, I had found solace in this balcony most evenings, sitting among my pots of bamboos, watching people in their cars below heading to somewhere while I stayed put. But tonight, tonight was going to be different. Tonight would be the last night that I would sit here. My mind was finally made up. There would be no turning back.

No turning back.

Robert was away on an overseas assignment for two weeks. This was my chance. I had already wasted two nights toying with this and that, trying to find the strength to do it. Do it while I could.

But here, I was still enjoying the wonderful peace and quiet of Sea Cove without Robert. Like a servant savouring his freedom without the master of the house at home. Without his loud television. Without his shouts and curses at soccer players or me. Without his yelling for me when I showered or used the toilet. Without his liquor and imminent anger like the threat of an approaching thunderstorm. The unpredictability of his temper had scared me.

But tonight was such a beautiful night. Like a blessing the sky was awash with an ethereal light from a watery moon smiling down upon the ships. I would miss this familiar scene. Miss the sea and sky. Miss this balcony and pots of bamboos I had cultivated for years like the many children I could not have.

With a sigh, I got up and went into Janice's bedroom. The large teddy bear that Robert had bought for her on her sixth birthday was still on her bed where she had left it. Should I take it with me and send it to her in Vancouver? But Janice might not want it. I sank into her armchair, and for a minute I felt my resolve softening. I had held this family together for so long. Built my whole life here in Sea Cove. And now was I letting it go?

You might not get another chance, the voice in my head warned.

I looked around my daughter's room. Something had changed over time since Janice's departure. Although I had made sure everything looked the same as the days before she left, the room had gradually felt empty and hollow as if her spirit and memories were no longer here. But the large stain in the upholstery of her armchair was still here. Indelible and painful. The stain made when she threw up during her illness. She had starved herself in the year when she fought a relentless battle with her father. A traumatic year that destroyed the family.

My eyes rested on the large, framed poster of *The Butterfly Lovers* hanging over her bed. The poster of the opera that changed our lives. I had bought the poster for her when we watched the opera together in Hong Kong on the holiday when it was just Janice and I. Robert, who could not take leave, did not join us that year. How happy we were – mother and daughter. We went to watch the Cantonese opera one night.

The Butterfly Lovers so mesmerised Janice that her eyes did not leave the stage all night. She was captivated by the wilful courageous girl who dressed as a male scholar to study for three years at a boarding institute that prepared young men for the imperial exams. The singing, the music, the costumes, and scintillating wit of the scholars' exchanges enthralled her, even though at twelve she did not fully understand the literary Cantonese of the opera. The finale of the tragic death and transformation of the girl and the young man she loved into a pair of butterflies so moved Janice that she begged me to let her watch the opera again.

'But you know the story already, darling. Won't you be bored?'

'I won't, Mummy. The performance will be different.'

'What an acute observation from one so young.' The lady seated next to us smiled at me. 'My friends and I often watch the same opera two or three times each season. The singing and acting are different each night. The quality of the singing is different. The performers often speak off the cuff and joke with the audience. The great Yam Kim-fai was very engaging that way, teasing the audience and drawing us in if it were an operatic comedy. It's wonderful watching her as the young scholar wooing Miss Bak Xuet-sin in *The Purple Hairpin*,' the lady said. 'Go watch it. *The Purple Hairpin* is showing in a theatre in Kowloon.'

That holiday, Janice and I binged on Cantonese opera. Without Robert herding us, we were free as mountain goats. We watched a different opera every evening. My young daughter's keen interest in the operatic arts thrilled me to no end. Would she follow her maternal great grandparents' footsteps? I was determined to keep an open mind. I bought her several videotapes of operas by Yam Kim-fai and Bak Xuet-sin, the two brightest stars in the Hong Kong Cantonese Opera constellation.

Thinking of my daughter, my strength and resolve returned. I climbed on to her bed and took down the framed poster of *The Butterfly Lovers*. Then I looked for some newspapers to wrap it in.

When we returned to Singapore Janice had pestered Robert to let her take classes at the Singapore Chinese Opera Institute. Amused by his daughter's persistence, he agreed.

'A childish whim. Let's see how long she lasts. It's good for her ECA record. Schools like this sort of extra-curricular mix. Eurasian girl singing Cantonese opera. It might even get her picture into the papers.'

Three years later he wasn't so amused when Janice refused to go to Raffles Junior College.

'Are you out of your mind? The top JC offers you a place and you reject it? Who do you think you are?'

'But Dad, Hwa Chong has the best facilities for the Chinese operatic arts.'

'For god's sake! You're not going to college to be an opera actor!'

'But what if I want to be?'

'I will never allow it! You listen to me!'

'Rob, my grandparents...'

'Stay out of this, Yin! *My* daughter is not going to follow your grandparents' footsteps! Chinese opera is just street wayang! We Palmerstons are not street performers. We are professionals. Since my great great grandfather, we have been in law or medicine.'

'But Dad, you are not in law or medicine.'

His hand slammed into Janice's face. The swiftness of it! The sudden explosiveness of it! It shocked the three of us. I saw the terror in my daughter's eyes. The stricken look in Robert's eyes. His hand had hit her right cheek barely missing her eye. Her cheek swelled up at once.

But Janice did not cry. She fled to her room and locked the door. Robert reached for his drink. And I sank into the armchair.

Judge Magnus had expected his three children to be doctors, lawyers or engineers. Not civil servants. Robert's elder brother was a neurosurgeon and the director of a top hospital in New York. His sister, Ruth, was a barrister and a partner in a top London law firm. And Robert the youngest was his father's great disappointment.

'A mere Assistant Director in the civil service. Poor Rob! The runt of our litter,' Judge Magnus had chortled one Christmas dinner not long after my marriage when Janice was still in my womb. Robert got up and left the table. He did not return till his mother went out to the garden to comfort him.

For days, Janice stayed in her room. She refused to come out or eat.

'Dinner is growing cold!'

The more Robert yelled the more Janice retreated behind her locked door. He knocked on her door. At first gently, then louder! I knew he was ashamed. But he could not admit he had been violent. What? To his only child? The princess of his heart? The daughter he was so proud of? He just could not bring himself to acknowledge what he had done. Instead, he shouted at me and banged on her door. When she refused to answer he turned on me.

'What kind of mother are you? Tell her to come out! Useless!'

I bore the brunt of his rage and shame.

Then one evening Janice threw up and fainted. A good thing I had a spare key to her room. I found her on the floor and took her to the hospital.

'Why the hell didn't you force her to eat? Before things get to this stage?'

During the three days Janice was in hospital, he would not visit her. I knew he was afraid his daughter might make a scene. His presence might provoke Janice to tell the doctor what her father had done.

I took leave and stayed home to nurse my child back to health. Robert moved in and out of the apartment like a shadow. Home became quiet as a grave. Late one night when we were in bed, he said to me,

'Tell the girl to get well. I don't care where or what she studies.'

Janice went to Hwa Chong Junior College when the school year started. And she continued to attend the Chinese Opera Institute. Robert blamed the institute for bewitching his daughter. He refused to pay the fees. Janice turned to me, and I gave her the money.

'Bitch! You're undermining my authority!'

He gripped my wrists one night, yelled into my face his hysterical insistence on being the head of the family.

'It's a curse to have a wife who betrays you!'

Objects were flung across the room. A chair broke against the wall. He squeezed so hard, marks appeared on my arms. To this day I could still hear his snarling ugly accusations, incoherent and unreasonable. But I would not, and possibly, could not recount exactly all that was said and happened that night. I had tried to forget. But it was impossible to forget. No. I was not proud of myself that night I had to admit. I had crumpled before his overwhelming onslaught. Drowning in the tsunami I was stripped of all care for my self-esteem. I placated him, yielded to him, and begged him for forgiveness on my knees. I clung to him. Endured the blows that rained on me. In silence. Till his fury petering out, he helped me up, and in silence, he kissed my blue-black arms and rubbed my body with medicated oil.

I didn't tell Janice. I didn't have to. My daughter was no fool. She must have known even before this happened though we had never spoken all these years of her father's meltdowns. It was very difficult for the both of us. I didn't know where or how to begin or even if it was the right thing to do if I opened my mouth. It was not something a mother could talk easily with her child nor could she ask me directly or even ask a relative. Ours was an educated, discreet, middle class family especially on Robert's side where such things were not supposed to occur, where silence marked boundaries in the family's history that were never crossed for years, where silence was the mark of respect for another's privacy, the mark of a child's respect for her parents' privacy. A respect ingrained in children from a young age like never asking questions that would make your elder feel ashamed, and never opening your parents' bedroom door when you hear noises from within.

Looking back to that time, I couldn't be sure if my silence was a selfish, self-protective act or a silence meant to protect my daughter, or my husband or myself or all three of us. But what I do remember was the feeling of being trapped inside a thick grey fog for years. My mind was so befogged and muddied, I couldn't see or think clearly. I was fearful, shameful and half blind. Possibly wilfully blind! And deaf.

I let out a heavy sigh, then wrapped *The Butterfly Lovers* poster with newspapers, and wrapped the parcel once more with several large bath towels to protect the glass frame. Then I packed it into the box with the books I was taking with me to Jin Swee Estate. I would send the poster later to Vancouver after I had settled down.

Janice was nineteen the year she won the Arts scholarship to Canada after her 'A' Levels. Four years later, I flew to Vancouver with Robert for her graduation. By then he was very proud of his daughter. When the two of them met, they spoke to each other like two acquaintances newly met, slowly easing into longer exchanges over meals with neutral topics like food, work and the weather. But the ease of the past, the teasing and the ribbing between father and daughter did not return. All the same I was very thankful on that trip. Thankful that the three of us even managed to take a week's holiday together in Nova Scotia after which Janice told us she was staying on in Vancouver to pursue a Master's in Theatre Studies. We visited her again a couple of times together. But after her Master's, Janice said she had other plans.

She didn't come back to Singapore. She stayed on in Vancouver, and with the help of a generous grant from the Hong Kong Cantonese Association of Vancouver, she worked on her PhD in the development of Cantonese opera.

'I'm wondering how useful would a study on Cantonese opera be?' Robert asked her on our last trip.

I held my breath, fearing he might dismiss it as a useless, time-wasting project. But his question was genuine and his tone was polite.

'Cantonese opera, Kunju opera and Beijing opera are the three types of Chinese operas recognised by UNESCO as the Intangible Cultural Treasures of the world,' Janice said, and left it at that. She did not elaborate, and Robert did not ask her again.

17

It was very late by the time I finished my packing. I went out to the balcony to water my beloved bamboos and ferns one last time. These plants were a soothing balm on my daily pains. Watering these plants had always calmed me after an explosive episode with Robert.

'Madam, emerald jade green bamboos last forever,' the man at the nursery had laughed when I bought them. True to his word, after twenty years the bamboo was still arching gracefully over the two cane chairs and a small table I had placed under it. I had bought the chairs when I was still hoping that Robert and I would sit under the bamboos in our silver years to enjoy a pot of tea, and perhaps a moon cake or two on the night of the Mid-Autumn moon. But that hope had long fizzled out.

A small breeze whispered among the leaves. Their shushing above me made me look out at the calm dark sea. Last year, its dark waters had almost taken my life. I pushed that memory away and went into the bedroom I had shared with Robert for more than twenty years. I gave my chest of drawers a last check. Just to make sure I hadn't left behind any papers or my notebook. I sat down on my side of the bed, but tears threatened to brim. I stood up. I would not weep. No, I wouldn't cry on the night of my impending freedom. Nothing in life is permanent. Changes occur. Minute changes we hardly noticed go on as the present slips into the past even as we breathe or stand still.

Other thoughts crowded in. I thought of the Sunday dinner at his parents' house when Ruben had called from New York. Judge Magnus was very happy when he put down the phone. He opened a bottle of his best wine and insisted all of us especially Robert should drink a toast to his brother.

'Ruben said his hospital has appointed him the head of neurosurgery,' he announced. 'The hospital is one of the most renowned research hospitals in New York State. The *Straits Times* will run an article on him.'

'That's good news, Dad.'

'He and Sue have also moved into their new home.'

'A lovely brownstone with five bedrooms,' Mrs Palmerston added. 'And Sue has invited your father and I to stay with them this Christmas. I meant to tell you both earlier. And Ruben has promised your dad some very good wine.'

'Ah well, well, our Ruben knows his wine,' Judge Magnus laughed. 'Come, come, Robbie. Don't look so glum. Fill up your glass. This is my best bottle.'

I thought it was a happy dinner. Robert drank with his father all night. Judge Magnus even brought out more of his prized wines to show Robert. I did not sense anything amiss. Robert looked happy that night. During Christmas, with his parents away visiting Ruben, Robert and I went to church on Christmas Eve as usual. But we slept in late on Christmas Day. We went to one of the hotels for dinner and shared a bottle of red the sommelier had recommended highly. Robert, pleased with the attention of the sommelier, declared he liked the wine.

'Bring me another bottle to take home.'

'Rob, it's very expensive buying wine from the hotel,' I whispered.

'It's Christmas, honey. And we're happy. In fact happier celebrating Christmas on our own. The bill, please.'

Not long after that dinner, bottles of red, white, cabernet, merlot, Shiraz, and other wines started to make their way into our home. Then – I couldn't remember when it started – bottles of single malts, prized whiskeys and bourbon started lining the shelves in the living room. When did his wines turn into whisky, I asked myself. When did the change occur? I thought of the many nights I had taken empty bottles down to the recycle bin centre, too angry and frustrated to speak. As more and more empty bottles gathered under the sink something hard and knotted clumped inside my throat, a rock for which I had no name. It squatted in my chest so hard and heavy at times that it was difficult to breathe some nights when Robert, intoxicated, fell heavily on me.

At first, I had pleaded and argued till our arguments turned into quarrels that eventually led to blows. Then I tried patience, persuasion, obedience, silence and compliance to avoid inebriated arguments and explosive tempers. It worked for a while. But inevitably, eventually some small thing I did or failed to do or said or did not say or if I did say had said it too softly or too loudly or too late when it should have been reported to him at once would rile him. Sometimes the accusation was about my silence. Or my reply that showed slowness of mind. Or stupidity. Or dullness. Or lack of wit. Or lack of manners and grace or lack of something that exasperated and infuriated him. Enraged, he would yell, 'Your utter stupidity drives me to the bottle!'

Not true! I protested inside my head. Outwardly I said nothing lest it provoked worse things to occur.

But accusations, repeated often enough, repeated daily, repeated over time, ground my spirit down. Caused me to search my conscience and examine my guilt on nights when sleep eluded me. Accused and blamed often enough, day in and day out over the years, guilt seeped in like damp creeping up the walls, like termites gnawing the woodwork unseen until one night lying in the dark, eyes fixed on the ceiling, I heard the termites. My fault, my fault, my most grievous fault, I fell on my knees and prayed for forgiveness and tried to change my habits.

I started to sit in the balcony after dinner where he could see me whenever he looked for me. For a while I even stopped reading or writing on weekends. I tried not to talk to Por Por on the phone when he was around. I stopped taking phone calls from friends when I was at home. In the dark, I yielded in bed like a good wife. And there was peace between us. We attended official events together, went grocery shopping together, watched a movie of his choice together on weekends, and sat in the living room after dinner watching mindless American soaps and sitcoms. Once he even took me to a wine tasting event, which he usually went without me, and returned with a case of several bottles.

'Hobby. Everyone must have a hobby. Mine is liquor sampling,' he roared, and agreed to let me drive us home.

Then one evening all of a sudden he flung his mobile phone at me over something I had said or did not say. He accused me of not loving him.

'You don't put me first! I'm your spouse!'

'But I do.'

'No! You're always somewhere else!'

'I'm here.'

'Your body is here. Your mind is thousands of miles away! And you're writing. Hell! Who knows what your bloody mind is thinking when you write?'

'Thinking is natural. Thoughts occur even when I don't write. Thoughts come and go whether we…'

Piak! A slap on my face.

'Stop arguing!'

I had tried to dam that energy. That desire to put words on paper. Tried hard not to think and scribble. But it was impossible. The more Robert sought total control over me, over my thinking, the more I thought, the more that energy slipped out. It had a life of its own. It wandered off, imagining and dreaming of things without my being conscious of it sometimes. And I had to admit I did scribble secretly. I couldn't stop. I enjoyed the movement of mind and hand. Immersed in the happiness of words coming out of my head flowing through my fingers into the pen or laptop or whatever instrument at hand, I could escape Robert's tyranny, escape the present.

'Rob, I did try!'

'Liar!'

His phone hit my arm. I held my tongue and stayed still. Some books had counselled silence and stillness in the face of anger. Similar to not running away from an angry dog. Sometimes such a response worked. Most times it didn't. Sometimes out of the blue, in a rare ruminative mood late at night, he pulled up my sleeves, kissed the dark purple bruises on my arms and legs, and rubbed them gently with medicated oil, murmuring apologies all the while as he held me in his arms, murmuring *my poor darling, my sweet, sweet darling*, until the mattress beneath us squeaked and bounced again and again.

The next morning, he made coffee and toast. And while he read the papers, I changed for work, putting on long pants and a blouse with long sleeves. For the next few days or weeks or months, as the dark marks faded, hope rose once again in my breast. *We've turned a corner*, I thought, and went to the church on East Coast Road where I lit a candle and gave thanks to God. But then all of a sudden, another thunderstorm broke out! Fresh marks appeared on my upper arms and replaced those that had faded.

I told no one. Not even my grandparents when they were alive. I couldn't bear to see the pain in their eyes. It would break their hearts. So I told no one. Besides who would believe me? Not his gracious mother. Not Judge Magnus. Such a thing would never happen in a judge's family. Not the people in church where Robert was a churchwarden for the early morning Sunday mass, and such a kindly man to the old folks who came for the early mass.

'Change takes time. God's time is different from our time,' the priest said one Sunday. 'Neither love nor prayer could hasten His pace. Let us pray...'

Late one night in bed, Rob kissed and stroked my hair and I, shocked more than surprised, started to cry.

'Now, now, darling, I love you.'

The more he said 'I love you' the more I cried. And the more I cried the more I heard his unspoken plea – please, please never leave me – a plea that had been played and replayed again and again till my heart once again softened so many times over the years. Again and again and again, my tears falling.

I looked out at the pink dawn breaking over the sea outside the window. Its pink light fell upon the wall where the poster of *The Butterfly Lovers* had hung, and I heard once again the rational voice in my head.

Is this the pendulum you want to live for another twenty years?

I went out to the living room and my hand reached for the phone. I heard my voice say, 'Taxi to Jin Swee please.'

18

In the Hokkien dialect, Jin Swee means Very Beautiful. When I was six, the new housing estate on the edge of Chinatown was a much desired public housing estate. Its twelve-storey blocks painted a light green and grey jutted so high and modern into the blue sky above the surrounding old shophouses were desired by many. When Grandfather received his letter from the Housing Development Board, he shouted, 'We won! We won! We got our flat in Jin Swee!' Waving his letter above his head for all to see as though he had won the lottery.

Fellow tenants and neighbours crowded around to congratulate us. That night Grandfather took Por Por, Great Grandfather Wu and I out for chicken and roast pork dinner to celebrate our good luck. In those days in the early years of Singapore's independence in the 1960s, the demand for housing in Chinatown was so great, getting a flat was like striking the lottery. Our attic in Great Grandfather Wu's shophouse was cramped and dark like all the rooms in the three-storey tenement. My grandparents had the bed while I had to sleep on a mattress under the spiral staircase to the alcove where Por Por practised her singing.

There was great excitement on the morning we moved out. My grandparents' opera troupe came to help. When they carried our furniture into the new flat such *oohs* and *aahs* of surprise and delight greeted us. Used to living in dim cramped quarters, used to sharing one kitchen, one bathroom and one toilet with several other families, our three-room flat on the tenth floor of the twelve-storey block thrilled everyone. Its walls painted a pale cream and sunlight streaming in through the windows greeted the movers. The sheer luxury of having two bedrooms, a kitchen and a living room for just one family of three adults and a child was unimaginable.

'Wow! So much space!'

'So bright and airy!'

I danced and raced from room to room.

'Xiu Yin! Yin girl! Come and look!' Great Grandfather Wu called.

The chrome faucet and the ceramic toilet in the bathroom were gleaming wonders to us. Water gushed out when I pulled the metal chain.

'No more smells, Great Grandpa!'

Laughing, he pulled the chain. 'No more smelly bucket latrine!'

'Hey Sifu! Don't waste water!'

Grandfather came over. And he pulled the chain too.

'No more dung for the nightsoil man to collect!' he laughed. 'We won't need night soil collectors soon in Singapore!'

'Just think! One toilet for just the four of us! Our government is generous. Didn't I say vote for Lee Kuan Yew at the election? He will look after us! Didn't I say so? Didn't I?'

Great Grandfather Wu shouted above the noise and laughter of the troupe. The new flat gave us so much joy. Every member of the troupe wanted to apply for a flat. They had brought food and bottles of beer to celebrate my grandparents' new status as the owners of a much-desired HDB flat.

'To our good fortune! *Yum seng!*'

'*Yum seng!* To our success! May all of us own a new flat next year!'

'Hahaha! A song! A song! Sister Kam Foong!'

Grandfather played his erhu, and Por Por sang a popular aria welcoming the God of Good Fortune. Members of the troupe joined in, and I, seated on Great Grandfather Wu's lap, was clapping to the melody. We were all so happy.

But some thirty years later, on the morning I moved back to Jin Swee, the estate appeared dull and dingy despite its new coat of paint. A sense of failure clung to me. I paid the taxi driver, and he helped to push my two boxes into the lift lobby. I went up to the tenth floor and pushed the boxes out of the lift. A musty air greeted my nostrils when I opened the door of the flat. It had been shuttered since Por Por's death. I threw open all the windows to let the sun in and spent the rest of the day washing and cleaning.

That first night, exhausted, I slept on my grandparents' bed, troubled by dreams I could not recall when I woke up the next morning. After breakfast, I returned to Sea Cove to collect my bags and more boxes of my books and clothing. By the third day, I was exhausted but relieved. I had managed to take all my things out of Sea Cove. I had escaped, but I felt no elation.

In the evening I ate my dinner, a box of takeaway noodles, in front of the old television set with my legs propped up on one of the boxes. Thankful I had a home to come back to; thankful my grandparents had left the flat to me, and thankful that the flat was some distance away from the busy main road, and there were angsana trees and other greenery all around muffling the noise of the city.

Over the next few days I was anxious. Robert would be coming home in the evening. He would get a shock when he saw my cupboard emptied of clothes. I imagined him striding into the study and stopping short when he saw the empty bookshelves. Fuck the woman! What has she done? He would shout into the air. I felt ill thinking of the scene.

The next day it was sunny with a cloudless blue sky. My head was burning with a fever. I drank two cups of water and went back to bed. My anxiety was getting the better of me. *Calm down. Calm down. You've done nothing wrong.* I took two Panadol to bring my fever down and slept.

In the evening when I woke up I felt better. Craving for something soupy, I ventured down to the coffeeshop for dinner. I walked past the children's playground, and my mood lifted at the sight of children playing on the swings. Elderly men and women were chatting on the stone benches outside the supermarket. They smiled a greeting, and I smiled back. Glad the neighbourhood was still friendly.

Two traditional Chinese pharmacies, the optician's, a doctor's clinic and a florist were among the shops facing the main road. Jin Swee was unchanged. It was still a small residential estate with an electrical and plumbing services shop, a watch and clocks repairer, two dressmakers and a cheongsam tailor who had stuck to the traditional tailoring service.

The city's double-decker buses rumbled past as I walked to the coffeeshop at the corner of the block. It was crowded with diners. The telly on the wall was on, but no one was watching. Groups of workingmen were talking and laughing, many with their shirtsleeves rolled up and shirts unbuttoned down the front. The men were seated around the red plastic tables arranged on the covered walkway and open space next to the road.

With beer glasses in hand, they were exchanging the news of the day, chatting up the beer ladies tottering on their high heels in red shorts and tight, white tees. The women, giggling, parried off the men's jokes and filled their glasses with more beer. Bottles of beer stood in pails of ice on the tables, the empty bottles gleaming like bowling pins reflecting light from the overhead bright lamps. Bursts of laughter punctuated the warm evening air. The Hokkien and Cantonese voices of the drinkers could sound raucous to those unaccustomed to the raw joy of male comradeship. Everyone here from the beer ladies to the drinkers and food vendors spoke in loud voices. All of them were polyglots, conversant in Cantonese, Hokkien and Teochew, switching to Mandarin or Singlish if an outsider could not understand their dialect speech. Like all other coffeeshops in Singapore this coffeeshop was a bastion of Chinese dialects. Loyal customers were treated like *ga-gi-nang*, a Teochew phrase meaning 'we from the same clan'. Said in Cantonese, it's *ji-gei-yan,* and in Mandarin, *zi-ji-ren*. When the government banned Chinese dialects, many in the coffeeshop here, like my grandparents, were unimpressed.

'Ban or no ban at home we will speak Cantonese as usual. In the theatre we will perform Cantonese opera as usual,' Por Por huffed.

Smiling at the memory, I was glad I could still speak Cantonese and Hokkien to the residents here.

'*Oi!* Sister Xiu Yin! Good to see you! Eating here or buying back?' Khim called out to me in Hokkien, the lingua franca in Jin Swee.

'Eating here!' I replied similarly in Hokkien, and sat down at a table, aware of other diners' oblique glances and smiles.

The coffeeshop had been my grandfather's favourite. Its food stalls sold the hawker fare my grandparents and I loved to eat. Fried turnip cake in sweet dark sauce. *Char kuay teow* fried with lard, cockles and slices of sweet red *lup cheong* sausage. *Bak cho mee* mixed with chopped garlic and minced pork slathered in a dark vinegar gravy. And my two favourites – a peppery pig's organ soup and innards braised in a brown garlicky soy sauce – food that Robert detested. For the sake of marital peace I had stopped eating them. My mouth watering now, I ordered a plate of the braised pig innards.

The taciturn old lady pulled out a string of browned entrails from the pot of rich gravy. Then *chop, chop, chop*! She chopped, scooped and ladled gravy onto the organ meat and handed me the plate without a look or smile. I helped myself to chilli sauce and fresh minced garlic, and returned to my table.

'Drink?' the tea lady asked.

'Iced chrysanthemum, please.'

When my drink arrived, I took out my phone, snapped a photo of my dinner and sent it to Janice. Seconds later, a thumb-up sign. Its arrival comforted me. I was not alone though I was eating alone.

Nothing is so sad as supping alone
On the night of Chang Er's moon.

With Great Grandfather Wu's song playing in my head, I drank some chrysanthemum tea to ward off the threat of tears. My great grandpa had doted on me. Had never laid a hand on me. I was his treasure. When I was thirteen, he suffered a bad fall and a long illness, which forced him to retire. Confined to his wheelchair he missed the opera stage and took to singing in the middle of the night. Irate neighbours used to yell, *Quiet, you old fool!* But stubborn and irascible he sang louder. Some nights, the neighbours even called the police. Yet when he died, hundreds of opera fans including the irate neighbours turned up for his funeral to honour the opera singer who had refused to bend his knee to the Japanese conqueror during the Second World War. On stage, he had won fame as Lord Chief Justice Bao and as the monk who locked up Madam White Snake for ten thousand years in the pagoda.

A tear fell on my plate. I had not eaten alone for years. And tonight was the night of the Mid-Autumn Festival. I looked around the coffeeshop. Everyone was sitting with someone or in a group. I was the only one eating alone. I felt even more exposed and vulnerable when the sudden thought of Robert walking into the coffeeshop hit me. The vision of him shouting at me here in public sent a cold shiver down my back. The sudden fear of an encounter with him killed off my appetite. I could no longer enjoy my plate of braised innards. I drank more chrysanthemum tea and ordered a bowl of fishball soup instead.

I thought of the many wasted anxious nights before this, anticipating and planning what to say and what to do if he were to turn up at my front door. Unnameable fears had troubled my sleep. Anxiety dogged me as I counted down the days of his return to Sea Cove and found me not there. I dreaded his sudden appearance in Jin Swee. He would overpower whatever presence of mind I had. His caustic tongue would shred whatever defence I put up. His arms would overpower me. I wanted to avoid confrontation at all cost. I dreaded the looks of strangers. Hated and feared the scenes he could create. Yesterday my heart jumped when I saw the back of a man who looked like him. I had planned to send him a note earlier but each day had passed without the note being written. I dreaded what would come out of my head if I were to write. My temples started to throb just thinking of it. I couldn't drink my fishball soup. I took a deep breath. Calm down, calm down, I said to myself. I tried to recall what the books had said. I had done nothing wrong. Hadn't broken the law. I could go to the police if necessary. I had nothing to fear. Besides no one knew me in Jin Swee except Madam Soh, my next-door neighbour, and Khim.

'Hey Sister Xiu Yin!' Khim hurried past with a tray of glasses. '*Aiyohhhh!* Eating innards, are you? No good! No good! Organ meat is *baaad* for your heart! Can cause high blood pressure, you know!'

'*Oi!* You minx!' the taciturn old lady yelled in Cantonese. 'I've been eating innards even before you were yanked out of your mother's womb! And I'm still here! Strong as an ox!'

The queue in front of her stall cheered. The beer drinkers outside joined in. The innards stall was the most popular in the coffeeshop.

Undaunted, Khim shook her head. Mischievous eyes glinting, her silver earrings dangling and flashing in the fluorescent light, she yelled, 'Ah Por! Lucky the gov'men didn't hear you! They want every Singaporean to eat healthy!'

'Let them hear, *lor!* The gov'men rule the country! I rule my body!'

'Hear, hear!'

Whoops and cheers greeted the old lady's spirited retort. Egged on by their supporters, the two women's words, at times mocking, at times witty and sarcastic, lobbed back and forth across the shop like tennis balls. The men at the beer tables banged on their tables and cheered! Their glasses clinked; the bottles of beer emptied fast.

'Give her a beer! Give Ah Por a Tiger!'

'More beer over here! Here, my lovely!'

The beer ladies laughing moved swiftly from table to table. Pouring drinks, clinking glasses, and joking with the men. More customers crowded into the shop. By the time I left, I was laughing with the rest of them. My fears forgotten.

At the supermarket, I stopped and bought a box of moon cakes. Then I strolled up the slope behind the supermarket to the park. There were few visitors tonight, and I was disappointed. Where were the children? This was the night of the Mid-Autumn Festival when children used to walk around the park with their lanterns. Grandfather used to bring Noodle Boy and I here on such a night when the moon was round and bright. For a moment I saw my childhood friend's grinning face. We're standing on the stone bench under the spreading arms of the rain tree, holding our lanterns high above our heads, belting at the top of our voices,

O bright Lady in the Mooooo...oon....

Two crazy eight-year-olds baying like hyenas at the full moon while the other children laughed.

A cat sprang all of a sudden out of the bin. I jumped out of its way, shaken by the black cat and its startled green eyes. The cat's look reminded me of the scowl on Noodle Boy's handsome face years after we outgrew the lanterns. We were in our twenties.

Social climber, he'd hissed when I kissed him goodbye under this rain tree. Furious, I turned away. I was in love. I left him standing under the tree, and ran down the slope towards the sports car where Robert was waiting.

'Honey, what took you so long?' Robert planted a kiss on my cheek.

Several years later in the crowded food court of Parkway Parade I recalled this. By then Robert no longer called me Honey; his face was scowling.

'What took you so long?' He stalked off weaving recklessly between the tables. Almost knocking into an old man carrying a bowl of hot soup.

'Come here and sit!' He pointed to the table and walked off.

Several minutes later, he returned with two plates of roast pork and rice. I detested fatty pork. But I was resigned.

'I'll get us drinks.' I stood up.

'Sit down! Sit!'

Diners whirled round, shocked at his bark.

I kept my head down. Avoided the curious stares and sympathetic looks. Such humiliation was not new to me. There had been others before. Others and others. I struggled to eat the fatty pork.

'Can't you eat faster? You're such a bloody pain. I had to queue to buy food for myself. And if I have to queue again to buy something else for you, we'll be here the whole night. Can't you understand?' He stood up and walked off.

I remained at the table.

'Excuse me. Can we share your table?' Other diners came by to ask.

But Robert might come back with dessert and drinks, so I shook my head and remained seated at the table, aware of the stares of those milling around with their tray of food, eyeing the empty seats next to me while they looked for a place to sit and eat. But I... I dared not let them sit at the table with me in case Robert returned. He would blast me later if I'd let others share our table.

'Sorry, no,' I said, ashamed.

Such a simple act of kindness yet I dared not do it. Memories of my helpless mortification in the food court and other public places came crowding into my mind as I meandered through the park. I stopped by a bristling clump of clipped bushes and sobbed. Shocked that there was still so much tears and weeping inside me. So much humiliation lying in wait for me. So much pain ready to pounce and claw at my heart. Hurt hidden in the recesses of the mind, secreted in the ventricles of the heart pounced when I least expected it. I blew my nose and hurried down the slope back to my block.

The flat was full of boxes. I stood in the living room and took a deep breath. Boxes were stacked along the walls in the two bedrooms. On top of the cupboard and under the beds. Boxes of opera and stage memorabilia my grandparents were unwilling to part with. My boxes and bags were piled in the living room. My return was sudden and unplanned. I had not had time to clear away any of my grandparents' belongings before moving in.

I went into the kitchen and washed my face. Took two moon cakes out of the box and put them on a plate, determined to celebrate the Mid-

Autumn Festival. I had to honour the woman who flew to the moon to escape her husband. I should have bought a lantern. I used to light lanterns and walk around the grounds of Sea Cove with Janice. Her little hand gripping mine she squealed with a child's fear and delight when shadows loomed in the bushes as she swung her lantern. I held her close and kissed away her fears. Back in our apartment later, I told her the story of the Lady in the Moon.

'A courageous woman, Lady Chang Er stole the elixir of eternal life from her husband, the tyrant Emperor Houyi. She drank the elixir so that he couldn't have the power to rule forever. The emperor was so furious he took out his sword and tried to kill her. But Chang Er jumped out of the palace window. Instead of falling, she flew up to the moon because of the elixir she had drunk. Since then, Lady Chang Er had reigned as the Goddess of the Moon.'

'Bewa-aaare, Jannie girl, beware! Mummy and her grandparents worship the big rock in the sky. Are you praying to the big rock tonight?'

'Mummy! Are we praying to a big rock?'

'No, no, darling, don't listen to Daddy. He's teasing you.'

I bit into one of the moon cakes filled with sweet lotus, my lips tasting the salt of tears. How happy our little family had been on that balcony.

I took a photo of the moon cakes with my phone and sent it to Janice. But there was no response this time. I fought off the impulse to phone her and drank some tea instead to shake off this neediness and clinginess I was feeling tonight. Outside the kitchen window the lonely moon was a bright silver disc hanging in the strip of night sky between the apartment blocks. I thought of my balcony in Sea Cove with the pots of bamboos looking out at the dark silent sea with the bright moon above. I missed my daughter tonight.

Two a.m., still sleepless, I stood at the window in the kitchen.

The night was quiet save for a distant rumbling of traffic, and the faint murmuring from Madam Soh's tv next door. The night was as close to silence as was possible in a public housing estate. The windows of the neighbouring flats were dark. And the estate, like the city, was still. There was a special quality to this nocturnal stillness in the city after the shops had closed, and the homeless had spread out their bedding of cardboard along the darkened walkways. Above them the silver moon shone, a night lamp filtering its feeble light through the clouds like a half-hearted blessing on the city's displaced and dispossessed. I thought of the folks in the flats above and below me, asleep with their sorrows, or awake on their narrow beds staring bleak-eyed at walls streaked with light from the fluorescent lamps in the corridor. Night was never completely dark in Singapore's housing estates. Never completely silent, never completely bereft of the presence of other folks nearby. Yet there were many a night when an elderly resident, living alone, unvisited by family or friends, had lain undiscovered till a putrid odour from their body had seeped out to the common corridor.

I shook off my morose thoughts. Sat down at the kitchen table I used as a desk and switched on my computer. My heart skipped a beat. And I switched off at once. Among my emails was one from Robert.

19

'Dear Honoured Ancestors, Wah Jai and I survived the bombs. I thank Heaven and the gods for their protection.'

After the bombing, we left Chinatown. The Teochew family in the lorry with us took us to Ow Kang where their uncle has a farm. Liang Pek and his wife, Liang Soh, are very kind. The old couple took us in. They let us live in their shed. Once used for storing animal feed, farming supplies and equipment, the shed has no window. A big gap between the roof and the wooden partitions lets air in. We push aside the hoes and spades, the sacks of grain, the boxes and barrels, and make a wooden platform that serves as our bed. A small hut behind the shed once used for cooking pig feed is our kitchen, and the outhouse is an even smaller hut. We are very grateful to be alive. Kind neighbours have given us a grass mat, some old clothes and some plates and spoons. So we have a home at last. Thank the gods in heaven. The pig and vegetable farms here in Ow Kang have escaped the bombs of the Japanese planes. Honoured Ancestors, please protect us.

Wah Jai was very ill when we arrived. His knee was swollen like a ball. The wound was filled with a lot of pus. Liang Pek showed me how to wash and bind his wound with herbs. Daily I boiled the herbs that old Mrs Liang gave me, and I fed him the brew spoon by spoon for days till his fever came down.

Now he walks with a limp. He helps Liang Pek with the planting and harvesting of vegetables, and the daily collection of nightsoil from the outhouses in and around Ow Kang. The work is hard and smelly. But we are grateful.

The nightsoil is dumped into a large pit behind our shed and left to fester and ripen. Then it is used as manure for the vegetables and fruit trees. On hot days the stench is unbearable. The smell of rot, urine and dung seeps into our shed. Manure clings to our clothes, gets into our hair and skin, and even into our food. It has seeped into our bodies but we are getting used to it. Back in China, Wah Jai and I had grown up in farming country.

'The smell of dung is better than the smell of bombs,' Wah Jai said.

'Better than the smell of fear,' I added.

'Better than the stench of burning flesh.'

'Better than oozing pus and scorched hair.'

We laughed, grateful to be alive. Grateful we have a roof over our heads. And fortunate to have benefactors like Liang Pek and Liang Soh.

Gratitude fills my heart each morning as I water the vegetables and feed the chickens and pigs. I help Liang Soh cook the pigs' feed in the morning and evening. Some days in the midst of work a terrible ache grips my heart. Are my parents alive? Will my family survive the bombing in China?

Jade Emperor in Heaven, can you hear our prayers? Can you hear the prayers of mothers for their son's safety? The prayers of the wives for their husband on the run? Every heart in Ow Kang is filled with worries. Wah Jai's knee still gives him a lot of pain each night. Please heal and protect him. He's all I have in this world.

∾ — ℚ

As the anxious days creep away, Wah Jai grows better. He feels at home here. He's a pig farmer's son after all. The stench of nightsoil does not bother him. But it bothers me day and night. I am full of grumblings these days.

'How quickly you forget,' Wah Jai says.

'How quickly you forget,' I say. 'Once I was a member of the perfumed world.'

I walk out of the shed and stand under the papaya trees, and weep. Longings and memories of the stage assail me. How I miss the theatres, the performers and the brilliance of their costumes. I miss the music of the orchestra, the dramatic singing and acting each night. And how I miss my mentor Master Wu. May Heaven protect him and keep him alive in these dangerous times. I yearn to hear his stern voice once again and feel the sting of his cane. Most of all I long to sing.

Gok-gok-gok-gok-gokkkk! I call to the hens each morning, singing up and down the operatic vocal scale as I fling out handfuls of grains.

Ah, ah, ah, ahhhhhhh! I sing to the pigs each evening to keep my voice and throat supple and strong.

Gok-gok-gok! The village children laughing mimic me each morning.

Their shrill *ah-ah-ahhhs* fill the evening air and make their parents laugh.

'Kam Foong! Louder! We can't hear you!'

The adults laugh and shout, *Gok-gok-gok!*

I am glad I can bring some cheer to the community. So I sing to the banana trees, and to the fowls and pigs as though they are my fellow actors. I pretend I am a poor scholar reduced to feeding pigs while I wait to earn enough to make the journey to the capital to sit for the imperial exam. How I long to tread the boards again.

When night comes Ow Kang falls silent and dark. The village is pitch black. Everyone stays inside his darkened house. No one dares to go out. Wah Jai and I huddle in our shed as military planes roar overhead. The sounds of bombs and ack-ack guns make us tremble in our bed, unable to sleep. Lodged deep inside my fears I think of the woman with a baby in her arms.

Dearest Intimate! Are you alive? Are you?

౪ — ౧

Yesterday the sky fell! Everyone ran to Liang Pek's house. Like an avalanche, the news swept through all of Ow Kang.

'The Brits have abandoned us! They're leaving Sing-ga-pore!'

'The *gwai-lo* and their families are fleeing like rats from a sinking ship!' Liang Pek's eldest son shouted.

'True or not? Where did you hear this?' we asked.

'I heard the news on the radio in town and cycled home at once. The British have surrendered.'

Liang Pek, who is also the village headman, was too despondent to go on.

Wah Jai was so distraught he uttered not a word at the meeting. He had been so sure. So very sure that the British would protect us till the war ends.

'What will happen to us now?' Scared and confused, we asked each other.

Then, in one accord, we knelt down and prayed.

'O Majestic Jade Emperor in Heaven, pity and protect us, the people of Sing-ga-pore.

The next day another bombshell fell.

'Japanese soldiers are killing us Chinese,' a villager reported. 'Hundreds have been shot. Others were beheaded. We have to prepare for the worst.'

The whole of Ow Kang fell silent that evening. The next morning the village was half deserted. The young men were gone. Only the old and the crippled like Wah Jai were left. The young and agile had fled.

'But where can they hide on the island? Can they escape up north into the jungles of Malaya?' I asked Wah Jai.

He shook his head. 'The sea around Singapore and the Causeway are heavily patrolled by Japanese boats. These invaders are ruthless.'

Liang Pek called a meeting that night. Behind locked doors and shuttered windows, we crowded inside his house. Thick curtains covered the windows to make sure that no light could seep out. An oil lamp on the family's altar was the only light in the room where we crouched on the floor with the children and listened to the men's moving shadows exchange news of what they had gathered in town.

'All of you listen carefully,' Liang Pek began.

Mothers hushed the little ones.

'Be very, very cautious of what you say outside your home from now on. The Japanese are the new masters of Singapore now. Their spies are everywhere. Their soldiers are beasts. They rob and ransack homes. Rape wives and daughters. And I heard…' Liang Pek's voice dropped to a whisper. 'Even grandmothers are not spared in some homes. When you see a Japanese man, stop what you're doing and bow low. When you see a Japanese soldier, kneel and kowtow at once. Don't be arrogant. Act stupid and you will live. Act clever and you will die. Their swords are sharp. Your head will roll to the ground before you know it. And if you steal or hoard food your head will be speared and displayed on a spike. And young women, make yourself ugly if you don't want to be taken away to the Japanese comfort houses. Cut off your hair.'

Wah Jai cut my hair, and I put on his clothes.

The next day the village was full of men with bad haircuts and muddied faces. We giggled when we saw each other. And I stopped singing to the pigs and fowls.

And so our days passed, uncertain and fearful.

The wind brings the sound of gunfire and the acrid smell of smoke and burning. The world is on fire. Monsters are abroad. The news and rumours that thousands have been caught, tortured and killed because of spies make us wary and fearful even of neighbours. We know not which day we will join our ancestors. Dearest Intimate, are you alive? Please do not die. We have many things to tell each other. To forgive each other. Please stay alive. Even if this life is the dream of a butterfly I want to go on dreaming. As long as I have breath, I will look for you after this war. I am filled with remorse. If only I had not walked out of your shop in such haste that day. Regret gnaws at my heart like a rat each night. I can't sleep. I think of you and your son. I promise I will look for your shop as soon as it is safe to travel out of Ow Kang and go to town. It will be difficult. Wah Jai clings to me. He will not let me leave Ow Kang.

In our windowless home filled with farming tools and the foul smells of dung and pigs, we lie in the pitch dark side by side on our platform bed. Each night he holds me tight, and I let him. Who else does he have if not me? Who else do I have if not him? I hold him to my breast. I do a wife's duty. The war has changed everything. My anger demons have fled. They fled the day the bombs fell and I thought I had lost him. Now all I want is for everyone to be safe.

Stay alive, stay alive, my dearest friend and sister intimate. What does it matter what we call each other? Words do not matter now. What matters is life. What matters is destiny. Once you were the goldsmith's wife. Today you are the goldsmith's widow. And I? I am a poor cripple's wife. Tomorrow I do not know what we will be. Will we even be alive? So I hide in the kitchen shed to write. What else can I do? I need to write to stay calm.

The air of Ow Kang smells of fear. We tremble at the sound of marching boots. The pigs wail. The chickens cluck anxiously. Even the trees shiver at the sound of Japanese boots stomping down the road. Only the Earth God remains calm. He has blessed Ow Kang's fertile earth. The sweet potatoes and tapioca Wah Jai and I planted are flourishing. The long beans are green and tall. Spinach and *pak choi* fattened with manure are growing luscious in the sun. Wah Jai is growing sweet potato, tapioca and yam. We cannot depend on Liang Pek and Liang Soh to feed us. They have a large family of relatives and grandchildren to feed. Wah Jai and I eat what we grow and what we manage to catch in the rivers and swamps. We dare not hoard food. Last week a man was caught hoarding a small sack of rice he had bought in the black market. The soldiers shot him in front of us. The children were so frightened they peed into their pants and dared not utter a sound. No one made any sound until the soldiers had left. Then the man's family wailed. Calling out to Heaven and Earth. The babies joined in. And that night the children had nightmares.

The price of rice on the black market is sky high. Rice is rationed. It's not enough to fill us. We eat tapioca, yams or sweet potatoes mixed with just a little rice each day to make our rations last. I am learning from Liang Soh how to make tapioca and sweet potato noodles. Wah Jai and I dare not eat too much. We have to make our food last. We are lucky that we are not starving but we don't feel full. I am tired all the time but I continue to write. If I don't, I will go mad. The hush of brush on paper in the hot silence of afternoon calms my fretful thoughts. Ink and paper do not resist the press of fingers. May my honoured Ancestors forgive my wretched brush strokes. If I go on writing, everyone will go on living. This is what I believe. Bless my brush O Lord Buddha.

I hide in the kitchen shed to write after Wah Jai has left to collect night soil each afternoon. Then I stuff the pages, brush and ink stone into an old biscuit tin. And hide the tin among the pots and pans. Since he doesn't cook, he will never find the tin.

ℰ — ℭ

Ektch! Ektch!

I throw up again. I feel so sick these days. I have been throwing up after breakfast every morning. Nothing stays in me for long.

Wah Jai brings me a towel.

'Here. Eat some of these noodles.'

I shake my head. My stomach feels bloated all the time. I feel nauseated.

The red aunt that visits women every month has stopped coming.

Ektch! I throw up again.

I have been throwing up after every meal. Wah Jai's anxious eyes follow me. He pushes the bowl of tapioca noodles towards me.

'You have to put something in your stomach.'

'Stop fussing!' I yell at him.

My temper is short. My abdomen is extended. I have stopped cutting my hair. Stopped wearing men's clothes. Nothing can hide the belly of a woman with child. I long for a bowl of rice gruel with a sprinkle of salt. Months of eating tapioca noodle is making me ill.

છ — ૭૩

Dearest Intimate, if only you are here. I have good neighbours but none is a dear friend I can confide in. I mourn. I wail. I have been sobbing till I have no tears left. A lifetime has passed since I last sat here in the kitchen shed and wrote about my nausea. The biscuit tin in which I keep my brush and ink stone has grown rusty. Dried carcasses of houseflies and beetles have gathered in dusty corners. When the wind blows in, their corpses fly about. Death is everywhere. The days of my mourning will never end.

Today is the first day I am out of bed. The first day I sit in the kitchen shed on my own. With great care, I lay out my papers, brush and ink stone on the wooden box I use for a table. It has been such a long time since I greeted my three old friends. I pour a little water onto the ink stone, grinding the ink stick on the wet stone as drops of my tears fall onto it. Sobs choke my throat. I stop grinding. Let myself grieve; grieve for what I have lost. Mixing tears with water and black ink, I dip my brush in grief. In grief I write the words of Li Yu, the emperor-poet who lost his kingdom.

How much grief you ask can be harboured in my breast?
As much as the rivers in spring flowing eastwards without rest.

Bereaved, accursed and unblessed, Wah Jai and I mourn for our son in grief-choked silence every day.

In silence I watch him leave on his round to collect night soil. In silence he limps past with a heavy pail hanging at each end of the pole on his shoulders. He tries to hide his pain from the world and straightens his shoulders when he sees others. His limping has grown worse. He has lost weight. At night he cries out in his sleep. Like me he is plagued by nightmares. A bad aura clings to us.

Guardian God of the Earth, please protect Wah Jai and keep him healthy and safe as he goes on his rounds. Each evening I burn joss papers, and light joss sticks and red candles to ward off the baleful spirits that seem to haunt our home. Guardian God of the Earth, forgive us if Wah Jai and I had sullied your abode. Forgive us if we had disturbed your peace with our digging. We meant no harm. We only wanted to plant our sweet potatoes and tapioca and yam. I should not have railed against the gods when I was in labour.

My pains began on the morning the storm broke. A flash of thunder and lightning felled the papaya tree. A bad omen I ignored. I was not superstitious. The child inside me kicked hard but it wasn't due yet. All morning it struggled in my womb like some alien being trying to break free. It was no longer a part of me, this thing with a will of its own. At times it kicked so hard hot flames seared my insides, burning my guts. The pain twisted and bit hard as if a tiger was clawing inside. I yelled and cursed above the thunderous roar of the storm.

When Wah Jai dabbed my brow with a warm towel I grabbed his wrist and bit his hand as another wave of searing pain tore through my belly. The walls of the womb tightened and burned. The muscles were pulled taut. The child kicked and jabbed like a boxer so hard I felt my womb would burst. I knew then it was a male child. The veins in my legs were swollen with the strain to contain him. Another scorching wave of fire. I clutched Wah Jai's hand. Bit the rolled-up towel he held out. Then something burst. I felt wet, very wet between my thighs.

'Wah Jai! Put the kettle on! Push Kam Foong! Push!' Liang Soh yelled above the raging storm. 'Bring the tub and towels in! Go quickly! Stop shaking! Go! Go now!'

I heard him lug the tub into the shed. Saw him place the towels on a stool. His face was ashen. His brow was furrowed, and his eyes were anxious when he looked at me. He didn't know that a woman had to endure such pain giving birth. He came towards my bed but Liang Soh pushed him out of the shed.

'Don't worry. I've delivered many babies before.'

The door shut.

He stood outside listening to my screams. He was drenched. The rain had come down hard all morning. He took shelter in the hut used for cooking the pigs' feed. Stood in the doorway staring out at the rain streaming down the attap roof. He thought of his mother who had given birth to him and his brother who had died fighting the bandits, and the sister who had jumped into the river after she was raped by marauding soldiers sweeping like locusts through the village. He thought of his father who died of a broken heart. His parents and siblings would never see his child. His firstborn.

The rain stopped. He stood outside the shed and waited a long time for a child's cry that never came. When Liang Soh opened the door, he came inside. The shed was warm with the smell of afterbirth and blood. He stood watching Liang Soh gather up the sodden bloodied towels and sheets. Then I heard his hoarse whisper.

'Son or daughter?'

'Son.' Liang Soh's reply was soft. 'Your wife has lost a lot of blood.'

In the ensuing silence, Liang Soh went out and closed the door of our shed. He came and sat on the edge of our bed, his face taut and stiff as plaster. With no words of comfort to offer each other, the silence between us hardened.

ഋ — രു

Then three days later the aroma of rice cooked over a wood fire filled our shed. The steam rising from the pot carried hints of the fragrant earth and brilliant sunshine.

'Here, eat.' He held out the bowl.

I sat up in bed and stared at the blue and white bowl filled with gleaming white pearls. It had been such a long time since I ate sweet clean fragrant rice. When he placed the bowl of steaming white rice in my hands, my tears fell.

'Eat with me,' I begged him.

'Eat up while it's hot! You're weak!'

He stalked out.

And I wept for him. And wept each time I pushed the warm steaming white rice into my mouth. I knew why he had to leave. How else could he resist the bowl of steaming white rice topped with a fried egg?

Such a rare heavenly treat.

And so unexpected that I howled like a sow but I ate. My chopsticks shovelling every precious white grain into my mouth. It has been more than a year since I ate such beautiful white rice. Gleaming like freshwater pearls, each grain was whole and clean without weevils, without insects, without bits of sand and grit. Throughout this year Wah Jai and I had seldom felt full. He is thin as a bamboo stalk. Grief and hunger have hammered him into a thin grim man. The once smooth sun-browned skin and ready smile of the young butcher who had locked me in his bedroom was gone. There was no sign of the sweet humour, grins and laughter that used to irritate me to no end in Ipoh. Holding the bowl of gleaming white rice, so warm and fragrant in my hand, Liang Pek's words were jangling in my head. Each word a nail rattling in a rusty tin.

'When he told me he dug graves for the Japanese army, I wanted to spit on him. That's how he got such top grade rice to feed you.'

He walked away.

For shame, for shame, for shame I wept for the wife who had failed him.

80 — 03

And so the hot dry days pass followed by hot wet days.

We keep ourselves busy. Try not to think too much about what we have lost. Day in, day out we eat tapioca noodles with vegetables and a sprinkling of dried prawns or a bit of salted fish. After the harvest of our sweet potatoes, we eat sweet potato porridge laced with broken grains of rice, rationed out by the Japanese government people. Our sweet potato leaves and sweet potato stalks I will fry them with a little oil and soya sauce to make a dish. Nothing is wasted. When our hens' eggs are collected he makes me eat a half boiled egg in the morning. Once a week he serves me a small bowl of the white rice he has earned from his digging. And sometimes we share the bowl of white rice and have an egg each to go with the rice. Such meals keep us going through the bright empty days. And I don't ask him about where he got the rice.

We rarely talk. We keep busy. We go about our work during the day and avoid each other's eyes. In the night, lying side by side in the dark shed, we are silent, and he does not touch me. We avoid talk of the child who has slipped away. My heart weeps each night, but my eyes are dry as sand.

Last evening when the sun was sinking, and the ghost of a breeze was blowing, I saw him sitting under our papaya trees. A thin lonely figure, he sat on the wooden bench he had knocked together with a few planks. His arm was bowing as though he was playing on his two-string erhu the sad music in his head. It made me tear up to see how he had missed his erhu all this while. Yet we have never spoken of it.

We have secrets. He doesn't know that I know he is working as a gravedigger for the Japanese army. It breaks my heart. I have failed him. Yet he works so hard to feed me. Despite the shame, he digs for the enemy to earn a small bowl of white rice for his barren wife. Such kindness from a spouse merits a thousand years of gratitude. How can I ever leave him?

I pray for his health every day. I pray that you and your son are alive. That our families are living. Strange as it may sound, my heart believes my writing will keep everyone alive. Keep us connected till this wretched war ends. War and its horrors will not destroy us. Music and art will sustain us. This is what I wanted to tell Wah Jai last evening as I watched him bowing his imaginary erhu. But I could not open my mouth. The air had suddenly hushed. Children stopped running. Young women sank out of sight. Wah Jai pulled me into our shed and shut the door. We trembled as a Japanese army patrol marched down the lane.

₭—‛Q“

For days there is a blue cloudless sky. Dry winds are blowing away the empty days like dry brown leaves. Mute, Wah Jai and I keep busy in our silent home. I water the sweet potatoes and yams around the shed. I feed the fowls and pigs. Clean their pens and cook their feed. I wash and mend our clothes. Cook and serve him meals of tapioca or yam noodles, which he eats in silence.

Last night he was late coming in. I lit the oil lamp in our shed. Ate half the rice and half the egg and left the rest in the bowl on the table for him. Then I left and went over to Liang Soh's house. When I returned, the shed was dark. When my eyes had adjusted to the darkness, I saw the bowl was washed clean and he was asleep. I lay down on the platform bed beside him. For no reason I could think of at the time, tears started to roll down my cheeks. Just knowing that he was beside me each night when army patrols marched through Ow Kang made me feel safe. As long as he is beside me I have courage to live. A time will come when this war will be over. Then he and I will eat together like husband and wife. I hate to see him so choked with grief, so darkened by the sun, so gaunt and limping in pain as he carries the pails of night soil each evening. An erhu will comfort him. The two-string erhu and bow will bring the music he needs to heal. I have to grow more sweet potatoes.

$\wp - \wp$

Misfortune has fallen on the Liang family. Last night there was loud wailing in Liang Pek's house as soldiers came and took away their eldest son. Their second son-in-law was killed when he tried to run.

'The two men shouldn't have returned,' neighbours whisper to one another.

A pall settles on Liang Pek's house. The women's wailing is the only sound I hear. Neighbours stay away. Fear of trouble makes us lock our doors. The village is quiet. Not a soul is out watering their vegetables. The young ones have not come out of their houses. No one shouts or calls out 'Good morning'.

Liang Soh is ill. So I work alone.

Alone I wash the pigsty and feed the pigs. Feed the fowls, chop up the banana trunks and cook them as the pigs' feed. I wash our clothes and mend Wah Jai's torn trousers. In the evening I water the sweet potatoes I have planted. *Gok-gok-gok-gok*, I sing softly to the chickens. And one more day has passed. When will this war end? When will the monsters leave our land?

ഔ — ൠ

New Year came and the village was silent as the grave. No one had the heart to celebrate like before. Everyone is fearful for someone in the family. The Liang household, still in mourning, did not celebrate. What was there to celebrate?

On New Year's Day Wah Jai went to the river mouth and caught some shrimps. I fried the shrimps and made a green papaya soup with some dried fish, which Wah Jai and I ate with tapioca noodles. Later I took some of the noodles over to Liang Pek and Liang Soh. And they shared it with their grandchildren. The youngsters ate the noodles with such joy and hungry relish that we felt the God of Fortune had visited us! I was happy until I thought of the boy who would be crawling or learning to walk by now if he were with us.

ഔ — ൠ

Yesterday I sold some vegetables and bought a bundle of paper. Then I sat in the doorway of the kitchen shed with brush and ink stone, and wrote, longing for the emerald green rice fields shimmering in the sun of Saam Hor, and boys flying kites and girls washing clothes in the river. Not yet twenty, I am already an old woman dreaming of bygone days

20

My courage is wrestling with fear. I steal out of bed.

Wah Jai is still asleep when I step outside. The sky is full of stars. The trees are glistening with dew, and the air feels cold and brittle. I walk to the Sixth Milestone and wait. When the shadows walk past, I join them with my basket of sweet potatoes. Each shadow is carrying a shoulder pole with a heavy basket hanging from each end. The farmers of Ow Kang are walking to Chinatown. I trudge behind them in the dark silence. Talk is forbidden. That is the unspoken rule. No one wants to attract the attention of the Japanese soldiers patrolling the route. We keep to the dirt tracks. As we walk the only sound is the slither of feet on stones. There are no street lamps, no cars, and no lorries when we reach the main road. The Japanese army had ordered a blackout. All vehicles had been confiscated. Even old tricycles were taken away.

My hair is cut short again. I wear a shirt and rolled-up trousers. I know I can pass off as a man. I have done this before in the opera troupe. I can do it again. *There's nothing to fear in town. Nothing to fear.* I repeat the words in my heart as if they can ward off evil. In my rattan basket are the purple sweet potatoes I hope to sell.

We pass streets of shuttered houses too fearful to open their windows, ghostly shapes of men and carts along the roads. The stars disappear as the sky lightens and turns grey with streaks of pink by the time we reach Chinatown. I am exhilarated and exhausted until I see the streets of bomb-scarred shops. I race down the road looking for your goldsmith shop. Up and down I run. Where is it? Where is it? I cannot remember.

Down Buffalo-Cart-Carrying-Water Road I run. Up Theatre Street and Temple Street I race. Heart thumping, my head turning right and left, I search for your shop. In and out of black ruins I clamber and run till I reach Sago Lane or Dead Man's Street. Then exhausted, I turn and walk back slowly through the same streets searching for your shop. What is your shop's name? I was so sure I would know your shop when I see it.

Where is it? Where is it? I keep asking my frantic self. I can't remember. Tears cannot wash away my anguish and stupidity as I stand in front of the bomb scarred shops. I had been such a fool. I was so excited on the day I visited you I didn't even notice your shop's signboard or the name of the road. I want to cry aloud. Call out your name. Once again down the covered walkways I walk slowly this time. I poke into the charred skeletons of shop after shop. Stumbled down the pitted, potholed steps and pavements. Darted into houses with caved-in roofs and charred walls. Scoured the roads over and over again asking passers-by if they know the whereabouts of the goldsmith's widow with a baby son till a man yells at me.

'You crazy? War is on! Hundreds of shops bombed! Thousands of widows with babies! Which widow are you looking for?'

'Young Dog!' A voice calls out.

I whirl around. 'Sifu!'

Master Wu arches his brow and looks me up and down. Grey and gaunt, his shirt hanging loosely from his bony shoulders, he is like a scarecrow.

'Ha! Still in man's attire!'

'*Hush!* Not so loud, Sifu. Got to avoid the devil's troops.'

That shushed him. I ask if he knows the whereabouts of a goldsmith shop or the goldsmith's widow and her baby son.

'Young Dog, look at these bombed out shells. Who can tell if the widow is still in this world? Hey now, now, don't you cry. Goldsmiths are rich. She could have fled. Taken her gold or buried it somewhere. Many rich people have escaped to Indonesia, India. Some even to as far as Australia.'

'Then I'm too late! Too late!'

Master Wu let me cry.

'Is she your relative?'

'We grew up together in the same village,' I sniff.

When my tears stop, I ask him about Big Boss and the opera troupe.

'Dead! They're dead. Today is not yesterday. Today there's no troupe. From now on don't even call me Sifu! I'm not worthy to be your mentor. Look at me! A beggar!'

He holds up the coconut half shell he uses as a begging bowl.

'Beggar or not, you're still my teacher. Were it not for your training, I would still be emptying spittoons.'

'Ha! The training I gave you isn't worth two bits now.'

A voice yells from across the road.

'Wife! Wife! My wife!'

Hollering and limping like a crazed idiot, Wah Jai is pushing through the crowd shouting, 'Wife! Wife!'

Is the idiot blind? Can't he see that I'm dressed like a man? Fearing that he would make a scene, I turn to Master Wu just as the idiot reaches us. Before he can open his mouth, I say, 'Sifu, meet my mister. Just call him Wah Jai.'

Master Wu smiles and lets out a long drawn *Ahhhhhhh*. So this is your honourable mister. The same honourable mister who rushed backstage looking for his wife in the grandest theatre for opera! The right honourable hero who fought so valiantly with my troupe! Aye, that wasn't so long ago, was it, honourable sir? Not too long ago. I am very honoured, very honoured indeed, to make your honourable acquaintance, most honoured sir. May our opportune meeting this beau-ti-ful morning bring us good will and good fortune, my most honoured sir!'

I try hard to keep a straight face. Master Wu has caught on. Wah Jai is completely overwhelmed bowing at each 'honourable'. Despite his dirty shirt and dishevelled hair, Master Wu carries himself with the dignity of a gentleman scholar.

'Honourable Sir, as you can see for yourself your manly wife here,' he says in his low gravelly voice, 'your manly wife has very kindly brought me some sweet potatoes.'

The sly old fox! He stares at my basket. But hunger knows no shame. My hope of selling the sweet potatoes and buying an erhu for Wah Jai sinks. Meekly I hand over my basket.

'What excellent sweet potatoes! I thank your wife and you, honourable sir, for your generosity. Look here. I managed to beg some coins this morning. Let me treat you and your wife to a cup of tea.'

'Ah no, no, sir! These are just a few rotten potatoes.'

'Listen, young man. Acting is over. Let's drop the honourable right now! As the ancients say, if we're destined to meet, we will meet despite a thousand li apart. Here we are on this fine morning, the three of us meeting despite war and bombs! So! Drink a cup of tea together we must! Who knows on whom the bombs will drop next? There's an excellent tea stall over there. Come with me.'

And that is how over a cup of tea one thing led to another.

When Master Wu found out that Wah Jai could play the two-stringed erhu he is ecstatic. He pumps Wah Jai's hand up and down, patting his shoulders as though he's greeting a long-lost son or brother. Wah Jai is so taken aback that he falls off his stool, and his thin grim face cracks like parched earth when he heard that I had actually come to Chinatown to sell the sweet potatoes so I could buy him a second-hand erhu.

'Kam Foong, you wanted to buy me an erhu? You walked all the way from Ow Kang to buy me the erhu? My wife...'

'Hey, hey! Stop cooing like lovebirds. There's no need to buy! I have an excellent erhu for you. The three of us can earn a living together. I will play the drum. You, Wah Jai, will play the erhu and Young Dog will sing.'

'My wife can sing, *meh?*'

'Of course, your wife can sing. She was in the opera troupe, wasn't she? Have you forgotten? I trained her myself to sing and act. She's a *xiu sung!* Look at her. Isn't she handsome even in these rags? In those days we thought she was the most handsome lad in the troupe. We didn't know the handsome rascal was a woman.'

'Sifu!' I put up my hand. 'The troupe didn't want a woman. Remember? The troupe threw me out.'

'So they did! So they did! But where are they now? A war is on. And they are gone. Big Boss is dead. You are my disciple. I am your Sifu. Who is to stop me if I say you can sing in my troupe? Times have changed, Kam Foong. In Macao and Hong Kong, women in the opera troupes are performing male roles. Didn't you know?'

'But I haven't sung for a long while.'

'*Chieh!* Small matter! You have a good voice and a solid grounding in the four skills and five methods. With practice, your singing will improve. With performance, your skills will expand.'

I turn to Wah Jai shaking his head.

'But by the rules of discipleship, I cannot say no to Sifu. He is my mentor. I should obey him like my own father.'

Wah Jai turns to Master Wu. 'Honoured sir, in Ow Kang we have a roof over our heads, and kind friends and neighbours who help us. It's where I can earn extra food.'

'How so? Doing what?'

'He digs graves for the Japanese dead,' I blurt out.

Master Wu's eyes narrow like a tiger's. Then his fist hits the table.

'You fucking worm! Is this how you honour our people? Is this how you honour the heroes who gave their lives for country, family and worms like you? Have you no respect? No regard for your ancestors?'

'Sir, sir! I do respect our heroes and ancestors.'

'Then honour them! It is in such trying times that we hold our heads high! Play our music! Tell our stories! Sing our songs! Write our histories! Preserve our humanity. That is what our arts are for. Never, never for one moment forget who we are even when we are forced to bow to a foreign emperor!'

'*Shhhhh!* Hush! Lower your voice. Someone might report you.' Wah Jai tried to shush him.

'Bugger them report! Let them report! Thousands have been massacred. Our land taken! Our ancestors' tombs desecrated! Our villages destroyed. Our wives and daughters raped. Our sons killed. Heaven has shut his eyes. Turned a deaf ear to our cries! And you! You bury their dead while our dead lie unburied! And un-mourned! Desist! I order you. Play your erhu! We must sing! Sing so loud that the Jade Emperor in Heaven is forced to open his ears and hear our people's cries! And take pity on those...' he looked around before roaring at the top of his voice, 'Take pity on those forced to sing the devils' propaganda songs! Hahahahahahaha!'

Disbelieving eyes stare at this foolhardy beggar. His uproarious laughter thundering like the voice of Lord Bao Gong, the black-faced Chief Justice celebrated in operas and songs. Those sitting around us, their faces pinched with fear and hunger, forget their fear and they applaud. *Ho-yeah! Ho-yeah!*

My heart fills with pride for my courageous teacher, the old fox who takes my sweet potatoes and shames Wah Jai into agreeing.

'Sir, my erhu playing is only so-so.'

'Skill comes with practice, Wah Jai. Practice, practice, and more practice! Which musician is ever good without practice? Look. The three of us have *yueen fen*. An invisible bond made in heaven has drawn us together. If it were not Heaven's will, we wouldn't have met this morning. If it weren't Destiny, I wouldn't have bumped into Young Dog. Look here. I can offer you a room in my lodging house. It's better than your cow shed. Don't look so surprised, Kam Foong. I was a great *xiu sung* before this bloody war. I wasn't poor then. I am a beggar now. Even then I can still offer you a roof over your head. And I won't charge you a cent. All I ask is that the two of you join me to form a troupe. Opera is my lifeblood. Much more important than a daily bowl of rice.'

Overwhelmed by the onslaught of words Wah Jai nods dumbly.

And that is how the Golden Phoenix Cantonese Opera Troupe was born on the morning I ventured out to sell sweet potatoes and look for you.

Isn't Heaven full of mischief?

21

Yesterday Wah Jai and I went to the temple to give thanks and asked Buddha to bless our new life.

'Let the attic be our permanent home,' he prayed.

'It will.' I assured him.

His tired eyes looked at me, and he smiled.

I took his hand, rough and work worn with carrying buckets of Ow Kang's waste, and we knelt down. With head bowed he asked Buddha and the patron gods of the Pear Garden, the patron saints of opera and theatre to bless our new venture and new home in Keong Saik Road.

That evening for the first time in many months since our son died, Wah Jai and I ate together. Like a family we sat down to have dinner with Master Wu, and there was conversation, hope and laughter.

ℰ — ℜ

Our attic in Master Wu's three-storey tenement shophouse is up three flights of stairs. Lit by a skylight it is more comfortable than the windowless shed on the farm. Yet after a few nights I miss the quiet spaciousness of our days on the vegetable farm in Ow Kang. Keong Saik Road is all noise and movement and crowds. It buzzes with activities day and night. The air is agitated. Japanese patrols march down the road. Airplanes roar overhead. Motorcycles rattle past. Bicycles ring shrill warnings and hawkers yell. Mothers shout. Their children fight and run about. The road bulges with brothels, sundry shops and herbalist stores, tenements and lodging houses with bed-sits for single men, and rooms for families of eight or more. Grandparents often had to sleep in the corridors where young mothers nurse their babies. Sometimes when I see a child in his mother's arms, the dry barren sorrow that had never vacated my heart chokes my throat. I feel the hollow in my womb as if a hot dry wind is howling through it.

In Ow Kang I had lived among neighbours who spoke Teochew. Here in Keong Saik Road everyone speaks Cantonese, which makes me feel at home. Hawkers, trishaw riders, shop assistants, out-of-work musicians, actors, singers, stagehands and prostitutes are our neighbours now instead of farmers. And most of them live in rented rooms.

'Will people have money for opera, Sifu?'

'Don't worry. Money comes money goes. Among the poor, we're all brothers, we will survive,' Master Wu laughs.

He is the landlord of tenants who often cannot pay rent. His three-storey tenement is divided into small rooms rented out to impoverished families and bachelors. Yet he is happy, and his optimism is infectious. Wah Jai and I feel blessed. We live above his warren of sub-lets. Our attic is more spacious. It even has a spiral iron staircase leading up to an alcove overlooking the rooftops. Each night I come here to look at the night sky and think of you and your son. May we gaze at the same moon each night and stay alive.

℘—℆

My dearest intimate friend and sister, the days have flown off like swallows. There is so much to learn, and so little time to learn. How to give shape to my new life?

Daily I thank our Honoured Ancestors and ask them to continue to protect us. Wah Jai is doing well. Now that he does not have to dig graves and carry buckets of night soil, his leg is better. He is playing his erhu again, and Master Wu is teaching me to sing. There is so much to learn and re-learn for Wah Jai and I.

'Practise, practise, practise!' Master Wu shouts. 'I have plans for us to perform in the market square. Kam Foong, memorise this aria even in your sleep. You're like a buffalo that needs the whip!'

I feel the sting of his teaching stick. Yet I am grateful. Very grateful that I don't have to sing to the pigs and hens again.

This afternoon while Master Wu is taking a nap, I've stolen up to this alcove to 'talk' to you. How wonderful the mind is that it can bring you to me as I write under the eaves of the roof and blue sky. I dip my brush into the ink and think of us back in Saam Hor. As I write I see the two of us crouched under the window of the village school. We are writing on the sand, copying the words that Old Teacher has written on the board. Our brothers and the other village boys, bloated with boy privilege, are whispering to one another, unaware that we are under their window stealing their learning right under their noses. You are giggling beside me. Your eyes are shining with mischief as we copy their words, moving our sticks in tandem in the sand as though these are our writing brushes. If our fathers had found out about our thieving, they would whip us. But the gods shielded us from our fathers' sight. When your eldest brother returned from Canton, he spoke of girls in the city learning to read and write with the boys in school. What a revelation that was. We pestered him. Is it really true that the girls went to school with the boys? Did they sit with the boys? What did they learn? What did they wear?

The two of us dreamt of running away to Canton. We didn't know then that the learning we stole would one day be my doorway to the opera stage.

We will go and watch opera in the Canton Opera House, you said.

First, ask your elder brother to teach us to read more, I said.

Marry my brother, you said; then he can always teach you to read.

But I don't want to marry your brother, I said.

Then marry me, you said, and ran away, blushing and giggling.

Weren't we foolish? We should have run away together. I miss you so.

℘ — ℭ

'Master Wu has been feeding us on the meagre rent he collects. We have to start earning some money soon,' Wah Jai said one night after a long day of practice. 'We have to practise harder.'

I nodded. What else could I say?

Master Wu is training me to sing several arias from popular operas. Wah Jai is learning the music for them on his erhu. He surprises me. He was so reluctant to move away from the farm. Yet once he is here, he plays the erhu day and night as though this is his life's calling. Master Wu has found him a very strict erhu master to mentor him.

Loke Sifu was with an opera troupe before war broke out. Before the bombs fell on Temple Street. Before he lost his legs and family. When the pain and anguish strike him, he curses the Japanese conquerors and swears at Wah Jai.

'Block of wood! Where's your heart? Have you no heart? No feelings? The erhu has a heart! Play her like a woman. Listen to her cry when you draw your bow across her strings! Like this, blockhead! Make love to her. Play her till her strings yearn for your fingering. Plunge her into the depths of despair. Bow her strings till she cries to the heavens for mercy. This is what the aria demands! Now play that line again. Our rice bowl depends on her, blockhead!'

Poor Wah Jai.

His hands tremble. His erhu quavers and the melody chokes. Master Loke barks at him again. 'Blockhead! Are you tone deaf? Play her again!'

Ten times. Twenty times. Thirty times, he plays the same tune. Seeing him practise so hard, I practise harder. Fortunately Master Wu knows I am a woman. He doesn't hit me as hard as before. But he yells! Oh how he yells. The children fled out of the house. And the women scatter.

'Hold that note! Hold it! You're a *xiu sung*! A scholar with lily smooth hands! Not a peasant wielding a hoe! Watch those movements of your hands. The expression in your eyes. Movement and expression must suit the lyrics. Good acting accompanies good singing. That's opera. Words flow out clear and natural. At times, loud as a waterfall. At times, smooth as a brook. Soft or loud, each word is clear. Every sound is music to the ear. Every move is dance. That is opera. Have you forgotten?'

His cane stings my back.

'Now start again. Hand on your *dan tian*, near your belly button. Now breathe in and out. From tomorrow onwards go up to the rooftop each morning. Practise controlling your breath. Open up your voice before you come down to me.'

෨ — ൬

The next morning at five, I trudge up the spiral stairs to the alcove. A cup of warm water in my hand, I look up at the dark sky as I gargle.

'*Ah-ah-arrrraaaaaaaah!*' Up and down the operatic scale.

A tin mug flies out of a window. 'Bitch! Stop your howling!'

Vulgarities and curses streaming out of several windows. Babies wail.

'*Arrrraaaaaaaah…*' I try softly.

'Stop your screeching! Or I'll throttle you!'

'Fuck the lot of you!' Master Wu sticks his head out of a window. 'Kam Foong is my disciple! She must practise before dawn! If you lot don't like it, move out! Kam Foong! Gargle!'

෴

Every morning up and down the vocal scale I gargle the way Master Wu taught me. Watering buried seeds in my throat. Seeds that will sprout someday.

On rainy mornings I face the walls in the attic and practise. On sunny mornings I stand in the alcove, facing the rooftops and sing my scales. Then with face to the sky, I let my voice rise and rise.

'No straining,' Master Wu says. 'Let your voice flow out.'

But it is hopeless. Cooing a whole year to the chickens and pigs was not enough. My voice has grown tinny and timid. Master Loke guffaws each time I sing. And some tenants join in. But laughter will not deter me. I must strengthen my vocal chords before I can sing before an audience.

'Patience, Kam Foong. Don't force. Don't strain. Like the bamboo, growth is taking place beneath the earth. One day we will see new shoots.'

Master Wu's words are comforting even though his cane stings my back. He must have seen some talent in me. But I am impatient and afflicted with doubts. Isn't doubt a sign from Heaven that I should not be in opera? This thought troubles me. Is doubt a sign that I am not fit to sing the major *xiu sung's* role? Not fit to act the scholar? The judge? The mandarin? Or the filial son who passes the imperial exam? O Gods of the Pear Garden, Patrons of Opera, please give me a sign. Each night I stand in the alcove and utter the same prayer.

෴

'Kam Foong! Come downstairs!'

O God of the Earth, open up a hole and swallow me.

'Now!' Master Wu yells.

How can I face him? I have let him down. And Wah Jai down. I have let this whole tenement house down. Tenants and neighbours are whispering among themselves. They know what happened in the market this morning. I want to crawl into a hole and die like a worm.

'Kam Foong! Come down! Did Buddha become Buddha in one day? What did you expect?'

The morning had begun with such bright hope. The sky was a beautiful pink at dawn. After weeks and weeks of practice, my vocal chords had finally felt less tight. I went up to the alcove. I stood straight and still, and placed my palms on my abdomen at my *dan tian*, and took several deep breaths.

Ah-ah ah-aaaaaaaahh… the notes streamed out clear as the morning dew.

Surprised, I sang again till the notes went rolling over the rooftops as the sun rose. The chords rising and falling, flittering and flying like the swifts with such beautiful ease. Surprised, I sang the entire aria of "The Blind Beggar's Plea", which I had been practising for weeks.

'Kam Foong!' Master Wu called up the stairs.

I could hear the joy in his voice. 'The bamboo shoots have sprouted! Come down and eat! You are going to sing in the market after breakfast!'

Master Wu was very pleased. The tenants wished me luck when I left the house. I was nervous. Very nervous. I had sung in front of large audiences in the theatre before the war. But that was only a few lines for minor roles. This morning it would be different. Whether we earned enough for a meal or not, would depend entirely on my singing.

I dishevelled my hair and put on the beggar's robe. The opera had been very popular before the war. "The Blind Beggar's Plea" was the signature aria of its hero, the starving prince who was blinded by his enemies and reduced to beggary.

I walked to the market with Wah Jai while Master Wu walked in front of us, beating his drum. When we reached the market, a crowd had gathered in the large open space near the vegetable stalls. I tied a blindfold above my eyes and held out a begging bowl. Wah Jai began to bow his erhu playing the familiar opening chords, and the crowd clapped.

I began to sing.

'Good hearts, good souls of this city, have pity!
Pity this blind hungry beggar; spare him some stale rice, please.'

The crowd fell silent, drinking in the words of the popular opera. Passers-by stopped to listen to the sorrowful tale of defeat and betrayal as Wah Jai's erhu weaved its sad notes through the silent crowd. Some women dabbed their eyes and my confidence soared as I sang. But halfway through my singing, people started to edge away. At first it was just two or three. Then a few more, and a few more moved away till the crowd eventually thinned to about ten by the end of the sorrowful tale. And then these ten walked away too.

Wah Jai started to pack up his erhu and Master Wu put away his drum. Neither of them spoke.

The moment we reached home, I fell on my knees.

'Sifu, cane me. I was not good enough.'

'Damn you!' Master Wu banged his fist on the table. 'Are you insulting me? If I, your Sifu, say you are good enough, by heaven! How dare you say you're not good enough!'

Shocked tenants and children came running into the front room.

'Please, Sifu, please sit down. Don't get so upset.'

'Why shouldn't I be upset? Is my endorsement not good enough?'

Wah Jai made him sit down and poured him a cup of hot tea.

'Let's think calmly, Sifu. "The Blind Beggar's Plea" is a very good aria. An excellent aria. But it's a sorrowful aria of defeat. In the days of prosperity before the war when people were happy, tragic operas were popular. Now life is a misery. No one wants to hear sad operatic songs. We have chosen the wrong aria to perform. People don't want to be reminded of their defeat, hunger, sorrow and loss. We should sing happy songs. Songs that raise our spirits. You say right or not, Sifu? Right or not, you people?' Wah Jai appealed to the tenants.

I have never heard him speak so eloquently before. The tenants agreed with him. Master Wu sighed.

'You're right, Wah Jai. The fault is mine. I chose the wrong aria. In future, you choose. Kam Foong, listen. I am going to say this to you only once. You are not the first opera singer to fall. Nor the last. As the ancients say, when your horse dies, get up and walk. Greatness comes to those who fall and pick themselves up. Wah Jai! Choose us a new aria to perform. We will start again.'

22

The next day I didn't open Robert's email. I was very cautious. In the morning I went to work as usual. But instead of taking a taxi as usual, I took the bus. I reckoned there was safety in numbers. When the bus stopped opposite the National Archives building, I alighted with those who were working in the same building and crossed the road with them. I walked with them and entered the National Archives office in the company of my colleagues. I made sure I was not alone that day when I went out for lunch. I didn't want to be alone in case Robert was waiting for me outside. After so many years I knew his ways and his tenacity. All that day I felt the onset of panic. By evening when all were packing up to go home, I thought of Robert and feared he might be waiting to accost me downstairs.

'Mrs Gupta, can I take a lift from you to the National Library?'

'Sure, Xiu Yin. I'm going there anyway to pick up my son.'

Inside the car, the deputy head of department asked, 'Are you feeling all right? You've been looking very tired today.'

'I'm just very stressed.'

'I guess as much. Work or family?'

'Both.'

'Aye… everyone feels stressed these days. Let me know if you can't handle that project alone. I'll ask Juliet to help you out. The director has been asking me about it.'

'Thanks. Please don't ask Juliet yet. I've already started on it. I'll let you know if I need her assistance.'

I got off at the library and breathed a sigh of relief. I should have expected Mrs Gupta would ask about the heritage project. But thank God I'd escaped Robert's surveillance if he was waiting for me back at the Archives. I was not ready to meet him. Not yet. Not so soon. I had left Sea Cove. I didn't want to be accosted by him.

I borrowed several books from the library on how to handle domestic violence and abuse. Then I hailed a taxi.

By the time I saw the lights of the coffeeshop in Jin Swee, I was relieved. I felt safe. This was my territory. The estate where I grew up. I took the lift up to my grandparents' flat with the bag of books and a take-away dinner. When I went in and locked the door, a sense of triumph flooded me. That night I had a good night's sleep after many nights of disturbed sleep.

The next day, I followed the same routine. But in the evening, instead of asking Mrs Gupta, I asked Jeffrey for a lift, and he dropped me at the library near his house in Queenstown. I borrowed a book from the Queenstown Library and had dinner at the hawker centre nearby before taking a taxi back to Jin Swee. But by the time I reached home I realised this was no way to go on. I couldn't evade Robert every night. One of these nights I was bound to bump into him if he was indeed waiting for me outside the Archives' office. But then on the other hand, he might not. Wouldn't I be silly then? Why should I act like an ostrich hiding my head in the sand refusing to see what was in his email? Stupid woman. I turned on my computer.

Yin.
Imagine my shock. You didn't even have the courtesy to leave a note! Since you choose to remain silent, I am forced to send you this email. You sneaked away like a thief in the night. This shows you are a coward. You have no respect for your spouse. You didn't even have the courtesy to inform me and seek my concurrence first. No doubt you must have left to chase your wild dream of being a writer among the Dickens and the Austens. Don't think I haven't noticed your sneaky habit of scribbling and reading late into the night hiding in Janice's room. Come home at once!

The next night there was another email.

Xiu Yin.
I don't know what's your game. You left while I was away. By now you have been gone without a word for more than two weeks. If you persist in staying out, and do not regard Sea Cove

as your home, I will have no choice but to take some action that will embarrass the both of us. And our daughter too. Have you thought of her? What game are you playing???

Robert
I am not playing a game. I left while you were away because you would have …. I could not …. I was afraid for years I had dreamed of ….

Delete. Delete. If it were the old-fashioned typewriter, the floor would be littered with a whole lot of crushed papers.

I spent the whole night trying but failing to type an adequate response. My mind was suddenly so befuddled as though faced with a huge axe and given sixty seconds to type the response before the axe fell on my neck.

The next morning, eyes puffy from lack of sleep, I left the house at six-thirty. After work I took a lift from one of the clerical staff and went to the Bedok Library. Late that night, I saw another email.

Mrs Palmerston!
What is wrong with you? What have I done to deserve this???
Your husband has worked for nation and family all his life.
What is wrong with that? Is it wrong for a man to devote his life to the security of his country? I warn you my tolerance has a limit. Let me make it very clear. I did not throw you out.
YOU CHOSE TO MOVE OUT.

Several emails of a similar nature came in quick succession over the next several nights. I was so distressed I could not pay attention during work meetings. My project suffered. I had to ask for an extension of time. Mrs Gupta's email was terse.

The director wants to see your draft asap.

I could not sleep. Robert's emails, more frequent now, came at the hour when he usually had his last few drinks before getting ready for bed. That he was sending out these emails after several rounds of drinks worried me. An angry man under the influence of drink could do anything. The moment I got home from work I locked myself in. I double locked the front door and metal gate as though I was under siege. The windows facing the corridor were kept shut. I grew paranoid. His pride was at stake. But then, on the other hand, I thought it was unlikely he would come to Jin Swee to look for me. To come here would look as if he were begging me to return home. And that would be a loss of face. No, no, he wouldn't come, I assured myself, opening my box of chicken rice. Jin Swee was my territory. It was also my grandparents' territory. This flat had been their home for years. Neighbours knew one another. Robert wouldn't come, no, he wouldn't unless I taunted him. Yet my heart pounded each time I heard footsteps outside the door. Was it Robert? What if he were to come? What if he made a scene? Turned up, banged and kicked the front door?

I dished the chicken rice onto a dinner plate. Poured chilli sauce and thick dark soy sauce onto the rice and sat down to eat. No, not likely. He's an educated man and a civil servant. I drank some of the chicken soup to calm myself. That means nothing. You're his wife. And precisely because you're his wife he might turn up, another part of me rebutted. He needs to exert control over his wife. Didn't some of the books from the library describe how some men's obsessive need to exert control over their spouse had led to violence and abuse?

I pushed away the plate. I had lost my appetite. I could recall many instances of Robert hammering my door at home.

Bang! Bang! Bang!

Come out! Are you so full of shit? You've been sitting on that toilet all day! He kicked opened my bathroom door.

Phew! How you smell!

He tried to diminish me. Make me feel filthy and unworthy.

I got up. I could not finish my dinner. The more I thought of his behaviours the more stressed and anxious I became. Memories and imagination brought up more explosive scenes of rage. Especially after Janice had left, and he blamed me. Nightmarish dreams of banging and shouting at my front door woke me up in the middle of the night. The next several days I suffered from broken sleep. I dreamt of neighbours awakened by Robert's banging at my door. But the neighbours, fearful of being sucked into a stranger's domestic altercation, stayed inside their apartments. They would not come out. And I was left to face the raging bull alone. *Cowards!* I screamed and woke up.

Three a.m. I got out of bed and had a drink of warm water. The dream was so real. The warm drink calmed me. I returned to the bed and phoned the Helpline for advice. The calm friendly voice at the end of the Helpline spoke with me for several minutes.

'Don't panic. If you hear actual banging on your door, don't open the door. Check who is outside. If it's your husband, stay calm. Stay inside. Don't answer him. Don't open the door. If things get worse, call the police.'

I was glad to go to work during those weeks. Work was a welcome distraction. When I answered office emails, took phone calls, attended meetings or chaired meetings, wrote and edited papers, discussed and reviewed editorial changes, I forgot my fears and worries. In the quiet of my office cubicle in the National Archives, the fury of Robert inside my head quietened down. I was very careful not to let my feelings show or my thoughts stray to other thoughts during meetings but many occasions I failed.

One morning I walked into the washroom, looked at the mirror and was appalled at the grim sallow face gazing at me. I made an effort to smile. At a meeting later, I strained to make a comment or two and tried to smile. In the afternoon, the director called me into her room. In her hand was my report of the heritage project.

'What's this, Xiu Yin? This is after two extensions. Not your usual standard of work. Do these look like typos to you?'

The hum in the general office outside ceased when at last I emerged from the director's room. The colleagues around my desk were quiet. I wanted to cry. I left the office early, wondering if I was breaking down.

When the weekend came I stayed home. All Saturday, I refrained from switching on my computer. I looked for other things to do. But after the cleaning and sweeping, the watering and pottering among the few pots of plants I had bought and arranged along the common corridor, I was dismayed it was only still mid-morning. There was not much else left to do except to gather up the week's clothes and towels and stuff them into the washing machine.

In the evening when the air turned cool, I went out to do the week's grocery shopping. I did not linger and returned home as soon as I had finished, and double locked the door and gate.

I ate dinner and watched the news on tv. After that I made a cup of tea and settled down to read Por Por's journal in the living room where I didn't have to look at the computer. Por Por's Chinese characters with their fluid brush strokes and flourishes, tiny as a sunbird's footprints, transported me to another world. An old world in which my grandmother, a young woman, was strong. And I recalled that I too was strong when I was in university. Before I married Robert. What had happened to me over the years?

I suppressed my thoughts and feelings. I kept quiet when I should speak up or disagreed, but I gave in. For the sake of peace I acquiesced; I yielded; I bowed; I kneeled; I diminished my self bit by bit. Tears flowed. I brushed them off. Piddling self-pity!

The next day was Sunday. I stayed an hour or so later in bed. A luxury I was not allowed to enjoy in Sea Cove. Robert had insisted I must attend the Sunday church service with him at seven-thirty because he was the churchwarden.

I sat in bed with the Sunday papers and a mug of coffee. But damn it, the world is unfair. It did not give me the pleasure I had yearned for. I resented it. I resented how one person's absence or threatened presence could deprive another of such a simple pleasure as reading the papers in bed. The irritability brought on tears again. Which made me even more irritated.

Do something else! Why cry for god's sake?

His absence should have brought pleasure and relief, but it brought this constant anxiety instead tailing me in the small apartment that did not yet feel like home. All morning irritable, restless and lethargic, I got in and out of bed, and finally, slumped into Por Por's old armchair in the living room.

Later after a quick lunch of Maggie noodles and vegetables that I hardly ate, I was slumped in the armchair again bathed in a feverish lethargy in the humid heat. My eyes fell on the boxes. My grandparents' stuff was everywhere. They had to be sorted and put away, or given away. Several of my boxes were stacked along the wall of the living room still unopened.

There was so much to do on weekends, and I had no energy to do it. I couldn't understand my reluctance to unpack. Was a sliver of hope still lurking in some dark corner of my heart? I had to admit I missed Sea Cove sorely. Missed its lush greenery and view of the blue sea. The changeling sea that had heard my prayers and longings for years. The dark merciless sea that had almost sucked my life.

The ceiling fan creaked. The afternoon heat was turning me into a restless caged beast. I padded from the kitchen to bedroom and sitting room, and back to the kitchen. Dug up the brochure stuffed into the letterbox a few days ago and phoned the neighbourhood electrical shop.

'Ya, ya, install air-con. No problem,' the man said in Singlish. 'When you want to come and choose? Many brands in my shop.'

'How do I address you, mister?'

'Just call me Raju can, *lah!*' the man laughed.

'Mr Raju. I have an old ceiling fan that…'

'Ah, I know! Take it away. No problem! My workers can take it away. You just pay them direct, okay.'

'Oh, that's good. I'll visit your shop this evening.'

'Buy your air-con this evening. Tomorrow my workers can install the air-con for you.'

'Good! That's fast.'

'Our service is very fast, *one!* Life is very fast. Many people want to buy aircon now. Weather very hot. Climate change.' Loud laughter again.

'Thank you, Mr Raju.'

The shopkeeper's alacrity and laughter gave me a shot of energy. I put down the phone and took a shower. After that I sat under the creaking fan and made a list of all the things I needed to buy, and another list of things to get rid of if I were to make this flat my home. I was very thankful that my grandparents had given it to me.

Near evening the doorbell rang. I froze.

The bell rang again. I steeled myself. Recalled the Helpline's advice and looked through the peephole.

Then I opened the door. The delivery boy from the Instant Florist was outside with a large bunch of red roses.

'For... ahh, Mrs Palmeer-stone,' the teenager grinned.

'Thank you.'

I unlocked the iron-grille gate, took the roses from him and quickly re-locked the gate and door again. Being extra careful. A report in the papers this morning about a man who had stabbed his wife in the corridor of his in-law's Housing Board flat had sent a warning shiver through my heart as I drank my coffee. He was very upset that his wife had wanted to divorce him.

I read the white card tucked among the red roses. As I read the two words, written large in caps with a red felt pen, Robert's peremptory voice echoed loud and strong in the living room.

COME HOME!

I held the bunch of furious red roses away from me. At arm's length. Trying to keep the voice as far from me as I could as I searched desperately for a vase. Failing to find one, I ran into the bathroom, filled a pail with water and dumped the bunch into it. The white card fell into the water.

A sudden peaceful quiet descended upon me.

The peremptory voice in my head stopped its shouting.

I stood still in the bathroom. Petrified as though I had landed a blow on Robert. Then I recovered. Everything had taken no more than a minute or two. I took in a deep breath. The card inside the pail had started to curl as water began to seep into its hard edges and the bright red ink from Robert's two words ran curling like blood from a deep wound.

I turned away, suddenly aware of my hunger. But I would not go down to the coffeeshop. Robert might be lurking nearby. Who knows what arrogance and fury might do. I stayed in and cooked myself a simple meal of instant noodles with an egg and vegetables. Then holding the bowl in one hand and chopsticks in the other, I slurped up the noodles slowly as I stood at the window, listening to the life going on around me in the neighbourhood. Enjoying the shouts and laughter of children playing 'Catch' in the playground, I felt what I imagined a mountaineer must have felt after having successfully crossed an unexpectedly difficult mountain pass. In the blue distance beyond the blocks of flats and the shopping mall, huge white cumulous clouds were beginning to turn orange and pink. The climb ahead though just as difficult as before did not look as formidable or impossible as before. And Master Wu's advice to my young grandmother returned to me — *You are not the first opera singer to fall. Nor the last. As the ancients say, when your horse dies, get up and walk. Greatness comes to those who fall and pick themselves up.*

Later that night, I sat down at the kitchen table and faced the computer once again. I switched on my email and read.

Yin.
I hope you like the roses. I apologise for not sending you flowers earlier. I am wondering if you have met someone. I suspect you are NOT acting independently. You have never been a leader. You were always a follower. Who is advising you? You have been seduced into a state of madness, which because of my patience all this while, I did not nip in the bud earlier. I hope and pray the madness will take its course and you will see the light of day and come home. My mother reminded me that you left because I had raised my hand against you. That is an exaggeration. She's on the brink of Alzheimer's. And Dad pursed his lips. Not a word out of the justice's golden mouth. In all honesty I have forgotten that incident. I understand you had to see a doctor. If I had known you were hurt I would have apologized and brought you to the doctor myself. Why did you keep quiet? You can't blame me for not attending to you if you fail to tell me. I admit I had failed to contain my anger at times. I am not a saint. Even Jesus showed his temper at the temple. And I am sure you are aware that you yourself had succumbed to the temptation of provoking me to violence on several occasions. But my violence had been feigned. If I had used my full strength I would have maimed you by now. But I did not. I wanted to give you a scare. Teach you a lesson. Your grandparents in their ignorance had spoilt you. I believe you were never punished for impertinence when you were a child.

I went into the bathroom, took the bunch of roses out of the pail and threw them down the rubbish chute. *In all honesty* (he had) *forgotten that incident?*

How could he? He had hit me. Dazed, with ears ringing with tinnitus, I had clung to the sofa's arm when he pulled me. Pulled me into the bedroom. And switched off the lights.

No, Robbie, please stop... oh please... no, no....

The next morning his electric toothbrush was whining in the bathroom as usual. I brushed my hair as usual. The hangers in the closet rattled as usual as he pulled out a shirt and tie. He was always fastidious about his dressing.

At eight sharp, both of us took the lift down as usual. We walked through the car park. Greeted our neighbours going to work like us. As usual. We got into the car and drove out of Sea Cove, and he waved to the guard.

Inside the car the voice of the BBC filled the silence. When he stopped at the National Archives, he said, 'Pick you at six as usual.' Then he gave me a peck on my cheek as usual. The habit of our years. I wore long sleeves that day. And thereafter every day until several weeks later when the bruises on my arms turned a sickly yellowish green that reminded me of his vomit when he drank on weekends.

That night he lay on top of me again, the bed bouncing under us. I waited till he fell into a deep slumber before I extricated myself from under his inebriated hump. I dressed and left the apartment. Took the lift down and walked out of the back gate to the beach.

A late-night somnambulant ambling in the ghostly glow of the beach lamps. Shame and self-disgust dogged me like two diseased mongrels. I loathed my body. Loathed my lack of fight. Loathed my very self. My gaze turning inwards, I was horrified at the dark bottomless void I saw inside.

What have I become? O God, what have I become?

But God was silent, and the night had no answer.

A sudden strong sea wind tore through my hair. The casuarina trees soughing and sighing as dead leaves and plastic bags eddied past me. Sand got into my shoes and eyes. I kicked off my shoes. Barefooted, I walked down the beach towards the heaving waves as fat drops started to fall. Somewhere the branch of a tree cracked and crashed in the gust. Rolling white waves rushed ashore. I waded into the dark churning waters as the waves rose to my calves and knees. The waves licking my chest, my head was spinning. The earth was spinning. The storm broke above me as an undercurrent gripped my legs. Merciless rain slanted down like daggers. Spears stabbed my cheeks and eyes. A sudden undertow dragged me down under the waves. Dark waters rushed into my nostrils. Seawater flooding my eyes rushed into my lungs. My body was sinking, sinking, surrendering to the heavy pull into a dark silent watery world when a sudden deafening clap of thunder, lightning and Por Por flashed before me! Waves and voices pounded in my ears.

Wake up! Wake up!

A burst of energy pushed me up into the thunderous night and pouring rain. My legs kicked and kicked against the tenacious undertow trying to drag me down again. Arms flailing I fought off the terrifying grip of the current pulling me out. Rain pelted my eyes as I swam with the weight of the ocean pressing against me. Swimming against the waves pushing me further away from shore. Against the fierce winds and driving rain I kept swimming. Heaving, panting, sucking and gasping deep lungs full of air, I fell at last onto the beach. Vomited out seawater and bile. Spitted out sand. Wretched and choked and dripping wet, I tottered up the beach towards the gate of Sea Cove.

Back in the apartment, I fell against the balcony railings, leaning into the storm letting the rain wash the salt out of my hair.

In the bathroom, I turned the shower on full. Soaped every crevice of my body till the air was filled with the warm scent of lemongrass. Then towelling dry I gently patted the dark bruises on my arms and legs. Dabbed dry the sore region between my thighs and dressed. A snore from the bedroom made me stand still. I waited till the tremors in my body died down. Then quietly, very quietly, I went into Janice's room, locked the door and texted my daughter.

'I have to move out of here.'

23

Sky, oh, sky, answer me.
Is she looking at the same night sky as I?
Does she know I am thinking of her?
Is she still alive?
Is it true that those we remember will live?
Those we forget will die?
When will this war end?

Tonight I dip my brush into the inkpot by the light of an oil lamp and think of her and all our families.

Singing, acting and recitation practice fill my days. Music practice fills Wah Jai's. He is playing the erhu and learning the gaohu. Master Loke is training him to be versatile.

'Our troupe is small. Wah Jai must know how to play more than one string instrument,' he says.

Master Wu and Master Loke are relentless exacting teachers. Their standards are high. Their words are harsh. Their teaching sticks are thin and sharp.

Whack!

'Straighten your back! Only slaves and hags walk with bent backs. Scholars walk with dignity and wide strides!'

Whack!

'Cowhide lantern! No matter how many times you're lit, you don't brighten! Do you need a hundred years to learn how to talk like a scholar? Modulate your voice!'

Nothing escapes his ears. A word mispronounced. A quaver misplaced. And his stick descends. My shoulders and legs are streaked with red cane marks.

At night in the solitude of our attic, Wah Jai and I rub each other's back with medicated oil.

'We have to eat bitterness before success,' he whispers in my ear when I succumb to tears. Under the blanket of night he holds me close. I let him do what he wants. It comforts him. Sometimes it comforts me.

Oh, when will the God of Opera smile on the two of us?

ഇ — ൙

This morning I sang in the market a happy cheerful song. People did not move away. They stayed throughout my performance and applauded. And they threw coins into our coconut bowl. The takings were slim, but Master Wu was pleased.

'Never forget this morning, Kam Foong. The poor parted with their coins. Big as cartwheels in their eyes, yet they gave you their coins because of your singing.'

'We've made enough to buy tapioca today, Kam Foong. Tomorrow we'll earn enough to buy roast pork!' Wah Jai teased me.

'Roast pork and roast duck. My mouth is watering!' Master Loke laughed when he heard of our success.

That evening our dinner of tapioca noodle soup flavoured with salted fish tasted extra sweet. It was so good to hear the three men laughing as we ate.

ഇ — ൙

Dearest Intimate, we are beginning to earn a small living through our singing and clowning.

Each day I wake up before the sun rises. While Wah Jai sleeps, I go up to the alcove. Standing under a starlit sky I exercise my vocal chords. The tenants and neighbours used to my caterwauling by now sleep on. No one throws things out of the window at me anymore. I have become part of the pre-dawn sounds of a grey world.

After a quick breakfast of boiled sweet potatoes, the three of us go to the market. Every day I pray that the coins thrown into our bowl are enough for our meals. When the market closes we return home to rest, to cook and do the laundry. In the hot humid afternoon when the house is quiet, I come up to the alcove to write and rest. The hot days and our meagre meals make us tire easily. We have to rest. And I come up to the alcove to write and think. May my words and thoughts keep you and our families alive.

In the evening Master Wu and I try out new arias or new scenes from the operas to expand our repertoire while Wah Jai practises the music for them with Master Loke. And so our life goes on in the hot muggy days flowing like sluggish ditch water.

Food is in short supply. People are impoverished as the war drags on. When our takings in the morning is small, we skip the evening meal, and drink a soup I make out of the potato and tapioca skins I have dried and saved for days like this. But some evenings we strike gold when our good neighbours in the pleasure houses along Keong Saik Road, Madam Fong and her young ladies, manage to cajole their clients to engage us for a few songs.

'More!' the Japanese bigwigs from the army shout.

And we perform another excerpt while they fondle the ladies serving them drinks. When the army men get tipsy, they can be very generous. Sometimes we earn enough to buy rice and meat even after we have shared our takings with Madam Fong and her young ladies.

Wah Jai and I regard these young women as our village sisters as though we are from the same village of Saam Hor. If our parents find out, will they be ashamed of us? Will they think we have descended so low for a morsel to eat?

I do not think so, Wah Jai said. War and hunger have erased old boundaries and bring new friends. Who is high? Who is low? Who has a good reputation? Who cares these days? This is wartime. We are all slaves on this island. Long distance from home has changed our thoughts and beliefs. It does not matter where we come from or how we earn our living. It does not matter if our skin is yellow or brown. What matters is our heart. Help one another to appease the monsters among us. This is Wah Jai's mantra:

Yan yan wai ngo; ngo wai yan yan. Everyone for me; I am for everyone.

He reminds me again and again to thank the ladies in the pleasure houses. 'If it weren't for their services, more daughters and wives will be raped,' he says.

Listening to him some nights in our attic, I wonder if I had married a philosopher instead of a pig farmer's son. The tenants here respect him even though Master Loke shouts at him.

෪ — ଔ

Enough to eat.
Not enough to eat.
Earned enough to buy rice.
Earned not enough to buy rice.
This is how I mark the passing of the days.

Yesterday for the first time since we started performing in the market, we earned more than enough for two meals. The amount we collected could buy a cup of good quality white rice without broken grains, sand or grit mixed in it. I cooked the rice with two yams and a bit of salted fish to give it taste and bulk. It was enough for our family of four to share. The white pearly grains and yam eaten with a dish of fresh greens fried with a bit of sesame oil and soy sauce tasted heavenly.

'Oh, I feel as if we're celebrating the New Year. This is a feast.' Wah Jai slapped his belly. 'I'm so full I can't eat any more.'

Master Wu and Master Loke praised my cooking. The three men ate up every grain of rice and licked their bowls clean.

That night before we went to bed, Wah Jai and I lit a joss stick each. We gave thanks to Lord Buddha and the patron gods of opera for the rare bounty.

Eating clean white rice is a treat. I am reminded of how hard Wah Jai had to slog and dig graves to earn it after I had given birth. Rice is rationed and controlled by the Japanese, and by those who work for them. In the black market, a cup of good quality rice bought at an exorbitant price is a cup of white rice grains without broken bits, without grit, dirt, sand and weevils in it. With our earnings we can usually afford to buy broken rice. Before I cook, I have to pick out the bits of grit and weevils and other insects before washing the rice clean. Then I cook rice porridge with chopped yam or tapioca or sweet potatoes to add bulk. Broken rice porridge with weevils is often what everyone eats if they are lucky. Most of the time our meals are still tapioca noodles, tapioca bread and sweet potatoes. Yet I still count us among the fortunate and blessed. We are no longer as hungry as before. Wah Jai has even put back some of the weight he lost when he was digging graves. And he talks more and laughs often.

꿍 — 꿈

Last night I dreamt of you. You were eating a bowl of pearly white rice as you watched us perform in a theatre full of Japanese soldiers. I called out to you but you dared not answer. The soldiers and their guns was the great wall between us. Suddenly the soldiers pulled you out of your chair. No! I cried and woke up. May Lord Buddha protect you! I dare not think what this dream means. So I will write of happy things.

This is how Master Wu begins our theatre in the street.

'Madammmm... Mistress... Towkay,' he sings. 'And you who labour and slog! Take a rest! Stop a while for a song and a smile!'

Thum, thum thum! He drums out a catchy rhythm.

A crowd gathers around us. When Wah Jai plays his erhu, Master Wu and I stride into the circle formed by the crowd.

'Listen, listen to our joyous songs! Songs that make you laugh. Songs that celebrate love and family. Songs that honour heroes and country!'

Master Wu and I sing a duet of two heroes toasting each other after a victorious battle. It is a popular song and the crowd join us in the chorus.

'To victory! To victory we march!
The monster! The monster we've slayed!'

After that I woo them with a love song reminding them of a time when there was beauty, honour and righteousness in the world. On good days, people throw Japanese dollar notes into Master Wu's coconut bowl. Some days we earn enough to buy a thin slice of pork about the size of my four fingers. A bit of meat is a wondrous addition to our usual diet of vegetables, beans, yam, tapioca and sweet potatoes. I will not say ours is a stable living. We are not rich goldsmiths. We live from hand to mouth but we are not starving. We do not beg. We do not steal. We earn our food with our music and opera songs.

Lately we have begun to put on excerpts from popular operas. Singers and musicians from disbanded troupes have asked to join us. Master Wu is generous. He lets them join our troupe even though it means we have to share our meagre earnings. More performers mean we have to change our programmes as well. We put on more excerpts from the operas so everyone will have a role. And this is how our street theatre has grown bigger and more popular, and the crowds have grown larger. Sometimes we perform at night too, to increase our takings.

Fortunately at this time the Japanese government is allowing such entertainment. It is good news. Temples have begun to invite us for their festivals. More out-of-work opera actors have asked to join us.

'Sifu, too many actors will eat into our earnings,' Wah Jai warns.

'What a worrywart you are! The poor must help the poor.'

But not everyone in the city is poor. I am not blind. I have seen many who live comfortably even though food is scarce and exorbitant. It shocks me that elsewhere outside Chinatown many families can still afford to eat good quality white rice, drive cars, and live in the big houses in Katong and Bukit Timah. At night many visit the gambling dens in the Great World Amusement Park. They dine in fine restaurants, dance in nightclubs, and the men visit brothels and teahouses with their Japanese clients and friends. Gossips in the coffeeshops say that those who have good relations with the Japanese military, who work for Japanese companies, or who operate factories and run businesses under the Japanese can afford to live very well. Others not so kind say those who lick Japanese arses live even better. The higher-ups in the Japanese army and navy also live very well. Wah Jai says the authorities are eager to show that life under the Japanese is better than life under the British.

Singapore has been renamed *Syonan-to* – Light of the South – shining like a bright beacon in Asia, Japanese newspapers and radio declare. All these things I have learnt from Wah Jai. When I ask how he knows so much, he laughs and shows me a Japanese newspaper. Many of the words are Chinese characters that the Japanese call Kanji, he says. And true enough I can read many of the words.

The Japanese government wants life to return to normal. Shops, restaurants, theatres, cinemas and amusement parks have been ordered to open. Nightclubs and teahouses are also opened. The Great World and Happy World amusement parks have become gambling dens attracting crowds of men each night. Religious festivals and celebrations are encouraged. It is not a good sign. It looks as if the enemy will rule us forever. Dearest Intimate, look after yourself and your son. He must be a big boy now. I have never stopped thinking of you. I am sure you too are thinking of me. Wherever you are, we live under the same heaven. This is my consolation.

ℴ—ℙ

It is dawn. High in the square of blue sky outside, a lone bird flies. Down in the streets below, a white flag with a red sun is flapping in the breeze. Today is the Emperor's birthday. Loudspeakers yell for us to come out of our houses.

In the streets we stand in straight rows. At a command, the whole street shouts 'Banzai!' three times and bow to the flag with the red sun and pointed rays. As the true sun rises above the roofs, the Japanese national anthem is broadcast from loudspeakers in every street corner. Like hundreds of fishes we open and close our mouths pretending to sing. When the song ends an army captain reads out a long speech in Japanese. Then a Chinese man translates what he had read into Cantonese. I was so amazed that the man knows Japanese.

'Today is a holiday. Everyone should go out to enjoy the day. Visit the temples. Pray for the good health of the Emperor and the glory of Japan. Visit the cinemas where there are free shows today. Banzai!'

Banzai! The Japanese soldiers shout.

Banzai! The entire street shouts and bows as the Japanese contingent leaves. The ceremony is over.

Phooi! Master Wu clears his throat and spits into the drain. Back inside the house, he and Master Loke take out their small drums. Drumming a rhythmic beat, the pair of them breaks into song.

'Who wants to watch free shows?
Not I, chirp the sparrows.
Who wants to listen to foreign songs?
Not I, meow the cats.

Don't the devils know?
Out here in Chinatown
An old singer, a young erhu player and his wife in men's rags
Are playing to large crowds? Sing that out! Sing out strong!
Sing to our heroes long gone!'

Boomg! Boomg! Boomg! Wah Jai beat the big drum as loud as he could to drown out the pair's dangerous song.

'Stop it! Stop your song!' I shout with our tenants banging on their pots and pans.

But the two subversives go on singing and dancing like two silly old beards without a care in the world. And the street sombre and solemn a minute ago is now filled with the banging of pots and pans, and the people's singing of popular Chinese songs.

80 — 03

And so the hot muggy days pass into wet miserable days.

Daily thunderstorms are adding to our misery. Flooded drains have brought armies of cockroaches. Rats invade our homes. Everyone sets traps. The house smells of damp and dirt these days. Clothes take days to dry. I escape to my little alcove whenever I can. Standing under an umbrella I sing in the rain training my voice to sing out loud without straining my vocal chords.

It rained all day yesterday. Wah Jai was not at home the whole day. These days he often slips away like a shadow. Sometimes he is gone for a night or a day. No one knows where he goes. Not even Master Wu or Master Loke, which is strange because Wah Jai talks to them more than he talks to me. When I ask Master Wu, he sings softly. 'It's better not to know than to know where a man comes and goes, and so the saying goes!'

These two old blokes get on my nerves. They must think I am an idiot. Well, we will see.

24

My hands gripped the bars of the window as though the limbs belonged to someone else. An ache was coursing down my back. How long had I been standing at the kitchen window? Night after night I grieved. Weeping the angry, self-pitying tears of the disillusioned and betrayed.

What had gone wrong with me these past twenty years?

Once I was so full of courage and energy. Once I had batted life as though I was playing tennis. I made and returned phone calls, wrote and replied to faxes and emails, one after another all morning, and still had time to stop for mid-morning coffee and go for lunch with colleagues, and in the afternoon, I attended meetings, took notes, wrote up the notes, held consultations at the National Archives, all the while half my mind was thinking of Robert. Light and joyful, I didn't know fatigue then. I was in love and was loved. Now my days had become burdensome. No longer was it possible to separate the working part of my day from the personal. My mind kept wandering off during meetings, making it difficult to attend to what others were saying, and they could be making a point of relevance when in fact, preoccupied with thoughts of my fractured self and marriage, I had lost the thread of the discussion.

Bitter memories came and went as I stood at the kitchen window gripping its bars like one accused of a crime. The casements of the neighbouring blocks stared at me with accusing eyes. A light breeze was rustling the angsana trees. Waking up late one night I had seen Robert snoring on the couch in our living room. The curtains were billowing and rain was coming in. I shut the balcony doors and the noise woke him.

'Why didn't you come to bed?'

'Didn't want to wake my darling,' he had mumbled half awake, ambling into bed. He pulled me under the sheets and stroked my hair, licking the nape of my neck, my breasts and smelling of whisky. Softened by his whisperings of endearments, I revelled in the wet kisses and exploration of tongue and hands on breasts till suddenly forceful, he pushed and forced himself into me, yet then, even then, I had thought, might not this be another facet of lovemaking? There was something erotic in a man's strength and power in bed, a power that had attracted and repulsed, and secretly excited thousands of women till a ripping of blouse and panty had shocked and terrified them, and revealed all of a sudden the vulnerability of a female's body bared against its will. It did not matter that the hand that had torn off our clothes was the spouse's hand. Not a stranger's hand. It had the same raw power of the male to terrify and dominate.

Stop! Please stop pleeeeease!

But the bed heaved and shook, and heaved heedless of our pleas.

The memory shamed me. Solitude had forced honesty upon my memory, forced it to admit that what is so abhorrent now was what had once been revelled in. I banged my head against the window grilles.

I was so ashamed that I had failed myself. Failed my body and my soul. Failed my grandparents. Failed all those who had believed in my potential. I had failed to fulfil the promises and vision I had before marriage. I was no longer the courageous woman I once was in my youth. A deep sense of shame filled me as I stood at the window. The night had grown chilly. I pulled a wrap over my shoulders. But it could not cover my shame. My humiliation.

Glistening dew had settled on the tops of the roadside trees. Street lamps cast a spectral glow on the cars ten floors below. Despondently I watched a cat pounce on a leaf and melted back into the shadows. My hands were cold and my knuckles stiff and pale when I let go of the grilles.

I turned on the tap and filled the electric kettle. When the water boiled, I made a mug of chamomile tea and sat down among my boxes in the living room and wept.

I wept for a long time. As though all the grief I had bottled up over the years were flowing out through my eyes and nose. When my weeping finally stopped, I became aware of the comforting presences on my grandparents' old red altar. Sun Wukong the Monkey King was standing next to the porcelain figurines of Lord Mun Cheong the patron saint of literature and Kwan Yin the Goddess of Mercy. These familiar and reassuring presences of my childhood seemed to be looking at me with sympathy. I had treasured them on the old red altar. A profane and sacred piece of furniture, sometimes the red altar was the abode of the gods at home, and other times, it was a prop in the theatre when the troupe ran out of money for new props. Yet as a child, I had never felt poor. Neither had I seen my grandparents despair over the lack of money.

'With a roof over our heads, what is there to fear? Next season things will be better,' Grandfather always said.

A bowl of rice and a roof over their heads, a benevolent government and a country at peace – that was my grandparents' measure of a happy life. And sharing the same bed with the same person till the end of their days even if husband and wife hardly spoke with each other was still marital bliss. Opera was the leitmotif of their lives. And while Por Por was the star on stage, Grandfather was content to sit with his erhu in the wings.

Each according to his destiny, she sang to the music of his erhu.

A head taller than Grandfather, she walked across the stage like a man proudly displaying her large wooden opera boots.

The rich bound their daughters' feet. The poor did not, so their wives and daughters could work in the fields and fight against bandits alongside their men. With unbound feet, I had sailed the ocean wide. Travelled from China to Malaya fearing nothing but the betraying heart, she had written in her journal.

I thought of the years I had wasted. Years of placating a spouse I no longer loved. When did that love slip away? It was hard to tell. How many could claim to know love truly? We knew passion and sex and thought that was love on fire. Till violence doused the flames. I thought of what Robert had done on drunken nights. And the dark hollowed out shell that had walked into the sea. And I wept again.

When I finished weeping, I sat down at the kitchen table, switched on the computer and wrote to Robert.

25

Wah Jai is mute again. His silence reminds me of our days in Ow Kang, when grief-stricken over the loss of our son he had stopped talking. I keep an eye on him but last night he slipped off again. And the box in which I keep our medicine and ointments is gone. That's when I realise the poor cripple wants to do his part in this war. Well! I know whom to blame if something dire happens to him. But for now my words are useless. The men will not listen. Worrying will not help. All I can do is pray. He is all the family I have in this world. Please, protect him from his enemies, Lord Guan Gong, God of War.

$\wp-\text{\reflectbox{$\wp$}}$

I had nightmares.

But last night I had a good dream. I saw you carrying your son in your arms. You are alive. Alive! Someday we will meet.

It is raining again. This morning we could not go out to perform, and Wah Jai has vanished again. Instead of answering my questions about Wah Jai, Master Wu sat in the front hall drinking tea. And the old fox lectured me about Cantonese opera.

'Remember, Kam Foong. In Cantonese opera, words are more important than music. Clear enunciation and voice control are more important than movement. No point waving your sleeves about when you can't sing.'

He sips his dark pu'er tea.

'Flashy movements cater only to vulgar taste. But when your words are clear, the singing precise and the movements controlled yet graceful, then! The combination of song, music and movement will convey strong emotion. Pay attention to voice. There is music in words, cadence in speech. The timbre of your voice, its pitch and tone, and the pause – these mark the difference between mediocrity and excellence. Remember this.'

Before I can speak, he raises his hand.

'Small movements and gestures can bring great results if well timed. A small change of tone, well timed, will change the meaning of an aria or speech.'

'Sifu.'

He ignores me.

'The length and timing of a pause adds emotional depth to a song. Listen and learn from your elders. They have secrets that will help those willing to learn. Be humble. Every performer has something to teach us. And be grateful. Thank Heaven for your talent and respect your craft. Do not give up on yourself. You are still young and green. An opera performer must have hundreds of performances under her belt before her skills and voice mature. When this stupid war ends, you will perform a full-length opera.'

His words 'full-length opera' distracts me. I let go of my worries. I forget about Wah Jai and think of the hours of practice I have to put in breathing in and out from my *dan tian* to strengthen my breath so I can lengthen the note of a musical phrase. The crafty fox.

Now daily I do memory work, singing different arias and solo pieces from different operas. Some mornings before dawn, I walk out to the wasteland on Pearl's Hill. Looking out at the rooftops, I recall the ancestral spirits in that dark and vaporous graveyard on the outskirts of Kampar. As I sing to them, I drink in once again that bowl of bird's nest soup Master Wu had given me in the cemetery. How heavenly sweet and warm that soup is in my memory. Since that time in the cemetery my voice has grown stronger.

'It is a voice the crowds in the market identify as male. But they know I am a woman. Yet as soon as I don the robe of a scholar or a peasant's rags and sing, they see me as the male character I am performing.'

'That is the magic of theatre. The magic of the moment when the gods of opera sprinkle stardust on the audience. They see what the actor wants them to see. It is a wondrous power. Treasure it. Never abuse it. Do you understand?'

'Yes, Sifu.'

Rain, carry on! It is on such rainy days when Wah Jai vanishes that Sifu teaches me his philosophy of opera.

ℰ — ℛ

... Ai-ya-yaaa... the prelude is all sound and fury!
The actual break-up is a silence – so vast –
So vast... it swallows everything in the house!

I listened, spellbound, to the powerful voice, the controlled emotion in his singing, and watched the movements of his hands. The veteran actor, Hor Fei Foo, was performing an excerpt from a popular opera with Master Wu.

Their performance on the temporary stage in the market square is paid for by the stallholders to honour the poor hungry souls during the Seventh Lunar Month of the Hungry Ghosts Festival.

Our little troupe of three has expanded. Four veteran opera singers have joined us. Each time they perform with Master Wu I watch and listen to their singing closely. To the way they lengthen a musical phrase or bite a note or hold a pause. I watch how they step across the threshold of a palace, enter a lady's chamber or mime going up a flight of stairs. Eight steps up must be eight steps down; their movements are clear and precise. I am stealing their skills, as the opera folks say.

Stealing skills – that is how young performers learn from the masters, who do not tell or teach us unlike Master Wu. Whenever they perform, we must watch and learn. The folding and unfolding of their long white water sleeves, the opening and closing of a scholar's fan, the twist and turn of his fan, all add meaning and significance to an act in the hands of a master as he sings.

Each time I act with one of these veteran performers I learn something new. I suspect Master Wu has brought them into our troupe to give me the chance to learn from other opera masters other than himself, and gratitude fills my heart at the thought. The more opera singers I perform with the more skills I pick up.

Most of the opera actors in our troupe are literate. But there are some who cannot read, yet they can sing from memory entire arias and duets from several operas and act without reading the script. Entire operas are stored inside their heads. Their memory is astounding. Like Master Wu, many of the veteran artistes were born into opera families. They grew up watching operas from the time they were babies. They went on stage with their parents as soon as they could talk. Master Wu had gone on stage when he was only three or four. He had studied only three years in school, yet he is highly literate, well read and knowledgeable about the classics due to his years of opera training.

I am learning to read the opera scripts that Master Wu keeps in his rosewood chest. Heaven willing, someday I will perform one of these operas. And I will sing and act in the *xiu sung's* role. I have learnt to move across the stage as I sing, striding out with dignity when I act the judge and fling my mandarin robe when I take the judge's seat. I have yet to master the stylised movements of a penniless poet and that of a successful scholar riding his horse. There are so many set roles and excerpts to learn and memorise. So many arias and duets to remember and practise. The more opera excerpts I perform with these veterans, the more skills I learn. And the more skills I learn, the more I want to perform. Opera has become my passion. Its music flows in my blood. Someday you will see me in an opera theatre when this war is over.

26

Shhhh!

Wah Jai placed a finger on his lips as he limped up the stairs one night. It was very late. All the tenants were asleep.

I turned up the oil lamp and covered my mouth to stop the scream rising up my throat. Wah Jai's face and knees were bleeding profusely, and he was covered with mud.

Without a word, I brought a basin of warm water into our attic. We did not speak as I cleaned his bleeding face and knees. Master Wu crept up the stairs. He handed me the bottle of medicated oil, plasters and bandages, and left. No words were exchanged between the three of us. I knew the two men didn't want the tenants to know that Wah Jai had come home bleeding at this ungodly hour. While the rest of the house slept, I wiped him clean. He winced and grimaced as I cleaned and bandaged his knees. Throughout neither of us spoke a word. The walls are thin wooden partitions and sound carries at night.

After I had cleaned and bandaged him, he fell asleep at once. He was so exhausted. But I could not sleep. I lay beside him, wide-eyed. I kept thinking of what I would say the next morning if any of the tenants asked. Oh stupid blind man, I would laugh. The idiot fell into a drain while looking at a pretty woman. Serve him right! This is what I would say if tenants and neighbours were to ask.

∽ — ∾

A week later, I whispered, 'Don't go.'

'*Shhhh!*' He limped down the stairs.

Dearest Intimate, I am very worried. The wounds on his knees are still red and watery. He did not tell me what happened, and I did not ask. But I am not stupid. He must have run away from a place he was not supposed to be in. Then chased by the devils with guns and dogs, he must have fallen into a ditch and crawled out of the enemy's reach. Those devils' dogs are ruthless beasts. Aye, it's best not to say some things aloud. That which is not uttered will not happen. I pray for him morning and night. Danger lurks everywhere. Rumours and whispers buzz and hover like flies over rotting fish. Friends and family whisper behind locked doors at night when the children are asleep. A neighbour's daughter was dragged off the street the other night. So-and-so's son, or uncle or husband or cousin was taken away.

'Did you hear the cries and wails from the pleasure houses down the road?' the butcher's wife asked.

'*Shhhh,*' the women shushed her. They crowded in the corridor below my attic, a group of whispering anxieties.

'Horrendous tortures are taking place every day in a building in Orchard Road,' the butcher's wife said.

'*Hush!* Lower your voice for goodness sake. That's the Young Men's Christian Association building, now the headquarters of the Kempetai, the secret police. Those in there won't come out alive.'

Dearest Intimate, I fear for Wah Jai's safety. It is no use talking to him. He won't listen. His anger is deep. His courage is foolish. I fear the midnight knock on the door. What if a Japanese soldier…? What if Wah Jai is taken away like the other men? It is so hard to live a normal life these days. Yet we have to try. How else to go on if we don't? Everywhere ordinary folks go about their daily tasks despite their men's sudden disappearance. Despite the bombing and roar of warplanes. Despite the daily food rationing. Despite the sudden arrival of soldiers to search their homes and take away their menfolk. What can we do? But try to live as normal a life as we can. Children still run about. We still have to go out to work. We have to eat, shit and sleep even though a bomb might fall on us while we sleep. What else can we do? What else, I ask myself? Wah Jai is all I have. Some people work for the Japanese enemy. Can we blame them? Collaborators. Traitors. So people say. Who are we to judge? Wah Jai dug graves in the Japanese cemetery but he did it for me. For me.

Meanwhile we will continue to perform, continue to bring a smile to the sad faces around us. We have to eat after all.

ℰ — ℛ

Several days passed. The wound on his knee has not yet healed.

"Don't go,' I beg him one night.

He places a finger on my lips and slips out of the house with the medicine box again. My poor, brave cripple. His determination to help the Resistance is so strong. Lord Buddha, please keep him safe. Honoured Ancestors, protect your only descendant.

After writing, I stuff my papers into the rusty biscuit tin and push it under the woodpile in the alcove. Then I place the chamber pot that Wah Jai and I use as our toilet at night in front of the woodpile.

May our piss and shit keep the devils away from my journal, I pray. Keep them away from this house. And away from Wah Jai.

On such nervous nights I cannot sleep. I wait no matter how long, I will wait till he comes home. At dawn he returns with the empty medicine box and a bunch of *choy sum* and bananas.

'From the farm in Ow Kang,' he says, and promptly falls asleep on our mattress bed on the floor. His feet are red and swollen when I take off his shoes caked with mud. And I wonder how far he has limped.

And so the nervous weeks passed till the monsoon rains arrive. The thunderstorms put an end to Wah Jai's trips for the time being. And I sigh with relief.

Yesterday afternoon while the rains poured down, the tenants and their children bunched into the front hall. Our Uncle Loke, the erhu master with the foul mouth and foul temper, surprised all of us. He was giving Wah Jai his family's heirloom. Everyone had heard how Uncle Loke had flung his body over the priceless erhu to save the heirloom from the bombs, and as a result lost his legs, his wife and two daughters. The priceless instrument had been crafted in the seventeenth century by his great, great grandfather, the most famous erhu master craftsman of Canton.

Wah Jai, speechless, stood in front of Uncle Loke who was seated in his wheelchair. I gave him a hard nudge and he fell on his knees.

'Get up, you fool! Get up!' Uncle Loke bawled at him.

'Hey, hey, Old Loke, calm down.' Master Wu patted his old friend's shoulders. 'Don't yell at the poor boy. Wah Jai is very grateful. Look at him. His face is all red. He wants to thank you. He will be like a son to you and make you proud of him someday!'

Now it was Uncle Loke's face that turned a bright pink. I poured a cup of tea and handed it to Wah Jai, still kneeling on his bandaged knees. Eyes tearing with pain, he served Uncle Loke the ritual cup of tea that disciples served their Sifu. Everyone cheered and clapped.

'Now we are truly a family of four,' Master Wu laughed. 'Circumstance and kindness have turned four refugees of this war into a family in Singapore. Old Loke, you and I are the elders of this family now.'

Everyone laughed. And Wah Jai's dark eyes were bright with unshed tears. His face had aged these past few years though his smile was wide as he cradled the prized erhu in his arms. And I was reminded of the young butcher cycling up the sizzling road in Ipoh, the crazed butcher whose grins used to irritate me. He looked so young and happy then.

That evening we celebrated the occasion with a dinner of plain white rice, vegetables and salted fish, and toasted our new family with cups of tea.

ℴ — Ⅎ

Rain pelting the window. Rain streaming down the eaves. The oil lamp was flickering. I was lying on the mattress waiting for Wah Jai to come home. Late in the night, drenched and dripping wet, he limped up the stairs with a bag.

'See what I've salvaged.'

'You went scavenging in this rain?' I sat up. 'What are you going to do with this guzheng?'

'We might need it later.'

'Our attic is already so full. Look at the room. When we first came from Ow Kang, we brought only a small bundle. Now we have a mattress on the floor for our bed and I have more clothes than I can wear.'

'I am very happy to hear my wife say this. You make me feel so rich,' he grinned, towelling his hair. Then he stripped off his wet clothes. I turned away. Though we are man and wife, we have always changed in the dark or alone. What was he doing? A glimpse of him in the corner of my eye. He was stark naked!

'You scavenger! Look at your musical instruments!' I hissed.

'*Shhh!* Not that many.' He sat down on the mattress beside me, pulling on a dry shirt. He was so at ease. I didn't know where to look.

'There is the erhu Master Wu gave you!' I tried to distract myself. 'Then the prized heirloom from Uncle Loke!' My heart was beating fast. My voice sounded shaky above the storm. 'And… and what about those instruments you salvaged from bombed houses – the drum, the gaohu, a gong, two pairs of cymbals, a pipa and now this, this guzheng. Are you building an orchestra?' My voice started rising higher.

'Wife, listen, listen to me.' He moved closer till his arm was touching mine. 'Our troupe is expanding. But look at the beautiful rosewood chest I lugged back for you. All the way from that empty house in Bukit Pasoh. All the men in that house had been killed. The two brothers had helped the resistance and the cousin killed two Japanese soldiers. The whole family had to flee.'

'Are you trying to scare me? People say such houses are haunted.'

'*Noooo.*' He leaned over and blew out the oil lamp, throwing the attic into darkness. 'These things I salvaged for you so you can barter for rice, salt and sugar later whenever we need. All for you…'

'My resourceful pig farmer's son.'

'At your service,' murmuring in my ear, he lay down and fell asleep.

$\wp - \wr$

Dearest Intimate, the weather has changed. Wah Jai and I are performing, learning and memorising new opera excerpts which keep us very busy all day. I fear I might have little time to write after this. Our troupe has expanded. And our audience in the market has grown large. We need new acts for the bigger crowds who come to watch us each morning. Yet Master Wu and Uncle Loke do not like the larger crowds. I don't understand these two men.

'Popularity attracts jealousy,' Uncle Loke grumbled last night.

'And jealous hearts will betray others,' Master Wu muttered.

Wah Jai and I frowned.

'What is eating you two?' I asked.

'Old Loke and I have seen things before you two came to live here.' Master Wu dropped his voice to a whisper. 'The Kempetai came to round up men accused of spying. And who had accused them?' His voice dropped even lower. 'Our own people.'

'Chinese were betraying Chinese. Jealous hearts are treacherous hearts,' Master Loke whispered. 'Move away from the market, we must. Large crowds attract louts.'

'But Uncle Loke…'

'Don't argue, Kam Foong. We have eaten more salt than you and Wah Jai rice. Old Loke and I talked it over. Our good run will end if we do not move.'

'But we are a cultural troupe,' Wah Jai said. 'The Japanese government favours Chinese opera because it is culture. Do you really think…?'

'Do not think, Wah Jai,' Master Wu cut him short. 'There are many troupes, many kinds of opera. Teochew opera. Hokkien opera. Hakka opera. Each troupe is vying for audience. Life is hard yet some troupes can afford to eat pork and pearly white rice. These troupes can travel freely. Can even cross the Causeway to Malaya to perform in the towns and villages up north. Why? You may ask. Because the dogs agreed to perform Japanese propaganda together with their operas. So they are paid sacks of rice. They are allowed to re-sell the rice in the black market for an exorbitant price. The black market has made them comfortable. But we are not them. Do you understand? We are not dogs. We are opera artistes. Singers and actors. Danger lurks for us. Troupes and singers who had raised funds for China's war effort have gone into hiding. Other troupes have disbanded. Actors have disappeared. Many have left the profession. If we are too successful, we will catch the attention of the Japs. They will ask us to help in their war effort. What are you going to do then? Do you two thickheads understand?

I looked at Wah Jai. He was silent. Suddenly life is more chilling than I thought. Why didn't Master Wu tell us about this before we joined him? If we had known of such things earlier Wah Jai and I would have remained on the farm in Ow Kang. But then… but then I would have no opportunity to sing in an opera again, would I?

Dearest Intimate, I write to tell you such things. No one else.

℘ — ℆

Has it been months since I last wrote the above?

I am so tired. We have been on the move. A different place on different days at different times. Like sparrows, we flit from branch to branch. Fly from tree to tree. A temple at three-mile stone or sixth-mile stone in Serangoon one day. A market in Queenstown, or Redhill, or Bukit Ho Swee another day. Sometimes we perform at night in a temple courtyard at a religious festival. Sometimes we sing in an open space under a tree in a village square somewhere. Sometimes it is a market in Bukit Merah. The next day it is somewhere else. We are never in the same place for more than two or three days. Wah Jai has stopped slipping away with his medicine box at night. He fears being tailed. For now, he is staying by my side. Learning to play the drum. He takes over the drumming when Master Wu joins me in the singing and acting. We are back to being a troupe of three. We no longer let others join us. But we have expanded our repertoire. Master Wu and I take on multiple roles. Sometimes I am the *xiu sung* playing the young scholar or poet. Sometimes I am the scholar skilled in the martial arts or a general skilled in the literary arts. Master Wu taught me some basic kungfu stances for the excerpts. The two of us perform brief stylised exchanges with a sword and spear. And as we sing Wah Jai rolls the drum. The audience is small, much smaller than before. We earn less, but enough. We keep our props simple. A flag represents an army. A whip, the horse, and the audience imagine the rest.

'This is opera theatre at its best, light-footed and imaginative,' Master Wu says. He and Wah Jai sound optimistic. But the two men do not need to tell me. I know they are worried. They have received word that the Japanese soldiers are looking in our direction for a certain person.

Dearest Intimate, wherever you are, please pray for my poor cripple. Honoured Ancestors, Goddess of Mercy, please protect my pig farmer's son. Bless my erhu player.

℘ — ℆

We carry on despite our worries. What else can we do? To stop might rouse suspicions. This morning in the market in Tiong Bahru, Master Wu played my idiot husband and made the crowd laugh. Yesterday he was the powerful eunuch in the imperial court, scolding me the young prince under his tutelage. In other performances he acts the old fool and clown. Sometimes he is the foolish innkeeper or the bumbling boatman or the inept court official. Seeing our stern teacher transform himself into a white-faced eunuch with mincing walk and speech, Wah Jai and I giggled.

'Ignoramus!' He turned to the audience. 'Look at the two sillies laughing at me. Poor fools! Do they not know the clown is the most revered character in the history of opera? The founder of the legendary Pear Garden of Opera was none other than the great Emperor Xuanzong of the Tang Dynasty. The patron saint of opera. And he often acted the clown! When operas were performed in court, Emperor Xuanzong often acted as the Chou clown. He had his face painted white to disguise himself. To this day, clowns in opera paint their faces white to honour Emperor Xuanzong. And mark this, people!'

A dramatic pause. The audience held its breath.

'During the ritual prayers before a performance begins, every performer has to kneel before the gods. Only the clown does not kneel. Why? Because the clown...'

Master Wu drew himself to a great height.

'... because the clown was once the Emperor himself!'

'Ho-yeah! Ho-yeah!' The crowd applauded him.

I looked at the three of us and the people in the street laughing at Master Wu, enjoying our opera excerpts. Is this happiness? I asked myself. Can we still be happy in wartime? Is laughter still possible when the enemy has occupied our country? Life felt like a dream at such times.

We are butterflies. Our performance is but a dream. A dream so real that actor and audience float out of their small lives into another life, tragic, vital, heroic, or comedic, while I, a woman, with a flick of my fan, change into a man, a prince, a judge or a peasant. An enchantment of the moment. We let its magic hold us. Who knows when this war will end? Where a bomb will fall next? Every day there are rumours and news of arrest, torture, rape and killing. People's hearts are fearful and anxious at the sound of marching boots. Yet when we perform an opera excerpt or sing a song, they forget their fears. They laugh and shout, *Bravo! Bravo!* For a few shining moments, terror and worries are vanquished. Hunger is conquered. Pain and sorrow banished. Laughter and fellowship reign supreme. We are a noble race again. Such is the power of opera and theatre. How can I not dedicate my life to the gift that Heaven has bestowed upon me? Lord Guan Gong, god of courage. Protect us please!

27

For two weeks after my email, I heard nothing from Robert. Just as I was beginning to calm down, the first of several emails popped into my Inbox.

Mrs Xiu Yin Palmerston, are you mad?????
     You have absolutely no grounds to ask for a divorce or separation! I categorically DO NOT agree to our living apart. Come home now. We can talk things through. Remember your marriage vow, the solemn promise you made before God. The Palmerstons' name has never been sullied in a divorce court. From the time of my great great-grandfather, a highly respected God-fearing judge, the Palmerston women have stayed by their husbands' side. Our PM frowns on divorce and other peccadilloes among those seeking political office. Are you so wicked? So determined to bring disgrace upon me? So vengeful as to deprive me of the chance to political office? I have put in years of voluntary work in church and grassroots committees. Admittedly I had spent little time with you to fathom your thoughts, hopes and aspirations. Am I to blame when you are so cold and judgemental in the first place? When did we last come together as man and wife? Answer me.

Ten more emails came one after another that night. Then they stopped. I knew he had fallen asleep. Sprawled on the sofa. The computer and tv still on, and his empty glasses strewn all over the carpet.
     The following night, I waited like a caged goat waiting for the butcher's knife. For three nights, there were no emails. And then they came.

Let me reiterate. We are not separated. Do not consider this a separation. This is a desertion! You deserted your spouse! I did not desert you. I admit I was selfish. Even pugnacious at times.

Competing so hard at work has made me so. In university we used to call it 'the dehumanising effect of an achievement-oriented society.' Remember? To get to where I am at the top tier of the Civil Service I have to compete hard and work hard. Very hard. I have to put in long hours. I cannot talk about my work. I serve the state. Nation before self. Community before family. Have you forgotten these values of our founding fathers? I thought you understood. Apparently you do not. In my work, silence is paramount. We are trained to keep our thoughts to ourselves. Never to trust anyone totally. I told you time and again never to question me. I do not think you appreciate the importance of internal security and national security. I have to maintain a professionalism that separates what I do at work from what I am at home. If you had not been so hard in your judgement of me, if you had not been so pugnacious, if you had not subverted my decisions so often (and I cite the most damaging example – turning my daughter against me) I might have trusted you, loved you, even enjoyed your companionship.

My patience is wearing thin. I hope I will not be forced to go to your office to bring you home. Do not say that you have not been warned. I am the husband, the head of the family. St Paul said in Ephesians 5:21:33, "Wives, be subject to your husbands as to the Lord." You are subject to me. Come home at once and I will forgive you.

I laughed out loud. I couldn't help it. He would quote the Bible. That he would. His email, hilarious and threatening, and yet at the same time, reasonable. A hardworking man, an ambitious man, he had set his sights on a political career, and I hadn't known, hadn't realised it. My guilt returning, I read his email over and over again. I was the deserting wife. I had misunderstood him. It was my fault. Then I read the last paragraph again.

I could not sleep. When I did fall asleep I had a nightmare. He was intimidating the staff at the front desk in the National Archives. He flashed his official card, ignored the security guard and charged up the escalator.

Barging into the main office he announced in a loud voice, 'I am looking for my runaway wife!' I saw the shock on my colleagues' faces and the barely concealed look of revulsion on my director's face as she yelled, 'Guards!'

I woke up with a start. Bathed in a cold sweat all sorts of possibilities rushed into my mind. The intrusion of my marital discord into the professional sanctum of the National Archives was a very real possibility. The migraine in my head started to throb again. The muscles in my neck felt tight. I paced from bedroom to living room and kitchen. Unable to sit down. Tumultuous clouds gathered as I stood at the window watching my neighbours drive out of the car park to join the morning hour traffic. I imagined the talk in the office among my colleagues and the clerical staff. The whispered conversation that stopped as soon as I approached. The mask of incuriosity that fell upon their faces as I walked past. Then a timid emissary would come to enquire how I was, or worse, to bring a summons to the director's office. I filled the electric kettle and made a cup of black coffee. While waiting for it to cool I switched on the computer and read his last email again. *Do not say that you have not been warned.*

Could my nightmare be a premonition of things to come? The thought made me ill. I poured away the coffee now grown cold and phoned the office to tell them I was not going in. I wasn't feeling well. It was not a good sign. Two days ago I had already missed an important meeting after pleading a dreadful headache. The phone rang.

'Hello. Xiu Yin? Are you all right?' Mrs Hassim asked.

'It's my migraine again.'

'Have you seen a doctor?'

'Not yet.'

'Tell the doctor about your migraine. Rest well. Remember. Help is just a phone call away. Call me if you need to talk to someone.'

'Thank you for your concern, Mrs Hassim, thank you.'

I put down the phone. I had never confided in anyone in the office. A colleague was a colleague. Not a friend. I had no close friends although a name did come into my head. I wished to God I had at least kept in touch with him and sent the annual Chinese New Year card. But I didn't all these years. Robert would have killed me if he found out that I had kept in touch with Meng. Our last meeting was in the park under the rain tree.

Then I thought of the lawyer who did my grandparents' will. I picked up the phone but put it down. If I called Mr Leong it would be a step of no return. I drank a glass of water. Be brave, I told myself, and dialled the lawyer's number. His office line was busy. After another attempt I gave up. Relieved. It was a sign from Heaven. I shouldn't do it. By then it was noon, and I hadn't had breakfast yet. I sat down at the kitchen table, undecided what to do. I got up, went to the bathroom, came out and pushed away the superstitious thought. I looked for the lawyer's email, found it, and typed out a brief note and pressed Send. Then I went down to the coffeeshop and bought a packet of chicken rice.

Back home, the chicken tasted flat. I couldn't finish the meal. I drank another glass of water and tried to settle down to read the day's newspapers. Nothing went into my head. At three, I checked my email; the lawyer's secretary had replied. Mr Leong would be in court this whole afternoon, it said, but if I left my phone number, she would ask him to call me on Monday morning. I sent her my phone number and switched off my computer.

There was nothing I could do to rush things. It was already Friday afternoon. Faced with a long weekend and nothing accomplished, I blamed myself. I shouldn't have procrastinated for so long. I should have called Mr Leong before moving out of Sea Cove. Should have talked to him after I had moved out. Knowing Robert I should have been prepared. Instead I was dithering. I had kept putting things off, blaming a heavy workload in the office, the pressure of a tight schedule and fatigue. Then after I had moved out, I was so relieved to be on my own at last that I was very reluctant to do anything that might stir a hornet's nest. Let things be. Take it one day at a time. That was my mantra, and the lie I comforted myself.

In truth I was deeply ashamed. Ashamed of the pain in my heart and limbs. Ashamed of my humiliated body and self. Ashamed of having been so helpless, so worthless for so long. So stripped of dignity by the man I had once loved, the father of my only child. Ashamed of what I had endured for so many years. How could I, a professional woman with a university degree, have been so weak, so stupid, so feeble for so many years? I felt so mortified I could not face myself. How then could I face a lawyer? Face the exposure of my private life in the office of a stranger, professionally kind in voice and competent in manner, seated with a pen in hand, taking notes as I spoke?

Ashamed I had fled to the National Library. The library had always been my refuge. I felt safe wandering among its shelves of books, an anonymous silent reader among other anonymous silent readers as I pulled out books on domestic violence.

I had no idea of the large number books published each year about spousal and domestic abuse – biographies, novels, poetry, memoirs, research papers and social workers' accounts, no idea of the thousands of children and women, and old folks the world over, who had suffered and continue to suffer abuse unseen and undetected by others, enduring years of harsh, caustic, derisive, sarcastic, scathing contempt, words that constantly put them down, that constantly cut them off and made them feel scorned, contemptible and unworthy. Sometimes as I read, I cried. Reading helped me to understand gradually how years of having one's intelligence, self-worth and confidence belittled and chipped off day after day for years could turn a woman into a mouse. The knowledge shocked and freed me. It became clear what Robert had done to me. For years I had thought the problems I had with Robert was my fault. For years I went through life muttering the ancient Catholic prayer, *'through my fault, through my fault, through my most grievous fault'*. Reading all those books opened my eyes. And especially after reading Por Por's journal, I realised what a strong forebear I had. Her blood runs in me.

The solitude and privacy in my grandparents' flat gave me the mental space to think of what I had gone through, what I needed to do, cry as much as my heart wanted and get into the proper frame of mind to establish some distance from my problems.

All that weekend I thought about Robert's email. He had threatened to go to my office to force me to return to Sea Cove. If that happened it would be a scandal. No, he wouldn't do it, I thought one minute. Next minute, it was yes, he could be mad enough to do it. Just to show how strong he was. These thoughts ding-donged in my head throughout the day and only ceased when I fell asleep.

It was irrational. It was driving me crazy. I resolved to resign from the National Archives. I had enough savings. I could earn a living as long as status didn't matter. I wrote a brief letter of resignation on Sunday evening. On Monday morning I posted it before I could change my mind.

Then I called the lawyer's office. His secretary remembered my email, and sensing the urgency in my voice, said she would check with Mr Leong and call me back. I was restless the whole morning waiting for her call. Now that I had made up my mind I was impatient to get things moving. Just before noon, the secretary called and said Mr Leong would meet me the following evening.

His office was cluttered with steel cabinets and shelves of files and books. Framed certificates almost covered one wall. Mr Leong's room was even more cluttered.

'Sit down, sit down, can I get you a cup of tea or cold water?'

'Thanks, Mr Leong. I'm fine.'

He was a kindly man in his mid-sixties, with thinning hair and eyes that hinted of sharpness when aroused. He had been a friend of my grandparents.

'I was your grandmother's fan. I attended all her operas. Aye, those were the days.'

Without seeming to, he put me at ease. We had a long meeting. He asked many questions, some of which I struggled to answer. But he was patient and did not hurry me.

'Don't worry. You don't have to answer now. You can take your time and email me later. My office will draft the letter of intention and send it to Mr Palmerston.'

His smile was warm and his words were reassuring. When our meeting was over at last, I walked out of the law office building and kept walking till I came to the Singapore River. I had done it. In the darkening twilight I stood on the riverbank looking down at the drift of black waters twinkling with the city's lights that had come on. The dark phase of my life was drifting out to sea like the dark waters. I could feel the weight that had been pressing on me for years lifting from my heart as I stood gazing at the flowing murky waters. The lightness felt strange. My fingers were tingling as I typed out a message and sent it to Janice. Minutes later my phone rang.

'Mom, are you all right?'

'I am.' I could feel the smile on my face. 'I'm divorcing your dad. I've just spoken with Mr Leong, my lawyer.'

There was a pause, then an explosive 'Oh Mom!!'

The words that followed took me by surprise.

'You did it! You found the strength to do it. I've been waiting for you to do it all these years!'

Hearing those words from my daughter, words that had travelled at light speed under the Pacific Ocean from Canada to Singapore, bringing me not just her words but her feelings that were so heart warming and so unexpected, something hard in me broke. Tears spilled out of my eyes. A sense of lightness and emancipation came over me. All these years my daughter had been so careful, so formal whenever she called home. She had kept to safe topics like her studies, her grades, her professors and food. I thought I had lost her. I still bore the guilt of having failed to protect her from her father's temper. But now for the first time, the first time in years, the two of us were talking of things close to our hearts, the things that had hurt us, and I was crying and sobbing into my phone.

A man walking his dog, a large Alsatian, stopped.

'Ma'am, do you need help?' he asked, looking concerned.

I smiled at him through my tears and shook my head.

'Talking with my daughter in Vancouver,' I whispered.

He nodded, smiling, and gave his dog a tug, and went his way.

'A kindly ang moh, German, I think, just asked why I'm crying,' I told Janice.

We laughed. And for the next hour or more till the battery in my phone died out, we talked, at times as mother and daughter, at times like two old friends crying and laughing for we had so much to cry about. So much to talk about. So many things we had held back.

'Mom, I want to hug you right now. Call me again. We haven't finished. Call any time, do you understand? I love you so very much. I love you.'

I put away my phone, and walked along the riverbank, stopping now and then to admire the sinuous lines of light in the dark flowing river and the lighted boats ferrying groups of laughing hand-waving tourists. There was light everywhere. Threads of golden light swimming in shape-shifting patches of glow on the river. Light spilling out from the numerous restaurants, bars and eateries along its bank. Light raining down from the coloured lamps strung round the branches of trees and awnings. Light shining on the people's flushed faces out enjoying a beer and a meal with family and friends. The city was aglow with light wherever I looked. Electric light, ambient light, coloured lights. I walked through the brightly lit streets back to Jin Swee and took the lift up to the flat. I showered, changed into fresh clean clothes, and went down to the coffeeshop and ordered noodles with braised innards for dinner.

'Hey Sister Xiu Yin! Good to see you eating here instead of buying back!' Khim called out.

'Give me a cold beer, Khim.'

'*Waah!* You touch 4-D or what?'

'Better than 4-D. Come! Share a bottle with me.'

28

'Mercy, mercy, mercy! Lord Buddha, have mercy on us.
Heal my Sifu's injuries. Keep those devils far from him.
Keep him alive. Make him strong again.
May all who live in this house be safe from the devils' guns!'

I light three joss sticks and implore all the gods in Heaven to heal Master Wu and keep Wah Jai safe from harm. What else can I do other than pray? And practise my singing when I am not brewing herbal medicinal soup for Master Wu. He will want me to carry on even though we have stopped performing.

The whole house is gripped by fear and anxiety. Everyone is quiet and heartsick. The butcher's wife has stopped shouting at her children. Uncle Loke sits in his wheelchair playing his erhu softly in the hall sending his erhu's fluid soothing notes into Master Wu's bedroom upstairs. Music will heal his wounds, I hope. Last night he was delirious. I kept sponging him to bring his fever down. When Wah Jai changed his bandages the amount of pus had shocked us. I thank Heaven his fever has subsided and he's sleeping at last.

Wah Jai and I are at home much of the time these days. He carries on his music practice with Uncle Loke while I sing up here in the alcove. We try to live as normally as we can. After drinking the bitter brew prescribed by Old Dr Wong, Master Wu is asleep again. A good sign. Sleep is good. It will help his body to heal. The house is unusually quiet in the afternoon. The children, bless them, no longer run in and out or shout for their mothers.

Wah Jai has gone out to buy food. While I wait for his return, I sit up here in the alcove and write my worries to you.

When I recall what happened I am frustrated. Why didn't Master Wu kneel? Neighbours and tenants ask me. Why did he remain standing when he knew it would provoke those Japanese scum? He wouldn't have been so badly wounded if he had knelt and kowtowed like the rest of us, they whispered to each other. He was the only one who remained standing. Like a nail waiting to be hammered down. Those soldiers could have shot him. Friends and neighbours shook their sorry heads.

'One moment's glory, a hundred nights of pain and worry,' the butcher's wife muttered.

No one understands Master Wu. My Sifu is not a fool! He has his reasons for not kneeling.

Now that I have time for a while, I can tell you what happened last week. Or was it two weeks? These anxious days have rushed by so fast.

That fateful morning we were performing in Temple Street. Master Wu was playing the great Eunuch Li, the imperial adviser to the young Emperor. How could the imperial advisor kneel to a mere army sergeant? In our act, Eunuch Li was lecturing his young emperor – namely me. Stroking and flinging the long grey beard hooked round his ears, his manner was both magisterial and subservient before his young imperial charge. His words at times angry, at times pleading, at times stern like the old palace tutor with the authority to berate the emperor. The crowd was thrilled. Everyone knew that his words were directed at that young spineless Son of Heaven in Beijing, who had become the puppet of Japan. As Master Wu sang out the words scolding the emperor for his weakness, for not fighting the enemy at the gate, the crowd roared and flung money into our bowls.

Banzai!!

The sudden harsh icy voice rang out. Soldiers rushed into the street, guns pointing. The crowd froze.

Banzai!!

In one body w knelt at once. But not my fearless Sifu. The great imperial eunuch turned, and gave the leader of the Japanese troops a courtly bow. The eyes of the Japanese sergeant narrowed like a tiger's. His claws lashed out, a sudden vicious kick. Loud screaming from the crowd. Master Wu's body landed among us. Wah Jai clamped a hand over my mouth to stifle my cries as a dozen soldiers pounced on Master Wu. They kicked him in the groin and belly. Kicked and hit him with the butt of their guns as he lay on the ground, hands covering his head, curled like a prawn. He did not cry out. No one made a sound. No one moved as we watched, horror in our eyes. Even the children dared not cry. Fear had frozen us. We knelt like statues.

A black van screeched round the corner and drew up. Six men leapt out of the van. They wore full black with black hoods covering their faces. And sinister slits in the hood for eyes.

Banzai! They saluted.

Banzai! The sergeant and his soldiers replied.

Banzai! We repeated, tears in our eyes.

My heart had turned to ice at the sight of the hooded men. Everyone knew such men worked for the Kempetai, the dreaded secret service of the Japanese Army. Dark eyes looked out of the menacing black hoods as the men in black walked among us. One of the men stopped in front of Master Wu. A soldier yanked him up by the hair. The hooded man looked at him, but pointed to the man kneeling next to him. Two soldiers grabbed that man who wailed like a pig being led to slaughter. He was shoved into the black van.

When one of the hooded men stopped in front of Wah Jai, my heart dropped. I thought I would faint. I breathed again when the man moved on. Shocked and relieved, I stared at Wah Jai. His face was smeared with white paint. He looked like the Chou clown. When did he paint his face white? Why did he do that? Questions. Questions swirled in my head as my eyes followed the men in black threading through the terrified crowd. A child wailed and was hushed by his frightened mother. She pulled up her blouse and thrust her breast into the toddler's mouth to silence him. A soldier walked over and squeezed the woman's breast. The other soldiers roared and guffawed. Then one by one, they shoved seven men into the black van. Loud wails and cries issued from inside the van. A sudden shot rang inside. The wailing stopped. The black van drove off.

Banzai! The soldiers marched off.

Banzai! Tears streaking down our faces we waited till the soldiers had left the street.

'Sifu! Sifu!'

I rushed to Master Wu. Blood was streaming down his ashen face. He was lying in a pool of urine and blood. Many of us had also soiled our pants.

The news had reached Keong Saik Road by the time Wah Jai and the men carried Master Wu home on a stretcher. Many came into the house to offer help. Old Dr Wong, the most respected physician in Chinatown, attended to him, and refused payment. Hour after hour people came to enquire about Master Wu. They brought nourishing soups and porridge, sharing with us what little they have.

'Let them die without burial!

Without family to mourn them!

Without descendants to remember them!

Without children to light a joss stick or say a prayer for them.

Condemned as nameless hungry ghosts forever! I curse them!

May their wives and daughters be barren forever!'

Daily loud curses and loud wailing fill the street and our three-storey tenement. The pipa player on the second floor has lost her only son. He was one of the men dragged into the van. No one knows if he was the one shot in the van.

Who were those hooded men? Rumours flew like black crows all over Chinatown. Last night a neighbour whispered that the pipa player's son had been helping the anti-Japanese forces and had supplied them with medicine. I swallowed the stone in my throat and kept silent, careful not to look at Wah Jai's face. The pipa player's cries and curses went on for days. Each night I pray that I do not have to utter such curses.

&) — CR

Daily Wah Jai washes, cleans and bandages the open wounds. Master Wu groans with such pain when he is moved, it sears my heart. His body is covered with bruises and bleeding lesions. His legs and arms are covered with gashes and lacerations where the gun butts had struck him. His body is so stiff and swollen in parts that he cannot sit up without crying out in pain. Every morning I make him drink the dark bitter brew that I had boiled with the herbs from Old Dr Wong. Every day I pray that the wounds in his groin will heal and the pain in his back will ease. Those dogs had stomped on his legs which are swollen an angry bright pink, and his knees have swelled many times their normal size. Fortunately Old Dr Wong is an excellent bonesetter. He shifted and massaged Master Wu's bones back into place, and bandaged the knees with a mixture of herbs in a cast held in place by two planks of wood.

'There! We have to make do,' he said. 'Don't let him move that leg too much. When he feels a great itch, don't let him take off the cast. The itch shows the wound is healing. But his leg won't heal well enough to kneel again.'

℁—ℂ

Yesterday I plucked up courage to ask Master Wu why he refused to kneel. Lying in bed with his eyes closed and a smile on his lips, he sighed.

'Do you still have to ask? Don't you know your Sifu by now? I had already walked through the invisible gate, the *Fu Doh Muen*. I was already Imperial Eunuch Li. I couldn't just get out of character because some dogs with guns appeared. The great Lord Li does not kneel to dogs. Besides,' he paused for breath, 'the spirit of Liu Gan San was in me that morning.'

'Liu Gan San? Who is he?'

'My poor ignorant fool! Ouch!' he groaned. 'I haven't taught you well. Liu Gan San is the most courageous of clowns in the history of opera. He used his performances to criticise corrupt officials in the Qing court. Even when he was beaten up and tortured. Ouch!'

'Those fiends could have beaten you to death. They could have shot you. If you are gone, what am I to do?' I started to sob.

He opened his eyes and stared hard at me. And then he laughed! A deep belly laugh that caused him to groan in pain.

'Don't be such a goose. Look, Wah Jai has come in. You have a husband. Who do I have? No wife. No child. If I die, I die. Now stop sniffling! I am not dead yet. If I had died that day, I would have died a glorious death. Died without kneeling to dogs and fiends and murderers. Died without dishonouring my ancestors. Unlike that arsehole you call Big Boss. His troupe of arse lickers. They kowtow to dogs! Ouch! Damn this pain!'

'Sifu, don't move. What did you say just now? Aren't Big Boss and his troupe dead?'

'Yes. In my eyes they are dead!'

'Now wait a minute. Are they dead or alive?'

'I told you! In my eyes they are dead! No longer alive! No longer human. They are running dogs! Dogs that lick Japanese backsides! Ouch!'

He tried to sit up, but I pushed him down.

'Don't sit up. Doctor's orders. Now tell me again. Are Big Boss and his troupe dead or alive?'

'I told you already! In my eyes they are dead. Here we are gnawing on sweet potatoes and yams. There they are eating pearly white rice and pork every day. Allowed to travel. Allowed to perform in every town and village in Singapore and Malaya. In Penang, Ipoh and Kuala Lumpur. The Japanese military gave them special documents stamped Actor. Those turncoats had agreed to perform the enemy's propaganda. They are blackguards and traitors.'

He shut his eyes, his laboured breath filling the room. For a long while he could not speak. Shocked, Wah Jai and I watched a tear seeping out of the corner of his eyes and roll down the deep runnels on his sunken cheek. His face was taut with the effort to stop his tears. I reached out for his hand, but Wah Jai stopped me. He shook his head. A battle was raging inside our Sifu.

'That night… when the bombs fell, we were in Ipoh… we were running for shelter… I was holding my son's hand, running… through the deadly air when… when he screamed… a piece of shrapnel had… had pierced his heart. My son… my only descendant… I cradled him in my arms. The child was in such pain. Another bomb fell. Smoke everywhere and cries. It was a nightmare and… and my wife… My wife, she went mad… she… she tried to kill me, said it should have pierced my heart. I wish it had… I truly wish the bombs had killed me instead of my boy.'

He struggled to sit up again. And I pushed him down again.

'That whore… that shameless whore… she sneaked off… with that… that son of a bitch. Your Big Boss… the bast… bastard!'

He lay so still and pale, not a muscle moved. After several minutes when he did not move, I shook his arm.

'Sifu! Sifu! Don't die! You have me!'

℘—℞

Dearest Intimate. I feel so alone.

Ever since the dreaded secret police came and the pipa player's son was whisked away, Wah Jai and I had avoided each other's eyes. I dared not ask why or how he painted his face white. Night after night we lie sleepless next to each other, silent as two gravestones. Last night, I could no longer bear it. Under the cover of darkness, I told him not to be a hero. He had done enough.

He turned away.

I hugged his back, hard and taut as dried cowhide. Our attic was dark without the oil lamp. I could not see his face. After a long while I heard his hoarse voice choked.

'It should have been me.'

I hugged his back, hard as rock.

'Stop what you are doing,' I whispered. 'I do not want to lose you.'

The muscles of his back and shoulders tightened. A baby wailed in one of the tenants' rooms on the floor below. A soft mewling cry like a kitten's. Its mother hushed her, and the night's silence thickened. *Chik!* A house lizard on the wall called. I heard a light snore beside me, and drew in a deep breath, my eyes staring into the dark.

Intimate, wherever you are, please stay alive.

It is a strange time to live. Wives do not know their husbands' whereabouts. Mothers do not know what their sons do. Young women dress as men and young men vanish into the night. Grief and fear patrol the city. Suspicions taint the air we breathe. Can we trust our neighbours? Accusations may lurk behind sealed lips. It is a fearful time to live. Honoured Ancestors, protect your sole descendant, Wah Jai.

৯০ — ০৩

There are big worries and small worries. Big thieves and small thieves. Yesterday I turned my back from the piece of pork fat I left in the kitchen for a minute and it vanished. Was it my fault? This is my home. A piece of pork couldn't have sprung legs and walked out of the kitchen. There are thieves in this house. Prices are soaring in the market and tenants padlock their food safe.

I had paid a lot of money for my small piece of fatty pork. I had wanted to cook it for Master Wu. So I was furious when that very night, I smelt fried lard wafting through the house. I searched every floor. In the corridor of the second floor, I saw Mrs Tung, the trishaw rider's wife feeding her hungry brood of five with fried tapioca noodles garnished with tiny bits of fried lard and pork. As I walked past, Mrs Tung averted her face pulling up her blouse to give her breast to the youngest child. Her children kept their big hungry eyes trained on me, wolfing down their noodles as though I was about to snatch away their food. I looked at the hungry eyes in the thin sallow faces of the children, swallowed my anger and walked away.

80 — 08

A month has passed since those hooded devils walked among us and the soldiers marched into Temple Street with their guns. Our three-storey house has grown strangely quiet. The tenants, usually rowdy, are silent and fearful. The pipa player no longer plays her pipa. And the actors and musicians who had clamoured to join our troupe have stayed away.

'Can't blame them. Everyone is afraid,' Uncle Loke says. 'But when our horse dies, we must get up and walk.'

Wah Jai and I have been walking. We no longer travel all over the island to perform. The two of us have stayed within the Chinatown and the Telok Ayer precinct where there are still many teahouses open. We avoid the morning market and Temple Street. Each night we stand outside the restaurants and teahouses in other streets and along the Singapore River, hawking my songs accompanied by Wah Jai on the erhu. Without Master Wu, we cannot perform excerpts and our takings are dismal. Some nights our earning is so miserable, our sisters in the brothels take pity on us. They persuade their Japanese clients to engage us and we are asked to go into the brothel to sing. Some of their Japanese clients are generous. But when they are drunk, they are worse than lewd. It is a good thing that I sing as a *xiu sung* and they think I am a young man. But that does not always stop some of them from reaching out to touch me.

'Some Japanese men like handsome Chinese young men,' the brothel sisters say. 'And you are so handsome.'

'Don't worry, don't worry,' Madam Fong comforts me. 'I will see that nothing goes beyond touching your face and arms.'

For a few dollars, I swallowed my anger and pride last night, and let one of the more persistent army brass plant a kiss on my cheek.

Anger flared in Wah Jai's eyes. I stopped him with a look. Then turned and smiled at the Japanese brass. He was drunk. Madam Fong and her girls fussed around him, made him drink and laugh till he let go of my arm.

'Never let a Japanese dog lose face,' Madam Fong hissed at Wah Jai in Cantonese. Then she turned around, and smiling, she and her girls bowed low singing like cheerful canaries, 'Domo arigato gozaimasu, sir. Thank you very much, thank you very much.'

I fear for Wah Jai's safety and the safety of Madam Fong and the sisters each time we go into the pleasure house. When these Japanese soldiers lose their temper, heads could roll. And so we smiled and bowed low, we the defeated, the conquered and the downtrodden. We eat humiliation and swallow anger like stones. The daily humiliations and deprivations a conquered people suffer are too many to record. But there is one I must record. If I don't spit it out onto this page, I might spit it out on a soldier's face. My heart shatters when I think of it. My hands shake. I want to kill the dog.

Three nights ago we were singing in a restaurant patronised by Japanese and Chinese businessmen. A rowdy group of Japanese soldiers barged in. I stopped singing. One of the soldiers saw Wah Jai holding on to his erhu. The soldier laughing seized his erhu, and Wah Jai sprang forward to retrieve his precious instrument. The soldier flung it into the air. It landed onto the lap of a customer, who dared not move. The soldier was drunk. He laughed, and snatched up a customer's bottle of liquor, and drank from it, dripping all over his boots.

'You!' He pointed at Wah Jai, shouted something in Japanese.

When Wah Jai did not move, the soldier took out his gun and fired a shot in the air. The shot shattered the restaurant's mirror.

'Get down. He wants you to crawl over and lick his boot,' a Chinese customer hissed at Wah Jai.

A second shot rang out.

'Get down or we will all die!'

I saw Wah Jai's shattered face in the mirror change into a stiff mask. He got down on his hands and knees. In petrified silence, the whole restaurant watched him crawl up to the soldier's boot. Licked up the wine on his boot, and wiped his mouth on his sleeve. Loud belching guffaws from the other Japanese soldiers greeted this.

'*Banzai!*' Those drunken dogs marched off.

As I helped Wah Jai to his feet, the Japanese customers in the restaurant came forward and stuffed our bowl with dollar notes. It was hard to believe. These Japanese civilians were sorry for us. Actually sorry for us. I was crying as I helped Wah Jai out.

When we reached home, we did not talk about what happened. We did not tell Master Wu or Uncle Loke. Speech would not change a thing. But words once written down will be remembered.

Back in our attic, I made him rinse his mouth several times with hot tea and spit into the spittoon. I wished I had a bottle of liquor to wash away the dirt clinging to his tongue, making him unable to speak. I brought in a basin of warm water and a towel. Gently I wiped and cleaned his taut humiliated body, especially his knees. Then I rubbed and massaged him with oil till he finally fell asleep.

I will not forget this night. Neither will Wah Jai. All our life we will remember it.

⁋—⁍

Dearest Intimate, I am scared. Wah Jai is gone. He hasn't come home for two nights. I pray and wait. I make sure these days that I have herbs, ointment and strips of cloth that I cut from old clothes. Whenever he leaves, he takes some of these with him. I do not ask where he goes. The few words between us have become fewer. Each morning, I look at the empty blue sky and white clouds and try not to think too much. But the mind would not stop thinking. I think of his family and mine. I think of the sisters in the pleasure houses hiding their sorrow behind their giggles. I think of the howling young girl naked to the waist being dragged the night before by a Japanese soldier naked from the waist down. Madam Fong did nothing. I did nothing. I want to tear my hair when I think of the screams I had ignored, the fear that rose in my throat at the sound of tramping boots, and that night, that night when Wah Jai had to lick a Japanese boot. For days, he could not eat or speak. Anger had stuffed up his throat. And mine. All sorts of cries rose in the middle of the night, ignored by Heaven and earth. And neighbours. What could the neighbours do? I think of Wah Jai's infrequent disappearances, limping home in the early hours of morn with an empty box that had contained the bandages and medicine I had packed. I do not want to think of the consequences if the dogs bite him. Would I kill myself? Could I live without him? Silence like a dark abyss sits between us. Yet life would be unbearable without each other. We have travelled so far, he and I, walking the same road under the same sky in the same shoes. Loss and gratitude bind us to each other. Silent and urgent he clings to me at night. In the dark I feel his ribs and he feels mine. We hold each other close. Before this war I had thought the human heart was small. But I was wrong. The size of a fist, our heart holds an ocean of love.

29

Dearest Intimate. How are you earning a living?

The Japanese dollar has shrunk so much these days that people call them 'banana notes'. Food prices are high as the sky. I have spent all the money we have to buy pork bones to make soup for Master Wu. He is recovering well. He can sit up in bed and is hungry for news of the outside world like the rest of us. I dare not ask how some people get their news from overseas. All the news that we can hear on official radio is about the victories of the Japanese fighter planes and bombers. No one is allowed to listen to other broadcasting stations. Those found tuning to other stations are severely punished or worse, beheaded. Yet despite the great risk, news of the outside world does trickle in through word of mouth. China is suffering. I long for news of my parents and brothers. I feel I have been separated from them and my village for a hundred years. Mother told me that in life we would taste the sweet, the sour, the salty, and the bitterness of life and memory. Wah Jai and I have tasted everything these past years. I dare not think what we will taste in the future if this war goes on much longer. I still fear for his safety. And there is something else I have not told him. I don't want to disappoint him again, so I have been withholding the news for as long as I could.

$$\wp — \wp$$

He knows. Last night, just before we went to bed he asked, 'Are you…?'

I placed a hand over his mouth at once.

'Don't say a word. Not even to Sifu.'

His gaze rested on my belly and his face started to crunch up. I thought he was going to cry and averted my eyes.

'Stop performing from now on,' he said. His voice was hoarse and he had to restrain his smiles from breaking out.

'What do we eat if I don't perform? Sifu hasn't recovered fully yet. And I need to eat.'

He sighed at the truth of my words. He has lost weight. He is so thin that his shirt flaps like an insect's wings when the wind blows. He asked if I crave for any food.

'Pork porridge,' I said.

'Then you will have pork porridge every day,' he grinned. 'You have to eat well from now on.'

His hand reached out but I pushed him away.

'Stop that! Pray.'

He knelt down at the ancestral altar we had set up under the skylight in our attic. I knelt next to him. Side by side in silence, we kowtowed three times to thank the gods and ancestors for blessing us. We did not voice aloud our wish. We have learnt that what is not said is far more precious than what is said.

₧——₦

Intimate. You will laugh when you read this.

Wah Jai has started to do the laundry. He washes our clothes and hangs them out to dry on the bamboo poles in the back lane. The women tease and call him, Twenty-four Hour Dutiful Husband! He smiles and ignores them. Yesterday he came up to the alcove with some planks and tools, and fixed an awning over the alcove. This morning he brought up a cane chair and a small table. Now I can sit during the day in the shade to sew and write more comfortably, and do my singing practice. If he knows that I write, he says nothing. He is good in this way. He does not probe. He waits for me to tell him when I am ready. If I do not speak, he does not ask. And he expects the same of me. A measure of silence and distance creates respect between husband and wife. I remember my parents were the same. They talked more to relatives and neighbours than to each other. But once a year when the harvest was in, my father would buy my mother a few yards of cloth or a nice hair clip, and she in turn would cook my father's favourite dishes. I suppose that is married life.

Each morning Wah Jai goes to the market at dawn and brings home a small bowl of pork porridge, which I eat, and promptly throw up.

'A waste, don't buy,' I tell him.

'But you didn't throw up everything. Some stayed inside your stomach.' He comforts me in a hundred different ways these days. At night, he massages my tired feet. He has also removed from our repertoire those songs and opera excerpts that require vigorous kung fu movements. In the evening when I go out with him to the teahouses and restaurants, he makes sure that the opera songs and arias that we perform celebrate family, friendship, beauty, fidelity and filial duty. Our earnings are less than before because he would not go back to the pleasure houses. 'Not in your condition,' he said. He was adamant. At any other time I would have fought him, but not now, not in my condition. Isn't it strange how a small disruption in our body can change us women?

The ancients said, 'In the winter of scarcity, food is a treasured gift.' Friends and neighbours give us food these days. The hawker's wife, the butcher's wife, Old Dr Wong's wife and Grandma Li, and others in the neighbourhood have been sharing what little food they can spare. Sometimes Grandma Li brings a bowl of herbal soup cooked with a thin slice of pork liver and ginger, or a sliver of pig's kidney boiled with dried pepper roots for Master Wu. And he leaves some of the soup for me.

If he has noticed the change in me, he makes no comment. Come to think of it, no one in these past months, not even the gossips in the house, has commented about the loose clothes I am wearing. Wah Jai must have warned them not to say a word. Talk might alert mischievous spirits.

Wah Jai leaves the house on some mornings and does not return till evening. He claims he has found work on the river as a coolie. But I think he lies. I suspect he has returned to digging graves for the enemy. I do not ask him. I need the eggs and rice he brings home now that I am in this condition. I think of you every day. You have successfully borne a son. He must be three by now. How is the boy? Do you both have enough to eat? Please stay alive.

You will be surprised to know that I still sing each night outside the teahouses while Wah Jai plays his erhu. We depend on goodwill and generosity, which is getting very thin. Some nights Uncle Loke in his wheelchair joins us with his erhu. What a sight then. Two cripples and a pregnancy. I am in my seventh month. Yet no one in the house has said a word about my condition. None of the tenants has asked how I am. And I am relieved. Careless talk is dangerous. Silence protects the unborn.

I have taken up sewing. Learning from Grandma Li how to sew diapers using the old clothes that neighbours gave.

Master Wu is much better now. The wound in his groin has healed. The swelling in his knees has gone down. On hot afternoons, he sits in the covered walkway outside, yarning with friends. He is growing restless as a caged tiger and dreams of performing again.

Yesterday as I sit up here writing to you, I heard him talking with Uncle Loke and their opera friends. The more these men talked the more they sounded as though they were drunk on opium instead of Iron Buddha tea. From up in the alcove, I could hear their loud outrageous talk and uproarious laughter while soothing strains of Wah Jai's erhu floated up the stairs.

'Listen! The Golden Phoenix Cantonese Opera Troupe will take to the sky once this shitty war is over. Mark my words! It will be over soon! Those devils cannot win forever.'

'Shush, Old Wu.'

'You shush! I will not! I will sing. And my troupe will perform. Go ahead. Laugh! You think this is empty talk? My goddaughter, Kam Foong, has not stopped her singing practice. All these years her singing has steadily improved. With her singing and Wah Jai's playing we have put food on the table. When the war ends, Kam Foong will be the troupe's number one *xiu sung*! The Golden Phoenix will soar with her!'

I felt the warmth rising up to my ears when I heard his words.

'Dream on. We drink to that glorious day!' Uncle Loke's voice rose above the other men's laughter. 'My disciple, Wah Jai, will be your master erhu player!'

'No, no! I can't accept this honour!' I heard Wah Jai protest. 'Uncle Loke, you are my teacher, my Sifu, and the master erhu player. You will lead the Golden Phoenix orchestra. I will be your assistant!'

'Well said, Wah Jai, well said!' I heard the older men praise him.

'Such humility in a young man is admirable.'

'Listen! I have chosen a stage name for Kam Foong. She has a strong voice. She needs a strong name. Her stage name will be Wong Mun Loong.'

'A very good name, Old Wu!' I heard Uncle Loke exclaim. 'The character, *Loong*, exudes the strength and nobility of Dragon. And *Mun* denotes a man of literary learning and culture. It will suit the *xiu sung* role.'

'An excellent name for the scholar, the noble judge and the poet. An auspicious name,' the others agreed.

Then I heard Master Wu ask, 'Any objection to a young woman with a big belly as the leading young man?'

There was uproarious laughter and much hooting. 'Not at all! Not at all! Such things change!'

Then one of the men said, 'The opera stage is changing. In Macau and Hong Kong female performers like Yam Kim Fai are already performing male roles even before the war. And men were acting as Madam Matchmaker and mothers-in-law.'

'It doesn't matter man or woman. It's all in the voice and movement.'

The talk is rekindling my flame. It is true I have not stopped my singing practice. Every dawn I still come up here to the alcove and send my voice out to the rooftops. No one throws things at me any more. Sometimes I even hear applause. I dream of performing a full-length opera but I must wait. Wait for the war to end. Be patient and wait. All things come to those who wait. Talk does not cook rice as Mother used to say.

₧—₧

I crave for durians. I can eat a whole fruit the size of a football. But I WILL NOT eat durian. No! Stay the course. Suffer the nausea and vomit. But do not eat it. The rich creamy fruit is bad for my throat. I must protect my voice. I want to sing for as long as I can. When I sing, the audience does not see a pregnant lady. They see the character I am singing and acting. This is the magic I wield. For a brief moment, song and gestures and Wah Jai's music cast a spell on the audience. I am addicted to the magic.

Dearest Intimate. I wish, truly wish with all my heart, you are here in front of me. Last night I dreamt of a little boy. If the dream comes true, my son and yours will be sworn brothers. If it turns out to be a girl, then my daughter will be your daughter-in-law. Wouldn't we be so happy if this happens? This was what our mothers had planned for us before we were born. If I had been born a boy, I would be your husband now.

℘ — ℂℛ

Did I hear what I heard? My ears are still tingling.

Master Wu praised me! Praised my singing, he who is so stingy with praise. He was listening as I sang an excerpt from *The Butterfly Lovers*.

When I finished, he said, 'Kam Foong, I could feel the pain of your loss.'

Those were my Sifu's words. *'I could feel the pain of your loss.'*

I could not believe my ears. I could not speak. My heart was so full. My Sifu, ever so miserly with praise, had never praised my singing before. I wanted to kneel and cry. Does anyone understand how this feels?

℘ — ℂℛ

Call me superstitious. I have collected old towels and old clothes from women who have given birth to several children. Such women are very blessed. Every night, I use one of their towels to wipe my belly so that their good fortune would rub into my womb. I cut up these women's old clothes and sew them into baby shirts, socks and diapers.

Last night much to my annoyance Wah Jai said it again. 'You must stop performing,'

'If I stop, can you earn enough to feed another mouth for long?'

The insult hurt his male pride.

'If anything happens to your belly, you bear the burden!'

Choy! Choy! Choy! I waved my arms vigorously to dispel the bad aura of his words. 'Beware of what you say in anger!' I hissed. 'The invisible ones can hear you!'

That pulled him up. His face turned a little pale. Just two days ago we had heard that the noodle hawker's wife up the road had a miscarriage. He quickly lighted an incense stick and knelt in front of the altar to beg his ancestors' forgiveness and seek protection for his unborn child.

Seeing him kneeling before the square of moonless sky in the window, all the memories of our first loss came rushing back to me. Head reeling, I knelt beside him. He reached for my hand and held it firmly in his. It felt so strange. We had never held hands like this before.

∞ — ∞

My days are so full. I have had no time to pick up my writing brush. Cries of joy fill our three-storey shophouse to overflowing! I am writing as fast as I can to let you know how very happy and blessed we are.

On the night of the Seven Sisters' Festival, whispers of Japanese losses and defeats were buzzing in the coffeeshops like flies. For days the news had fluttered around the market. *The end of war is imminent!* The latest news on clandestine radio said the British forces are winning.

Hope has been rising and sizzling on the night of the festival. People were very eager to part with their Japanese money. But my spirits were low. I have been feeling dull all day. I thought the dull ache was due to the longing in my heart. The Seven Sisters' Festival always reminded me of the time when the two of us had acted and sung as the Cowherd and the Celestial Maid. Master Wu asked me to sing *The Ballad of The Cowherd* to entertain the festive crowd. He dug out from his opera chest a large loose-fitting peasant costume and asked me to put it on.

'I will look like a fat cowherd, Sifu.'

He laughed. 'With so many things going on, who will look at you? Just sing.'

That evening the crowd was larger than expected. The whole of Chinatown was out to celebrate as if the war was over. The noise at times drowned out Wah Jai's erhu. And as I strained to sing louder a sharp pain stabbed my belly. I carried on. The stabbing pain grew worse. I ignored the sore tautness between my legs. Heartache and body aches, and a superstitious fear that you have left this world had crept into my heart as I struggled to sing the familiar words of the song. My voice started to quiver. The pain was becoming unbearable. Wah Jai glanced at me once or twice. I sang on until an excruciating stab hit my lower back and I felt a warm fluid streaming down my legs. I stopped singing and Wah Jai rushed to my side.

'Help! Help my wife!' Wah Jai yelled at the milling crowd.

'Move back! Move back! I am a doctor!'

I remember seeing a Japanese man pushing through the crowd shouting in fluent Cantonese just as another huge dark wave of excruciating pain swallowed me into darkness.

When I opened my eyes I was in hospital, and Wah Jai was by my bed.

'Are you all right? Thank the gods you are safe. We owe the Japanese doctor a thousand years of gratitude. Because of him a jeep rushed you to this hospital. Because of him, our precious little one came into this world safely before she was due. The debt we owe that Japanese can never be repaid in this life, and we do not even know his name,' Wah Jai said.

There was a soft cry. I glanced at the white bundle and tiny head in the cradle next to my bed. The little one's cries brought tears to her father's eyes as he carried her up. Wah Jai could not stop smiling as he cradled our treasure in his arms.

'Such tiny pink fingers and toes, so tiny, so perfect, so precious,' he whispered, his voice cracked with emotion. 'My wife. You… you have given the Chan family a descendant. What… what shall we call her?'

'You are the father. You decide.'

I was very tired after the birth. I had almost lost the baby and my life if not for the doctor. And I was thinking, from now on I could no longer look upon the Japanese as the evil ones or dogs.

'I had not thought of a name,' Wah Jai whispered, careful not to wake up the little precious gem curled so trustingly in the crook of his arm. 'I dared not think of the future when you were carrying her. Did you?'

I shook my head. Both of us stared at the sleeping bundle. After our experience when the first one was snatched from us, we had been extremely cautious throughout this second pregnancy. Spirits were such capricious entities, and we feared giving them the slightest cause for offence. We avoided all talk about the child in my womb and did not even think of a name for the child in case the spirits thought we were being too presumptuous.

'Well then, we will follow tradition.'

With a broad smile Wah Jai turned to Master Wu. He had been so quiet I did not notice him.

'Sifu, here is Kam Foong your goddaughter, who has given birth. So that makes you our baby's maternal grandfather. So please Grandpa, give your granddaughter a name.'

For once my eloquent Sifu was silent. Open-mouthed, Master Wu stared at Wah Jai and I, and his face contorting with pain he turned his gaze to the baby sleeping so peacefully in her father's arms. I knew he was thinking at that moment of the loss of his only son killed by bombs, and the wife who had deserted him, and his other women who had left him childless and bereft during the great bombing of Ipoh. His hand reached out to stroke the tuft of fuzz on the tiny head. The baby stirred, and opening her eyes she looked straight into the old man's eyes as though she could fathom the darkness and sorrows in the old man's soul. And to our surprise this barely a day old babe smiled at him, a smile that was like a ray of sunshine into this grey weary world. He had not thought the wicked world was still capable of such wonder and beauty. That such a soft bundle of delicate limbs and flesh could move his hardened soul. And he bit his lip as a tear fell on the little one's head like a blessing. Never in his wildest dreams had he dreamt that he would be a grandfather someday. Never had he expected that Wah Jai and I would honour him like this. And another tear fell on the baby's head.

'I will give her a good name,' he mumbled.

He knew the importance of names. As the traditional saying goes – fear not a life of suffering; fear more a life of bearing the wrong name. A name could make or break an actor's fame.

'Choi Wan, Beautiful Cloud,' he choked, and smiled at us.

'That's a lovely name,' Wah Jai said. 'Choi Wan – a name that embodies the beauty of clouds that bring life-saving rain. Choi Wan she will be.'

The birth of Choi Wan was our happiest day in the war. Dearest Intimate. Be happy for me. Now at last I know why you had clung to your little son. How can we not love the babe we had carried for nine months in our womb?

'Quick! You can't stay here any longer. Hurry. You must leave,' a Chinese nurse came in to tell us. 'The entire hospital is in chaos. News from clandestine radios and rumours of Japan's impending defeat has affected all the nursing staff and doctors.'

ℰℴ — ℛℐ

Three days after Choi Wan's birth, news of a strange beautiful mushroom cloud spread throughout Singapore.

'A cloud so immense, so massive it blotted out the sky over Japan. A cloud so enormous, so powerful the Japanese emperor surrendered at once,' radios all over the island announced, the broadcasters' voices filled with awe, wonder and joy. And the good news was announced on radio swiftly all over Singapore.

'The guns fell silent. The dreaded marching boots stopped. An unfamiliar silence fell over the city,' Wah Jai said.

Up in my attic where I was being confined till the baby's one month birthday, I say a grateful prayer to thank the gods in Heaven. Downstairs there was great commotion and celebration.

'The war is over! Peace is here!' Master Wu yelled and danced a jig. 'The cloud has ended the war! I had felt it the morning Choi Wan was born! That is why I named her Beautiful Cloud. Good fortune will follow my granddaughter wherever she goes! Where are the red eggs, Wah Jai?'

'But the one month confinement is not over yet, Old Wu,' said the butcher's wife.

'This is special moment in history. And my granddaughter is born of this historic moment. Bring out the red eggs, Wah Jai! We have to celebrate!'

Eggs are a luxury. Yet Master Wu celebrated his granddaughter's three days after her birth as though it were the birth of a grandson and the end of my confinement month. It was unprecedented. Every family in the three-storey tenement shophouse received a red egg. Then carrying Choi Wan in his arm, he poured three libations of rice wine onto the floor, and gave thanks to Heaven and Earth for the peace, and he asked the Patron Gods of Opera to bless this special child. Then facing the gathering of his friends and tenants, he held Choi Wan up.

'Behold the youngest star of the Golden Phoenix Cantonese Opera

Troupe, which will rise from the ashes of war! Didn't I predict that earlier?' he laughed.

Thunderous applause woke up the baby who kicked and yelled in protest.

'My, my, this little Cloud has a strong voice! Hey!' Uncle Loke was so surprised when Master Wu placed Choi Wan into his arms.

'You're her Granduncle, Old Loke!'

'Am I? Am I?'

'Of course you are! We're family!' Wah Jai and I assured him.

At this there was loud applause from everyone in the house.

'Opera and war have brought us together as family,' Wah Jai laughed. I had never seen him so happy.

'Opera and peace will bring us prosperity!' Master Wu shouted.

My three-day-old baby daughter went on sleeping in her granduncle's arms. How beautiful she looked as she was carried in turn by her father, her grandfather and her granduncle. How beautiful she looked, everyone said.

Uncle Loke, seated in his wheelchair, was blushing. He had not expected such happiness as he held Choi Wan asleep like a kitten in his lap.

The tenants started to peel off the red shell of their egg, and their children waited eagerly for their parents to divide up the egg. The small eggs were shared out and consumed with great relish. It was such a luxury. I don't know how Uncle Loke and Master Wu had managed to procure the twelve eggs at this time of scarcity.

'We have our means, Kam Foong. We have friends everywhere. Hahaha!'

That night in the quiet attic where I continued my confinement I prayed to the Ancestors.

'Honoured Ancestors. Dear Mother-in law and Father-in-law, beloved Ma and Pa, wherever you are in this world or the next, look upon your granddaughter and bless her. Look at the baby nestling in her father's arms and forgive her mother. Honoured Ancestors, forgive and accept me back into the family fold now that I have given Wah Jai a descendant. When I die, do not let me end up a homeless hungry ghost in the netherworld.

'I seek too your blessings for the Japanese doctor who saved little Choi Wan and me. Let the good man return to his family safely now that war is over. This blasted war had made devils of us. Compassionate Buddha, please forgive and guide us on to the path of compassion.

'Honoured Ancestors, look upon the sleeping child. Bless her and keep her safe. Choi Wan my little Beautiful Cloud!'

Who could have foreseen that her name would be so apt?

30

I never knew that my mother's birth was celebrated with such joy on the day America dropped the atomic bomb on Hiroshima and thousands of Japanese died. Years later when I was working at our National Archives, I went on an official visit to the Hiroshima Peace Memorial Museum and found out how thousands of children, burned by radiation and heat rays had crawled to their death seeking water in the rivers and wells. I wondered if this was why, throughout my childhood, my grandparents never talked about my mother or the war. The only time my grandfather talked about the war was when I was in university working on my final year history project, and I said I was going to visit the Japanese cemetery as part of my research. Grandfather, who had just recovered from a long illness, asked to go with me. That was when, to my shock and bewilderment, I found out that he had been visiting the Japanese cemetery on his own every year. Knowing how stubborn and tight-lipped he could be, I did not press him for a reason but waited for him to tell me.

The Japanese cemetery in Singapore was a quiet park behind a private estate of terraced houses in Hougang. Known to the locals there as the place of a thousand forgotten souls, few people visited it.

'The Japanese cemetery in Hougang,' I said to the taxi driver.

'Hougang!' Grandfather scoffed as he got into the taxi. A spark of fire in his aged eyes. 'There was nothing wrong with its original Teochew name. Ow Kang sounds so much better than Hougang. So much more familiar. So much more meaningful to those of us who had lived through the war. Ow Kang bears the scars of Singapore's past. So much history was in that name. Ow Kang was where many young men went into hiding and never came back. Ow Kang was where your grandmother and I took refuge during the war. Where she toiled growing vegetables and I carried night soil and almost broke my back digging.'

He fell silent. His old eyes turning inwards to a past I could not share.

Our taxi stopped outside the gate. I helped him out, making sure he remembered his walking stick. His limp was getting worse. He was often in pain. We walked slowly past the row of grey stone Jizos, and stopped in front of the small Shinto shrine, a dark brown wooden structure shaded by two tall angsana trees. As we stood there a sparrow flew into the shrine with a sudden furious fluttering of wings and flew out again. Surprised, Grandfather took it as a sign from the other realm and made a deep bow before the shrine. Leaning on his stick, he stood before the shrine for a long while. I stood beside him, listening to the distant humming of traffic from behind the rows of terraced houses, and thought of the hundreds who went each year to the War Memorial Park on Beach Road in remembrance of their family members killed during the Japanese Occupation. I wondered why Grandfather chose to come here instead.

The place was quiet in the hot languid afternoon. The air was still and humid. I followed Grandfather's gaze to the rows of graves standing in the bright sunshine. Beads of sweat formed on his brow and rolled down his cheeks. He fumbled for his handkerchief and wiped his face. Seeing that he looked tired and drained in the heat, I led him down a path to a stone bench in the shade of the trees. And as we sat in the shady silence, I told him of my intention to research and write a paper on the Japanese Occupation of Singapore. He patted my hand, proud that his granddaughter had made it to university.

When I was thirteen, he had put his foot down when I wanted to join the opera troupe. When Por Por encouraged me, a huge quarrel erupted between them. It scared me. As far as I could remember my grandparents had never raised their voices that loudly at each other before. Grandfather was a quiet man. He had always given in to Por Por, who always had the last say. But that evening Grandfather's eyes flashed fire.

'Kam Foong! Listen to me! Xiu Yin is my Little Swallow. She will fly higher than you and I. Higher than an opera troupe. I will never, never let you sacrifice her to the opera stage. You have sacrificed your heart and life to your art. You've even sacrificed our daughter! Choi Wan might have…'

Their bedroom door slammed shut! But before the door closed, I'd caught a glimpse of Por Por sobbing at Grandfather's feet. That vision shocked me. And the memory of that made me glance at the tired old man beside me. There was much I did not know about him. While he rested meekly on the bench beside me, I gave him a brief history of the Japanese cemetery.

'In the nineteenth century, Singapore had many Japanese prostitutes. Many were too poor to return to Japan. In 1891 a Japanese brothel owner donated a part of his land for a burial ground for these impoverished prostitutes. During WWII hundreds of Japanese soldiers, airmen and marines killed in Southeast Asia were also buried here. After the war, the one hundred and thirty-five war criminals executed by the British government were also buried here.'

Grandfather's eyes rested on the neat rows of head stones standing like soldiers on parade in the late afternoon sunshine.

'What had these soldiers gained from their country's war? Nothing but a hole in this foreign earth,' he sighed.

'More than fifty thousand Chinese were killed in the Sook Ching massacre. And there's something else, Grandpa. It's said the Japanese army and the Kempetai secret police were not the only ones who had killed the Chinese in Singapore.'

He looked at me, his eyes revealed nothing.

'Some people said that those killed were betrayed by their fellow Chinese. Their betrayers wore hoods over their faces and pointed out their victims to the Japanese soldiers. This dark blot in our history is rarely talked about. Never written about. And if written, never published as far as I know. That's why I have to… ' I stopped.

Grandfather's steely cataract gaze was unnerving. His tone was unusually sharp when he asked, 'Are you going to write about it?'

'I don't know. I'm digging around, doing research. I might if I find out more. Do you know anything about it?'

He looked up at the trees. A warm breeze was rustling the branches and a few sparrows flew up to the angsanas.

'Must you dig in the earthen pot till it breaks? What good would such research do? Maybe you might win some praise but your writing won't bring back the dead.'

'So you don't approve?'

He kept his gaze on the rows of gravestones in the sun.

'Thousands had died – Chinese, Japanese, Malays, Indians, white people from Australia, Britain. War is a strange wild beast. It bites and changes us. Fear, hunger and greed turned many into animals.'

His eyes closed, perhaps to shut out what his memory had brought up. A light breeze blew through the cemetery. A bird gave a loud chirp. He opened his eyes and remained silent for a long time watching a little brown sparrow pecking in the grass. When he finally spoke, his Cantonese was more formal than usual.

'In war, terrible things happened. Horrible unspeakable things worse than death itself happened. After the war, we worked hard, very hard to forget these things. We looked to the future for the sake of our children and grandchildren. The past was locked away. If people had secrets, those secrets died with them. If people had suspicions, those suspicions died with them. If people had spoken out, we Chinese would have been torn apart. Careless speech,' he paused, struggling to catch his breath, seeking the right words. 'Careless talk and rash accusations would have turned neighbour against neighbour, relative against relative, family against family. Silence.'

A long pause while he wiped off the sweat on his face.

'Silence gave us respite. Silence gave the next generation peace. Not the poison of vengeance and enmity. We had suffered enough during the war. We didn't want to suffer again during peace. We didn't want the next generation, that is, your generation, to suffer because of our desire for revenge, because of old men's memories of what happened. Let go, the Buddhists say. Let go. You are still young. You may not agree. But in life, even our closest relationships suffer from betrayal.'

As he stood up, his face was scrunched up in pain. He refused my help and leaned heavily on his walking stick. His limp had become more pronounced with the onset of arthritis. I walked behind him as his stick crunched down the stony path between the gravestones.

'Your generation is the silent generation, Grandpa. The generation that had censored out so many things in war and politics. Singapore's stories are always narratives of the upward path, rarely do they take the plunge into the darkness and corruption of the human soul.'

'Little Swallow. You speak well. All my life, I have read the newspapers. I have followed the difficult relations between China and Japan, Korea and Japan. The enmity of WWII is still with them to this day. Their younger generation are still burdened by the humiliation and defeat of the older generation. You may think of your grandparents as the silent generation. But our silence has freed those who came after us from the burden of history.'

He stopped to rest his bad leg. For a long while, the two of us stood listening to the swishing of the branches of the angsana trees above us. I felt his annoyance and we did not speak. Finally he pointed to the large black polished boulder, the largest gravestone in the cemetery.

'What is that? Do you know?'

'It is a memorial set up by a group of Japanese prisoners-of-war. A carpenter and two stonemasons had carved this boulder to honour their General and fellow soldiers. Especially those in the lowly labour force of the Japanese army and navy.'

Grandfather studied the highly polished black boulder and shook his head. 'So cruel in war. So loyal in peace. Poor misled souls. They were cannon fodder.'

He walked on, determined to limp past every gravestone in the cemetery. Then he stopped and turned to me.

'I had dug some of these graves,' he said in a soft voice. He gave no hint of the whippings and beatings he had endured. And I did not know about them at the time. It was only years later after his death when I read Por Por's journal that I knew what he had suffered at the hands of his Japanese abusers.

But that day as I stood beside him, he had only praise for the Japanese doctor who had saved his wife's life and delivered his daughter. Sitting on the stone bench under the angsana tree to rest his bad leg once more, he told me that when he found out that the good doctor had killed himself after Japan's defeat, he was very sad. And a little angry.

'He could have gone home to serve his own people. His death must have caused his family in Japan immense sorrow. I come here each year to remember him,' and he quoted a saying.

'*For a gift of flowers, a hundred years of thanks.*
For a gift of life, a thousand years of remembrance.'

I squeezed his mottled, wrinkled hand.

'If not for the good doctor, would I have a granddaughter today?' he smiled. Leaning on his walking stick, he stood up. 'Time to go.'

PART 3

31

My phone rang. It's a video call from Janice.

'Happy birthday, Mom. Hold the phone closer to your face. *Hmmm*, still smooth, no wrinkles yet. The year of living alone has done you good.'

'Thank you, darling. I wouldn't have been able to live through it without your support and honesty.'

'Brutal honesty you mean.'

Then silence.

I held on to the phone, and took a deep breath, listening to the dark immensity of the universe between us, praying that the thin line connecting mother and child would never ever break. Please God hear my prayer.

Janice was silent for a long while but I was used to her long silences by now. The past year had been a year of very difficult conversations between the two of us. The hinges of her door long shut against her parents had grudgingly creaked open, and she could finally express the anger and pain she had suppressed for years.

'What did you do to help me? What? Nothing,' she had sobbed one night.

I was forced to face myself. Face up to the knowledge that my cowardice and weakness had hurt my daughter deeply. And my heart broke. Not that it hadn't been broken before. But this time it was different.

'Did you not know how vulnerable I had felt? I was only sixteen. Only sixteen, Mom. And Dad was drunk that night. He came into my room insisting it was his room. After that night I locked my door every night. When he banged on my door, what did you do? What *did* you do? Nothing! You were useless! And blind! Wilfully blind! And weak! Were it not for college, opera school and Saturdays with Great Grandma, I would have jumped down from our flat.'

'No! I love you.'

'You loved me??? I wouldn't have survived all those years without Great Grandma loving me, pampering me.'

'Did your dad… did… did he…?

'No!'

'You're sure.'

A burst of derisive laughter.

'Your husband did not touch your daughter if that's what you're thinking. And if he did, you're years too late in asking.'

She cut me off. She was offline for days. I could not reach her. I rang her. I messaged her. I emailed her. And then I was forced to wait. And wait. And wait. The waiting was hell. I had to discipline myself. Control my hand. Refrain from dialling her number. Restrain my neediness to connect to the child I had failed to protect. The daughter I thought I had lost. Give her space, I kept reminding myself. The time and space I had needed. Two long weeks crawled by; it felt like a whole year. Then she called. And we started again. Started to yell at each other again over the phone. Ploughing and pushing through the hard, caked mud of years of suppressed pain, we sobbed and wept. The phone pressed to my ears, my daughter's voice alternating between angry and cruel, distant and intimate. Then suddenly a memory would make us laugh through our tears, and we began to talk again of the past till our talking escalated to shouting once again, each trying to make the other see her point of view. And so on and on it went. That was how it had been the past year. I was tossed like a lonely wretched leaf in the ocean, crying to Heaven for succour, to Earth for relief. Yet at times when I least expected it, I had felt blessed. So very blessed as a mother. My daughter, my only child who left home at eighteen, could have turned to drugs and sex in Canada. It was every mother's fear and nightmare. But she didn't. Thank God, thank Blessed Mary Ever Virgin, she didn't.

And now after years of polite speech she was talking to me so fiercely and so honestly. I was so proud of this strong independent young woman who had come out of my womb. There are few times in a mother's life when a family's dark past is pried open in such fierce honesty between mother and daughter, and settling after years of ferocious battles into the quietude of reflection and conversation because each had struggled hard to listen to the other with the deep empathy of shared pain and hindsight.

'I've been thinking, Mom, that you and I have changed. When I look back on the past now I realise we're no longer the same person who lived that past. I'm so glad you joined that women's support group in AWARE.'

'I had to. I wanted my daughter back.'

Silence at the other end of the line. Then minutes later, a gentle reply.

'I never left you, Mom.'

I held on to the phone, pressed hard against my ear. I wanted to hug her. Hug my daughter. Many times I had wanted to fly over to Vancouver to be with her. But she said, no. She preferred to talk on the phone. Some nights, with the headset pressed to my ear, I heard her voice quaver at the other end of the line. Coming from the depths of the Pacific Ocean, her soft voice was firm yet intimate with nuanced pauses at times, an indrawn breath and quiet sobbing at other times. With the phone she could call me anytime she was ready to talk, she said. And get off the line when she needed to.

'And I needn't have to worry about you. If you were to visit Vancouver, I would have to worry about where to put you up, take you out for meals or shop, or whether to stay in and cook, or wash and do a host of such daily mundane mumsy things. Because nobody can talk about emotional stuff the whole day, you know,' she laughed. 'Or I would have to take you sightseeing, or worry if you were to drive around on your own. No, no, please don't come.'

She was busy with term papers and rehearsals, and she was taking extra classes with veteran Hong Kong Cantonese opera star Loong Gim Sung who had left Hong Kong and settled in Vancouver because of the impending handing over of the island and its territories back to China. Besides she was already talking to her campus counsellor. I shouldn't worry about her.

Then back to the present, she said, 'I love you very much, Mom. And I wish you happy birthday and another good year ahead. It's too bad I have a full day of lectures and rehearsals tomorrow. I won't be able to call you. Enjoy your birthday tomorrow. I'll think of you but I won't call you. Okay? Good night, Mother dear. I love you.' She hung up but I held on to the phone a little longer, reluctant to let her go.

32

My birthday was the anniversary of my mother's death. Throughout my life, it was a day to get through, a day to pay my respects to the dead.

I woke before dawn, got dressed, and took the lift down. It stopped on the sixth floor and my heart skipped. The man who entered the lift had a grey crew cut and wore rimless glasses. But this same man in my memory had been young and wore a ponytail.

'Xiu Yin?' His smile was shy.

'Meng.'

He saw me glance at the Down button and pressed it. His eyes were on me while I kept mine on the lighted numbers, unable to think of what to say to him. We had not spoken for years. Almost twenty-five. And we didn't speak in the lift till it reached the lobby and we stepped out.

'Yin. How are you?' he asked in Cantonese, his tone polite and formal.

'I'm well. Thank you. And you?' I responded similarly in Cantonese.

'Neither torn nor broken.' A small smile on his lips as though pleased he had stopped sounding formal. 'More than twenty years, is it not?'

'I heard you were in Hong Kong.'

'I moved there after…' His words trailed off. 'I must say you're very early this morning.' He changed the subject.

'Well, I live here now.'

'I know. Madam Soh told me. More than a month ago.'

'Why didn't you call on me?'

'I would have if I was sure of the reception.' An edginess in his reply.

'Meng, I would've welcomed you. This is an early morning surprise.'

The corners of his eyes crinkled with a hint of mischief.

'From a thousand *li* we meet,' he quoted half of a popular saying, leaving out the half about the destined affinity that drew two persons together.

Not sure how to respond to that, I said, 'I'm going to the market.' And started to move off.

'I'm going to the porridge stall. And you? Which stall?' He fell in step.
'Fresh flowers.'

'Did Madam Soh tell you why I came back?'

'She didn't tell me anything. You're the one she favours, not me.'

He laughed. And the sudden memory of those long ago times when the two of us used to compete with each other for the attention and approval of opera artistes and theatre audiences made me join him. Then turning serious, he said, 'I came back to look after Tony.'

He looked down at his flipflops, the cheap rubber thongs that he used to wear when he helped out at his father's noodle stall in the coffeeshop. It didn't surprise me that he was still wearing them. He had always clung to the cheap and comfortable. Customers used to call him Noodle Head because of his straight long hair, which was his pride and a sign of his rebelliousness at a time when the government banned long hair for young men.

'Anything wrong with Tony?' I asked.

'Cancer. Fourth stage.'

'Oh no, I'm so sorry, Meng. How is he?'

We stopped in the middle of the path, time flowing through us like a stream as we talked of the past. His elder brother used to tease the two of us when we were in the opera troupe.

As if he had read my thoughts, he said, 'Remember Tony used to call us Jade Girl and Golden Boy? Noodle Head and Spatula? He gave you that horrible name, Spatula.'

'No, you did.'

'No, no, he did.'

'No, it was you.'

'No no...'

And we laughed again. Our argument was so inconsequential. Just like when we were in our teens. Still laughing, we parted, he to buy porridge for Tony, and I to buy flowers for my mother.

'Happy birthday, Yin!'

I turned around surprised that he remembered after all these years. But he was gone. I stared at the space where he had stood a minute ago. The man I did not marry. The young man I should have married instead of Robert. The young man I had rejected under the rain tree in the park on the slope more than twenty-five years ago. And now he had greeted me 'Happy birthday'. Sudden tears blurred my vision. I was glad no one was close by as a cool dawn breeze pushed past me. I waited till my feelings had subsided. Then I walked through the market towards the flower stalls where bunches of gold, pinks, reds and whites stared at me. Few customers were about. It was still early. I bought a bunch of golden chrysanthemums and a bunch of white lilies and red roses. The flower seller was so pleased with his first sale of the morning that he added baby's breath and ferns for free.

'Your face is full of smiles, madam,' she remarked in Hokkien, handing me the flowers. 'Have a good day!'

Surprised, I called out to all the flower sellers. 'Good business, everyone!'

Wide smiles greeted me.

'Have a good day. Come again, madam!' the flower sellers called out as I passed them on my way to the taxi stand.

The temple was in Upper Changi. The old nun in charge of the temple led me down the familiar dim corridors to the Hall of Eternal Rest. A dawn visit on my birthday to this temple that housed my mother's ashes was an annual ritual during my childhood. It was how my grandparents marked the day of my birth each year. The day that brought them no joy. I did not think they blamed me for I was never told about the circumstances of my mother's death. Yet throughout my childhood a kind of emotional osmosis must have taken place such that I had always sensed with the sensitive imagination of a lonely only child that my mother had died because of me. If I had not been born, she would have been alive. And the weight of this guilt had sat on me like a boulder since I was a toddler of three or four. I was a solemn quiet child until I met Meng or Noodle Head as he was called then.

Inside the dim, silent hall, I placed the flowers into two vases – the roses and baby's breath for my mother, the chrysanthemums and lilies for my grandparents. Then I knelt down before their memorial tablets and kowtowed three times. After their death, I had placed my grandparents' memorial tablets together in the same temple with that of my mother so that my grandparents would be with the daughter they loved and missed so sorely all their life.

I remembered on my fifth birthday Por Por had awakened me before dawn. While Grandfather packed a basket with food, candles and joss sticks, she dressed me in new clothes and combed and plaited my hair. Unlike other mornings, the three of us were quiet and spoke little. When we arrived at the Hall of Eternal Rest, I watched Por Por arrange the plates of steamed chicken, sweet meats and mandarin oranges on the altar while Grandfather lit two red candles and three joss sticks. Then Por Por stood me in front of the solemn tiers of dark wooden tablets and called my mother's name, her voice soft and tender in the still morning air.

'Choi Wan, my daughter, we are here again.'

She pushed me down on my knees. Tears coursing down my grandparents' faces, Por Por told me to kowtow before the tablet written with my mother's name.

'Choi Wan, my love, Papa and I have brought Xiu Yin to pay her respects to you. Watch over your Little Swallow. She's five today. It has been five long years, my beloved Beautiful Cloud, five lonely years since you floated away from us.'

Por Por wept. When she was in one of her foul moods at home, which was whenever the troupe was not performing, she would weep and blame Great Grandfather Wu for giving her daughter that inauspicious name.

'Choi Wan, Choi Wan, Beautiful Cloud! Beautiful Cloud! She floated away. Was the old man blind? Naming her after the world's most destructive cloud! How many did that cloud kill? How many?'

Heart-wrenching sobs heaving, I would wail with her in her arms. Grandmother and grandchild seated on the attic floor wailing and rocking to and fro in each other's arms. Our cries rising higher and higher in the three-storey tenement house. Our cries brought Grandfather limping up the stairs.

'Stop it, Kam Foong. You're hurting our Sifu.'

'Then you stop your bitter words. You think I didn't love our daughter. Didn't pay attention to her!'

'I didn't say that.'

'But you think that! I can hear those words rattling in your head!'

'You're scaring the child.'

He placed a hand on Por Por's shoulders, soothing her till she released me into his arms. My face wet with tears, I nuzzled against Grandfather's warm neck as he carried me down the stairs and out to the back lane where the hanging filigree roots of a banyan tree had curtained off the noises of the streets. Grandfather stood in this quiet green space under the banyan tree, his arms wrapped around me, cooing softly,

Fly, my Little Swallow, fly.
Your wings will write the clear blue sky.
Fly, my Little Swallow, fly.

Dappled sunlight and shadows of filigree roots and leaves dancing in the breeze as he sang. I burrowed my face into his shoulders, and dried my tears on his shirt collar smelling of musky sweat and the fragrant wax he used to polish his musical instruments. He had named me Xiu Yin or Little Swallow when I was born. And this was the song I heard him sing in his husky whispery voice when I was a toddler sobbing in his arms.

But now that I had begun to write, my memory of that scene had changed. Looking back to those years I realised that I had been listening to my grandfather's singing like a self-centred wailing child thinking he was singing my name. But I was wrong. All the while he had been singing my grandmother's name, Kam Foong or Golden Phoenix.

Fly, my Golden Phoenix, fly.
Your brush will write the clear blue sky.
Fly, my Golden Phoenix, fly.

He must have composed this song during the war when they were still living on the farm in Ow Kang. When I closed my eyes, I could see him still. Limping between the rows of vegetables in the brilliant sunshine, a straw hat slapped upon his head. He stopped when he saw his wife, looking pale and thin, sitting outside the kitchen shed. It was just after the loss of their first child. A writing brush poised in her hand her eyes were gazing up at the blue sky. Then bending her head, she started to write. He was taken aback for he had not expected this writing from his wife, the daughter of an illiterate vegetable farmer. Quietly he moved away. Pleased to have discovered this side of Kam Foong.

She could write, he told himself. For days he carried this beautiful secret in his heart. I have a wife who knows how to write, he thought, gazing at the bony curve of her neck and back when they were in bed. Since the death of their baby son, he had not smiled. But that night, lying in the dark beside her, he was smiling, his mind travelling back to the pig and rice farms in Saam Hor, where none of the village girls could even write their own name. And his heart swelled with pride. His wife was literate. Like the daughters of the gentry, she could read and write. How blessed he felt to have such a wife. And the thought nourished his starving body like rain upon parched earth. But at the same time he realised his wife's writing would always be a mystery, not meant for his male eyes. She was writing not for her husband's approval. He who could read and write too, who could have been the village schoolmaster if not for the war, he who loved music and poetry must pretend he didn't know his wife could write.

Back in the temple, Grandfather patted my five-year-old shoulders and helped me to stand up. I leaned against his leg, enjoying the comfort of his arm on my shoulders as we watched the flickering red candles cast a rich warm glow in the dim Hall of Eternal Rest.

Back at home later, Por Por cut up the chicken and gave me the two drumsticks for my lunch as a birthday treat. But lunch on my birthday was always a cheerless meal. My grandparents did not eat. Por Por stayed up in the attic's alcove all day long and Grandfather played his mournful music on the erhu in the front hall downstairs. Great Grandfather Wu had left our three-storey tenement house for the day. And the tenants had learnt to keep quiet on my birthday.

Alone and bored, I sat in the kitchen gnawing at my chicken drumstick.

After lunch, Grandfather stopped playing his erhu. He wheeled out his large old bicycle, used for ferrying theatre props and the roast pig for prayers on the opening night of an opera. My eyes lit up. Our cycling trip to the hills was the highlight of my birthday each year. He swung me up and sat me in the wooden box tied to the bicycle's back carrier. Then he mounted the bicycle, and with our face to the sun and a warm breeze blowing in our hair, we raced through the grey dusty streets of the city and headed for the green hills. I was too young to know which hill we went to but it was far, far away from Chinatown.

Grandfather was a strong and tireless cyclist despite his limp. He could cycle for hours without stopping. When we finally reached the foot of the hill, he carried me down from the box and parked his bicycle behind some bushes. I placed my small hand into his large one and we walked up the slope following a shady rocky path.

He rarely spoke during these walks. When I grew tired, he carried me on his shoulders. From the height of his shoulders an enthralling green world populated by monkeys, squirrels and birds opened up to me till he set me down when we reached the top of the hill. Then I looked for bugs and ants in the grass while he perched himself on a rocky outcrop like a lone brown monkey, looking ancient and timeless, smoking his pipe, lost and abstracted in thought. He sat all afternoon smoking on that rock. And though I was a child, I knew not to pester him with questions during such times.

Sometimes while writing my book at night, I would find myself thinking of him on that hill. Sometimes I would catch or thought I had caught a glimpse of him perched at my memory's edge. Perched like a brooding brown langur on its tree, its long tail hanging down in the early dawn.

Grandfather was a quiet man, a private man. Had it not been for Por Por's journal I would never have known of the deep love he had for my grandmother. For the two of them hardly spoke to each other when I was growing up, and I did not understand the language of love's silence then.

'Come, Little Swallow!'

He jumped down from his rock when the sun began to set and swung me on to his shoulders.

'Let's go look for Great Grandfather Wu, and go for dinner and ice cream. Would you like that?'

'Yes, Grandpa.'

When I turned six the following year the family had already moved out of the attic in the three-storey tenement in Keong Saik Road, and we were living in our new flat in Jin Swee Estate. On my birthday that year, I met Meng. That day I had taken my plate with the two chicken drumsticks out to the landing near our flat, sitting on the stairs, feeling lonely and sorry for myself.

'*Psst!* Are you eating snake?'

A grubby boy crept up the stairs towards me.

'Are you eating snake?'

Shocked. 'Chicken,' I said.

'It's snake. Look. The meat so white like a skinned snake.'

'I don't eat snake. Who are you?'

'Noodle Head. My pa sells noodle soup in the coffeeshop downstairs.'

The boy sat down beside me. I moved a little away, put off by the mucous creeping out of his nostrils like a green worm. He wiped it off with the back of his hand and grinned. His hair was long and his fingernails were dirt encrusted.

'You? What's your name?'

'Xiu Yin.'

'Ahhh! Little Swallow. The name suits you. You're so small and skinny. Quick, *lah!* Eat the snake meat. It'll make you strong.'

'It's chicken.'

'It's snake. I should know. Last night my family ate snake.'

'I don't believe you.'

'At first I thought it was a worm. Have you seen a worm this long?' He stretched out both his arms as far as they could go. 'Yesterday a worm this long had wriggled out of my bottom when I was moving my bowels.'

'Ugh! Don't bluff.'

'It's true! The worm ballooned into a big white snake. *Piak!* My mother chopped off its head with her chopper. That night we had snake meat noodle soup for dinner.'

'*Eeeeek!*' The thought of his family eating a snake that had come out of his anus was so disgusting. I stared at the pale white meat of my two chicken drumsticks and shoved my plate towards him.

'You don't want to eat this?'

I shook my head. With a wide grin, he bit into one of the drumsticks and quickly devoured both as I watched, fascinated and horrified that he could eat something so disgusting.

'Thank you, Little Swallow.'

His grubby face glowed. He wiped his mouth on his sleeve.

'This is the first time I've eaten two chicken drumsticks at one go. In our family my two brothers, two sisters and I have to share two drumsticks. We don't even get half a drumstick each. You have two drumsticks all to yourself and you look like you're at a funeral. Why?'

'It's my birthday. I killed my mother when I was born.' I started to cry.

'Hey, hey. Don't cry. Do you want to know a secret?'

I was sobbing and couldn't answer him.

'Hey, Little Swallow, don't cry. Please don't cry. Listen. My Pa almost died last night. He's not really a hawker, you know. He's not from this earth. He came down from heaven. A very long time ago. Before I was born. In heaven he was the Jade Emperor's guard. He wore a warrior's armour and carried a big sword. But one night he looked down from heaven and fell in love with my mother on earth. Just like the Cowherd and the Weaving Maid.'

My mouth fell open. I stopped crying. I had seen his father, the stocky, foul-mouthed, foul-tempered noodle hawker who was always shouting at his wife and children in the coffeeshop. He did not fit my picture of the Jade Emperor's noble guard.

'True or not?'

'Cross my heart. Because of my mother, my father was punished. The Jade Emperor banished him from heaven. He was sent down to earth to marry my mother. Last night, there was a full moon. Did you know that? No? The moon woke me up. In the moonlight I saw my father climb on top of my mother. He was stacking noodle bowls on top of her. One on top of the other up and up and up, he stacked the bowls. Higher and higher. Faster and faster he climbed up the bowls till my mother cried out. *Ah, ah, ahhhhhh!* Hundreds and hundreds of bowls were on top of her. And my father was climbing up the tower of noodle bowls to reach heaven. Then my father's spirit cried out, *Ah, ah, ahhhhh!* Just like my mother. Only louder. Then his body looked dead lying on top of her. I was so scared. I pulled the blanket over my head and went back to sleep.'

From that day on I was hooked. There was such magic in Noodle Head's stories. I started to share my food with him, and in return he told me stories. When Por Por found out that the two of us were eating on the stairs near the lift, she invited Noodle Head into our flat for meals and made him clean up and wash his hands.

One evening, his mother came with a large pot of meatball noodle soup.

'Madam Kam Foong,' she said to Por Por. 'I have gone to every one of your operas. Please I beg you, accept this pot of soup. I cooked it myself and, and I made the meatballs. I don't know how to thank you for feeding my rascal. He's put on weight,' she laughed, shy and embarrassed in front of my grandmother. The hero in so many operas.

'It's all right, your son comes to play with my granddaughter.'

'I hope Noodle Head behaves. He is my youngest and... and he's very keen on opera. I beg you, Madam. Please let him go with your granddaughter to the theatre. We can't pay. Let him work for you and watch you perform. Let him sweep and mop the floor for you. His father and I are poor people. But please come to our noodle stall as often as you like. Your family is very welcome to eat as many bowls of noodles as you wish. Forgive my rough and blunt speech. No need to pay a cent, Madam.'

And that was how Meng joined our troupe as a child actor.

33

The rains came in the early mornings in a soft mizzle, growing into a grey drizzly rain, then blown by sudden winds vast sweeps and veils this way and that way. These grey wet days made the whole house smell of damp. Clothes took days to dry. Diapers washed in the morning were still wet in the evening, draped over the ropes the men had strung all around the walls of the dank corridors and in their rooms where their babies were whimpering for their mother's breast.

Up in my attic I was suckling Choi Wan when an orange butterfly was blown in by the storm. Wings outspread, black dots on its wings, the poor butterfly was too drenched to fly. Barely pulsing, it lay in the palm of my outstretched hand and gave out its last breath.

I gazed at the now dead orange butterfly. Had the poor thing braved the heavy rains to come to me? Who had died? Oh, orange butterfly, harbinger of death, have you come to tell me someone close to me is dead? Dead? I dared not utter her name, but I wept and sang "The Requiem of the Butterfly" as the rains came pouring down outside the attic's window. My singing woke up the baby asleep at my breast and I had to stop. For now the opera singer is no longer the queen. She's just the mother. And not even a mother. Most times I am just the cow munching and chewing to produce milk for the little princess suckling at my breast. Each time I sing as she suckled, I felt like a cow mooing to the moon. For how could my baby understand that the war was over? And I should be happy? Happy that I had a little daughter; happy that Wah Jai was alive; happy that Master Wu was alive and bad-tempered Uncle Loke was alive. Our family had survived the three-and-a-half years of terror and had expanded to five.

And then I looked down at the orange butterfly in my palm. And all the stories and operas about how butterflies were the dead come to say goodbye flooded into my head. And my heart skipped a beat. Butterflies do not normally fly into houses and never ever fly into an attic so dim and high in a storm. Back in Saam Hor I had heard that a butterfly that flies into the house is the dead come to console the living and say goodbye. No, I pushed out the thought that Intimate could be dead. I refused to believe even as I buried the orange butterfly under the potted rose plant. I refused to harbour the thought or utter her name. Could silence ward off what I dread most? I could not be sure. A deep uncertainty filled me. Throughout the day I harboured a faint, weak hope like the fading lingering light of dusk. The uncertainty weighed me down in the coming days. I could not be happy. I could not celebrate the end of war.

Wah Jai could not understand. He had changed. He was no longer the grim man during the war. When news of the British gwai lo's return to Singapore reached our tenement last week Wah Jai leapt down the stairs and ran out of the house. As if his limp was healed. Filled with an energy that seemed to have electrified both his legs, he raced out of the house and limped down the street. Wild with joy! Wild with happiness! And he was not the only one. All the tenants in the house had run out to the street that day. Even the pipa player who had lost her son had run out with her husband and three daughters. Cradling Choi Wan in my arms, I too ran out to the street. But I had no heart to join in the wild celebration and festivities of the crowd that night.

After that wild day Wah Jai and Master Wu were out of the house every day, returning only in the evening. And every evening I asked them, 'Have you eaten?'

'We have! We're full,' they laughed.

Not once did they ask me if I had eaten. Day after day, it was the same. So why should it surprise them when I lost my temper?

'Hey, hey, calm down. We were looking up the musicians and singers we used to know', Master Wu said. 'What do you think we were doing while you sit at home all day with your baby?'

If he weren't my Sifu, I would have flung a soiled diaper at him. It made me so mad. Wah Jai tried to calm me.

'Listen, listen. Business has started again, Foong. From Telok Ayer to Redhill people are hawking all kinds of goods again. Shop owners have returned to their shops. They're opening for business. New shop signs are going up all over town.'

At once I thought of her then. Alive! She might still be alive! If she were alive she would come back to her goldsmith shop. I had to go and look for her at the shop. If there's one thing the war has taught me, it is forgiveness. We have to forgive. I have to find her and put right all that was wrong between us when we parted.

৪০—০৪

My hope was high. I didn't sleep all last night. Images of her in the goldsmith shop with her son in her arms and tears in her eyes invaded my dreams. I had to look for her.

When the rain stopped the next morning I left the house and my baby daughter who was asleep after her feed.

I walked down the roads and scoured the shops down the entire length of the roads and lanes from Keong Saik Road to Temple Street, from Dead Man's Lane to South Bridge Road and all the way to North Bridge Road as far as the Kallang River. I looked into every shop hoping to see her. I stopped passers-by to ask about a young widow with a baby son whose husband had owned a goldsmith shop in the neighbourhood. Her son should be three or four by now, I said. Several times I was directed to one shop or another, but came away disappointed. Several times I was also scolded, ignored or brushed aside by those who mistook me for a beggar, for the streets were crawling with scrawny women with their large-eyed hungry scabby children begging for food.

Food is still scarce and expensive in town despite the end of war and the British army's return to Singapore.

Every shop I glanced at I thought I had caught a glimpse of the goldsmith's widow with a white flower in her hair waiting for me. The spirits were teasing me till hot and hungry by noon I found myself in the unfamiliar Malay quarters of North Bridge Road. I stopped at a curry shop and begged for a cup of water. A young Malay woman wearing a white flower in her hair gave me a tin cup, and to my shock she also gave me a small packet of cooked rice. Such kindness was unheard of! The price of rice was still sky high. How could she afford to give me rice? No, no, I refused. I could not trust such kindness. I had heard too many stories of the Malay bomoh's black magic. Besides I understood not a word of her speech. And to my shame and regret to this day, I ran out of her shop with only one thought in my head – *She's dead!* The young Malay woman with the white flower in her hair must be a spirit teasing me.

When I reached home, drenched in yet another sharp downpour, Wah Jai's face was dark as the Thunder God's. And my poor baby was wailing in his arms. Without a word, he thrust our bawling daughter into my arms and left the house. He didn't even ask where I had been all morning. And I did not tell him.

₭—ߙ

It is the fifth day since Wah Jai and I stopped speaking to each other. He's still mad with me for leaving Choi Wan alone. I admit I had done wrong but if he doesn't speak with me I will not talk with him. If he wants to stew in righteous anger I will let him. I will not be the first to open my mouth.

Dearest Intimate. This is also the fifth day of my mourning. In silence, I grieve for you. In secret, I cry for the loss of hope. I have buried the orange butterfly in a flowerpot in the alcove and planted a cutting of rose in the pot so that I will never forget how a butterfly had braved the storm to comfort me. That morning I was too dense, too slow and too timid to accept the significance of the orange butterfly that lay dead in my palm. A part of me feared it was you. I pushed away the thought. I refused to accept that the butterfly was your soul's return to bid me a final farewell. I could not accept it on that morning of the storm. Not until I had made a final attempt to find you. Now I know you are gone. Gone.

O my beloved butterfly. Fare thee well, my dearest butterfly
I cannot follow you. ...

Like the grieving scholar in *Butterfly's Shadow on Red Pear Blossom*, I sang my sorrow till the baby's cries stopped me. And I have a baby daughter to feed the way you fed your little son. And a solemn vow to keep. The vow I made to Wah Jai never to leave him. But to you I vow, O Butterfly, no matter where or what you are, ghost or butterfly, I shall hold you dear in my heart, and write to you just as before, just as I had done throughout the war when I knew not whether you were dead or alive. Throughout the war I was writing to a memory. You were always in my head and heart. Death will not change this. You braved a heavy rainstorm to comfort me. Your effort will not be in vain. I promise you I will not despair. I will live. I will not be despondent forever, my dearest Butterfly.

℘ — ℭ

The seventh day.

O Butterfly, how can I not despair? Without hope of ever seeing you again, how can I banish this sorrow that squats on my heart like a heavy rock? What had sustained me throughout the war was the hope you were alive. Now the war has ended and you have left this world and me, how can I not grieve? How can I?

℘ — ℭ

Twentieth day of mourning.

I have not been able to write. For days I had no heart to take up my brush.

With no words or song in my heart, I had not the heart to dip my brush in ink. My feet drag. No longer can they dance as before. Last night I could not join in the festivities in the streets where crowds were celebrating the return of the British gwai lo as though they were the war heroes.

Are they really heroes? I am still furious when I think of how they had sent their own families away to safety, leaving us, the ordinary folks, to suffer the bombing of the Japanese, the hunger and torture. What heroes you tell me?

I think of the sisters in the pleasure houses, the sisters who had helped Wah Jai and I to earn a bowl of rice each night.

I think of the young girls naked to the waist, howling for mercy as Japanese soldiers dragged them into the cubicles in the pleasure houses, and I did nothing. Could do nothing.

I think of the screams and cries in the middle of the night. Screams that Heaven and Earth and the neighbourhood ignored. I think of the fear that rose in our throats at the sound of tramping boots and the knock on our door at midnight. Then I think of how Wah Jai was forced to lick the boot of the drunk soldier and the fury he had to suppress hard. My throat grows dry. As though stuffed with sand I cannot sing. I cannot hear the music of the erhu especially when I recall his sudden disappearances at night, and later his perilous return to the attic in the early hours of morning, limping up the stairs, holding the empty box that had held the bandages and medicine I had packed earlier.

Fear and fury grip my heart when I think of these.

Throughout the war, fear, fury and sorrow had intertwined his life and mine. What if the Japanese had caught him? What then? What if he were captured and tortured? Or killed? That would have ended his life and mine.

ﻬ — ﻬ

Silent and long are the dreary days. At night lying beside Wah Jai, I can't sleep. The night is humid. The baby is restless like me. I keep thinking of my orange butterfly. Restless and unhappy the days and nights creep past. Wah Jai still has not spoken with me.

Till yesterday morning, when all of a sudden he yelled, 'Kam Foong!'

The urgency in his voice made me rush down the stairs. Wah Jai was standing in the front hall, holding on to Master Loke's wheelchair shaking his teacher's shoulder.

'Sifu! Sifu!'

Master Loke was slumped forward. His head drooped low to his chest as though in deep slumber.

'Sifu! Sifu!'

Wah Jai's eyes were wild and desperate. He looked up when I touched his arm. 'He's left us,' I said softly.

'He's left us? He's left us?' Wah Jai repeated my words as though he needed convincing. 'We were about to have our lesson. I was just bringing him his erhu and tea.' Tears streamed down his face.

I wanted to hold him but I knew he would push me away in his grief. He reminded me of my youngest brother back home in Saam Hor.

'What happened?'

Master Wu ran in, and stopped short beside the wheelchair. Then he placed a hand on his old friend's shoulder. Confronted by death, the three of us were silent and grim. As if a thick black cloud had blanketed the entire house.

'Sifu,' I said but Master Wu did not look up. Like a statue, he stood beside the wheelchair and did not speak or move for a long time.

'Sifu.' I called him a second time.

'You bastard! The bombs did not kill you. Fear could not kill you. Having no legs did not kill you. How could you let your heart kill you? How could you?'

He gave Master Loke's shoulder a thump as though his old friend was still alive. 'You cannot go! You cannot leave me. I need you!'

A balled-up fist rubbed his reddening eyes. Then he turned to Wah Jai. 'You are leader of the orchestra now.'

A horrified look. Wah Jai shook his head. He could not take his beloved teacher's place. It would be like a son usurping the father's throne. He could not do it. No, he could not do it. He knelt in front of Master Loke's slumped figure and sobbed as though he had lost his own father. And refused to be comforted.

'Wah Jai, Wah Jai, listen. Listen to me.' Master Wu placed a gentle hand on his heaving shoulders. 'One life comes; another life goes. The young replaces the old. That is the cycle of life. The nature of life. Hard for all to accept. But Old Loke would want you to carry on. Come now. Stand up. You are his disciple. His *only* disciple. The one he gifted with his prized family heirloom. The erhu handed down the generations of males in his family. A clear sign he wanted you to succeed him. He knew he would not live long. He told me.'

'He told you?' Wah Jai looked up. He was still kneeling in front of the wheelchair.

'What do you think? Your foul-mouth teacher and I were brothers since the day we left China to roam the theatre world. In the floating world of shadows where all men claim to be brothers, he is the only one, truly my brother. Do you think your grief is deeper than mine? I have known this bastard for more than forty years. We grew up together. Played together. Acted together. Now stand up. Stand up! Do not let him down. Go and tell the brothers up the road to spread the word. Everyone in the opera world knows the master erhu player of Cantonese opera music in Chinatown. We will give him a proper send-off. We are his family. His living relations. Hell! Oh hell! You bastard! Sneaking off like this. Who is going to drink with me now?'

Master Wu knelt and wept.

On the day of the funeral, Wah Jai led the procession down Keong Saik Road as though he was Uncle Loke's son. His face stiff with grief he played the heirloom erhu in front of the slow-moving hearse, and led the opera world's musicians from erhu, gaohu and sanxian players to drummers and flautists of every school in the largest funeral procession that Chinatown had ever seen.

After that there was a large farewell feast held in the street. Master Wu saw to it that everyone who came to the funeral had a seat at one of the many tables set up by friends and fans and neighbours.

'A feast to celebrate our brother's life!' Master Wu declared. 'Let us toast the foul-mouth rascal!'

He sang and drank and was drunk. And still he sang and drank till the last guests had left before Wah Jai and I with the help of some tenants finally put him to bed.

That night, in the silence of our attic, I blew out the lamp and held Wah Jai close. He had hardly eaten anything all day. His body was hard and his limbs were stiff. I had no words to comfort him. I held him in my arms and soothed his rock hard back till he finally succumbed to tears and wept on my breast. And that night, wordless, we became husband and wife again.

34

A sombre air blows through the house. The three-storey tenement remains in mourning. There is no music and no shouting. The children no longer run from the kitchen to the hall, yelling for their mother. All day long Master Wu drinks alone in his room, and Wah Jai's erhu is silent.

Alone in the alcove of the attic, I mourn for Master Loke and my orange butterfly. And the only occasional sound in the afternoon is my baby's cry.

Sorrow has descended upon the house like a heavy mist. When I am feeding, washing, changing diapers, and doing the one thousand and one things that mothers with babies do, I do not feel like singing. And so the days pass.

℘ — ℭ

It has been more than a month. The two men are still cloaked in grief. I cannot bear it any longer. I have to sing or else I will lose my voice.

I start to hum a little. The next hour I start to sing a little. Just a few lines. Humming and cooing all morning, I begin to sing a lullaby to my baby. In the afternoon I sing another few lines again, and another few lines in the evening as I suckle the child, and all day the child was quiet and sweet and slept.

The next morning at dawn after my usual singing exercises, I carry Choi Wan up to the alcove and sing to her, the rooftops and sky of my grief and loneliness as I let her suckle at my breast. Again the two men are silent.

The next morning I sing again as though the three of us are out in the market square as before. And Master Wu is drumming, and Wah Jai is playing his erhu, his bowing hand flexible as a gentleman scholar waving his fan. And the memory of his erhu playing so stirs my heart I had to break into song just as an orange butterfly flies into a ray of morning sunshine, flitting among the two pots of roses sitting on the pile of logs. The sight lifts my heart. She is re-incarnated into a butterfly. I am comforted. I am not alone. Little Choi Wan cries. I run down the spiral stairs, pick her up from her cot, and still singing I feed her, and she gurgles and smiles up at me.

Each day I sing a little louder up in the alcove. Sometimes softly to my daughter. Sometimes loudly to the audience I imagine who will come someday to listen to my songs. Each day my voice begins to grow a little stronger. And so day by day I sing to my two-month-old baby daughter and my orange butterfly with the black dots on its wings.

Like leaves down a gurgling stream, the gloom in the house begin to float away and I sing longer pieces, letting the arias speak of hope and the possibility of joy.

Love half-forgotten rises in the heart
Pokes up its head like a little bean sprout, pale and delicate…

Then one day I hear Wah Jai's erhu playing the melody, and before long, Master Wu's voice is singing in the front hall. From up in the attic, I sing louder till voices and erhu music fill the three-storey tenement again and even the pipa player joins in strumming her pipa.

ဆ — ၰ

My dearest Butterfly.

It has been almost a month since I last wrote in this journal to you. Rest assured. Though I did not write you were never out of my heart. You are a spirit; you know my heart. And my heart does not lie.

Many things have happened. The gods and Master Wu were capricious. Our silent tenement house is noisy once again. Full of singers and musicians once again. Everything changed the day Master Wu rushed up to the attic.

'How is my little Beautiful Cloud?'

He scooped up Choi Wan from the mattress just as voices downstairs were calling for him.

'*Aiyah!* They are here already.'

Laughing, he handed the baby to Wah Jai and told the two of us to follow him downstairs. Musicians and opera performers and singers were milling around in the front hall, and more were crowding in.

'Old Wu! What is happening?'

'My friends! I have good news for you!' Master Wu roared. 'An old friend of mine is in charge of the Great World Theatre now. As you all know, the amusement parks were taken over by the secret society gangs during the war and turned into gambling dens. Then the Japanese army used part of the Great World Park to house prisoners-of-war. Even though the war is over now, people say you can still hear the screams of prisoners at night. True or not, few people dare to go and find out.'

'Hey! Uncle Wu! Have you invited us here to listen to you twisting a ghost story like a bunch of intestines?'

Loud laughter from the crowd.

'Patience, young man, patience! Let us not forget what happened during the war years!'

'You want us to remember, Uncle? Let us remember! –

Singapore bombed! People beheaded.
Troupes disbanded. Singers scattered!
But three stooges gathered…
To sing opera song in the market!'

Roars of laugher greeted the young actor's ditty.

'Well done! We three stooges sang and did not starve. You clowns were out of work,' Master Wu laughed. 'But today I have good news. Rich businessmen are re-opening the amusement parks and theatres.'

The crowd listened intently as he went on.

'Inside the New World, Happy World and Great World Parks theatres are going to stage operas again! My old friend, the new manager of the Great World Amusement Park, asked me how long would I take to put up an opera. A month I said! I need performers. So spread the word. Those of you who want work, see me tomorrow.'

Loud cheers all round.

When everyone had left, I turned to Master Wu. 'Sifu, the Golden Phoenix Opera Troupe has only you, Wah Jai and me.'

He grinned as though he was drunk, wagging his finger.

'Why do you worry? We will have an entire troupe. Including the orchestra by tomorrow.'

His airy drunken confidence frustrated me. His eyes were dreamy when he looked at me. I raised my voice.

'Sifu! Wake up from your opium dream! An opera needs singers, actors, people for costumes and props, musicians and instruments.'

'And training and rehearsals and money,' Wah Jai added.

'Hahaha! *So? So?*' Master Wu roared. 'All those who were here today are more experienced than the two of you. They don't need rehearsals. They know their operas like the back of their hands. As for props, we can buy from disbanded troupes. Wah Jai and I know where to find them. We have been going around. Once word gets out hundreds will come begging for work. They will work even for free. Just you watch.'

'Sifu, troupes need to eat. Where is the money?' Wah Jai tried to sober him up.

'The gods in Heaven! Look at these two grannies! I have eaten more salt than you have eaten rice. If small money does not go out, big money will not come in. I will mortgage this house if necessary.'

'What?!!! This is the roof over our heads!'

'No need to panic. Look. When you two first met me, I told you that opera is my life blood. What is a house? Mortar and bricks. Can you take this house with you when you die? We did not starve during the war. What more during peace? Kam Foong, you will perform your first full-length opera as the principal *xiu sung* of the troupe.'

My heart flew up to heaven at his words. Then it fell back to earth with a thud. The full responsibility of what I was asked to undertake. The weight of the trust he placed in me. And my responsibility to the Golden Phoenix Cantonese Opera Troupe. Could I do it?

My baby wailed. Master Wu stroked the tuft of hair on Choi Wan's little head.

'After the bombs fell in Ipoh,' his voice sober and gruff, 'I lost everything when I lost my son. Then I found you two. And you made me a grandfather. Now this grandfather wants to bequeath his granddaughter with more than a ton of bricks when he dies. A bomb will burn this house to ashes. But bombs and the Japanese army could not stop three stooges from performing. Why? Because we have skills. I want to bequeath to my granddaughter all the opera skills I know.'

Choi Wan wailed.

35

I closed the journal, rubbed my tired eyes and looked at the clock. It was way past midnight. I had been reading for hours. My limbs were stiff. I needed a walk and took the lift down and headed out to the empty streets. Walking where my feet took me, I watched my shadow gliding past the silent shuttered shops, slithering over the body of a man asleep on a shop's pavement, a piece of cardboard for a bed. His face was turned to the wall; and a small breeze was fluttering the forlorn edges of the newspapers tucked under his head. Not wishing to disturb the man's slumber I stepped out onto the road and into the neon glow of street lamps, and strolled down the wide spacious avenue empty of traffic except for an occasional passing taxi.

The quiet city was beautiful. The night sky above seemed so much wider without the crush of people rushing to cross the road at the traffic lights and the constant roar of cars and buses. I relished the sense of space and solitude down the quiet avenue under a starless sky and kept walking, admiring the chiaroscuros of light and dark along the pavements of the shophouses. A light cool breeze ruffling my hair, I suddenly realised I hadn't thought of Robert for weeks. My fear of meeting him or bumping into him no longer worried me. A feeling of freedom filled my heart as a faint fragrance of fried ginger and sesame oil wafted past. On a whim I followed the familiar scent down the street to the stall at the corner of South Bridge Road and Keong Saik Road. The only food stall still open past midnight.

On the pavement were a few tables of diners having a late supper. The smell of sautéed frog legs and fried ginger stirred my appetite. Frog leg porridge cooked and served in a clay pot was the stall's specialty. On impulse I ordered a pot of the porridge and a plate of bitter gourd fried with fermented black beans, and sat down at an empty table. That was when I noticed Meng, sitting with friends at another table, his back turned towards me. Suddenly self-conscious and vulnerable, I wished I hadn't stopped by the stall. I looked around. I was the only solitary diner. I moved my stool into the shadowy part of the pavement and was relieved when the waiter brought my food.

I bit into a piece of the sautéed bitter gourd. *It's bitter!* I heard two six-year-olds wail. Meng and I were inside the temple of the Goddess of Mercy with my grandparents. Meng, or Noodle Head then, was holding my hand. Fierce gods were gazing down at us from the temple's high imposing altar, and smoke from tall joss sticks encircled by dragons rose to the beams. The velvety red flocculent folds of the altar cascaded to the floor with embroidered fierce-eyed tigers standing on white clouds and dark green dragons clawing among pink lotuses. *Argaaaah!* All of a sudden the two of us were shoved under the altar.

Rigid as a stone frog we crouched in the sudden darkness not daring to move, while from far-off came my grandparents' voices urging Noodle Head and I to crawl to the other end of the altar. But the darkness looked impenetrable. I couldn't see him. *Noodle Head? I'm behind you.* His frightened whisper hissed behind my ears. As my eyes adjusted to the dark, I saw monstrous crossbeams thick as tree trunks were blocking our way. *Move,* he hissed. *I can't.* I wanted to tell him but my voice was gone. Then a sudden push! I fell flat on my belly. And dust puffs rose to my nose and joss ash tickled my throat. *Spirits will catch us. Move.* I plunged forward wriggling and snaking on my belly. Coughing and sneezing I inched. Sharp corners bit my head. Sharp fingers clawed my flesh. When Grandfather's hand yanked me out, I bawled! I thought the spirits had caught me. *Hush, precious, hush.* Por Por hugged and held me in her arms. *Goddess of Mercy has blessed you. You're her Jade Girl now. And Noodle Head, you're her Golden Lad. Both of you are blessed.* Por Por gave us each a cup of tea. *Bitter!* Meng and I cried. *Life is bitter,* Por Por replied.

'Yin. Yin. May I sit down?'

'Oh, sorry! Please do.'

His friends were leaving.

'They're members of the opera troupe at the community centre.'

'So you have a troupe.'

'Amateurs. Students from my classes,' he smiled. Then looking concerned, he said, 'I'm surprised to see you out alone at this late hour.'

'I'm used to it.' And winced at my defensive tone.

The stall was closing. I paid for my food, and the two of us started to walk back to Jin Swee.

'Like old times, isn't it? It's been twenty over years. Things have changed.'

'So what've you been doing these past twenty years?'

I surprised myself. What gave me the right to ask what he had been doing as if he had to account for his life to me? We hadn't spoken for so long. But he didn't look offended.

'Long story,' he said. 'I went to Hong Kong after the army. I worked in a factory for several months to pay for board and lodging. Then I waited on tables in order to train with a Cantonese opera troupe. After that, well, after many difficult years of training, I was accepted into a professional troupe, where I met my wife. We had a daughter, and I settled in Hong Kong. Several years ago my wife passed away. And I was left with my little girl. Last night my daughter and her husband phoned me. They are celebrating my grandson's birthday. And my grandson wanted to tell his grandpa he's going to nursery school.'

'What good news! You must be a very happy man.'

He rubbed his grey crop, the laughter lines on his face bunching up as he smiled. 'Thank you, Yin. It seems like not too long ago I was called Big Brother Meng. Now my troupe calls me Uncle Meng. Very soon some will call me Grandpa Meng. That's the story of life, isn't it?'

'A story of changing identities.'

'And a story of what could have been.' A brittle note in his laugh.

We walked on in silence. I was expecting him to ask about me. Instead he asked, 'Do you remember the opera about the poet Su Dongpo?'

'The name sounds familiar. But I don't remember the opera.'

'A scholar, a poet and a magistrate. He had a hard life. Imperial magistrates had to go wherever they were sent. And because he criticised imperial policies he was sent far away from home for years. By the time he returned to his village, his wife had passed on. His children had grown, some had died. Let me quote you a few lines of the poem we sung in the opera.

Ceaseless years have separated us,
Not often did I think of you.
My beard and temples are dusted with frost,
Would you recognise me if we were to meet?

I was sorry when he stopped. His recitation was so beautifully clear and pure; the Cantonese words sounded like music in the quiet night. I could see him on stage as the white-haired poet, bent with age and grief, I said.

We walked on in silence after that, side by side, wrapped in our thoughts with the night closing in on us, and did not speak again till we reached Jin Swee Estate.

'I'll see you home,' he said as we entered the lift.

He came up to my apartment, but stopped outside my door. Tipped his head, said good night and took the stairs down to his brother's apartment on the sixth floor.

I went in, locked the door, and started to search for Su Dongpo's poem among my books. His sudden recital of the poem had left me with a sense of curiosity and a little unease. I found the poem and read it through, wondering why he had quoted that particular paragraph. The ambiguity troubled me given our history.

36

My dearest Butterfly. Today is the day of the resurrection of the Golden Phoenix Cantonese Opera Troupe. I have to record this now or else there will be no time to write when the baby wakes.

This afternoon Master Wu took me to the teahouse where he had arranged to meet two sisters, Mei Lai and Mei Fong, who are *fah dan*, the principal singers in opera. The ground floor of the teahouse was full of men who looked like traders and merchants out to discuss business over dim sum and a pot of well-brewed tea. The proprietor who knew Master Wu conducted us up the stairs to the upper floor of the teahouse, which had no patrons in the afternoon.

'I'll look out for the two *fah dan* and tell them you're up here, Master Wu.'

'Thank you, Old Wang. I'll see that you get a free seat at the opera.'

'That will please my missus. I'll leave you now and send the waiter up with a pot of my best tea.'

It was so good to be out without the baby. I have not seen the inside of a teahouse since Choi Wan was born. To be honest, I am tired of being a mother all the time. I have done my duty by Wah Jai. I have given him a descendant. I cannot wait to return to the stage. The more I thought of the future the more excited I felt till Master Wu told me to calm down.

'As the *xiu sung*, you have to wait for the *fah dan*. On stage, man waits for woman. On earth, woman waits on man.'

'But once I return to the stage, I will wait on no one,' I said.

'Miss Mei Lai will be a good match for you.'

He had forgotten. I have never performed on stage with a woman before. When I was in Big Boss's troupe, all the female roles were sung by men. But things have changed since the war. In Hong Kong, Yam Kim Fai, the most popular woman acting the male on the opera stage, is leading the change. And what Hong Kong does, Singapore will follow.

'Mei Lai's high singing voice will be a perfect match for your contralto. But they are late so we wait.'

I could see my Sifu was not pleased. Opera actors and singers must be punctual. To be late is a sin. He hated waiting. We drank more tea. Then voices rose from the stairs.

'Master Wu! Master Wu! We are so sorry to keep you waiting!'

Two young women came running up the stairs. Mei Fong, the elder of the two sisters, explained that they had taken a wrong turn.

'After three years hiding in the rubber plantation in Malaya, we have forgotten the way here. Please, forgive us, sir. I am told you expect punctuality. Are you angry, sir?'

'No, no, please sit down.' Master Wu leaned over the bannisters. 'Waiter! Hurry! Another pot of tea! Make it fast!'

'Master Wu, please forgive us. This is my sister, Mei Lai.'

'It is an honour to meet you, sir,' the younger and petite sister murmured.

'Well, well, I am honoured both of you can come at such short notice. This is Kam Foong, the *xiu sung*. Her stage name is Wong Mun Loong.'

'Wong the Literary Dragon. What a beautiful name for a *xiu sung*.'

'And what a beautiful voice,' I thought. Mellifluous and sweet.

I caught Mei Lai's smiling eyes. When I first set eyes on her as she came up the stairs, I had felt something in the air had changed. As though a cool breeze had blown through the room. I was surprised she looked no more than seventeen, and her delicate features and bright dark eyes looked unscathed by the war. Her fair egg-shaped face was such a refreshing contrast to the gaunt faces of the women in the tenement and the ladies in the pleasure houses.

'Kam Foong will be performing her first full length opera. I hope both of you veterans will guide her. That is, if you, the *fah dan*, agree to join us.'

'Oh, Master Wu, you are far too humble,' Mei Fong said. 'Any disciple trained by you does not need our guidance. We will need your guidance instead. We have lost touch, you see. Our family hid in a village deep inside a rubber plantation in Johore. Far from the fighting and bombing. Even then, our mother shaved off our hair and smeared mud on our faces, and we worked as rubber tappers.'

While the elder sister was talking, Mei Lai was toying with her cup of tea, pretending not to know that I was watching her, while I was pretending that I was not looking at her. Both of us were so engrossed in this sweet game of pretence that all of a sudden Master Wu's words startled us. I was struck by the sudden formality and politeness in my Sifu's words and demeanour.

'Miss Mei Fong, as you know it is not so easy to agree at once. It's always very difficult to match performers to each other especially when they are the principal singers, *fah dan* and *xiu sung.*'

Master Wu shook his head and looked at the ceiling as he spoke, a hesitant note creeping into his voice.

'Naturally a lot would depend on Miss Mei Lai's vocal range and whether it matches Kam Foong's. We cannot force such things. And then there is the very important matter of relationship. It would not do for both of you to join us and then we part after one performance. Any partnership should aim for the long term. So, so… aye,' he let out a sigh, 'I must consider very carefully. Meet a few more *fah dan* first.'

I could not believe my ears. Why was Master Wu hee-hawing? We need a *fah dan*! He had promised to produce an opera within a month. I tried to catch his eye. But he had turned to Mei Lai who was leaning across the tea table, a worried look on her earnest face. Each whispered word out of her mouth sounded to me like a silver bell rung by raindrops. She was about to cry.

'Master Wu, I am very sorry my sister and I gave you the wrong impression. We did not mean to be late, sir. We really lost our way. My sister and I need the work badly. Our father… he is very ill. Our mother has pawned off all her jewellery.' With head bowed, and hands on her lap like a penitent confessing her sins, she went on. 'Sir, you need not worry. I can adapt. I have… I have been performing since I was four, and… and I did not stop performing during the war. I can adapt to Sister Kam Foong.'

Moved by the mention of my name and the earnestness in her faltering voice, I stood up. Facing the empty tables and chairs in the tearoom I sang the first verse of a popular duet so Mei Lai could hear the quality of my singing voice. A grateful smile lit up her face. She stood up at once and sang the response. Her eyes mirroring mine, verse replying to verse, we sang as patrons on the ground floor of the teahouse crowded up the stairs to watch.

When our duet ended, they cheered and shouted, 'Encore! Encore!'

Mei Lai took my hand, and the two of us bowed and bowed till the patrons eventually returned downstairs. Master Wu laughed.

'Well, well, well! It is settled then! Mei Lai and Mei Fong, you will be the two *fah dan* of the Golden Phoenix Cantonese Opera Troupe. But I warn you. Engagements are uncertain at the moment. I will do my best to get us work.'

'Master Wu, kind sir, in prosperity we share; in adversity we bear.'

'Well said, Mei Lai, well said.'

Master Wu was pleased.

After the two sisters had left, I asked him why he was hee-hawing earlier, and he gave a hearty hoot.

'You have much to learn, Kam Foong! Never appear too eager when engaging a performer. Else they will demand more than what you are prepared to pay them.'

'Why you sly old fox! Mei Lai cried!'

'*Chieh!* An actor's tears! Do not be so naïve. The sisters lied to us.'

'They lied? How do you know?' I was so surprised.

'I have my ways,' the old fox grinned. 'Did you not notice their hands? Those fair slender hands are not those of a rubber tapper's. They were in an opera troupe with their parents throughout the war. And Mei Lai herself said so later. I know their troupe had travelled to the villages to perform opera and Japanese propaganda. The top brass in the army have great respect for the opera arts. They tried to use opera to promote their Japanese notion of empire.'

'Then why do you accept them? You hate such troupes.'

'Aye, Foong, the war is over. The past is past. When forming a troupe, we must look for skill and art. Between art and politics, art must always prevail.'

'That is rot, Sifu! What if they were murderers?'

'But the fact is they are not. Context, Kam Foong. See things in context. These two sisters are excellent singers and seasoned performers. They have much to teach you. Just think. What would happen to them if they were to refuse the Japanese? Their whole family and the entire troupe would have been killed.'

37

I'm in a church. White hooded figures without faces are circling around the altar. I know these are the dark evil forces I have to get away from. I turn and run down the church aisle, which suddenly morphs into a maze with shut doors on both sides of its twisting passageways. As I run round the corner a huge black bear comes lumbering after me. Running faster and faster I bang on every door in the twisting maze, shake and turn every doorknob trying desperately to open one of the doors to get away from the bear. But none of the doors would open. The bear is coming closer. I run faster, heart racing, banging on the doors, turning left and right down the twisting passages of the maze. But none of the doors opens. The passageway is turning darker and narrower, and the bear is coming nearer. Then just as I see the huge beast turn the corner, I manage to push open a door into a room. I shut the door hard upon the large black paw that had thrust through the gap. A huge roar rose from the beast! Too terrified to scream, I lean the whole weight of my body against the door hard. And then I see to my horror I'm back in the chapel with the white hooded figures. Half the chapel is enveloped in darkness, and the other half in bright sunlight. Too petrified to move I remain standing on the dark side where there's a pair of swing doors like those in the bars of cowboy movies. My terrified eyes are fixated on the concrete floor on the other side of the swing doors where a hard thumping of boots is coming closer and closer. Just as the Devil in knee-high polished black boots is about to open the swing doors I somersaulted backwards and fall into the sunlit area.

I had to take several deep breaths to calm myself. My brain, which seemed to have flown out of my head, returned. I sat up in bed and started to scribble into the notebook I kept on the box of books that served as my temporary bedside table. I suffered from nightmares. At the AWARE Support group one of the women had suggested that I write them down the moment I wake up. Writing might help me to confront my suppressed fears, she said.

We think we are rational beings but nightmares suggest otherwise. We assume that as rational beings we have reasons to explain why we do what we do. But in many instances of our life we do not know why we do what we do. I do not know as I write this why I'm plagued by such nightmares. I cannot explain to myself why I fear so deeply the man I had once loved so dearly or why I had stayed so long and tried so hard to go on loving him. I cannot explain why I, a professional woman, had endured abuse for so many years. I have asked myself many times. Throughout history women had been hit and abused, and dared not complain because they lived in an oppressive patriarchal society. But these days women who are educated with professional careers still dare not or would not speak up even though the law is on their side. Something holds them back. A deep sense of shame and failure. They had failed themselves, failed their mothers, failed to fulfil the promises and dreams they had before they married. They feared what others think of them. And most of all they feared what they thought of themselves in the quiet of the night when even silence was an accusing voice.

Useless! Stupid, so slow! Where's your brain today? Beneath my appearance of modern femininity and efficiency I had felt worthless before such frequent onslaughts. When my marriage frayed and deteriorated to the point I knew I had to leave if I wanted to survive as a human being, I could not bring myself to leave him. Could not bear to leave the home and family we had built together. To give up more than twenty years of my life with another and live alone. I could not do it. I could not explain my fear of the solitary. Not to myself. Nor to anyone. It was irrational. But my fear was real. And large. It felt insurmountable. I was so afraid of leaving. So afraid of living alone. He had been taking care of every aspect of our life. I would not be able to manage on my own. Having lived in a cage for more than twenty years, I was afraid to step out. Afraid to fly out. But I have to fly out.

I read over what I had written and saw a glimpse of a self I used to know peeping out. To write is to be strong. I wrote all that morning, and once I had started I could not stop. I wrote every morning. Sometimes what I wrote were entire dreams. Often it was the remnants, the dark bits and pieces that had stayed in my mind when I woke up, and then greyed and faded from my memory the next day, and what remained were my scribbled words, the writing that later made no sense to me; and the few fragments that I could recall without reading my journal, I could make no sense of them either. Take this awful vivid scene in which I found myself slipping and falling in the streets flooded with human excreta all the way from Chinatown to the Bedok Jetty till I threw myself into the sea. What was the significance of that? A premonition of my near suicide? I could not explain. But this dream had stayed in my memory.

As the days passed there were mornings when I awoke without remembering having had any nightmares or dreams, and I was relieved and felt rested. On such mornings I went for walks. At the fresh food market, I bought a bunch of flowers to cheer myself and had breakfast at the noodle stall.

One morning I returned from my walk and breakfast, and sat down to read over what I had written in my journal, and I felt a clarity I had not felt before. Writing seemed to have quietened the incessant movement and noise inside my head, distilled the swirling mud, and my mind had settled and acquired clarity. And so April passed into May, June and July. I started to sleep better. And since I no longer worked at the National Archives, my days had acquired an expansiveness and freedom I had not felt in years. I had energy to do some of the things I had wanted to do before like visiting the art galleries, museums, and nurseries where I bought pots of dwarf bamboo and flowering plants for the corridor outside my flat. When I was working there was no time for hobbies or frivolities. There was always some worrisome tasks to complete or deadlines to meet in the office. At home, a grouch to appease, orders to follow, and at night a wife's duty to perform in bed, and all the while there was my rising frustration and irritation to curb and suppress every day, all of which had left me tired in mind and body. Over the years my horizon had shrivelled to that of a mouse.

It took a lot of courage for me to even say I wanted to divorce Robert and hold firm to my decision. Robert was furious.

'You can't do this to me! You're a vengeful woman!'

In a strongly worded letter to the lawyer, he called me a deserter. Declared he was against divorce. He was a Catholic.

I suffered from nightmares in the months before we went to court. I kept praying that things could be settled by the lawyers as quickly and as peacefully as possible.

Then on the day our case came up, I saw Robert standing before the magistrate, looking very subdued, like a schoolboy steeling himself for a dressing down by the principal. And it opened my eyes. Could it be this was how he had stood before the higher-ups in his department when they questioned him about things under his charge? Was this how he had stood before Judge Palmerston, his stern father, when his school results were not up to the mark? Were they not as good as his brother's? Or could he not explain his actions and defend himself?

He agreed to settle and also agreed not to flood my inbox with hostile emails. At first, disbelieving, I kept checking my mailbox whenever I switched on my laptop. Then as the weeks passed my eyes stopped searching for his name. Some nights just as I was about to fall asleep, Sea Cove still came to me in flashes of scenes that made me cringe in shame and pain. Some nights the ache in my chest still forced tears out of me, tears I did not want to cry. I could not understand my lingering despondency. The divorce was over, I kept telling myself. My anxieties were receding. I should be happy. Why wasn't I?

But life is a waxing of light and dark, I comforted myself. I noticed my moods change and wondered if it was part of post menopause. Part of the physical changes that afflict middle-aged women. Then as time passed there came days when I woke up before dawn, feeling quite cheerful and went for a stroll through the still sleeping city. Some mornings I walked a long way through the silent business district down to as far as the seafront at Collyer Quay to stand at the railings. A solitary figure watching the sun's rays paint the boats and waters a patina of gold. Later, I would stop at the old octagonal Lau Pat Sat market for a breakfast of toast with butter and kaya, half-boiled eggs and coffee before heading home to read and translate Por Por's journal into English, or to write my own. For the time being, I had no other plans. I was simply happy to pass the days lazing around, to read and write, or visit the National Library and the malls, or stay home to unpack my boxes leisurely or watch tv without someone ordering me to switch to the sports channel.

I grew to love the lazy expansiveness of my days and felt my heart opening. I made friends with my neighbours in Jin Swee. When the durian season arrived, I invited Madam Soh and Khim from the coffeeshop for a durian feast at the fruit stall. The young enterprising fruit seller, who was a cousin of the coffeeshop owner, had set up two tables along the side pavement of the coffeeshop and provided two pails of water for customers to wash their hands. Khim knew the young man well.

'Don't you dare overcharge Sister Xiu Yin. You heard me, Ah Huat? She's our *ga-gi-nang*. One of our own, and my good friend, and Auntie Soh's neighbour,' she said in her earthy Hokkien.

'I know, I know!'

Sporting a red bandana on his head, Ah Huat grinned at the three of us.

'Sister, don't worry. To live is to eat and enjoy, I say. When eating durian, do not worry about price. Eating is a blessing. Right or not? Later, when you're old, you want to eat durian, also cannot. Now Auntie Soh here is very blessed. She still can eat the rich creamy fruit. See? Her face still has the nice soft creamy skin like a baby's.'

'Go on! You naughty boy! I'm old enough to be your great grandma already. Not girlfriend!'

'Can you blame me? You look so young, *leh.*' Unfazed, Ah Huat grinned.

'Stop it! Go away!' Madam Soh, giggling, waved him off.

Ah Huat picked up a durian from his stall, felt the weight of the thorny fruit in both his hands, brought it to his nose, smelled it, and turned to me.

'For you, Sister, only the very best! I choose this durian from Segamat. And this one is from Thailand. Eat and compare.'

He cut off a small triangular piece of the thorny shell from the first durian and invited Khim to touch the flesh inside.

'Soft enough?'

Khim's finger prodded the soft yellow flesh inside, and she nodded. Ah Huat then knifed open the fruit and set it on our table with a flourish.

'Enjoy!' he grinned and opened the second fruit. Then he turned back to the stall to entice another customer.

We watched him invite a customer to pick a durian, feel its weight in his hands and sniff at the thorny fruit before he, Ah Huat, cut off a piece of the hard shell and let the customer touch the flesh inside.

'Guarantee! If no good, I don't take your money.'

When the man agreed to buy it, he knifed open the whole fruit and placed it on the table with a flourish and a shout, 'Ta-da! Enjoy!'

There was sequence in his selling and rhythm in his movements as though it was a performance, the music of which was inside his head. It was such a pleasure watching him and being cajoled by his good-natured cheerfulness that I bought a third durian and didn't mind spending close to two hundred dollars that night at his stall, especially when Joe Samad, his pal, came by with a guitar and serenaded us with a few evergreen Mandarin songs.

'At no extra charge, Auntie!' Ah Huat quipped. 'Joe is Jin Swee's poet and composer.'

'Who must sing for his supper,' Joe Samad laughed and introduced himself as 'Jin Swee's Number One Singer' and unacknowledged composer.

When the durian season was over, Ah Huat closed up his fruit stall. During the year-end school holidays, a small night market came to the neighbourhood bringing a merry-go-round for the young children and a game stall for the teenagers. There were makeshift stalls selling cheap tee shirts, knickknacks and street food like beef burgers, fried fishballs and banana fritters. I went down one evening with Madam Soh to walk around and saw Ah Huat hawking fried fishballs and curry puffs. Joe Samad wearing a bright red bandana was selling beef burgers, and a long queue was waiting for his Joe's Special.

'Hey Joe! Two burgers! Your Special! I'll collect them later!'

'Okay, Auntie! No problem!'

'The neighbourhood is so friendly, no wonder my grandparents refused to move away,' I said to Madam Soh.

'I too don't want to move. I'll live here till I die.'

'*Choy! Choy!* You'll live to a ripe old age, Auntie.'

38

In the weeks of hot dry weather the roadside trees blossomed yellow and pink. The angsana trees in the car park were aglow with golden yellow blooms, which attracted hundreds of kerengga or weaver ants. One morning during my walk I was staring at the long trail of these red ants in the park when I realised I hadn't had any nightmares in a long while.

To celebrate I visited department stores and bought some new clothes, a new computer, changed my email password, and started to change the pots and pans and crockery in the kitchen, getting rid of the old, chipped plates that Por Por had refused to throw away. After living here more than a year, I finally felt I had the right to throw away her things. Every weekend I chatted with Janice on the phone. At her urging, I gave serious thought to how I wanted to renovate the flat so that it would truly be mine. I did some research and engaged a design-and-build company and discussed plans with them to renovate the apartment.

Workers came and hauled away the old furniture. Everything except the red altar. Then came the weeks of knocking down, drilling, hammering, sawing and painting. The wall between the kitchen and the living room was knocked down in the first week. In the following week, the wall between the two bedrooms was torn down so I could have one large spacious bedroom instead of two small ones. The noise and dust was horrendous. Luckily, most of my neighbours were away at work during the day. By the time they returned in the evening, the knocking had ceased. But there were old people who remained at home, and I was grateful they were so forbearing. Madam Soh very kindly offered me her flat as a refuge.

'Come any time you like. Don't hesitate. If you don't come, I'd just go walking in the mall,' she said.

So I bought lunch for the both of us and we ate our meals with the windows closed tight to shut out the noise and dust. Sometimes in the late morning when the noise was impossible, I took her out to a restaurant for dim sum, and she was very happy.

'I'm so sorry for the noise and mess, Auntie.'

'No need to say sorry. Renovations happen. We Singaporeans like to buy and sell our HDB flats. That's how we poor people make money. We buy our first flat for twenty thousand. In twenty years' time we can sell it for more than a hundred thousand. Who wouldn't sell? It's sentimental folks like your grandparents and me who cling to our flat.' She laughed. 'Last night I saw the Bukit Ho Swee fire on tv. *Waah*, my heart was burning. Many of us, old people, still think that fire was deliberate. Done to clear out squatters. My family used to live there, you know. After our attap house was burned down, we had nothing. Not even a stick of furniture. We stayed for three weeks in a community centre with other families. Then the gov'men moved us into a two-room flat. Ten of us including my uncle's family and my grandparents crouched inside that box. At first the gov'men said no need to pay rent for six months. All the newspapers reported the good news. People were so relieved. But the gov'men was hanging up lamb's heads, and selling dog meat! The free rent was only for the first group of squatters they settled. After that, all had to pay! We were so furious! When the gov'men people came to visit our area, people splashed urine on them,' she said in her feisty Cantonese.

'Auntie, is this true or not? I've never read about this urine throwing in the papers.'

'Of course not, *lor!* Who dared to write? You want to go to prison?'

'But the government has done many good things.'

'And many bad things too!'

She put down her chopsticks. A dark flame burning behind her eyes.

'Xiu Yin, I'm already eighty plus. So don't mind me saying this. People like you always think the gov'men is good. Of course the gov'men is good to people like you. You have education. You have brains. The gov'men gives you high salary, gives you high pension or CPF. You and your family can choose which hospital or which doctor you want. And stay in first class wards when you get sick. In the old days, people like us with no education, ha! We had to depend on our pair of hands and feet. My husband had a pushcart selling fried noodles near the market. Both of us worked from dawn to midnight to feed our four children and send them to school. In those days there were no subsidies like now. With my youngest strapped to my back, I washed plates and took orders and looked after the children while my old man cut and fried and went to the market every morning at four. Our children ate and worked at the stall. The two older ones helped out. Every time just as we managed to save a few dollars, the *kapala*, those heartless hygiene inspectors, would come and slap a heavy fine on us! Once it was more than two hundred dollars! For two hundred dollars in those days I could feed my entire family for two months or more. We got into debt. Had to borrow from loan sharks. Which bank would lend to hawkers like us? All our relatives had no money to lend us. The gov'men in those days had no heart! Only wanted Singapore to be clean. And tidy and nice for tourists. Cared more about what foreigners think! Didn't care about people like us earning a hard living. Those hygiene dogs smashed our crockery. One year they confiscated our cart. My old man fell ill. He died the following year, leaving four young children for me to bring up. Two had to leave school. I will never forgive this gov'men!'

She coughed incessantly into her napkin, the rush of painful memories overcoming her. I poured her a fresh cup of pu'er, and the hot tea calmed her after a while. She dabbed her eyes and smiled.

'Don't mind me. No use crying after all these years. I learnt early on that tears didn't earn me a living. I was a widow at twenty-eight with four mouths to feed. I woke up at four each morning. Fried noodles and eggs. And went from floor to floor in the HDB blocks to sell. Heaven has eyes. No one reported me. My rice bins eventually grew up. Except for the youngest, everyone has a flat and family now. Come! Eat! Eating is our good fortune. Some wannae eat but cannae eat. I can still eat durian at my age,' she broke into her Toisan dialect.

Both of us laughed.

When the whole flat was finally refurbished, I ordered baskets of fruit for the neighbours on my floor and the floor immediately below and above my flat to thank them. Madam Soh was very pleased.

'There's no need for gifts, Xiu Yin. May I come in to take a look?'

'Come in, come in.'

'Your flat looks so much brighter and bigger now. And so spacious.'

I had a new bathroom and new cabinets in the kitchen, and the new white tiles made the floor look clean. There were new curtains hanging in the windows and Japanese styled furniture in the living room. I was proud of myself. These changes were the results of decisions I had made without having to seek another's permission. The renovation project gave me a new sense of authority and control. I loved the polished wood panels of the furniture I had chosen and the large closets where I could store away boxes of my grandparents' theatre things. With all their boxes put away and hidden, the flat had a comfortable spaciousness. The only old piece of furniture I kept was Por Por's red altar.

Two weeks later the air in the corridor was thick with the smell of fresh paint and the scent of the angsana flowers. And the sky was a flaming orange by the time I had finished giving the altar a fresh coat of paint. Sheets of newspapers with splashes of black paint lined the corridor outside my flat as I stood back to admire my day's work. Dark sweat stains had appeared under my armpits. My shirt clung to my back. The newly painted altar was gleaming in the golden glow of the setting sun.

The door of the lift opened and Madam Soh emerged. I saw the expression on her face suddenly changed. I quickly apologised but it wasn't the mess in the corridor that upset her.

'*Aiyah!* Why did you paint the altar black? Altars should be red.'

'But it's not going to be my altar, Auntie. It's my new bookshelf.'

'Bookshelf? Why not buy a proper bookshelf and throw this old altar away then?'

'No, no! I can't bear to throw it. See this panel here? See how intricately carved it is? The Eight Immortals are standing on the curling lotus leaves and flowers. You don't see such elaborate carving on the new altars any more. Besides this old altar is very special. It's a sacred piece of furniture. But sometimes it was used as a theatre prop.'

'Didn't that offend the gods?'

'I don't think so. Por Por always prayed to the gods first before moving them. I still remember her prayer. Merciful gods in Heaven, take pity on our plight. We have to use your altar again tonight. Then with great reverence, she moved the Goddess of Mercy, God of Literature and the Monkey King to our kitchen table. Sometimes even our kitchen table and chairs were taken away as props. Then the gods had to sit on our kitchen shelf for weeks. Especially when times were bad.'

'Aye, I remember her telling me that times were hard in some years. Young people were flocking to the cinemas. Hey, look. See who's here.'

Meng had come up the stairs with a plastic bag. He gave me a brief nod, took a packet out of the bag and handed it to Madam Soh.

'Chicken rice for you.'

'Oh! I didn't expect this, Meng. Thank you.'

'Have you been helping Xiu Yin to paint?'

'Ha! If I've the strength to help her, I'll say thank you to my knees! They've been very painful lately. Xiu Yin and I were just talking about the hard life of opera troupes.'

'It's a beggar's life, isn't it?' Meng turned to me, his look half conspiratorial and half searching as if seeking to connect.

I was surprised by the unexpected wave of pleasure that his look gave me. After our walk home from the porridge stall, we had not spoken in a very long while. Whenever I bumped into him by chance, he was always in a hurry either on his way to the hospital to see Tony or to a class, a meeting or a rehearsal. I felt he was avoiding me. Embarrassed perhaps by his Su Dongpo's poem.

'It's mostly the old who watch Chinese opera these days,' he said. 'The young want to watch *getai*. See girls prancing on stage in skimpy outfits, belting out Mando pop and Hokkien pop songs. Even the gods like it.'

His laugh sounded bitter.

'During your grandparents' time, the troupes were paid only seventy to a hundred dollars for a night's performance. Isn't it?' He tried to draw me in. 'The money had to be shared among the singers, actors, orchestra and stagehands. Each could end up earning just one to three dollars for a whole night's performance. Isn't that so? D'you remember?'

'Yes, but don't forget, the cost of living was very cheap then. A bowl of noodles cost only ten cents in the 1950s. And twenty to thirty cents in the sixties. Opera stars like Por Por were supported by rich patrons.'

'Ah yes, those opera dream lovers. That's what we used to call those patrons. They were not just fans but dream lovers with money. And there were plenty of them.' His tone had lost its earlier bitter edge and he sounded more enthusiastic now. 'Those rich *tai-tai* would buy entire rows of seats and fill them with their friends on opening night.'

'And they gave opera stars like my Por Por gifts of cash and jewellery stuffed into red packets,' I added, spurred by his animated recollection of those days when opera was the main entertainment of the local Chinese. 'The generosity of those rich *tai-tai* and their gifts added vastly to the opera actor's reputation and income.'

'Your grandmother was said to have received so many of such gifts that she could even afford to reject the gifts of a dream lover who had offended her. A certain woman in black. Did you know?'

'No. What woman in black?'

'There was this story about your grandmother and the woman in black that had spread to every town. The scandal press said there was a love story behind it. That love story in the tabloids added to your grandmother's fame. And mystique. Every *tai-tai* in every town wanted to be her opera dream lover. Even my mother,' he laughed. For a moment he was like a boy who had caught his mother out.

'You're making it up.'

'No, no, I heard it from the stagehands. I was slogging as a stagehand in your grandparents' troupe. Remember?'

'Oh? You were in the Golden Phoenix Cantonese Opera Troupe?'

'Auntie, I worked there without pay.'

'Nonsense, you ingrate!' I protested, laughing. 'Don't listen to him, Auntie. My grandparents fed him. And Great Grandfather Wu taught him the basic opera skills. They even took him to Malaysia with us. Not once but several times. The ungrateful boy.'

His eyes behind the rimless glasses lighted up.

'Those trips were great holidays. And such fun. I remember kneeling on the back seat of the bus. We kept trying to push each other off the seat. We made so much noise that Por Por shouted at us to behave or else she'd stop the bus and leave us at one of the rubber plantations along the road.'

'And she did just that! Remember? Both of us were so scared. We dared not even cry,' I laughed at the memory of the scene.

'I held your hand and we stood under a tree stiff with fright,' he said.

'I almost wet my pants. Did you know? When the bus came back we clambered up the bus howling like puppies.'

We laughed at the memory. Each of us seeing the child in the other. And Madam Soh was laughing with us too. Until finally I wiped the sweat from my eyes, surprised he had crouched down and had started cleaning the paint from my paintbrushes with some newspapers. Madam Soh trotted back into her flat and returned with two mugs.

'Here, you two! Drink this.'

From the way she called out to us 'you two', it was clear that she assumed that Meng and I were very close. I wondered if he had noticed it. I glanced at him sitting on my doorstep cleaning one of my brushes with a bunch of newspapers.

'It's chrysanthemum tea boiled with red dates.' Madam Soh pushed the two mugs into my hands.

'Thank you, Auntie. You've been very kind to me since I moved back.'

'*Chieh!* What a thing to say. Your grandparents and I were such old friends and neighbours. After they'd retired, we used to chat out here in the corridor like this every evening. Sitting in his wheelchair, your grandfather would play his erhu sometimes. Then your Por Por would sing softly. They missed the stage. Aye, they did, the two of them. When your grandfather became very ill, your Por Por took such good care of him. She bathed him, fed him and cleaned him up when he made a mess. She didn't complain or go out much. When I went to the market, she'd ask me to buy her some pork bones. Then she'd make him a nourishing soup and give a bowl to me. In the blink of an eye, they're both gone. Aye… that's life, isn't it? Good friends grow fewer as we grow older.'

We were both silent. The orange flames had gone out of the sky by now, and the evening light was turning dishwater grey.

'Auntie, I better clean up,' I said. 'I'm leaving the altar out here overnight for the paint to dry.'

'Well then, I'll leave you two to clean up.'

She went into her flat and closed her door.

In the gathering greyness before the lights came on in the corridor, I stood with the two mugs of chrysanthemum tea in my hands, acutely aware of a nervous humming in the distant traffic and Meng's silent presence on my doorstep. He had uncorked the bottle of paint thinner and was pouring some of it onto a rag. He wiped one of the brushes with the soaked rag and cleaned off the black paint with sheets of newspapers. When he had finished cleaning the brush, he laid it on a clean sheet and picked up another brush. He did not look up. Neither did he speak. His manner was focussed and concentrated. He worked without stopping till he had cleaned the three brushes. By then the fluorescent lamps in the corridor had come on. His hands were coated with thinner and black paint, and he was using several sheets of newspapers to clean his hands. I put down the mugs inside and came out with a clean rag but he didn't take it. He was gathering all the soiled newspapers from the floor, bunching them up and stuffing them into a large garbage bag.

'You better come inside to wash up.'

I had spoken without thinking. But once the words were out, the thought of him inside my flat brought a sudden fluttering. I could sense his tension too as he followed me inside. Then he rubbed his nose, and the sight of that smudged black nose made me giggle. He looked at me, puzzled.

'You look like Monkey King with your blackened nose. Better clean up.'

'Nose was itchy.' I heard him mutter as he followed me into the kitchen.

I hoped I had not offended him. At the sink, I handed him a bar of soap, a clean rag and the bottle of paint thinner. While he washed, I used another rag to clean my hands. We stood next to each other at the sink and did not talk. When his hands looked clean enough, he washed his face and I handed him a clean towel. Then he stood aside for me to wash at the sink.

When I had finished washing, he was standing with his back to me looking out of the kitchen window. I sensed his nervousness, and it made me nervous too. His straight back looked tense. His mood was so different from earlier on when we were talking to Auntie Soh. I wondered if I should invite him to sit and have a cup of tea. I stood next to him and for a while we watched the gathering shadows. He didn't seem eager to talk. So I didn't say anything. The kitchen had grown dark, so I touched a switch. The lights came on, and he turned around, and brushed against me.

'Sorry.' His voice tensed, his face flushed.

I thanked him for his help. 'Would you like a cup of Auntie Soh's chrysanthemum tea?'

'If it's not too much trouble.'

He sounded so formal. It made me more nervous. I led him to the living room that looked bare without the altar. Piles of my books were on the floor. He sank into one of the two armchairs and closed his eyes. His face looked so tired. I decided to let him sleep on, and took my time warming the chrysanthemum tea on the gas stove instead of the microwave. He jerked awake when I brought out the tea and biscuits.

'I'm sorry. I must've dozed off.'

He sounded less formal now. His apologetic tone gave me confidence to ask what he had been doing to get himself so tired.

'Tony hadn't been well. I was up with him the last few nights. I managed to catch some sleep this morning but then this afternoon I had to teach a class in the community centre.'

'Opera skills?'

'That's all I know.'

'It's valuable cultural work.'

He took off his glasses and stared at me, his dark eyes clouding with doubt. I thought of complimenting him on his dedication but decided to say nothing in the end. His passion for opera, or obsession as I called it then, had been a huge thorn between us.

'*Aiyah!*' he jumped up from his seat. 'I left your porridge in the corridor. No, no! You don't get up. I'll get it.' He rushed out of the flat.

When he returned with the plastic bag, he pointed to my door and gate. 'Do you always leave them unlocked?'

'Only if I've friends with me. And you're the first to visit.'

'Really?' His tired face broke into a smile. 'This calls for a little celebration. I should've brought wine.'

'No need. As the saying goes – dining with a bosom friend, plain porridge is more than enough,' I said.

'I think the original saying goes like this: Drinking wine with an intimate friend a thousand cups are too few. Talking to someone with no affinity half a word is far too many.'

We were speaking in Cantonese, the language of our youth and his opera art. Listening to his beautifully enunciated speech as he recited the two lines, something had stirred inside me. A feeling I had first felt when he recited Su Dongpo's poetry that night – an ache deep in the pit of my gut and heart. A feeling that had been buried deep in my being and left for dead for years was stirring to life again. Perhaps it was the mood of the evening. The simple pleasure of sitting quietly at the kitchen table with a friend, sharing the bowl of porridge he had brought. At that moment so moved was I by the poetry and clarity of his Cantonese I wanted to cry. His idiomatic turn of phrase and the rhythm of his words as he spoke, his enunciation and intonation, was making me feel how much I had missed all those years when such richness in Cantonese used to surround me as a child, when the idioms, the proverbs and witty play with words was part of my daily conversations. All that had been replaced by the English I had learnt and absorbed in school, and spoke at work and home throughout my married life. And a deep sense of loss brought tears to my eyes.

'Yin. Did I say something wrong?'

I shook my head. I could not speak.

'I should leave,' he said and stood up.

'No, please.' I placed a restraining hand on his.

He sat down again.

'I felt... it's like... I lost one of my senses,' I tried to explain. 'My hearing or speech... what I'd lost... the words, the vocabulary I had taken for granted in my youth. ... I need to... need to relearn the literary Cantonese I used to hear in the opera troupe.'

He finished his drink, and put down his cup before he turned to me.

'Yin, I never thought I'd hear you say this. I owe you an apology. All these years, well, all the years since I was in Hong Kong, I'd thought you hated Cantonese opera after... after you went to university and met...' He paused. Took up his cup and seeing it was empty, put it down again.

'Wrong, wrong, wrong,' he sang softly as though something had reminded him of an opera. 'I was wrong.' He looked at his cup for a long while. Then murmuring 'I was wrong', he looked up and smiled. 'There are many like you in Singapore. Those who join my classes in the community centre, they too wish to reclaim the treasure they had lost. It's not too late. Never too late to relearn a language. You're very welcome to join my amateur opera troupe.'

As he spoke about the troupe he started in the community centre, his face relaxed and he looked at ease. 'Come and join us. It's once a week.'

'You're not serious.'

'I am. You'll hear the Cantonese you're used to. Before you know it, it'll come back. Unlike some of my students who had learnt Mandarin in school. They read the words in Mandarin and then try to say them in Cantonese. So they struggle to get the pronunciation right. You won't have this problem.'

I smiled but said nothing.

'My troupe needs help with English surtitles for our year-end production. Our previous English translations are stiff. The Cantonese poetry was drained out of them.'

'Are you serious, Meng? I can't read Chinese as well as you.'

'But your English is far better than mine. Look. If we team up, surely we will come up with something better. If Cantonese opera is to survive in Singapore we need to broaden the audience base. We need good surtitles to attract the young and the English educated. My troupe needs help. If you help us... you and I working together...' Voice waxing with vigour and wistfulness at times and a host of other fleeting feelings in his eyes as he spoke.

I couldn't say no. In truth, my heart had leapt up to say yes! He had dropped his earlier formal façade. We talked for a long time, truly talking at last. And it was not the polite inane talk of acquaintances asking about each other's health and activities.

By the time he left, it was late. Almost eleven. I sat in the armchair he had sat on for a long time. I didn't know what to make of the tumultuous feelings in my heart. I didn't know what to think.

The next morning I stood in the doorway. As I waited for him I felt my youthful heart ticking inside a middle-aged body. And I laughed at myself. Before he left last night, he had promised to come by and give me a hand to carry the black altar into the flat. It was gleaming in the bright morning sun. I thought of how the black would highlight the white porcelain statue of the Goddess of Mercy, and the sea green robes of the God of Literature. And how I would arrange my volumes of the English translations of *Romance of* the *Three Kingdoms* and *Dream of the Red Chamber* next to them, and place *Journey to the West* next to the Monkey King standing on one leg holding his iron rod high above his head in one hand and scratching his ear with the other. An iconic pose immortalised by generations of artists, sculptors and opera actors. The year I turned eighteen, before I went to university and long before I met Robert, I had dragged Meng to the temple of the Monkey King in Tiong Bahru.

'Por Por said he's a saint. A *shen*.'

'And you believe her? Monkey King is just a character in *Journey to the West*. And you believe he's a *shen*?'

'Por Por said he had answered people's prayers. Why do you think they built this temple to honour him if he's just a figment of a writer's imagination? Come on.' I pulled him inside. 'Wu Cheng'en wrote that Monkey King saved the holy monk and learnt the Holy Scriptures on that journey.'

'*Chieh!* He's the author. He made that up.'

'*Shhh!* We're in his temple. The Jade Emperor bestowed on Monkey King the title of Sun Wukong, Lord of Emptiness and Seeker of Truth. So he's a *shen*. It's folk history.'

'Enough of history! Our future is more important!'

Laughing, he pulled me out of the temple into the dazzling sunshine. Blinded by the sudden brilliance of the noonday sun, I shut my eyes against the fierce white glare. He planted a kiss on my lips. All of a sudden the feelings in my breast were so intense and so mixed, the future was too dazzling to contemplate. Everything had happened very fast. One minute we were in the dark smoky temple. The next we were soaring into the blinding noonday sun and he was holding me in his arms.

I was surprised that I could still remember that long ago day in Tiong Bahru, and the young man with the ponytail boldly kissing me in full sight of passers-by. And now his ponytail was gone. The young man was no longer young. He had a greying crew cut and wore rimless glasses. And I had thudded back into the present, feeling heavy bodied and a little unnerved. Yet what was there to be nervous about? All he did was to ask me to join his opera troupe and work on surtitles with him. So don't you go getting ideas and imagining all sorts of things, Xiu Yin, I chided my overactive imagination. After so many years apart you scarcely know this man of many moods. He was just being kind. Should I make some excuses and decline?

I looked down the corridor towards the stairs and lift landing. He might not be in the mood to turn up this morning. The sun had already reached the altar. The earlier I brought it in the better. I rolled up my sleeves and went out to the corridor and started to shift the altar.

'*Whoa!* Wait! Wait! Madam Impatient, let me do it. Did you doubt I wouldn't keep my word this morning?' he laughed as he lifted one end of the altar and I the other end. 'Slowly, slowly, now heave!'

39

Dearest Butterfly. Time has flown past like a sparrow. I hardly have time to myself. Very little time to sleep and even breathe on some days. Everyone around me is so full of energy. Everyone in the troupe is an opera old hand. So experienced in what they do. Compared to them I am a baby bird still learning to fly. But I am happy.

Our three-storey tenement is filled with music and singing once again. The front hall is used for rehearsals again. And though the hall is small, everyone is getting used to performing in the confined space. A few words, a flag or two, coupled with the anxious booming of drums will transform the hall into a vast battlefield. In another scene, the plaintive music of the erhu will turn the hall into a quiet courtyard in the secluded Buddhist monastery where the Chief Minister's wife, her daughter and their maid are taking refuge from warring bandits.

Wah Jai is full of smiles. He is in charge of the orchestra and the selection of scripts. For our first performance he has chosen *Romance in the Western Chamber* (西厢记).

'The war is over. People want to laugh,' he declared. 'So no tragedy. No grand history. But a romance. A secret love blossoming in the western chamber of a Buddhist monastery in the hills. Between a poor scholar and the chief minister's daughter. Helped by the audacious maid, their love blossoms under the very nose of the arrogant chief minister's wife. The audience will enjoy it. The opera has love, beauty, intrigue and humour. It will bring the crowds.'

I have never heard Wah Jai speak so confidently and eloquently before. I know then that he too had been secretly yearning to play the music for a full opera with his erhu. I am to be the young scholar. Mei Lai will be the chief minister's daughter, and Mei Fong will be her clever maid. Master Wu, our director, will also take on the role as the chief minister's wife. I am looking forward to performing it. I have been studying and memorising the script, going through each scene to understand the scholar's feelings and sing his wonderful arias of love. My desire and doubt battle each other daily especially when I rehearse with Mei Lai. Will my singing be as good as hers? Will my acting match hers? Doubts assail me. I am a novice. Dearest Butterfly, spread your wings over me. Watch me. Protect me. I lack experience. I have never acted with a woman.

ဆ— craft

Enough! I want to yell

I have had enough of Wah Jai's nonsense! How am I to rehearse properly? How am I to even sing with feeling if I have to attend to the baby whenever she bawls? Oh Gods of Opera, help!

This morning we were rehearsing in the front hall when all of a sudden came the baby's wails. At the very moment when I was singing the most important aria in the scene declaring my love to the chief minister's daughter. What could I do? I ignored the wailing in the attic, and sang on. But the persistent crying broke my mood. Destroyed the lyrical poetry of the scholar's words. The music of the erhus and flutes stopped. The orchestra fell silent. Wah Jai had ceased to play his erhu. He put down his instrument and dashed up the stairs as though he had two perfect legs instead of a limp. The musicians, laughing, got up and went outside for a smoke. They are getting used to these interruptions. But I am not! I sat down. I refused to go upstairs. *Let the bloke feed and clean his child.* I was seething inside. With just two weeks before the show's opening, these frequent breaks are getting on my nerves.

I picked up the script and studied the aria I was singing. It is not that I do not know the words by heart! Not that I do not love my daughter. I simply want to rehearse without these feeding breaks. But Wah Jai is such an ass. He does not understand. He insists a mother should nurse her baby.

'But I need to rehearse the scene from beginning to end,' I argued with him last week.

'You know it already,' he said. 'And Mei Lai knows it. The orchestra knows it. The melody is familiar to all of them. And I have memorised the score. You have memorised the words. The musicians and I can return to the part where we stopped and start again. Why can't you do it? Is opera singing so very special?'

I had no answer. How to describe to this man the passion that creeps into a singer's heart when she is performing an aria with such depth of feeling that her heart feels like breaking? How to explain the working of the heart when strong emotions are stirred by the fusion of poetry, song and music? And in my case, by the added novelty and thrill of performing with another young woman whose presence has made everything fresh and youthful as spring?

In the end it was Master Wu who answered Wah Jai's question.

'Opera is indeed a special art. Cantonese opera, the opera of Southern China, is singing, acting, music, poetry, movement and dance. At any one time the singer has to do a combination of two or three of these elements. There are set movements for the expression of grief and joy and love that a beginner must learn from the masters of the art. But if she repeats the set gestures mindlessly as she sings, her actions will be stiff as a puppet's, and her performance will be mediocre.'

Wah Jai came limping down the stairs cradling the baby in his arms.

'Choi Wan was rolling in her poo,' he announced. 'I have cleaned her up and changed her diaper. Time for her feed.'

How righteous he looked as he thrust his daughter into my arms. I walked up the stairs with my baby, no longer the lovelorn scholar in the monastery now. Not even Wong Mun Loong the opera singer. I was once again Wah Jai's obedient wife, and his child's devoted mother. And I HATED IT!

Dearest Butterfly, I miss you! Only you can understand how I feel.

80 — 03

I did it, Butterfly.

I reclaimed my opera performer status!

Wah Jai will never know what happened between Mei Lai and I. After three years of serving three men during the war, it was so good to have another woman on my side.

Yesterday Mei Lai came up to the attic. She saw me seated on the floor trying to spoon some thin gruel into the baby's mouth. Choi Wan was wailing and flailing her little arms. Each time I gave her the spoon she turned away her head. I didn't know what to do. I had already rubbed my breasts and squeezed my nipples. But the drops that seeped out were pathetic. My poor child was losing weight. Mei Lai's soft hand tapped my shoulder.

'Let me,' she whispered, and took the baby into her arms.

Cradling the struggling wailing bundle firmly in one arm, she pulled up her blouse and bra with the other. Dipped a finger into the rice gruel and coated her nipple with the gruel all the while cooing and rocking and humming as she offered her breast to Choi Wan. Soon my little daughter was sucking her pale brown nipple. Still humming softly and rocking my baby, Mei Lai dipped her finger into the rice gruel again, and smeared her nipple again before letting my baby suckle her again. She repeated this again and again till a regular rhythm rocked and lulled the child's sucking, till the rice gruel was finished, and Choi Wan, satiated, had fallen asleep.

'I watched my mother do this during the war when she ran out of milk for my baby brother,' she smiled shyly, her face flushing as she handed my daughter over to me. My fingers brushed against her breast as I took over Choi Wan, and there was a quick intake of breath. I couldn't tell if it was hers or mine. I could hardly breathe. The accidental act seemed to have shifted my universe all of a sudden. I felt giddy as if the very air between us had changed as I watched her re-fasten her bra and pull down her blouse. That done, she looked up at me.

'There is no milk in your breasts, Sister Kam Foong,' she said, her voice as steady as though she had just said 'there is no fish in your basket'.

On hearing that plain-speaking voice, I felt the heat in my face receding and my heartbeat slowed.

'I don't know what else to do than give her the rice gruel. We cannot afford to buy cow's milk for her until we perform.'

'Even if you have enough milk, you cannot feed your child when the show is on. Men do not think of such things. We women in the theatre have to consider these things. A baby can affect not only your performance but also the entire troupe's performance. You are the *xiu sung*; I am the *fah dan* in the troupe. The success of the opera depends on us. The troupe knows it. Master Wu knows it, but he is the grandfather. How can he tell you not to feed his granddaughter?'

I wanted to weep. Such knowledge in one so young. And so divine. Her hand rested on mine.

'Sister Kam Foong. I will speak plainly with you. If we are to partner each other in this opera, and future operas, we have to be frank about all things that affect the both of us. And the show. We, women in opera, face more problems than the men when we become mothers. The great women in opera are usually childless, single or divorced. That aside,' a tiny smile playing on her lips, 'I have good news. My sister has found out a tenant here... Mrs Tang, poor woman. She has just lost her newborn. She has milk. Lots of milk. Let her be your baby's wet nurse. You have to concentrate on the show. This is your first full-length opera. And my first performance since the war. Do or die, we must succeed.'

The next day when Choi Wan wailed, I raced up the stairs. When Master Wu wanted to rehearse without me, I yelled from the landing.

'Sifu! Wait for me!'

Minutes later I ran down. Wah Jai frowned.

'Back so fast? Where is our daughter?'

'With Mrs Tang.' I faced him, and in a calm voice I said, 'Mrs Tang will be Choi Wan's wet nurse from now on. She has had several children and she has milk. She knows what to do.'

Then before he could recover from his shock, I turned to Master Wu and the orchestra.

'From now on we have to rehearse from beginning to end. This is my first full-length opera. My first performance with Mei Lai. And the first show of our troupe. Do or die, we must succeed.'

'Do or die we *will* succeed!' the troupe shouted.

'Start again! No stopping!' Master Wu grinned at me. 'We open in a week!'

ဆ—ဗ

SUCCESS!

It was full house every night. Wah Jai was grinning from ear to ear. His selection, *Romance in the Western Chamber*, was a great success. And I sprouted wings. I performed my first full-length opera. Sung eight solo arias and ten duets with Miss Mei Lai. My heart is full to overflowing.

On opening night the villagers from Ow Kang alone filled half the theatre. After the show, they came running to the stage. What a surprise! Wah Jai and I were so happy to see them.

'How can we not come to support our opera star from Ow Kang?' Liang Pek shouted, shaking Wah Jai's hand up and down.

'You know? When we saw your face in the papers, we said isn't she that *gock-gock* girl who sang to the chickens and pigs?' Liang Soh laughed.

'*Gock, gock, gock!*' The villagers sang and roared with laughter as they recalled my evening serenades to the animals and how the children imitated me. And the reporter in their midst lapped up their every word.

'And her husband is the erhu musician! *Aiyoh!* We were so blind! All of us had no eyes. Two dragons among us and we treated them like worms.'

'No, no,' Wah Jai laughed. 'Don't blame yourselves. Blame the war!'

Before the villagers left, Mei Lai and I sang a special duet for them to the strains of Wah Jai's erhu. And they were so happy they kept on clapping till the reporter asked them to pose for a group photograph with us. His report and photograph were published in all the Chinese papers the next day. And the publicity brought even more people to the theatre.

The city's hunger for entertainment after the war was palpable and the theatre was filled every night. The Great World Amusement Park management extended the troupe's performances by another week, and then to our surprise our troupe was engaged for a new opera for a longer season till the end of the year.

'You did well, Kam Foong,' Master Wu, my Sifu of little praise, grinned. What more do I want? My heart is full.

At the end of that first season, Master Wu led the whole troupe to thank the Patron Gods of Opera with a roast pig, a whole roast duck and steamed chicken, red candles and joss sticks. The next day Master Wu, Wah Jai and I with Choi Wan in my arms went to the temple to give thanks to the Jade Emperor of Heaven and our Ancestors for their protection of our little family of four.

Dearest Butterfly, that was why I have not written for so long. As you can tell, I am busy and well. You need not worry about me. Fly where you need to go. But I cannot follow.

40

I was standing on the escalator when Robert's real estate agent called. Perhaps it was the mechanism of my thumping heart then, or the state of my mind when I woke up this morning. Or simply the time of day. Or the fact that I was on the escalator going up to my ophthalmologist's office. But God knows I didn't want to be rude.

Weeks ago Robert's name had popped up suddenly in my Inbox. His email was curt.

It's obvious you no longer regard Sea Cove as home.
I will sell it.

There was no consultation. No discussion even though I am part owner of Sea Cove and it held so many memories and a large a part of my life.

When Robert had continued to live in it after the divorce, I hadn't minded. In fact I was relieved that I didn't have to discuss financial matters with him, or argue over his share or my share. It would have been life draining, and I had had enough of arguments to last me a lifetime. I was simply glad to get away. To escape, to flee from the cage that had imprisoned me for so long. I didn't want to go near Robert again. Not even on the phone or email. For all matters to do with the sale of the Sea Cove apartment I had already left word that his agent was to call my lawyer. So why was she calling me then?

I was already on the escalator in the Great World City Mall on my way to see the ophthalmologist. I was in no mood to listen, but the woman was so persistent and her voice bored into my ear like those pneumatic drills during road works. It went on and on about the mortgage and loan. The voice unsettled me. Once again memories of the years of fear and suppression and tension returned. The pain of dismantling and the fragmentation of structures, habits and relationships that had taken the better part of my youth to build cascaded into my head.

'I don't care about the bloody interest rate!' I shouted into the phone, and shoved it into my bag.

When it rang again, I switched it to silent mode. By then I had reached the clinic. I had cataract in both eyes. They had to be operated on, the ophthalmologist said. I had a morbid fear of surgery. Well, who doesn't? On hindsight I could see that it was fear and nerves that had blocked my judgement that morning. All I heard were his words, *as soon as possible.* The urgency shook me.

'Can I change my glasses first?'

'What for?'

'I would like to delay the op for a while.'

'Waste of money.'

His tone was so brusque. And dismissive. He didn't even look at me. And I was seated from just across his desk. Does the massive piece of polished wood that separated us give him such authority? Rage and hurt and I knew not what else shot through my head and down to my legs. I stood up.

'I need a second opinion.' I walked out.

The moment I stepped outside the clinic I was shocked at myself. I took a few deep breaths before taking the escalator to the ground floor. Then I walked into Starbucks, ordered a café mocha and sat down. And the rest of my limbs unwound and relaxed.

Well... I mulled over what I had done. Certainly as a patient, I had the right to seek a second opinion but did I have to be so rude to him? It's true in the past I would have obeyed authority. Let the ophthalmologist decide the fate of my eyes without question. I wouldn't have thought of seeking a second opinion. Where did this sudden decisiveness come from?

A bell sounded. I got up, collected my drink and sat down again. I took a sip of the mocha, sank into the café's armchair and started to examine my behaviour of the past several months since I renovated the flat and since I met Meng. How often I had caught myself like this, abrupt and decisive as though a rebellious young shoot had suddenly sprung out of me and grown into a hardy sapling. I took another sip of the mocha, mulling over whether I should call the ophthalmologist and apologise. But my limbs made no move. After several sips of my drink I was still seated, and my phone was still in my bag. And as I continued to sit in the armchair, I was beginning to feel rather pleased with what I had done. The guy had been arrogant after all. His tone had been so dismissive. These days, I was less and less ready to accept guilt and blame, something I would have done readily in the past. Anyway it's common sense one should get a second opinion before an operation. Consult another eye doctor. Why not call the National Eye Centre and compare the fees. I shouldn't let myself be bulldozed into making a quick decision. I took a deep breath. Picked up the phone, relieved that I could still read the small print though with some difficulty. I scrolled through Google, found the number and called the National Eye Centre. After a long wait, someone answered the phone, and I made an appointment. Then I sat back, gave myself a pat and drank my coffee while I waited for Meng. He had agreed to come and meet me for lunch. I looked at my watch. No, he wasn't late yet.

These past three months, he had been coming to my apartment two evenings a week, usually with an excerpt or song from the opera his troupe was planning to perform. We read and discussed the excerpts that he said needed English translations. We read and worked through the Chinese text phrase by phrase, line by line and, sometimes, word by word.

My grasp of literary Chinese was atrocious. But I was determined to learn, and he was a willing tutor. Sometimes on weekends he took me to the Chinese bookstores in the Bras Basah Complex, and we spent many pleasant hours together browsing through the books and old videos of Cantonese operas, stopping for tea or dim sum in the little cafés. Twice, he took me to the operas performed by troupes from Hong Kong. Sometimes on a Sunday evening he would ring, and come by with a video of a Cantonese opera, and we would watch it together and discuss it over supper.

I started to buy several Chinese-English and English-Chinese dictionaries till he stopped me.

'Slowly, Yin, slowly. No need to rush your learning.'

'Sometimes I have to check various dictionaries to see which English word would best convey the Chinese historical or cultural context of the opera text better. Since it's an aria, sound and rhythm play a part.'

'Agreed. In translating opera scripts, rhythm is sometimes more significant than being grammatical. Look at this. I think it's better to follow the original repetition and rhythm of that last line in Lu Yu's famous poem "The Phoenix Hairpin".

错，错，错！

I would translate it as Wrong! Wrong! Wrong! But a member of the troupe, an English language teacher, translated the line as, It was so wrong! Which do you prefer?'

I enjoyed these discussions with him. Sometimes in the middle of a discussion, he would recall a role he had performed in an opera and sing a few lines. Reliving that moment on stage, sometimes he recited or sang more than a few lines from the excerpt we were working on. Especially if he thought it might deepen my understanding of the scene or the nuance of an important poetic phrase since I did not know the opera's historical context. Sometimes after he had sung part of an aria in Chinese, I would read the surtitles in English.

Often our conversation strayed beyond the complexities of translation and touched on the personal. We swapped anecdotes of our teenage years together, laughed at each other's youthful foibles and forgave each other what we did in the past. Then like a wise old couple we skirted the dark holes in which our worms and snakes were buried, and left them locked in the heart.

'Some things are better left unsaid. I know you know,' I said.

'You know I know. Earth and Heaven know,' he laughed.

I looked forward to our evenings each week. Sometimes he surprised me when he brought over a dinner that he had cooked. And we ate it together, sitting at my kitchen table across from each other, like an old couple. After dinner, I walked with him to the community centre and sat in his opera class as an observer. He told the young men and women that he hoped one day I would join them in learning the basic skills of opera. And everyone applauded.

'Welcome, Xiu Yin *Jieh*!'

His class addressed me as 'Sister' in Cantonese as though I was already part of their group.

'Come more often, Xiu Yin *Jieh*. Teacher Meng smiles more often when you're here!'

'Nonsense!' he said, and the whole class laughed.

I drained the last of my mocha. Ordered an iced tea and looked around the mall. Still no sign of Meng. We had been working on the English surtitles for a scene in *Madam White Snake* for the past few weeks, and he said he would treat me to lunch. I looked around again. Sadly the Great World City Mall, once the site of Singapore's grandest amusement park, had little to remind us of its grand operatic history. Known to the Cantonese as *Dai Sai Gai* (大世界) and to the Hokkiens and Teochews as *Tua Seh Gai*, the Great World was famous for its many theatres built for different types of Chinese opera. It was especially famous for the large theatre dedicated to Cantonese opera where my grandparents' Golden Phoenix Cantonese Opera Troupe had soared to glory. And where Meng and I had performed in *Madam White Snake* when we were children.

I took another sip and glanced at my watch. He was late. It was past noon. Fierce sunlight was coming through the glass pane. Long queues were snaking towards the ticket booths of the theatre. Chatting housewives with their husbands and children in tow. Rich madams in embroidered *kebayas* and *tai-tais* in silk *qipaos*, their arms braceleted in sparkling gold. Next came the *ma-jiehs* with folded black umbrellas tucked under their arms, frowning at the giggling shop girls flirting with the young men manning the booths and entrances. Above the crowd, red satin banners with gold tassels swung in the breeze. Opera stars painted on giant billboards were lit up by electric bulbs. The opening show of the Golden Phoenix Cantonese Opera Troupe was *The Legend of Madam White Snake.*

Meng and I, dressed as tortoises, were prancing with the prawns and crabs and other sea creatures outside the theatre. We held each other's hand as we weaved in and out of the applauding crowd.

'Children! Quickly now! Quickly! Go in, go in.'

Grandfather shepherded all the sea creatures into the backstage.

Stagehands hurried past, giving the pulleys and coulisses a last-minute check. Actors in white undergarments sat in front of their mirrors putting on the last touches to their painted faces. Others put on their wigs and stuck jewelled hairpins into their hairpieces.

I ran to Por Por's corner, and stopped at the white chalk line that marked off her quiet corner from the rest of the busy backstage. Dressed in the male actor's white undergarments she was sipping her tea and going over her script in front of a small electric fan. When she did not look up at me, I knew then I must not disturb her. She was no longer my grandmother. No longer my Por Por. No longer the opera artiste. Her hair was already pulled up and twirled into a scholar's knot. Her painted face was that of a young man with the air and mannerism of a scholar as she sat in the cane chair with her right ankle resting on her left knee. Upon her feet were the black high platform wooden shoes she wore to give her the height and stature of a man. In a little while she would put on the scholar's blue robe and black cap. When the drums and cymbals sounded she would walk through the *Fu Doh Muen*, the actors' invisible doorway, and stride out onto the stage transformed into Xu Xian, the young scholar who fell in love with the beautiful Miss White Snake.

I ran back to join Meng and the other children behind the stage curtain. We peeped out at the hundreds streaming into the theatre filling up the seats. All the seats in the front rows were taken by the rich *tai-tais* except for one seat in the far corner. That seat was often empty. Sometimes a woman sat in it. She was always dressed in black.

'Tortoise! Tortoise!' The children in the audience screamed when they saw us. We quickly withdrew from the curtains.

The opening hour was drawing near. The excitement in the backstage was palpable. This was opening night, so everyone in the backstage must be calm. Opera folks were very finicky and superstitious about opening night. Any mishap on the opening night would affect the entire season and earnings of the troupe.

This morning to open the season, Master Wu as the head of the troupe, Por Por the *xiu sung*, and Grandfather the leader of the orchestra, as well as the guest diva from Hong Kong, Miss Mei Lai the principal *fah dan*, had led the troupe in a grand ritual.

'Stop giggling!' Grandfather scolded us. 'Pray properly, children, so that accidents will not happen. And don't forget to clean your face, clean off the makeup. Once a man acting the Monkey King had died. He was so drunk he fell asleep without taking off his makeup. At dawn his soul could not return to his body because he looked like a monkey.'

We shivered and fell silent.

Master Wu lit the pair of special red candles and joss sticks, and poured a generous libation of wine. The entire troupe knelt and kowtowed three times to the Patron Gods of Opera.

The big gong sounded once. A signal the opera was starting soon. The actors took their positions.

On the other side of the curtain, the audience settled down. A stagehand huddled us, the sea creatures, into the wings where we could see the stage without being seen by the audience.

The big gong sounded a second, then a third time.

The stage lights came on. Melodic music of the erhus, pipas and yangqin filled the theatre as the velvet curtains slowly parted revealing a river scene with weeping willows sweeping the riverbanks. In shimmering white silks the beautiful Miss White Snake, played by Miss Mei Lai, glided in, accompanied by Miss Green Snake radiant in sequinned green. Gliding and sashaying, the two women dancing, their long white water sleeves waving so gracefully that their white sleeves seemed to float in mid-air as the pair sang a duet rejoicing in their one-thousand-year-old friendship and successful transformation into human form.

'Hai! Hai! Hai! Boatman! Haiiii...!' Miss Green Snake trilled.

As the music of the erhus, flutes and pipas rose and fell like the river's swell, an old boatman played to great comic effect by Master Wu came rowing onto the stage. On board his imaginary boat was the handsome scholar Xu Xian carrying a rolled-up umbrella under his arm. On seeing the popular pair, the audience broke into loud applause.

'Hai! Boatman! Over here! Over hereeee!' Miss Green Snake sang, her high-pitched notes rising to the beams.

'I hear thee, Miss! Coming over! Overrrrrr!!!' The old boatman's sung reply reverberated round the theatre like echoes in the craggy mountains of China. Then the music of the whole orchestra swelled with the riotous beating of drums and clashing cymbals.

Rowing as fast as he could, the boatman and the scholar mimed the violent rocking of a boat caught in the river's rapids. Swaying from side to side, now backward, now forward, jerking so violently at times that the poor scholar Xu Xian had to cling to the old boatman's white beard for dear life.

'Bravo!' The audience roared their approval.

The drums dying down, the lyrical strains of a flute and pipa accompanied the boat as it glided into calm waters and reached the riverbank. The two women stepped one dainty foot after the other into the gently rocking boat. Miming the actions of four people crowding into the tiny boat, Miss White Snake stood close to Xu Xian and the pair exchanged shy glances and greetings. Accompanied by the flute and erhu Xu Xian sang a solo lamenting the vicissitudes of a poor scholar's lonely life in a grass hut, studying by the light of a lamp.

A sudden burst of trembling cymbals signalling a sudden shower, the music was rising with the wind. Xu Xian swiftly opened his umbrella and held it over Miss White Snake. Graciously, she sang her thanks as yangqin and erhu played. Then a sudden rocking of the boat forced her to hold on to Xu Xian's arm. With great gallantry he held her waist as flutes fluttered like twittering birds in the trees. The couple sang a melodious duet under Xu Xian's umbrella, rejoicing in the freshness of spring rain and the good fortune that an unexpected encounter brings. Like two mandarin ducks swimming on the river Miss White Snake's lyrical soprano set off Xu Xian's rich mellifluous tone, and the pair rejoiced in the arrival of spring and the awakening of new feelings in young hearts.

The boat reached land. The shower had stopped. Xu Xian closed his umbrella and everyone brushed off the raindrops with their sleeves and went ashore. Laughing with merriment, the mischievous old boatman and Miss Green Snake started to sing.

'For here is a match made in heaven, won't you say? Won't you say? They should marry, shouldn't they? Shouldn't they?'

'Well, well, well! The young man and young miss are so shy. Let this old grey beard be their matchmaker.'

The old boatman untied the length of red cloth wound around his waist and gave one end to Xu Xian and the other end to Miss White Snake. The young couple, shy and happy, sang their thanks, bowing first to Heaven, then to Earth, and to each other as thunderous applause filled the theatre.

And the red velvet curtains closed.

41

'So sorry! So sorry! Did you fall asleep waiting for me?'

Meng hurried into the cafe and sat down, mopping his brow with a large cotton handkerchief of light blue checks. Just like the kind my grandfather used to carry. It was so 1960, and I liked him all the more for it. So few men these days kept a well-pressed handkerchief in their trouser pocket to save the environment instead of using a packet of tissue.

'Relax. I wasn't asleep. Just dreaming.'

'Good, good. Well then, let's go.' He stood up and took a gulp of the water in my glass before we walked off. 'Never waste good water. My sister was late. It's her day to see to Tony's meals.'

'How's Tony today?'

'No better, no worse.'

He was walking ahead so briskly I had to run to keep up.

'The last round of chemo left him very weak. He has no appetite. Lost a lot of weight. My sister, Ling, cooks him soups. Remember her? She was late today. Then I missed the bus. I regret I didn't buy a car.'

'Aye! You could've postponed our lunch. Why didn't you call me?'

He didn't answer but walked ahead to a taxi waiting outside the mall. He opened the taxi door and waited for me to get in to the backseat. Then to my surprise, he went around and took the front seat next to the driver.

'Back to Jin Swee,' he said to the young driver, and turned to me. 'Meet Mr Hor Kah Leong. Taxi driver by day, Cantonese opera star by night.'

The young man laughed. 'Don't listen to him, madam. Uncle Meng is joking. He's my Sifu. I'm just his opera student. An amateur.'

'Kah Leong's father was in your grandparents' troupe.'

'Oh. We're family then,' I said.

Kah Leong's laughter was a rich baritone. 'Uncle Meng promised me a surprise if I cancelled a customer and drive him here. So you are the surprise. I'm very glad to meet you, Auntie Xiu Yin. My father always spoke very fondly of the Golden Phoenix Cantonese Opera Troupe. Very proud to have worked with your grandparents.'

Kah Leong dropped us back in Jin Swee and I thought Meng would take me to the coffeeshop for lunch. Instead he said, 'Hurry. My sister Ling and Tony are waiting to meet you.'

I was surprised. He had not said anything earlier. I followed him into the lift. When we reached his flat, he opened the door and called out.

'Tony! I've kept my promise! Look who's here!'

In the living room Tony was lying with eyes closed on a hospital bed. He opened his eyes and smiled. Lunch was set on a table next to him.

'Please make yourself at home, Xin Yin!' His sister called from the kitchen.

'Hello, Ling! Hi, Tony.'

'Hi, Spatula Face,' Tony grinned.

'He's been waiting to call you Spatula Face ever since Meng told him you've come back to live here.' Ling laughed as she set down her tray on the table. She had brought out four bowls of soup.

'Hey, you said you'd finish the pork bone soup if I bring her. She's here. Yin, here's your soup. Let's tuck in.'

Meng pulled out a chair for me and sat on a stool next to me. Confident and at ease.

'Here's my sister pouring her heart into cooking this soup and Tony wouldn't drink it. Oh no, he wouldn't until I bring you. The man is still as wilful as always. Still bullying this young brother.'

'What rot! Don't listen to his young brother nonsense, Yin. It's him who drives Tony and me up the wall with his opera singing. That's why Tony sleeps all the time,' Ling laughed.

Tony sat up with Meng's help. Propped against his pillows, he was smiling and pointing to the soup. Meng handed him a bowl and spoon, and signalled we should all drink our soup together with Tony. I was pleased with the lack of formality. I was not treated as a guest but as part of his family. Just like in the old days when we used to run in and out of each other's home and eat our meals at each other's tables.

The living room had a messy homeliness. Beside the hospital bed, there was a sofa of well-worn leather, a shelf with stacks of DVDs, a tv set and a video player by the wall. We ate at the small table next to Tony's bed by the window, which had a view of blue sky, trees and greenery. Above us an old ceiling fan was turning slowly with a regular creak. Time seemed to slow down as we ate and chatted about old times, their noodle stall, the theatre and opera. At the end of our simple meal of steamed fish, soft green spinach and rice, Ling brought out a large plate of cold slices of red watermelon for our dessert. We ate the melon with our hands, letting the red juices run down our chins, laughing at the mess we made, and left the green rinds on our plates.

'It's been a very long time since I've done this,' I sighed. 'I used to cut watermelon into cubes and eat them with a fork.'

'*Waah!* So fussy *meh!*'

The three siblings laughed at my pernickety middle-class ways, and I accused them of ganging up against me. Then Tony lay down, and Meng and I cleared the table while Ling went into the kitchen to boil water and make a pot of Chinese tea. We left Tony in the living room to rest while the three of us chatted in the kitchen, keeping our voices low as we did the washing up. I felt very comfortable drying dishes at the sink with Meng and catching up with his sister. And as we spoke in hushed voices, it struck me then that these were the people I grew up with, the people I outgrew and left, and like a salmon I had come back at last to where I grew up.

The three of us returned to the living room with the pot of hot tea and cups. Tony opened his eyes and tried to sit up.

'May I?'

He let me help him as Meng watched. Gently I placed a pillow behind his back and helped him to sit up and lean back.

'Thanks,' Tony gave me a smile. 'My brother said you're writing the English surtitles for *Madam White Snake*. Any favourite scenes?' he asked, his voice raspy with the effort for such a long speech.

'The highlight for me is the flooding of the Abbot's temple.'

'Tell me. I… haven't… seen the opera.'

'Oh Tony, you've got to get well and see Meng's staging of it.'

'I'd love to. Can't prom…mise,' he coughed.

His cough sounded hard and must be painful for him. Ling tried to rub his chest but he pushed her away. 'Des…describe it to me.'

'Ah well. Imagine an empty stage with a painted backdrop of blue waves. The drums and cymbals are sounding the battle cry. Children dressed as tortoises, crabs and prawns rush onto the stage, rolling and somersaulting.'

'*Attackkkkkk!* Tidal Waves! Flood the temple!' Meng yelled and joined me in the telling. 'Madam White Snake's high soprano cry sent out the Tidal Waves dressed in blue, brandishing long swathes of blue cloths and blue flags. Stagehands with kungfu skills leapt and somersaulted over these cloths and flags as the booming drums kept up a loud rhythmic beat.'

'Meng and I were tortoises when we were children. Together with the crabs and prawns we tumbled and rolled across the stage floor attacking the Abbot's temple walls. Fight! Fight! Children in the audience shouted to us. The Abbot had separated the scholar Xu Xian from his beloved wife, Madam White Snake,' I said.

Meng snatched up the yellow bath towel on Tony's bed and declared he was the Abbot waving his saffron cloak with the red brick design. He stood up on my chair and sang in his loud baritone.

'*Ocean and Earth are in turbulence!*

The honourable scholar Xu Xian has been seduced by a white snake! We have to save himmmmmm!'

'Bravo!' Ling and I applauded him.

Waving his saffron cloak, he turned to Ling and sang.

'*You vile snake! You have crossed the boundary between beast and man! Punish you I must! I must!!!*'

The air in the room shook. There was incredible power and passion in his singing. Things changed. The yellow towel became the saffron robe. The ruler held high in his hand turned into the Abbot's sacred staff.

'The Abbot holding his staff high above his head brought it down upon Madam White Snake. Wounded, she fell,' he said.

Ling sat on the floor.

'The other monks formed a wall behind their Abbot and fought off the Tidal Waves,' I continued. 'The stage lights dimmed. Defeated, the tortoises and other sea creatures retreated with the Tidal Waves. Madam White Snake coiled in pain on the stage floor. Wounded and alone on the darkened stage, she sang the heart-rending farewell aria of a wife and mother, which made the women in the audience weep.'

'*Wife! O my beloved wife!*' Meng sang as the scholar, Xu Xian, picking up the story where I left. 'Carrying their newborn son in his arms, Xu Xian rushed across the stage towards his beloved wife. But the Abbot's staff blocked him. The Abbot tore Madam White Snake away from her grieving husband and newborn son and locked her up in the Thunderous Wind Pagoda for another one thousand years.

Bleak, bleak, bleak is the silent moon in a wintry sky.
Bleak is the lonely scholar pining for his wife…'

'*Shhhhh!* Tony's asleep,' Ling whispered, getting up from the floor.

'No, please go on.' Tony opened his eyes.

Outside the flat, the sun had gone behind the angsana trees. The afternoon light had turned a neutral cool. A light breeze came into the living room, fluttering the curtains at the window. Several children from the neighbours' flats were peeping in. Ling got up and parted the curtains. She opened the door and let the children in. And they sat on the floor by the door.

'The curtains parted for the final act,' Meng went on. He threw off the yellow towel and bending slightly, he said, 'The erhus are sighing when Xu Xian came on stage. He had lost his youthful looks. His scholar's robe is drab and grey. His unkempt grey beard and the languid movements of his water sleeves showed the passage of years and underscored his poverty, grief and loss. Slow and dejected, he walked across the stage to the Thunderous Wind Pagoda. Behind him trudged his young son.'

'Meng and I took turns to act as the son in this scene, Tony. All we had to do was to wail and cry Mama! in a loud voice,' I said.

'*Ack!* I remember that wailing. I was the one who acted. But Yin! She cried real tears on the first night,' Meng grinned. 'Real crying on stage.'

'I was only six and very nervous! Kneeling in front of all those people on opening night in the Great World Theatre. Kneeling in front of the pagoda, I was thinking of all the children in my school with mothers. I was the only child without a mother. The only child who had never known her mother's scent, or heard her mother's voice, or felt her mother's arms around her. I was so sad that night. Sadness overwhelmed me in that moment when stage and life merged in my six-year-old head. I wailed for the mother I had never seen, the mother I had killed at birth. So bitterly did

I wail on that first night....' I laughed and pushed away the memory of that childhood sorrow.

'Tony, if you had been there you would have seen the children in the audience crying with Yin. Her wails were so overwhelming that opening night. Your performance was superb.'

He put his arm around my shoulders, the reassuring gesture surprising me, and took over the storytelling.

'The orchestra played louder and louder to drown out the children's cries. Cymbals clashed! Drums boomed! Lights flashed, and all of a sudden the Thunderous Wind Pagoda collapsed. Loud cheers from the audience. The music stopped. The audience held their breath. The theatre was silent as a lone erhu played. Madam White Snake emerged from the ruins of the pagoda in a white shimmer of silks.'

'Mama! I, her son, rushed into her arms!' I got into the spirit of Meng's storytelling. The two of us sang the chorus.

Mother and child, husband and wife
Embrace and reunite.
This story of their miraculous love
Has transcended boundaries.
It will live for generations to come!

'Bravo! Bravo!' Tony and Ling applauded. And so did the children sitting by the door. *'Bagus! Bagus!'*

'This is Chinese *bangsawan*,' the old Mak Cik next door told them as she herded them away. *'Bagus*, Meng,' she said in Malay 'I used to watch Chinese opera when I was a child. Every year the opera would come to Joo Chiat market.'

'Thank you, thank you!' Tony was rasping. For a moment, pure joy invaded his gaunt face and banished his pain.

We drank the strong dark Iron Buddha tea that Ling had brewed.

We were exhausted. And so was Tony. He was still rasping, trying to thank us.

'Stop it will you and listen! Such is the magic of opera. Singing, acting, music, and the audience's imagination created the performance each night,' Meng said, fanning himself with one of the paper fans he kept on the bookshelf.

'I remember that season in the Great World Theatre. Every night the Golden Phoenix Troupe was inundated with baskets of flowers and red *hong bao* stuffed with money for Por Por and Miss Mei Lai. Both were no longer young actually, yet they still had such youthful voices and thousands of fans. Aye! Those were such wonderful days, such glorious days of Chinese opera.'

His eyes had become wistful.

'The opera is so different than the movie version I saw. The movie was like soft porn,' Ling said. 'Madam White Snake and Miss Green Snake were scantily clad. No wonder some of my Christian friends condemned *Madam White Snake* as a tale of bestiality.'

'That's the bloody problem! It's the interpretation! Interpretation and adaptation destroy art and literature when there is no integrity. A change here. A change there, and the opera or play is no longer what the writer intended. That's why I want to work with original scripts. Adaptations and rewrites can be terribly dishonest sometimes.' Meng turned to me. I had never heard him speak with so much passion. 'Do you remember what Great Grandfather Wu said about *Madam White Snake*?'

'No, what did he say?'

'He said what made *Madam White Snake* so powerful and memorable is that it is not about evil snakes, or good and evil. But about love and fidelity. Her husband Xu Xian did not stop loving her even when he found out she was a snake in human form. Xu Xian remained faithful. He taught their son to love his absent mother. And the boy's love for his mother was so great that his anguished wails brought down the walls of the Thunderous Wind Pagoda. I remember to this day how Great Grandfather Wu instructed us during rehearsals. Wail as though you're wailing for your own mother, he said. Remember? That's why you wailed like that.'

'You remember everything Great Grandfather Wu taught.'

'That's… (Cough! Cough!) because he wanted to be in opera. And… and you didn't,' Tony's rasping laugh sounded painful. He looked very tired and weak.

Meng placed a finger to his lips, and gestured we should leave him and go into the kitchen.

'More tea, Yin?' Ling got up.

'Thanks, but no. It's almost five. I've been here for hours. I'd better get going. Thank you for such a lovely lunch and afternoon.'

'Come and eat with us again,' Ling said, keeping her voice low.

Meng walked up to the tenth floor with me. At my door, he suddenly asked, 'Can I come in for a while?'

'Of course, Meng. You're very welcome.'

He looked tired and spent. He sat on the sofa, hands clasped between his knees, his head bowed as though in prayer. I brought out two glasses of warm water and placed them quietly on the table next to him. Then I sat in the armchair and closed my eyes too.

After a long while, he sat up, gulped down his water and took out his handkerchief, mopped his brow and stood up.

'No, don't go yet. Rest awhile more. You are tired, Meng. That was a long performance of storytelling, acting and singing. An excellent interactive performance with full audience participation.'

An impatient wave of his hand. As though my compliments were pesky flies. But he sat down again. Drank the second glass of water, put the glass down and let out a sigh.

'An excellent performance, you say. What good is that? What use is opera? What use is music, acting, singing or any form of art? If I had trained as a nurse or a doctor, I'd be far more useful. An opera performer, what can I do for him? He won't last long. The doctor told us. Another two to three months. I've had to engage a night nurse for him this last week. Ling and I can't cope.'

'You've helped Tony forget his pain this afternoon. Stop beating yourself. Doctors and nurses are not miracle workers. Lie down for a while. Stretch out your legs. You have to teach at the CC later, don't you?'

I went into my room and took out Por Por's journal. I searched for the entries she had written during the war.

When Meng woke up from his short nap, I read out to him the words that Great Grandfather Wu said to my grandparents about preserving our arts during the Japanese Occupation.

It is in such trying times that we hold our heads high! Play our music. Tell our stories. Sing our songs. Create our myths and histories. Preserve our humanity. This is what the arts are for!

A weak smile. 'I hope we didn't tire out Tony.' He stood up. 'You've been a great partner this afternoon. Thank you. See you tomorrow.'

A peck on my cheek. And he was gone.

42

Three weeks after our impromptu performance, Tony grew worse. An ambulance took him to the hospital. The next day, another ambulance brought him back.

'Tony's wish,' Meng said when I brought lunch down to the flat.

I went down every morning after that and stayed with Meng till Ling or the night nurse came to relieve him. Tony was very frail by then. He couldn't eat except for a drop of soup or a spoonful of soft-boiled egg. Sometimes fighting through his morphine modulated pain he tried hard to join us in our conversation in a rasping disjointed way. But as the monster tormented his skeletal body more and more, he simply lay on his bed groaning in a grotesque noisy half sleep which reminded me of Por Por's last days.

Then early one morning, Meng rang. 'Tony passed away,' his voice choked.

After the funeral was over, I did not see him for several days. I thought he needed solitude and time to grieve. I stayed away.

Two weeks passed. Still there was no word from Meng. I tried to phone him. Then I went down to his flat and knocked on his door. There was no answer. I wondered if he had gone back to Hong Kong.

But if he had, why didn't he tell me before he left? Could he have gone to stay with Ling instead? With Tony gone, the flat must have felt very empty. But why didn't he come up and talk to me? I was hurt.

One evening I asked Khim at the coffeeshop if she had seen Meng.

'Oh, he came down last night. Very late. We were about to close,' she said. Pride prevented me from questioning her further.

The next day Ling phoned.

'Xiu Yin. Can you please go down and knock on my stupid brother's door? That man hasn't picked up his phone for days.'

I went down to his flat at once. Stood outside his door and dialled his mobile. I left it ringing while I kept banging on the door till I heard a husky voice shouting, 'Coming! Coming!'

The door opened. He stood by the door, a hand rubbing his head as though he had bumped hard against something. I stepped inside. He closed the door, but remained standing there, bare-chested in his pyjama pants staring disconsolately at his bare feet. He looked so forlorn I wanted to hug him. He had lost a lot of weight.

'Why didn't you call me?'

A shrug. 'I don't know what to say.'

'You don't have to say anything. Now please go and wash up. Take a shower and change.'

While he was in the bathroom, I opened the door and windows. Turned on the ceiling fan to blow out the stale air. The fan creaking with insistent regularity as I stripped the hospital bed, which had been left in the same state as it was in the living room as if Tony had just left it. Then I picked up all the empty cups and plates and brought them to the kitchen sink.

Meng came out. He had changed into a clean pair of trousers and t-shirt.

'Ah! You look better. Now go and tidy up your bedroom.'

He made his bed while I swept the floor. Like a robot, he did everything he was told, and then he washed up the pile of cups and plates in the sink, and even tidied up the kitchen while I cleaned the living room.

When we had finished, we locked up the flat, and he followed me up to my apartment. I made him sit down at my table in the kitchen and gave him a cup of coffee, a slice of buttered toast and a banana for his breakfast. Like a child he ate whatever I placed in front of him. Later while he spent the rest of the morning looking through my library, I cooked him minced pork porridge for lunch. When I told him to eat, he finished the whole bowl. Watching him wolfing down the porridge, I was surprised that he could be so obedient and I, so commanding. But he seemed happy to let me do the thinking and ordering. At least for the time being. He had other things on his mind. I did not pester him with questions during lunch the way Ling would have done. And I left him alone after lunch. While reading one of my books, he fell asleep on my sofa. If sleep was how a man grieved, I thought, then Meng was in deep grief.

I phoned Ling.

'He's fine.'

'Did he tell you?'

'Tell me what?'

'He's hiding. Hiding from us.'

'Hiding from you?'

'No, lah! Hiding from his family and relatives.'

'Why? What happened?'

'Long story. After the funeral, there was a huge uproar among us siblings. Over our parents' flat. Years ago Fred and Lai Leen were already very upset when Tony was the only one who inherited the flat after our parents passed away. Tony was the eldest son. My parents favoured him. But then Tony had no children. So Fred and Lai Leen had expected Tony to give each of us, his siblings, a share of the flat after he passed on. That would be fair. But Tony, that ingrate, gave the entire flat to Meng. It's clearly stated in his will. When those two found out, of course, they went after Meng. To tell you the truth I was very hurt and angry too. As you know, I had looked after Tony when he was so ill. Cooked him soups and all. But what can I do? The flat was Tony's and it's his decision to give to whosoever he wanted. I know Meng knew nothing about it until the lawyer told him. But that stupid man! Just because I'm angry he thinks I'm angry with him just like the others. He will not talk to me. He thinks all his siblings, including me, and our relatives are coming after him because of the will. That's why he's hiding.'

When I put down the phone, Meng was awake. He sat up, gave me a wry smile and shook his head.

'Now you know everything. A long story of sibling rivalry and jealousy. I'm tired. Will tell you my side another day.'

I didn't question him. He spent the day quietly reading and scribbling, and when he was tired he lay down on my sofa and napped. I left him in the living room and carried on with my own reading and writing in my room.

Later that evening, at my suggestion, he stayed for dinner, and after dinner, we watched the news together, and then to my surprise, he asked if he could spend the night on the sofa in the living room.

'I can't bear to go back to that hospital bed. I keep thinking of all the nights I had sat up with him before the night nurse came.'

And all those mornings and afternoons too, I thought to myself.

'Tomorrow, ring the Salvation Army to take away the bed,' I said. 'I'm sure Tony doesn't want you to mourn for him like this.'

The next day he called the Salvation Army, and spent the day in my flat again, and slept on the sofa at night again, curled on his side like a prawn. Sometimes his legs stuck out at one end of the sofa, which must be uncomfortable. But he made no mention of any discomfort when he woke up. He was very quiet and spoke little during breakfast.

On the third morning, we went down to his flat on the sixth floor after breakfast and spent the whole day cleaning the two bedrooms and then the living room, clearing out the unwanted medicines, and packing away Tony's saxophones, and bagged his clothes and other possessions for various charities. Then Meng went into his bedroom and emerged with a bag of his own clothes, a towel, toothbrush and a pile of opera scripts.

'Yin, I hate to ask but…'

I stopped him. 'You're very welcome to stay as long as you wish.'

'At least till the hospital bed and the wheelchair are removed. They said the earliest date is next Wednesday.'

'Whatever day. It doesn't matter. You can stay with me as long as you like. But I insist on one condition. Let me buy you a foldable bed.'

'No, no, the sofa is fine. It fits me. Or I can fit it,' he grinned.

'I'll place the foldable bed at one end of my bedroom,' I continued as though he hadn't spoken. I found out that was the only way I could overrule him. 'You know that my room is originally two bedrooms. It's large and air-conditioned. You'll sleep more comfortably there. The nights are very warm. And you're exhausted. You've been nursing Tony through so many months of sleepless nights while working. I want you to have a good night's sleep. A good sleep will preserve your singing voice, your agility and youth. You will live longer.'

'Madam Bulldozer!'

'Yah, yah!' I laughed.

That very evening we went to the shops to buy his foldable bed and he carried it home, that is, my home.

'For the time being, it's your home. You know where everything is, so just help yourself. I don't have to serve you.'

He stayed almost two weeks before he returned to his own flat, and to teaching his classes at the community centre. By then the two of us had gotten used to each other's habits, used to waking up early to go out for a walk at dawn. After the walk, we headed up the slope to the park where he tried to teach me tai chi. After the tai chi exercises, we returned to either his flat or mine for a leisurely breakfast. If we chose a breakfast of cereals, toast and coffee that morning we would go to my flat. If I wanted an Asian breakfast, we would buy freshly steamed *chee cheong fun* and return to his flat where he brewed coffee for both of us. Then we sat down with our chopsticks and ate the steamed rice rolls made fragrant with sesame oil, soya sauce, sweet red sauce and a liberal sprinkling of toasted sesame seeds. *Chee cheong fun* being both our childhood comfort food was like a healing balm for grief on some mornings when darkness and memories threatened to invade our breakfast conversations.

After his fortnight's stay with me, Meng continued to take refuge in my apartment intermittently throughout his family's uproar over Tony's will. There were frequent phone calls from Fred and Lai Leen or an aunt or uncle, which he refused to answer, or if he did answer, his answers were monosyllables. Sometimes a finger to his lips, he held the phone near my ear so I could hear his brother's blustery voice and Lai Leen's scolding monologues recalling past slights and injustices.

When the lawyer had completed all the paperwork, and the noise and grumblings had finally died down, Meng returned to his flat. And all at once, like a balloon, I felt deflated especially in the nights.

Throughout the troubles, he had kept in touch with his daughter, and one night, he stayed on after dinner.

'I've decided not to return to Hong Kong for the time being.'

I nodded. I didn't tell him I was relieved. I had been dreading the day, and now it wasn't going to happen. Life had already changed for us. Each morning we woke before dawn, went for a walk together along the silent Singapore River, followed by tai chi in the park and breakfast before we separated for the day. I read and wrote alone at home. I never asked what he did at home or where he went. In the evening we met for dinner. If he had no classes that evening, we might go for another walk, and then after a quick shower, take a taxi to one of the many hawker food centres that he said I should visit, and he made sure that each time we went somewhere I hadn't been before so that dinner on his good days became a kind of game to see if he could surprise me with a new place and a new dish. On those nights when he was struck low by his memories and withdrew into himself, I cooked us a simple meal at home, which he ate in silence. At such times, I left him alone.

Three times a week he continued to teach his opera classes, and twice a week he continued to read and translate opera scripts with me.

When Chinese New Year came round, he was still in mourning so we spent the fifteen days of the celebration quietly in each other's home till the visiting, eating and drinking festivities were over. Chief among the superstitions, death was like a terrible infection. Relatives, friends and neighbours stayed away. No one visited us. On our part, we didn't step into Auntie Soh's flat next door. And I noticed that this year, Auntie Soh had pasted on her front door bright red paper with auspicious greetings to ward off bad luck and welcome good fortune.

'So that's that. Superstition and myths still lurk beneath the skin of modern Singapore,' Meng laughed and pointed to the book he was reading. 'In *History of the Three Kingdoms* Lord Gwan Goong, or Guan Yu, said the important thing is to make sure that our actions whatever the intention do not harm others.'

43

After the Lunar New Year, the mornings in Jin Swee Estate were noticeably cooler, the air suggestive of moisture. At noon, the sun was no longer sharp as a knife, its glint rendered less brilliant by a covering of clouds. Pedestrians looked up at the sky, hopeful for relief after two weeks of dry brown grass.

'Even just a drizzle will cool the pavements,' I said to Auntie Soh as she watered her roses in the corridor, and I, my pots of bamboo greens.

'Rain is on the horizon, Yin. I can feel it in my old bones,' she squinted up at the columns of white clouds.

That night the sky released its pent-up heat. The rain came pouring down in sheets. In the kitchen, Meng and I were seated across from each other having dinner as usual. I got up to close the kitchen window against the torrents of slanting rain pouring down from the dark grey skies.

'That bloke should have come to Hong Kong to see me perform.'

'Who? Tony?'

He didn't answer my question, but stared out of the window at the watery lights of the apartment block opposite. Since Tony's passing and the troubles with his siblings, I had witnessed Meng's various moods when he came for dinner. Most nights he was quiet. Hardly saying a word sometimes. Other nights he would lie on the sofa in the living room after dinner reminiscing about his opera days in Hong Kong. The celebrities he had worked with, names I had never heard of. Some nights he made me laugh when he recalled the magical days of his childhood as Noodle Head and his misadventures with Tony and how they were caned together by their father.

'Our old man wielded his cane like a ringmaster...'

'What? Can't hear you.'

'I said our old man, he made us dance while our mom screamed at him, and the young ones cowed in the corner. Dared not make a sound in case he turned his attention and cane on them. He was a beast,' he growled.

Tonight his mood was dark as the thundery sky. We were eating the meal he had cooked and brought up from his apartment. He had been doing this each night since my cataract operation and we stopped going out for dinner for the time being. At his suggestion I had the op done at the National Eye Centre, and though both my eyes were better now, he continued to cook dinner for the two of us. A gift I accepted but never thanked him. To express my appreciation would have embarrassed him. I suspected he needed a reason to come up for dinner with me every night and stay the night. When he did not answer my question again, I did not press him. Now and then he would fall into a long silence when he came up, and I just let him be. With each passing night without realising it we had grown comfortable with each other's silences.

He missed Tony's presence in his flat. Yet if he were asked, he would never admit it. The two and a half years of taking care of Tony had brought him very close to his elder brother. By now his other siblings, nieces and nephews had left him alone after the arguments over Tony's will and had stopped their visits. Ling was the only one who continued to visit him occasionally. Sometimes at my invitation, she would stay for dinner with us, and I was happy to see Meng's face light up.

He was picking at his rice with his chopsticks. A few grains at a time. As if his mind was wandering somewhere faraway. Perhaps towards that faint horizon where sea meets sky, where thunderstorms and turbulence occur, and where he dreams and comes most alive when he performs. I knew by now that he had this private space inside him that none could enter, a private intersection between his inner self and the outer persona, the real and the imagined.

'But then what is the real? Who is the real person inside each of us? I don't know. The world doesn't know. Only God, the singer and lyricist know. Hahaha!' he had laughed one night when we were talking in bed.

He had told me earlier that an opera troupe from Hong Kong was coming to Singapore to perform *Madam White Snake* and they had asked him to take on the role of the Abbot again. He must be itching to reprise the role, I thought, and went on eating. His fingers were drumming on the table. A sign that he was thinking. Thinking of his brother perhaps. Missing Tony more than he cared to admit. I poured some hot pu'er tea into his cup.

He sipped the hot tea absentmindedly, his eyes staring at the runnels of rain streaming down the windowpane. He put down the cup, fished from his shirt pocket a newspaper clipping and spread it out on the dining table. It was an aerial photograph of the Guan Yin Temple standing in the middle of the flooded Yangtze River. Days of heavy storms had inundated the whole countryside in that region of China.

'Look, Yin. This is how I envisage the Abbot's scene in *Madam White Snake*. This picture of the flood will be projected onto the back of the stage. The Abbot is standing on a table against this backdrop. A lone man standing against the elements on the last remaining wall of his flooded temple. Against the music of the rising tidal waves with cymbals clashing. The drums booming! And the pipas strumming, going mad against the leaping somersaulting blue men waving long swathes of blue cloth surrounding him and the wall. And the children, the sea creatures, leaping onto the stage trying to topple the Abbot's wall.'

'What a fantastic scene!'

'The director has agreed to do it. I was so happy when he told me this morning. The one thing I regret is that Tony will not be here to see it. He did not see my performance in Hong Kong either. I was the Abbot. But he refused to come.' A bitter laugh. 'The arrogant asshole. So he was in his younger days. He was into jazz. Did you know?'

'No, but go on.'

'The saxophone was his thing. He used to laugh at my old-fashioned art. Saw himself as the modern man. He had plans. He wasn't going to sell noodles all his life, he said. Every night after helping Pa close the stall, he jumped onto his motorbike and raced down to the Blue Parrot. His girlfriend's brother was leader of the jazz band there. The guys let him play his sax during their rest periods. Sometimes they even let him play a few numbers with them or stand in for one of the musicians. On weekends he'd be jamming somewhere else.'

'Tony could have been a jazz musician?'

'If it weren't for me.'

He fell silent, still holding his bowl of rice and chopsticks. Outside, the rain had petered out to a drizzle. I finished my dinner. Took my bowl to the sink and sat down facing him to drink my tea.

'No need to tell you Tony was our Pa's favourite. The favourite eldest son. The one with the most common sense. The intelligent one. The musical one. The old man wouldn't even loan me three hundred dollars for my expenses when I went to Hong Kong. But he gave Tony several hundreds to buy a new saxophone. And he already had two! Even paid for his music lessons for years. Can you imagine how I felt when I found out? I hated my father. I hated Tony. After Pa died Tony as the eldest had to help our Ma with the noodle stall. Good, I thought, payback time. He was the one who had received all the goodies from Pa. Ling, Lai Leen and Freddy were still in school then. Tony ordered me to return home. What? To sell noodles? I refused. He yelled at me. Scolded and blasted me over the phone. Like he was my pa. Oh, so many times he yelled! But I stood firm. A good horse never returns to old pastures. I wanted to gallop forward. I had finally succeeded in getting into a good opera company in Hong Kong. I wasn't going to give it up. I had worked my butt off for years without a cent from the old man. Because Tony was always jeering at my singing Pa didn't lift a finger to help me. Said I would never succeed. And now my acting and singing were beginning to be noticed and appreciated in Hong Kong. I was getting engagements and contracts. Beginning to enjoy a modicum of success. And Tony ordered me to stop. To come home and sell noodles. The hell with him! But Ma was on his side. I was so furious. I kept cursing him. I had no patience each time he called. Jealous of the success I had worked so hard for. Damn it! And without Pa's help too. Ugly things were said between us. Ma often grabbed the phone from him and shouted at me. Countless times. I accused her of bias, of loving her eldest more. I could hear my younger siblings wailing in the background. When I shut my eyes, all I saw was chaos at home. But I couldn't shut out their screeching voices. So I sent home what money I could spare. I stayed in Hong Kong. Opera became my refuge. I was in thrall with the art. In thrall with its classical language. With the opera artiste's ability to take a lyricist's words, slip into character, and bring him alive each night. The art was so alive. And magical. Opera became my lifeblood. The theatre was my home. The troupe my family. Deep down I knew it was an illusion. But illusion was so much better than life then.'

He gulped down his tea, and was silent for a long while, picking at his food. I filled his cup. He drank without pausing to savour the fragrance of the fifteen-year-old pu'er tea that he had praised so highly when he gave it to me on my birthday.

'Did I tell you that when Tony got married, I didn't come back for his wedding?'

'No.'

'When I got married, none of the family came to Hong Kong for my wedding. Not even Ma. Not even the one who gave birth to me. And I had sent money home. When Ma died I did not come home for the funeral. I blamed Tony. I blamed him for every single thing. He and I did not speak for years. Not till he got divorced and my wife died. He came to Hong Kong for her funeral. Met my daughter for the first time. But he didn't stay with us. Aye...' A long sigh. 'Such fools we were! The two of us behaved as if we would be young forever. Alive forever. Wake up, Wong Kok Meng, wake up!'

He slapped his forehead hard like a Zen Buddhist waking himself up at an awareness retreat. I put a hand on his.

'Don't beat yourself. You came back to look after him when none of the other siblings here could do it. Tony had no children. He appreciated that you left your only daughter in Hong Kong and stayed with him till he passed away.'

'So then he gave me his flat. Should I be happy?' The look he gave me was miserable.

'Tony, wherever he is, is happy now. Most likely he was grateful that you came back to live with him. That you sacrificed more than a year of performances to look after him. As the saying goes, for a debt of flowers, a hundred years; for a debt of gratitude a thousand years of remembrance. Do you remember my first lunch with Tony? That lunch when Tony asked us to tell him about *Madam White Snake*?'

'How could I forget? That's the opera I had asked him to come and watch in Hong Kong. I told him I was performing a major role for the first time. But he didn't come. Neither did my mother. I never forgave them. Not for a long time. But you know what?' He gulped down more tea and grinned at the past. 'A good thing they didn't come to watch me. They might have jinxed me if they came. That role boosted my career. I was so successful that many were jealous of me.' Another gulp. 'What excellent pu'er tea.'

'You gave me the pu'er.' I was glad his mood had changed. 'But coming back to that lunch, Tony must've known he wouldn't last long. That's why when you performed the Abbot's part for him with that yellow towel he was very moved. He had tears in his eyes. Did you realise that?'

'How could I not?' A weak smile on his lips. '*Madam White Snake.* What a load of heartaches! The trouble that opera gave me.'

'Me too.'

'You too?' And he waited for me to go on.

But I was already regretting my outburst. 'It's nothing,' I said.

He reached over and took my hand in his. 'Look here. For months, I've been pouring into your ears every night. The least you can do is to pour something back into mine. Fair? Madam?' He gave my hand a squeeze, his hand warm, and his eyes loving.

'It's just a memory. Just Robert,' my voice was starting to shrink. 'I… I wanted to take Janice to watch the opera. He forbade it. Like Ling's Christian friends, he said the opera was about bestiality. I disagreed. We had an argument, and…'

'And what?'

'… and…' I was struggling to form the words '… and… he slapped me hard across my cheek. Janice saw it. My daughter was just seven, maybe eight. I forget her age, but I'll never forget the horror in her eyes. The poor mite didn't cry. She just looked at her papa and me, then turned and fled. I… I was… I was…' I was trying not to cry.

Meng came over to where I sat, and held me, pressing my head against his warm belly.

'He hit you.' An angry tremoring in his voice. 'I should've married you, Little Swallow. I should have…'

I stood up. 'Dreamer,' I smiled, tears pooling in my eyes. 'It wouldn't have worked. You were dreaming of being a great opera star. And I had other dreams. Remember? And it didn't include being the wife of a poor struggling Cantonese opera singer.'

We looked into each other's eyes. The two of us were no longer the impetuous young man and woman we once were. Then we looked away, conscious of what could have been in our misspent youth. Standing in the kitchen, he held me close. And then closer till our bodies were pressed hard against each other, and I could feel his heart pounding against his ribs. Neither of us spoke. Over the course of the many evenings he had come for dinner and stayed the night. He had told me about his wife and their hard life as second tier performers when they were both starting out in the same opera company. But I had told him little about my life with Robert and nothing about the abuse I had suffered. He was sensitive when he felt my reticence and did not try to probe. And for this I was grateful. I still could not speak about it except for the little I told Janice and the counsellor I saw infrequently. But things had begun to come out in bits and pieces now and then. I had started a journal and I was beginning to write them down.

I felt his hand stroking my back. The rhythmic movements made me realise how tensed and stiff my body was, how taut my muscles, and how coiled up the ache inside my heart. I thought of those nights when I had cried aloud and shaken the bed, and he had reached over and held me in his arms, murmuring, 'I'm here; I'm here,' soothing my night fears away. As he went on stroking, the tension in my back started to ease, the clamped rigidity in my bones loosening as I sobbed on his shoulders the sudden sorrows that had arisen. The neighbours' televisions down the corridor and the shouts in the playground sounded distant and faint. Outside the kitchen window a crescent moon was appearing and disappearing among the curtains of grey after the sudden storm. He bent down to kiss my lips. A kiss that was so deep and long. So much unsaid feelings passing from mouth to mouth as he held me, as the world and sounds of the neighbourhood receded further and further till we pulled away from each other. Away from the terrible intimacy of our kiss – its strangeness precious beyond words.

'I'll brew us a fresh pot of tea,' I mumbled.

'No, let me make the tea.' His finger gently brushed away the strand of hair near my eyes. 'Why don't you go and look for the original script of *Madam White Snake*? The one...' A slight trembling in his voice. 'The script that the Golden Phoenix Troupe had used. That script should be performed. Some day.'

I left him in the kitchen to wash up the dinner things and make tea, and I went into the bedroom. I needed time alone. My heart was pounding so fast. I started pulling out box after box of Por Por's opera costumes and other stuff. I could hear the tap running, and then heard him pottering in the kitchen, putting away the bowls and plates. A neat housekeeper, he knew by now where I kept everything.

Por Por's boxes were stashed in the closet. I could not remember where I had put away the opera scripts. My mind was in a mess. As I pulled one of Por Por's costumes out of one of the boxes a crushed piece of paper fell out.

I smoothened the page. Read it quickly and yelled, 'Meng! Come and look at this!'

44

When we got down from the bus Meng took my hand. We left the busy main avenue and walked down a quiet smaller road, passing the gated lawns and lighted windows of terraced houses. Pink and white blooms on the Rose of India trees scented the night air with a faint sweet fragrance after the rains. The night was cool. The two of us were glad to get away from the traffic and strolled under the trees without speaking. For a fleeting moment a young Robert flashed before my memory, holding my hand under the trees in the Botanic Gardens when I was in university. And I shrank from the memory.

'Nervous?' Meng turned and smiled.

'Just a little.'

'Her daughter said night is the best time to visit. Madam can't sleep at night. That's when she likes to talk. Her daughter says Madam talks incessantly of her opera days as she grows older.'

We turned down a lane and walked on. Though the night was still early not a soul was in sight. Not even a cat. Quietened by the silence in the lane both of us stopped talking. The quiet mornings we enjoyed at home came to my mind. After breakfast, three mornings a week, he left for the community centre to teach Cantonese opera singing. On other mornings, we worked on the English surtitles of the operas his troupe might perform next year. One performance a year is not enough, he said. The more performances the more opportunities for students to improve. But staging an opera is expensive. The subsidies are not enough, never enough, he grumbled. I had learnt from him how to read the surtitles of various Cantonese operas better when we watched videos of operas at night. I knew by now that when we parted for the day, he often went back to his flat to write or practise his singing. Our quiet way of life, living quietly and companionably, had an air of calm gentility and gentleness that was very different from my previous life of the past twenty years. Some nights as I closed my eyes, lying beside him, I thanked the God of the universe for this unexpected gift in my autumn years.

'This is the house,' he said softly.

The porch light had been left on. He let go of my hand and unlatched the gate of the two-storey bungalow. We walked up the driveway and at the door, he pressed the bell. A plump middle-aged woman with neatly coiffured hair opened the door. After Meng had introduced us, Madam Mei Lai's daughter turned to me with a wide smile.

'Madam Chan. Welcome, please come in.'

'Please call me Xiu Yin.'

'Xiu Yin. Little Swallow. What an unusual and beautiful name. Few can forget such a name. But I'm sure you've forgotten mine. Do you remember speaking to me once?'

'No, I'm afraid not.'

'Do you remember shouting at a real estate agent on the phone when your Sea Cove apartment was being sold?

I looked at her. 'No. Don't tell me it was you.'

A loud burst of laughter. 'Small world, isn't it?'

'Oh no, I'm so sorry, so very sorry,' I said, heat rising in my face.

'Oh please don't worry about it. It's past. I'm just being mischievous,' she chuckled. 'Real estate agents, we have skins thick as cowhide. We get bombarded every day. I've been through a divorce myself. I know how traumatic it is. How it makes us do foolish things. Come. Come inside. Mother is expecting you both.'

The room was spacious and high-ceilinged with a floor of pale polished wood. A large floor-to-ceiling wardrobe with see-through glass doors covered one entire wall. Chock full with opera costumes. On another wall facing the bed were framed coloured photographs of a young Madam Mei Lai in various opera outfits.

Waiting for us on the bed was Madam Mei Lai in white silk pyjamas and a cotton wrap over her legs. She looked pale and frail in the soft lighting of the room. But when she spoke, her voice was clear and vibrated with the energy of someone younger than her frail eighties.

'Come closer, Xiu Yin,' she said in beautifully enunciated Cantonese. She turned a knob by her bedside, and the lights in the room grew bright.

'There! I can see you much better. You look happier now than when I last saw you at your Por Por's wake. I have been waiting since then for you to visit.'

She pointed to the two chairs next to her bed. Meng and I sat down, and her daughter left us. A Filipino helper brought in a black lacquered tray with a pot of tea and three cups, and set it on the small table beside her bed.

After Meng had told her the purpose of our visit, Madam Mei Lai let out a loud theatrical sigh.

'Meng, oh Meng my dear man… why are you speaking for Xiu Yin? Surely the granddaughter of Kam Foong has no difficulty speaking for herself? Hmmm?'

She cocked her head at us like a white cockatoo in bed. Meng and I laughed. Relieved that this wasn't going to be a difficult evening, I reached into my bag and took out the piece of crushed paper I had brought.

'Madam Mei Lai, this is what I found among my Por Por's things. Meng thinks you can help me.'

'Aye, my eyes are useless these days. Read it to me. Loudly. I'm a bit deaf.'

Voice quavering, I read aloud.

Vixen with heart of wolf and lung of dog! I curse you and your son. May he meet an untimely death! May your shadow never fall upon my granddaughter! She-wolf! Witch! Why didn't you kill me? You should have killed me. I would have happily taken Choi Wan's place. What wicked deed did I do to you? Have I knifed or killed or murdered or robbed or stolen or cheated your family? What wrong? What wrong have I done to you? What crime? Tell me! Why didn't you rip out my heart and let her live?

Oh Gods in Heaven! Can you hear me? What crime did I commit in my past lives that I have to suffer like this in my present? Why did my daughter have to die like a poor bitch??? What wrong did her father do? Look at Wah Jai. He has turned into stone.

When I finished Madam Mei Lai's eyes were closed. I folded the piece of paper and returned it to my bag. Meng handed me a cup of tea and I drank it thirstily. Several minutes passed. Madam Mei Lai did not speak nor move. We wondered if we should wake the old lady or take our leave. I got up.

'Sit down, Little Swallow. I wasn't asleep. Just thinking of those far-off days after the war. Your mother, Choi Wan, was barely two months old when I gave her my breast to suckle. And became her godmother. You're my god granddaughter. Did you know?'

'I'm afraid not, Madam. Por Por never mentioned it.'

Meng poured out another cup of tea and handed it to me. His eyes indicated I should serve it to Madam Mei Lai. I took the cup. With both hands I offered Madam the ritual cup of respect and addressed her as Grandma. She smiled and accepted the cup.

'Your Por Por should have told you. But she was secretive and conservative to a fault. Not me. I was a rebel. Ahead of my time. Now time has caught up. Society's attitudes have changed. And I am old. So I will let you know. Your Por Por and I were very close. This close.'

She held up her hand. Her middle and index fingers were crossed to show how intimately entwined they had been.

'We were a couple onstage and offstage. But we didn't crow about it. Didn't flaunt it like the young fools today. Baring their love and angst for the whole world to see. Your Por Por and I didn't flaunt. And people didn't talk about it. They knew it. Your grandpa knew it. The whole troupe knew it.'

For a moment. Just a moment. I was shocked. Madam Mei Lai looked so old and frail in bed. My grandmother, on the other hand, the grandmother in the journal was a young and vigorous woman.

'This must have happened long before Xiu Yin and I were born,' Meng smiled, and gave me a look.

'When I was growing up, there were many nights when Por Por was away, returning only after lunch the next day. Nobody commented on it. But then I was still a child. I don't recall Grandfather had ever said an unhappy word about it. The other adults around me, the actors and singers, had thought nothing of two women spending nights together during the opera season,' I said.

Madam Mei Lai didn't look like she had heard me. Her thoughts were already far away.

'Madam. Madam. Do you know the story behind this note?' Meng pressed her.

She woke from her reverie and wagged a finger at him.

'Always the impatient one, our Meng! Can't you wait? Let Xiu Yin do the asking. Aye, now I'm thirsty!'

She drank some tea. And so did I to calm myself. I was thinking of the nameless woman, the 'Dearest Intimate' in the journal. Did she kill my mother?

'Madam, who is the she-wolf?'

'Ah, well! The she-wolf. Kam Foong and the she-wolf grew up together in China. And wait. This will surprise you. The two of them were betrothed to each other while still in their mothers' wombs. Don't look so surprised. Such things were common in rural China since ancient times. Their two mothers were very close friends. Could have been distant cousins. Kam Foong's mother, that is your great grandmother, thought she was going to give birth to a son. Well! As you can see, she didn't. But that story of being betrothed to each other while still in their mothers' wombs had fired their daughters' imagination. The two girls grew up together. As close as bees to honey. They slept over in each other's houses and shared the same bed. Right till the time they married. Kam Foong was incredibly loving and loyal. Loyal to a foolish fault. If she weren't so foolish and loyal, she would have left with me for Hong Kong when I asked her. But she couldn't leave your grandfather because of a vow she had made to him. So I left her. Aye, I wasn't foolish. I left Kam Foong. She was such a loyal soul. Such a romantic waif in her youth. She gave her heart and soul to that she-wolf.'

Madam Mei Lai fell silent. Meng put his arm round my shoulder.

'Is the air-conditioning too cold for you, Madam?'

'This tea is too cold. Go and ask the girl to make us a fresh pot, Meng.'

After Meng had left the room, Madam Mei Lai beckoned.

'Come closer. Let me take a good look at you. Forty-five? Fifty? You still look young. My daughter tells me you're divorced. That's good. I knew your marriage wouldn't last when I saw your husband at the wake. When a man is rude to his wife's guests, when he gave her no face, then something is wrong. And I was right.'

'That's in the past. I don't think of it anymore.'

'That's good, my dear. Look to the future. Meng loves you. Very much. I can tell. I've known him for years. I've acted with him. Taught him a few things. Saw how he struggled in Hong Kong after his wife died. He's a good man. Marry him. He will take good care of you.'

Taken aback, I changed the subject.

'What happened to my mother?'

But her eyes were closed again. I wanted to shake her. I was annoyed at her uncalled-for intrusion. The door opened and she woke up with a start. I wondered if she had been acting. Or had dozed off like very old people were wont to do. Meng put down the teapot and the flask he had brought.

'Madam, your daughter reminds you to drink your ginseng tea.'

He poured a half-cup out of the flask and gave it to her.

She took a few sips.

'Where was I, Yin?' She looked at me like an old lady who had forgotten what we were talking about.

'I was asking you about my mother,' I said, sorry now that I had been annoyed. 'All I know is that she died at sixteen. My birth had caused her death.'

'Oh no,' she reached for my hand. 'You didn't cause your mother's death. No, no, you didn't. You mustn't think that. Poor child. All these years. Imagine thinking you'd killed your own mother all through your childhood to adulthood. How unbearable a burden for a young child. And no one told you? Por Por didn't tell you?'

Her words made me both teary and angry. No one had spoken to me like this about my mother. Meng took my hand while Madam Mei Lai finished her ginseng tea. She leaned back into her thick pillows. Revived by the tea, she started to speak at length.

'Your mother, Choi Wan, was a very talented girl. Very precocious. From the time she was a toddler, her curious intelligent eyes had followed our every movement as we rehearsed. The stage was her playground wherever the stage happened to be. In a temple courtyard, a market square or the theatre in the Great World Park. Your grandparents took her with them everywhere. She loved music. When she cried, the strains of her father's erhu could quieten her. When she was tired, she would clamber into her crib in her mother's corner of the backstage and slept to the sounds of drums, flutes, pipas and cymbals. Opera music was her lullaby. Everyone adored this precocious child. Master Wu loved his granddaughter to the core of his heart. Choi Wan would sit at his feet and watch him teach. While other children played, she watched and listened to the musicians and singers. She loved opera. The singing and acting. The sounds and rhythms of Cantonese opera filled her world from the time she was a baby. Like a sponge she absorbed everything. From the time she was two, she was trying to sing and act. Imitating the *fah dan*. Flinging scarves and water sleeves and walking like one with bound feet. All these stories I'm telling you now are the stories I had heard from your Por Por over and over again. Years after Choi Wan had passed away. By then I had returned from Hong Kong. I had married and had settled down to start a family, never to sing and act again.'

Madam Mei Lai was smiling. Smiling at the past that was still so clear and bright in her aging memory. Meng poured more ginseng tea into her cup and urged her to drink. She sat up and took several sips of the drink that had given her strength to talk at length.

'Your Por Por told me this story. One day Choi Wan stood in front of the mirror in the backstage and sang. Her singing shocked everyone. She was only seven at the time. Yet she had memorised, and was singing an aria that had challenged even experienced singers like the *fah dan* who had taken my place. Not only could she sing the high notes in perfect pitch, she had also mastered the stylised movements that conveyed the meaning of the tragic song. Dabbing her eyes at the right part of the aria with the flowing sleeves of the *fah dan's* robe. From that day on, Master Wu took charge of her training. A teacher was engaged to give her voice and singing lessons. Another teacher was engaged to teach her to dance. By the time she was sixteen, she was a very attractive young *fah dan*. Very popular with audiences. So she was given major roles. The opera that made her famous was the opera in which she played a young lady poet who got drunk and spent the night with her lover in a boat. Her song on the morning after won great praise in the papers and tabloids. Her singing and acting as the drunken young poet made her name famous throughout Singapore and Kuala Lumpur, as far as Ipoh and Penang.'

She took another sip of ginseng tea, sat up straighter and sang in a thin high-pitched voice.

No feathery brushstrokes can describe the hand
That wandered among my lotuses last night.
Alas, alas, I am lost, lost, lost!
My lotuses have withered.

I coughed. Her reedy singing stopped.

'Now I'm truly lost. Where was I?'

'You were telling us about my mother playing the young poet's role,' I said, and hoped she had not detected my impatience.

'Ahhh! The irony of life. The mischief of the gods. It was in Penang where your mother was lost. Truly and tragically lost. And no one knew at the time. The night she was playing this beautiful tragic poet she met the handsome young man with a car. Now in those days, the car was a great luxury. Only the wealthy could afford it. Not many young men had a car in those days. When the Golden Phoenix troupe was performing in Penang, this rich young man came to the theatre to watch Choi Wan. Every night he came to the theatre. But he couldn't get near her. So smitten with her was he that he followed the troupe when they returned to Singapore. At this point of the story, your poor Por Por would wail each time she recounted the story. She had failed as a mother. Failed as her daughter's protector. She didn't know when the fox came into the chicken coup. No one knew how the two of them met. Till one day Choi Wan was gone. Just gone! Without a word to anyone. Not even to her beloved father. Not even to Master Wu, her beloved grandfather. Abruptly the opera season for the Golden Phoenix Troupe came to an end.'

She took a deep breath and drank more tea.

'Chaos broke out. Meng, please go to my chest of drawers over there. Look in the top drawer. Look for a green velvet box. Take out the news clipping.'

At this point, I excused myself. I couldn't take it anymore. I had been holding back tears. I went to the washroom. When I came out, Madam Mei Lai's daughter stopped me in the hallway.

'Would you and Meng like some supper? Mother can go on all night. You might get hungry later.'

'Oh no, thank you. We won't stay that long.'

I hurried back to the room. Meng looked up when I opened the door. His sheepish face puzzled me.

'Show her the news clipping,' Madam Mei Lai said.

He handed me the Chinese newspaper clipping.

INTERVIEW WITH A NIGHTINGALE
FAMED CANTONESE OPERA *FAH DAN*,
MISS CHAN CHOI WAN

Miss Chan, 16, is making her debut at the Majestic Nightclub in Kuala Lumpur this New Year season. Born in Singapore, she says, 'Singing comes naturally to me. I have been singing since I was in my mother's womb. When my mother sang, I followed. When my godmother sang, I followed. I grew up singing all their opera songs. Now I want to sing my own songs. The songs of the young and free, and dance the Cha-cha-cha.'

'This news had come months after she disappeared,' Madam Mei Lai said. 'It caused a furore in the troupe. No doubt the young man had lured her with these lurid dances like the Cha-cha and modern pop songs. And Choi Wan though talented was very naïve. She knew nothing of the world outside opera. The life and lights of the nightclubs dazzled her. Given a choice she chose the nightclub instead of the theatre. The news broke everyone's hearts. Her parents tracked her down from Kuala Lumpur to Penang. To a goldsmith shop in Campbell Lane. But it was too late. I was in Hong Kong when I heard the terrible news. I phoned Kam Foong several times but she couldn't talk. Just could not talk. Each time she opened her mouth, she wailed and sobbed into the phone. It was terrible. Terrible. And I couldn't come back at the time. I had several performances back to back that year. I wrote to your grandfather Wah Jai, and to your great grandfather Master Wu. Finally, a year later Master Wu wrote to me. Meng, show her the letter.'

Mei Lai,

You have to come back. Kam Foong is a wreck. Wah Jai is a mute. And I have lost my heart. I don't know what to do. The troupe is about to disband. We are barely surviving. If not for Little Swallow, their granddaughter, Wah Jai and Kam Foong would have killed themselves.

They brought Choi Wan home in a hearse. The two of them sat inside the hearse beside their daughter's coffin, holding their newborn grandchild. When I saw them and the coffin in that black hearse, I fainted. My precious princess had died such a piteous death. How could I not curse the young man who got her into trouble? How could I not curse the young man's mother who would not shelter my precious princess? Choi Wan was cabaret trash in her eyes. Her goldsmith shop was not a maternity ward, she said. She banished my precious to a mattress on the floor in the kitchen shed. And that was where Kam Foong and Wah Jai found their daughter. Lying on a bundle of blood soaked rags.

Vengeance! I cry to Heaven.

That night Kam Foong's heart was knifed a second time. It turned out that the mother of the young man was the woman Kam Foong had loved since they were children back in Saam Hor. Is this not dark Fate? The work of dark spirits? How do we cope with such malfeasance? Were it not for the kindness of strangers and Wah Jai's strength, Kam Foong could not have lived through that night. Were it not for the cries of the baby in her arms, she couldn't have made the journey back to Singapore in that hearse.

$\wp - \wp$

45

It was very late by the time we got into bed. The rains had started again on our way home. Though exhausted, sleep had eluded me all night. I was haunted by ghosts I hardly knew. Beside me in bed, Meng was snoring softly, his presence warm and comforting as an old blanket.

It was not yet morning when I opened my eyes. I lay beside him listening to the soft pattering on my potted plants outside the corridor where the rain was coming in. Thunder was rumbling in the distance. A thunderstorm was approaching. Snippets of last night's meeting with Madam Mei Lai returned. A mix of sadness, anger and resignation stirring my heart. Why didn't they tell me? Why didn't they? I could not understand my grandparents' silence. Grandfather, by nature, was reticent but Por Por? She should have told me. She should have.

I thought of the two photos that had sat on the dresser in her bedroom. The first was a coloured photo of me at six years old. Serious and unsmiling, I was wearing the iconic blue pinafore of the convent school where Grandfather had enrolled me. Standing between him and Por Por, I had placed a possessive hand on each of their knees to show the world that they were mine. An orphan laying claim to family. I was an insecure child even though I knew my grandparents and Great Grandfather Wu loved me. Grandfather had been so pleased he had succeeded in enrolling me in the English convent school that day, he had insisted on a family photo to mark the occasion. Afterwards he and Por Por took me to the temple where I was gifted to the Goddess of Mercy to serve as one of her celestial Jade Girls. Meng who had come with us was also gifted to the Goddess of Mercy as a Golden Boy. The second photograph in shades of sepia hues showed a lively little girl dancing in a long skirt and blouse with flowing water sleeves like a fairy in a Chinese opera. A finger rested lightly on her cheek, her head had turned to smile coquettishly at the camera. *Your mother was flirtatious even as a child*, Madam Mei Lai had said.

The soft patter of raindrops changed to a heavy downpour. I got out of bed to check if rain was coming into the kitchen. I didn't put on the light in case it woke Meng. I went to the kitchen and closed the windows leaving a small gap for cool air to enter. The rain was coming down hard. Making a loud din. It was impossible to go back to bed. I switched on the reading lamp in the living room and settled down in my armchair to re-read the letters that Madam Mei Lai had given me together with the news clipping and Great Grandfather Wu's letter. Her generosity had surprised me, and I was very touched.

'I don't know why I had kept these two letters for so long. All these years, Kam Foong had never written to me before. So these two letters written in her old age are very precious. You will know why when you read them. I believe now that the holy spirits must have directed me to keep these letters till time would bring you to me. Take them, my dear. My days are limited. These letters should go to you.'

On our way home, Meng said, 'Madam is a very devout Taoist. She believes there is a time for everything under Heaven.'

'Oh you mean like the writer in the Old Testament who wrote, for everything there is a season, a time for every activity under heaven,' I said.

'Ah, something like that,' he smiled and took my hand. 'We better call a taxi. The heavens will open up soon and we'd be drenched.'

I took Por Por's first letter out of its envelope and read it again.

My dearest Mei,
I think of you tonight. Though we are no longer intimates, I
have not stopped thinking of you. Not every night, I confess.
But tonight, tonight you are in my thoughts. Are you awake like
me? Insomnia, this affliction of the old, the very old, keeps us
awake. Memories we had suppressed when younger await us each
night. Mine are standing in line staring at me, waiting, till I take
up my pen to write.
    It has been years since I wrote. Years too many to count.
It was impossible to write when the heart was so broken. And
the mind busy, filling it with opera and success to help it forget.
But how could a mother forget the fruit of her womb? It was

impossible to forget what happened to my darling Choi Wan. My precious child. Not a day all these years.

Yet I have not forgotten the promise I made to you long ago. And I will not break it now in spite of these arthritic hands. We do not have that much time. You and I. Soon I will be eighty-five. And you are not that far behind.

I still hear the Cha-cha-cha some nights. I imagine things. I see my daughter and the young man with the foxy face. Remember the young man who came to the theatre every night? He was visiting his uncle who had a goldsmith shop here on South Bridge Road. One day Choi Wan had gone there to buy a gold ring for my birthday. And he recognised her. I saw you perform in Penang and followed you here, he said to her. Flattered, she laughed but she did not believe him. He invited her out. She declined. But her heart was fluttering. That night and every other night, she looked out for him in the audience. He sat in the front row of the theatre. Later he told her that he had watched her perform every night. But he could not afford an expensive front row seat every night. So he sat in the back of the theatre where the seats were cheap. Moved by his sincerity, she accepted his invitation to the Majestic to watch a film. It showed Ge Lan, the Hong Kong film star, dancing the Cha-cha. He taught her the dance, holding her close as they sang the songs of carefree youth.

During the troupe's rest season while I played mah-jong, Choi Wan slipped out of the house with the younger members of the troupe. They went to the Majestic one night. Quick, quick! I don't want to miss their arrival, I could imagine her saying. The bright lights and modern pop music mesmerised her. The huge crowd shocked her. The crowd was so much larger than the crowds at the operas. There were policemen everywhere directing traffic, ordering people to move out of the way. There were shouts and screams and applause when the glamorous film stars from Hong Kong arrived, and the police had to push people out of their way.

I do not know if such things are the idle imaginings of
my aging brain. The shadow of the black she-wolf haunts me
tonight. I feel murderous tonight. So to the Buddha and tobacco
I turn for mercy and company.

I search my drawers. I had hidden the packet from Xiu Yin.
My granddaughter nags me. No more smoking, Por Por. The
doctor says… Every time she visits she throws the doctor at me.
I lock my lips. I do not say a word. I don't want to go back to the
hospital. I would rather die at home.

Where is my tobacco, Wah Jai? I asked but he is silent. Ghosts
are supposed to know things. He is a useless ghost. I miss my
hand-rolled cigarettes. Ter-li-za that dreadful girl must have found
them again. She has been nothing but trouble ever since Xiu Yin
brought her home after my fall. Aye! I blame these old bones.

The morning sun has come into my bedroom. The light
hurt my eyes. I had told that girl to leave the curtains drawn.
The monkey! Even to my dying day must I deal with curtains
raised and lowered, parted and drawn? Take another curtain call
when the monkey gave me no time to wipe the drool from my
mouth? I check my pyjama pants. Are they wet or dry? Do they
smell of pee? Such indignities the old have to suffer. Even an
opera star who had thrilled the multitudes is not spared. If only
you could see me now. Once I was the young handsome
xiu sung on stage, the conquering hero of women's hearts. Now
I am a withered willow branch draped with dried tofu skin. Of
what use is success then without one's youth?

Death has mellowed me. After my darling girl and Master
Wu's departure the spark in my singing went out. Till hate
fanned it later into a fire when that woman in black walked into
the theatre. To make amends? How dare she try? Try to see Xiu
Yin? My granddaughter is mine! And Wah Jai's. Nothing to do
with her! Murderess! My singing sparkled hard as a diamond the
night she came. My acting burned with a ferocious energy that
made me a star among stars again. But it could not last. Old age
knocked on my door.

Good morning, Por Por.

Here is Miss Trouble again. She has come to help me out of bed, and into the bathroom. I shut the door in her face. I will safeguard my dignity yet. If only I can get up once I sit down on the bowl. So many things we took for granted in our glorious youth. Heaven punishes us now. I had told Xiu Yin, no helper. I don't need a helper. Yet she brought me this chirpy bright-eyed bird from the Philippines. To mollify this cranky old lady, she declared, Teresa has worked in Hong Kong before, Por Por. She can speak Cantonese and even cook a few Cantonese dishes for you. What could I say? Complaining, the recreation of the old, was snuffed out of me with a smile.

Your pills, Por Por.

Foolish child. Xiu Yin clings to hope and medicine. But pills will not help. The decay is relentless. But for now I can still complain and yell. I will not wet my knickers. My hair is still on my head. Combed. My fish porridge still has taste. No nausea or vomit yet. So thank you, Heaven and Buddha, for these little mercies. My table is a mess. I am trying to clear the boxes of old theatre bills and posters. Here is one of you.

Aye, those were our happy days. Droves of dream lovers of the theatre in every town. I was feted and feasted by both lovers and mistresses of the rich. I thought of the various women I had after you left for Hong Kong. I won't say I loved them. They had attracted and distracted me. Soothed me. Took care of me. That was enough. And I in turn tried to return a measure of their affection. But it was difficult, Mei. My heart was never wholly there. I was always glad to leave them when the troupe moved to another town. I was like my Sifu. Master Wu had a woman in each town. In my youth I had judged him callous, heartless, but it was more.

My punishment. I should have watched my precious jewel. Never take my eyes off her. But too late. Regret is always late. She is gone. Dead! Wah Jai's silence was the silence of the tomb. Remorse and regret snuffed out. I don't think he ever forgave me.

I am grinding my teeth. The pills do not work. Roll about the bed. Try not to yell Ter-li-za! Instead I think of the theatre. The operas we sung together. Ah! Tall and confident I had sung to the heavenly music of my Butcher's erhu. And the bowls of sweet bird's nest soup the *tai-tais* brought to soothe my throat. Think of the first time I drank bird's nest. It was in that cemetery on a misty morning. Since then other even more expensive decoctions had been delivered to my dressing table. While I painted my face, the mistresses and *tai-tais* fed me. Beautiful hands fanned me. Soft lips kissed me. Fame! Fleeting as a bree-eeze… Master Wu sings through my shooting pain. Aaaaah! The monster is going to kill me. Make it soon. Make it tonight. Kill me!

Goodbye, my dearest Mei, goodbye.

A deep breath, I closed my eyes.

Por Por was in the bright blue robe of an imperial judge and the black hat with side wings. Resplendent as a peacock she stood on stage while the audience shouted, *Bravo! Bravo!* Throwing roses and red packets of money onto the stage. This was how I wanted to remember her. I took out her second letter.

My dearest,
The monster let me live. How long? Who knows? Monsters are fickle.

Tonight I sit at my table in the kitchen. Watching ants coming after the bits of food I had dropped. Scurrying to and fro at the edge of the table, they remind me of the comings and goings in the house in Keong Saik Road. Divas and singers with egos bigger than the moon. Actors and their hangers-on. Humble pipa players. Twittering flautists. And those loud-mouthed drummers. Anyone who could bang out a tune, mutter a line or wield a sword could come and stay. Such flexibility. Unheard of now in theatre troupes. I miss them all. The ones who came and stayed a while. The ones who performed with

us a while. And those who stayed with the Golden Phoenix
for years. Through sorrows and joy. These were loyal and true
to the core. I miss these brothers and sisters. Their banter and
laughter. The click-click-clack of their mah-jong tiles in all-night
sessions. Most of all I miss my Butcher. I miss his cooking.
Wah Jai's pig trotters stewed in black vinegar and old ginger
was incomparable. His chicken soup with a sharp aromatic tang
could warm your heart and lungs on a chilly night like this.
Tonight I miss his ghost. I miss his silent presence by my side.
I live alone now. Ter-li-za does not count. The family that he and
I had gathered during the war – all scattered now. Gone.

1. The first to go was Uncle Loke who died in his
wheelchair. Such a shock to Wah Jai who inherited his erhu.

2. Then came the departure that shattered my heart. Choi
Wan, my Beautiful Cloud, floated off. Sudden and abrupt.
And cruel. A deep stab of the dagger into our hearts. It almost
killed her father. Wah Jai lost his tongue. For months he could
not speak. Choi Wan's birth had brought such joy. Her birth
had heralded the end of war, yet her future had ended on a pile
of rags on a kitchen floor. Aye… of her I will not dwell. My
daughter is alive in my heart still. Alive in the granddaughter she
left me. My Little Swallow so bruised and sallow-skinned these
days. I grieve each time Xiu Yin visits me. Her eyes are so sad.
Such dark wells of sorrows in there. I know not how to ask her. I
cannot help her. May the gods protect her and give her strength.

3. Master Wu, my Sifu, my almost-father, went off in his
sleep. A good death. A peaceful death. Though a shock to us
all. Famed for his roles as the boatman and the powerful Abbot
in *Madam White Snake*. And as Lord Bao Goong in the opera
of Chief Justice with the Black Face. You should have seen him
as the Imperial Eunuch during the war. The great Eunuch and
tutor to the Emperor. He refused to bend his knee before the
Japanese. Oh my beloved Sifu, you old fox, how I miss you.

4. The last to leave me is my Butcher Bloke. My erhu player,
my Wah Jai. I never let him forget his humble origins. Butcher!

I yelled at him even as others addressed him most respectfully
as Wah Sifu or Master Wah. His erhu sits on the kitchen
table before me. Gently, I wipe off the dust on it each night,
stroking his beloved instrument. Listen. I hear the soft strains of
"Autumn Moon Over Calm Lake", his favourite tune. The night
he went, I had sat in the ambulance with him, holding his hand.
The hospital room, dimly lit, had a view across the city. He was
lying on his back, his mouth slack, saliva drooling at the corner.
I sat on a chair by the bed. Took his hand and called him,
Husband, softly. The first time in our long years together that
I addressed him in the formal way we do in opera. Husband, I
whispered in his ear as though I didn't want anyone to hear me.
Dearest Intimate, my tears fell, and I called him louder, voicing
the love I had withheld from him when he was alive. There was
a slight, very slight movement of his hand; his fingers twitched
and closed on mine, then slackened, they lay on the blanket.
Alive, I thought. He is alive. Not dead, not dead. I brought
his hand to my forehead and held it in both mine. Husband, I
called him a third time. Wake up. We will walk the same road
as always, walk under the same umbrella as always, share the
same pair of shoes, silent as always, my Dearest Intimate, my pig
farmer's son, my Butcher Bloke. Loss and absence grip my heart
tonight.

'Still thinking of last night?' Meng called from the bedroom.

I put away the letters, went in and sat on the edge of the bed and kissed
him. 'Did I wake you?'

'I was already awake, thinking of the young man, your father.'

'How strange. I've never thought of him.'

'Madam said he had rushed out of the goldsmith shop after phoning
your grandparents.'

'Leaving my mother and me, the newborn. Coward, don't you think?'

'Madam said his car went up in flames. In that same night Por Por lost
her only daughter, and your other grandma her only son.'

He sat up, pushed a pillow behind his back and took both my hands.

'In that same night, you lost both parents when you were born. In those days the Chinese gave away such babies or drowned them. Your grandparents saved you.'

I thought of my grandparents sitting in the hearse, Por Por cradling me in her arms and Grandfather, mute, beside her. I could not cry. Meng took me into his arms and held me like a child.

Shuddering dry sobs coursing through my limbs, he held me close till tears broke through, and I saw his car bursting into flames, the young man's body burning and screaming. It took a long while before my shuddering sobs subsided. He handed me a tissue and brushed the strands of wet hair from my face.

'Breakfast?'

When I came out of the washroom, he was in the kitchen making two cups of coffee. A spoonful of sugar for his and a lot of milk for mine. I took out the jam and butter from the fridge, and sat down. He placed two slices of toast on the table and sat facing me. He buttered our toast and took a bite of his. I drank my coffee slowly. We ate in silence.

'More toast?' He got up.

'No.'

He toasted another slice of bread for himself.

'I've seen my other grandmother before,' I said.

'The woman in black?'

'We were having dinner in the backstage. The adults were talking. Suddenly, their bantering stopped. A stagehand had staggered in with a large basket of pink lotuses, lotus leaves and lotus pods. Flowers of the Goddess of Mercy. He put down the basket and handed Por Por a red packet. She showed it to my grandfather and he gave it back to the stagehand. Tell the lady we don't want her money, he said. I remember running to the stage curtains and sticking my head out. The woman in black was out there. I had seen her in the front row before. Always in the same corner seat. Always looking very sad. When she saw me, she waved and smiled. Por Por pulled me back and closed the curtains. Don't let that woman see you again. She is a she-wolf. She will eat you, she said. I burst into tears.'

'Phew! That must have been scary. How old were you?'

'Maybe four or five. The incident has stayed in my mind.'

We drank our coffee in silence again. The sun had come out. The clear blue sky promised the day would be bright and hot after last night's storm. A woman in the opposite block was sticking her washing out of her window into the bright sunshine.

'Will you be okay today?'

'Why wouldn't I be? The she-wolf must be dead.'

'She's also your grandma.'

'I feel nothing for her.'

'Feelings are like clouds. They change. If you meet her, you might feel differently.' He smiled and got up. 'I'll be back for dinner.'

A peck on my cheek. And he was gone.

I went on sitting in the kitchen listening to the shouts of children in the playground and the intermittent hammering of the mortar and pestle from a neighbour's flat. Someone was making chilli paste for a hot curry. I cleared the breakfast things, tidied up the kitchen table and washed up. My pace was unhurried. I loved the relaxed rhythm and spacious solitude of these mornings when Meng was out of the flat.

I returned to the living room and took out Por Por's letters to Madam Mei Lai. Settled in my armchair, put on my reading glasses and read the last letter again, searching the white spaces between the vertical rows of Chinese words as if these were the roads my grandparents had travelled together, the narrow byways where their love had hid. So much of their life had been lived side by side, never touching yet never apart. If not for this letter and the journal I would never have known how deep their love was for each other. As far as I could remember, they didn't speak much, and never directly to each other, talking always in the presence of others. So much of their love lay hidden like a rock among rocks under the sea, so much was unspoken. I would have been a silent child throughout my childhood if not for the gregarious noodle boy who told me I was eating snake and delighted me with his tall tales.

Last night in Madam Mei Lai's house when I had read the letters with Meng, he had said little at the time. But when we were walking to the main road to catch the bus, he turned to me.

'Your grandparents,' he began, paused, searching for the right words.

'Theirs was a deep love. Not sex. Not passion. But an intimacy of the heart. Beyond others' gaze. Beyond words. Intimacy was what had kept them alive besides you.' He squeezed my hand.

I thought of what Meng said. My grandfather had not left any written word. He had slipped away one night without any last words for Por Por or me. Just the strains of his music lingered on, straying into my memory from time to time. I thought of the solitary man perched on a rock up the hill, and the old man limping in the Japanese cemetery, who bowed to the Japanese dead, who rejected vengeance and left his granddaughter with the story of the kind Japanese doctor who had saved his wife's life. A man who valued peace and silence. I thought of Por Por and him. Love and sorrow could manifest such strange shapes. I doubted we ever knew truly those who brought us up.

I read Por Por's last letter again. Slowly this time.

46

It had been almost a week since our visit to Madam Mei Lai, and Meng's face had been frowning whenever he was unaware that I was looking at him. Something of great import seemed to be worrying him. What it was I couldn't tell. His silence reminded me of Grandfather. And it worried me.

'If Meng has a problem you have to wait till he tells you,' Ling had told me during one of our dinners. 'Don't let yourself get worried if he doesn't tell you. He's like this. People who get worried only make themselves sick.'

Funny how some things stuck in our brain. I let another week go by as I waited patiently for him to tell me. Then I had to ask him.

'You know...' he began, and paused.

'What?' I asked, trying to curb my impatience.

'That night when we visited Madam Mei Lai... she... she spoke to me while you went to the washroom.' He was so hesitant. It was unlike him.

'So what secret did she tell you?' I teased him.

He took up his cup, drank some tea and carefully put down the cup.

'She said... she said we should get married.'

'Oh that! She's such a busybody! She said the same to me too.'

'What? Did she? When? You didn't tell me.' His face was crestfallen.

'When you went to get the ginseng tea for her, she told me to marry you. It's none of her business. She just wants to play matchmaker. I didn't bother to tell you.'

His face flushed. Then a miffed look came into his dark eyes, he muttered, 'Don't you want to marry me?'

'What? Suddenly we have to marry just because the old Madam told you to marry me?'

Confusion in his eyes, he protested. 'No, no! She made me think of the future. Not that I haven't been thinking. We're not getting any younger, Yin. I want... I thought of going back to Hong Kong. I want to see my grandson. And my daughter is about to give birth to her second. I would like you to come with me. Meet my daughter and son-in-law. So shall we get married?'

'No!'

We sat facing each other across the table, the hum of traffic from the main road and the cries of children in the playground reaching us from a great distance. Sweat was sliding down his face and clouding his glasses. He cleared his throat, pulled out his checked handkerchief from his trouser pocket, took off his glasses and started to wipe them. He didn't look at me.

'Are you ashamed of me?'

'What? You've been sharing my bed night after night all these months and you ask if I'm ashamed of you?'

'What do you want me to think then?'

'You can think what you like.' I stood up. 'You're still measuring success by degrees. Oh, Xiu Yin has a university degree. I don't even have a diploma. Poor me. And oh, she married a man with a Master's degree before. Listen Meng! I married an abuser and a drunk!'

I turned and walked off.

'Yin!'

A chair fell. I ran out of the flat, fled down the ten flights of stairs till I reached the ground floor. Fear, anger and a sudden spurt of energy speeded me past the shops and supermarket. For a moment back there I'd thought he was going to throw a chair at me. But no. Nothing of the sort happened. Meng was not Robert. Nothing was thrown at me. My fear subsided; then anger rose. For god's sake! We'd slept together. Showered together and eaten together! Didn't that tell him something? Is he so dense, so stupid? What more does he want? Irritation and anger swept me through the basketball court, the car park, another block of flats and propelled me up the stone steps to the park where we did tai chi every morning. Panting at the top. Panting in the dark silence under the rain trees, I stopped, breathless, angry and tired, I felt my heart was going to give. I was breathing hard. I looked out at the white florescence of flats in the distance. The park was deserted. No one was walking the dog tonight. No couples were making out behind its bushes. Not a single homeless body was asleep on its stone benches. My breathing slowed down. A light breeze was blowing through the trees. I sat down on the concrete bench under the largest rain tree, my mind returning to the scene I had just left and the feelings that had exploded in me like a sudden squall. I thought of Meng sitting alone in the kitchen. Idiot, I thought looking up at the old rain tree above me.

'Ee-jit!' I said the word out loud. 'He's an ee-jit.'

The leaves of the rain tree rustling above me in the light breeze sounded as though they were giggling. This brought me a smile, and fanned by the breeze my anger started to cool down. I remembered the young woman seated here years ago waiting for her young man. I was glad to see her, glad to see that the rain tree that had arched over her all those years ago was still arching over me, its branches spreading out like gnarled dark bony arms against the night sky. The young woman dabbed off her perspiration with the checked cotton handkerchief that the young man had given her. With anxious eyes, she watched him come running up the slope, his ponytail swinging behind him, his hand waving a sheaf of papers, he was shouting, Yin! Yin! I got the forms! Hong Kong! Mecca of Cantonese opera here we come! He reached her, hugged and kissed her, dancing around her, spilling out his plans like water from an overfull pail. Meng, wait, wait! She tried to stop his exuberance. I can't go. Grandfather wants me to go to university, she said. You're not going. You're coming with me to Hong Kong. He was still dancing around her. Stop dancing. You're not listening to me. I'm not going. But why? You agreed. I want to go to university. I can't disappoint Grandfather. She would not change her mind. Her answer was firm. Her grandfather had set his heart on her going to university, and she herself wanted to go. To and fro they argued under the tree. I watched the young man's face. So full of hope one instant. So dejected the next. And a sudden sharp pain stabbed my heart. Hadn't I stabbed him again tonight?

My eyes followed the rain tree's gnarled old roots that had broken through the hard concrete base and cracked my stone bench. One side of the bench was pushed up higher than the other. Seated on the higher side, I watched as the young man, his ponytail limp and weary, retreated down the slope.

Hand on my breast, I did not move. I remained sitting on the bench watching a young mother and her little girl coming up the slope, watching them walk past. The little girl reminded me of my daughter. When Janice was little, I used to bring her up here with Grandfather. Hale and healthy then, he had limped up the slope with us holding his prattling great granddaughter's hand as he pointed out to the curious toddler the little yellow butterflies flitting in the grass. Years later, after his stroke, he had to use a wheelchair, and Janice, now a twelve-year-old, helped me to push him up to the park. And this time, it's the great granddaughter who pointed out the yellow butterflies, and told him about her school, and made him laugh. Later we pushed him down to the coffeeshop where we met Por Por for dinner. Once, Robert had marched into the coffeeshop, visibly irritated. How long more do you want me to wait? He did not greet my grandparents but hurried Janice and I out to the car. As we drove off, Janice and I stuck our heads out of the car window and waved. Lodged in my memory still was the stoic look on my grandparents' face, the resigned helplessness we sometimes catch in the eyes of the old. The inevitability of old age.

A drop fell on my face. A wind had risen. More drops fell through the rustling leaves. I stood up, gave the old rain tree another look, and started to run down the stone steps, thinking of my grandparents who were no longer around. My daughter had flown the dismantled nest. Why then, why was I resisting him? I raced down the steps. Rain was pouring when I reached home, drenched.

'Meng!' I called. 'It's yes, yes!'

There was no answer. The dinner things had been washed and put away. He had gone back to his flat. I locked up my flat, and ran down to the sixth floor and pressed his doorbell. No one came to the door. I ran back up to my flat and rang his mobile phone.

47

I woke up in the dark to the empty space next to me. Lying on my side of the bed, I listened to the soft pattering on the potted plants in the corridor, wondering if it had rained all night. The light coming through was a dull slate grey. The morning was quiet except for the sound of the rain. I rolled onto my side, checked my phone on the bedside table. There was no message and no call. I sat up. My legs were aching from last night's running. This is the first time Meng hadn't returned my calls. He must be very angry last night. I was beginning to feel sorry for myself, sorry for running off like that last night. I glanced at the clock. Six. It was still early. I got out of bed, found my slippers and padded into the kitchen.

A drab bed sheet was dripping on a bamboo pole outside a window in the opposite block. I filled the electric jug and started to make coffee. I took the bottle out of the fridge. Opened it and drank in the fragrance of the Columbian coffee. My senses awakened, I spooned out a heaped spoonful of the instant coffee into my mug. Stirred, and stood at the window staring out at the rain coming down, I took sips of the hot sugarless brew wondering if Meng was awake. I returned to the bedroom, picked up my phone and called his number. After the tenth ring, I ended the call. The morning was cooler than usual because of the rain. He must still be fast asleep. He was a deep sleeper. I toyed with the idea of making another cup of coffee while I waited for him to wake. Then I wondered if he could have put his phone on silent. He had done this before many times, and then forgot to switch it back to sound. Ah well, let him sleep off his anger. I returned to the kitchen, made toast and ate it plain while it was still warm, watching the rain slashing the windowpane.

After breakfast, I washed up, changed and made the bed. At seven, I rang him again. One, two, three rings… at the tenth ring I put down the phone. Could he be ill? Was he caught in the rain last night? Drenched like me? Or did he take some sleeping pills and overdose himself? Don't be absurd. Stop imagining. It would be so unlike him. I should just go down to his flat and knock on his door. I poured away the rest of my coffee and washed up the mug. Then I took out the broom and started to sweep the floor to pass the time.

At seven-fifteen I rang again. Still no answer. He was probably throwing a tantrum, not answering until I go down to get him. All right, all right, mister self-righteous, if that's what you want. I locked my door and took the lift down to the sixth floor. My legs were aching. I rang his doorbell several times. No one came to the door. Could he have gone to the coffeeshop for breakfast? I could catch him there if I hurry. And forgetting my aches, I ran up the four flights to my flat for an umbrella and took the lift down.

But he was not at the coffeeshop. I rang his phone again and again until an automatic voice said his number was no longer in use. That made me so riled I switched off my phone. Two could play the game.

By mid-morning, my phone's silence was getting unbearable. So I switched it on and called Ling. She sounded surprised.

'He flew to Hong Kong last night. Didn't he tell you? Richard, his son-in-law, rang him. Suk Mei is in very difficult labour. It sounded like life and death. Meng had a huge shock. He hadn't seen his daughter for such a long time. He called me when he was waiting for his flight. Why don't you try and call his Hong Kong number? He must have switched to his Hong Kong phone. I'll text you the number now.'

I thanked her and hung up. I felt humiliated. And disappointed. I had expected to be the first person he would turn to in a crisis. My fault. It was my fault. I shouldn't have run off like that last night. I called Meng on his Hong Kong number. He sounded distant and distracted.

'I'm on the way to the hospital. I can't talk now. I'll call you later.'

But he didn't call. The day crawled by. There was no news from him. I told myself not to ring him. But to wait. He had to focus on what was happening to his daughter. If something similar were to happen to Janice, God forbid, I would do the same, and shuddered at the thought. He had not seen his daughter for almost two years because he was taking care of Tony. Then after Tony's death, he had stayed on because of me. I felt very guilty. I went to church and lit a candle for his daughter and the baby.

In the evening Ling forwarded Meng's text: *Suk Mei has given birth to another son.*

I called Meng to congratulate him.

'Thank you. We were very worried. It was a very difficult delivery. The worst is not over yet. I must go now.'

That was all he said. My head throbbed all night with those words. I couldn't sleep. I had to take two pills before I fell asleep at three in the morning. The next day I messaged him twice but there was no reply. I hesitated calling again. His voice had sounded very strained and tensed.

The days were long and grey. It rained almost every day. Braving the foul weather I visited the library, spending long hours wandering between the shelves of books, my eyes glazing over the pages of print. Most afternoons found me sitting like the empty-eyed elderly men and women occupying the armchairs, an open book on my lap. I was reluctant to return to my empty apartment.

Ling was no help. She had no further news, but plenty of things to say about her brother's character whenever we were on the phone.

'Stubborn and clam-mouthed. That's what he is. He was like this when he was living in Hong Kong. He treated us like enemies. We could never get him to talk. When he got married he didn't even tell Ma. Got famous, we didn't even know. Until a relative holidaying in Hong Kong rang to tell Ma one night. When his daughter and her husband came here they didn't call on us.'

I kept myself busy. I went to the market with Madam Soh and bought pork, chicken and vegetables, and cooked dishes enough for two or more. I ate what I could and gave the rest to an appreciative Khim and her brood or to Madam Soh whose youngest son had come back to live with her.

When I grew tired of cooking and eating on my own, I returned to having my dinners in the coffeeshop where there was the company of Khim and the cheerful beer ladies. I phoned Janice a couple of times, but we didn't talk as much as before. She sounded busy. She was living a full life now, she said. She was conducting rehearsals for an upcoming Cantonese opera production with the support of her university and the Chinese community in Vancouver.

'Isn't it great? I love this city. It's so multicultural. And, mom, I'm seeing someone,' she added.

I was happy for her, and a little sad that I might lose my darling girl soon.

The sense of imminent loss stayed with me all week like the foul weather. It was the monsoon season. It rained almost every day. Rain came into the lift lobby, and the residents' dripping umbrellas formed treacherous puddles. The weather was cool but miserably grey. I went out every day. When I grew tired of the National Library, I went to one of the museums or art exhibitions, wandering among the exhibits glad that Singapore had many distractions to offer. Meanwhile Por Por's journal remained unopened on my study table.

In the morning, I went back to having breakfast alone, watching the grey light dripping through the angsana trees as I buttered my toast. November came round and brought more days of blustery winds and rain from the north-east. The newspapers carried depressing articles on climate change and carbon footprint. Disastrous floods in parts of China, Indonesia and Malaysia. Typhoons in Korea, Japan and the Philippines, wild fires in Australia, and melting glaciers in the Arctic. In Singapore, the melancholic afternoons brought sudden squalls, brief thunderstorms and flash floods in Bukit Timah and Bedok. The news on the television at night showed stalled cars and buses, and trees felled across roads. A fierce typhoon was heading towards Hong Kong and China where thousands had to be evacuated. I prayed for Meng and his family.

It was raining again today with intermittent stops all morning. Rain was bearing down on the rooftops now and hitting the shuttered windows. I stayed home and tried to read, wondering what Meng was doing besides visiting his daughter in hospital. Was he leading a very busy life? So busy that he couldn't find the time to call or send me a text? Was he punishing me came another thought. Of course not. Don't be silly. He was just catching up with friends. Meeting his opera pals the way Great Grandfather Wu used to do over tea and dim sum in the teahouses. So it was very natural that he would forget my existence for long periods as he yarned over dim sum and drank tea in the teahouses in Mongkok or Tsim Sha Tsui, unaware of my loneliness, oblivious of my heartache and longing. I lay sniffling on the sofa, fighting my self-pity and a cold. Annoyed with myself. Why did I let myself grow so dependent on him? Distant rumblings of thunder added to the gloom and emptiness in the flat at night. I had failed myself. I felt unfinished and incomplete, haunted by the ghost of failure in the past, and my future seeming a foggy grey mass of dampened expectations.

Each night, I dreaded the return of the biting loneliness I had suffered in my first solitary year after I had left Sea Cove. When I had slept alone in dread that Robert would bang on the door and kick it down.

The neighbours here locked their doors early at night. The corridor was deserted after nine. I was suspicious of strangers, fearing someone might break in; fearing a man would know I lived alone and follow me home if I went out at night. Women had been murdered or raped in their apartment. And none of their neighbours knew. We often laughed at these fears but they were real, very real to those of us who lived alone. But as November slowly turned into December my courage returned. I went out for walks at night. And very late one night I even walked to the frog's legs porridge stall and had a bowl of porridge on my own.

The next day, I went out and bought a large lime green umbrella, the size of those umbrellas held by the doorman over the head of a hotel guest on a rainy day. The bright colour would make me easily visible to car drivers on a rainy night, and the large size would keep me dry against heavy rain. Despite the wet weather of December I began to take solitary walks in the city when rain kept others at home. The half empty wet streets at night were better than sun baked roads, full of people rushing for buses and taxis.

One wet evening I stopped outside the darkened Kreta Ayer People's Theatre, famed for its Cantonese operas. Years ago the theatre was not as grand as now. It didn't have a roof then. When the Golden Phoenix Cantonese Opera Troupe was performing there, its auditorium was open-air and only the stage had a roof. One evening it had started to rain during a crucial scene, and the audience got up and started to leave. As the drops fell, Great Grandfather Wu and Por Por went on singing. The orchestra led by Grandfather Wah Jai's erhu went on playing. The drumbeats grew louder and more anxious. On stage the defeated general Wu was dying in the arms of his son, the poet, a tragic role sung by Por Por with incredible precision and passion. As the rain came down she did not stop singing. The poet-son held the dying general in his arms, recalling his father's heroic deeds as the pillar of the kingdom.

He led his army. Saved the thousands of fleeing peasants!
Defended the kingdom's verdant valleys and rice fields!
I his son must stay and honour him!

He sang as the rain came pouring down. The music of the cymbals, drums and pipas rose above the clattering rain. The audience stopped leaving. Under their umbrellas they stood mesmerised in the roofless auditorium as Por Por's aria caught by the microphones soared and fought the elements. Cymbals clashed and thunder rolled. Meng and I huddling under our umbrella stood with the audience till the scene ended and the curtain came down to shouts of *Bravo! Bravo!* Meng and I joined in the shouting.

'What a way to end the scene! The general's son snatched victory from defeat! That's how I want to sing. Sing with such passion I can hold an audience in the rain,' Meng said as we ran to the backstage.

But the world was on the cusp of change. Soon audiences were flocking to the new cinemas and movies from Hollywood and Hong Kong. In Singapore, the huge audiences for Cantonese opera were beginning to shrink. One year, the company that had engaged the Golden Phoenix Opera Troupe to perform went bankrupt. There was no money to pay the troupe. Loud clamouring did not help. The bankrupt owner had run off. Everyone was miserable. In the milieu of traditional Chinese opera, the troupe worked on trust. A man's word was his honour. That was how Grandfather, the troupe's manager, had worked. But now that the owner of the company that had engaged the troupe could not be found, the troupe had not been paid. That night Por Por took off the gold necklace she was wearing. She brought out other gold necklaces from her jewellery box and asked Grandfather to pawn them the next morning. The troupe has to eat, and their families have to eat, Por Por said. During this period, without a word, Meng and his mother brought us pots of fishball noodle soup every other day and his mother refused to accept payment. As I turned away from the Kreta Ayer People's Theatre in the pouring rain, I missed Meng sorely. He was the only one with whom I shared such memories.

The next day I stayed in bed with a heavy head cold. I had caught a chill walking in the rain. I nursed myself with hot herbal drinks, and made a peppery garlicky pork bone soup and drank it steaming hot. But the soup didn't taste as good and peppery as when Meng had made it. Why didn't he call? Why didn't he? These questions plagued me all day. I fought off my need to call him, pushed off my cloying self-pity. Sickness makes us needy. I was forced to stay in bed and dosed myself with pills and more herbal drinks.

When I got well, and there was still no call from him, I was annoyed with him. Then furious with myself. I had allowed myself to depend on his company far too much. I must return to enjoy living alone again. Before he came into my life, I had expected to live a free and unencumbered life after my divorce. I had told myself some birds fly in flocks and pairs while others fly alone. Imagine the joy of flying high in the sky like the solitary Brahmin kite, unconstrained and unfettered, riding the winds. I feared being chained to another man again. No, I would not call him. If he wished to speak to me, he could ring me. If he were to check his Singapore phone, he would know the many times I had rung him. Enough.

48

One morning, the sun peeped over the rooftops. Dawn was golden and warm. I went out to the corridor to check on my plants, surprised that Madam Soh had not come out to water her roses. The days that followed soon grew hot and dry again. The city sizzled and fretted once again. The noise of pounding road works and impatient traffic snarling in the humid heat grated our ears again. The harsh sunlight whipped our skin again and drove hordes of office workers and shoppers into the air-conditioned malls at noon.

I felt better and started work on Por Por's journal again. Every morning after a walk and breakfast, I switched on the fan, sat at my desk and read through the pages of bird's feet print again. It took me more than a week to read the journal from beginning to end. Sometimes I needed the help of a dictionary I had bought when Meng was reading opera scripts with me. Sometimes I had to re-read a passage several times because of a word or phrase I could not understand without knowing its historical or literary context. Then I had to consult several dictionaries or references I found online. As I ploughed through the Chinese characters slowly during this second reading of the journal, their meanings emerged with greater clarity. They did not elude me unlike the first time I read the journal. In this re-reading, the passages began to yield meanings that added to my initial understanding, becoming something that I, the reader, was not aware of during my first reading of the journal. And this change began to shape my understanding of the text, of my grandmother's voice in the text. And it excited me. I was reading Por Por with new eyes. I could read her words with a deeper and different understanding. I could see her village environment and hear the voice of her youth more clearly as I read each journal entry. I longed to tell Meng of my new discovery, share with him my excitement and thank him for the time he had spent with me translating his opera scripts into English, which I realised now had taught me to read Chinese better, and to appreciate the fluid beauty and depth of meaning in the Chinese words.

I read daily, slowly, working through the Chinese words. Till my head was buzzing with the Cantonese used by my grandparents. Then I had lunch in the coffeeshop and went for a leisurely stroll to unwind, letting my feet meander past the shops and among the stalls in Temple Street and Trengganu Street, and down the shady lane, away from the tourists, strolling past the back of the old shophouses that led to Keong Saik Road and the three-storeyed shophouse where my mother, Choi Wan, grew up.

Choi Wan. Choi Wan. No translation could capture the beauty, splendour and tragedy of that name. When Por Por was in one of her foul moods, which often happened when the troupe was not performing, she would blame Great Grandfather Wu for giving her daughter that name.

Choi Wan. That Beautiful Cloud! What do you expect of clouds? They float away. She's gone! Gone!

Heart-wrenching sobs shook her as she held me in her arms, rocking to and fro on the floor as though she was wrestling with invisible demons trying to wrest me away from her too.

What a great scene for an opera, Meng said when I told him about it. I'm tempted to write the libretto for it.

Why don't you?

I've written things that never saw the light of day.

Show me.

No. You'll laugh.

No, I promise.

Another time. Let me dream. Don't look at me like this, Yin. Dreaming is very important. When we dream we are sending out messages or wishes to the stars and universe. No one knows what life forms are out there. One of them might respond to dreams. You never know. It's whimsical, I know. But what's life without dreams?

We laughed and stopped under the rain tree in the park, its gnarled branches outspread like a grandmother's arms welcoming her grandchildren.

I miss you, Meng. Why aren't you calling me?

Some nights, on my solitary walks I sought the city's quiet nooks where he and I had never been before, where I could get away from memories of him. Get away from his face, his voice, the warmth of his hand holding mine. Along the canals and lanes in other housing estates where the foot traffic was light and cars were few at night, I trudged. But it was impossible. Sometimes during these solitary walks, his voice came to me. Disjointed phrases and sentences, snippets of our conversations imagined or real would dart into my head like little fishes impossible to catch with notebook and pen. I had to let them go, hoping they would return when I sat down to type something out later. What it would be, I did not know yet. And it was this not-knowing that drew me to my desk night after night, and I sat down to scribble. Scribbling was what I had to do in secret back then in Sea Cove. Robert detested my scribbling and forbade it. But Meng, my dearest Meng, had encouraged it.

Scribble as much as you can. You never know what you are thinking subconsciously till you scribble whatever comes to your head and read it to yourself later, he said.

On a good night, words and phrases flowed into my head and down my limbs travelling from hand to pen, and transferred to computer screen. Meng and I sat in different parts of our flat, I in the kitchen and he in the living room, scribbling, scribbling, and typing till tired, we got up and went out for supper.

I missed him.

My mornings were spent re-reading and then translating Por Por's youthful Cantonese voice in the journal into English. The work was very slow and absorbing but it was not entirely new. When I was working in the National Archives, part of my job was to listen to the recorded recollections of old people and jot down what they said. My nights were spent scribbling after my walks, writing down what my memory recalled and what my heart felt.

And so the days passed with walking, reading, re-reading and translating in the morning. In the evening, another walk and then scribbling, writing and typing out my own thoughts and memories late into the night. Some nights I forgot that I was waiting for Meng's phone call.

One evening I opened my post box and extracted a letter with thumping heart thinking it was from Meng till I saw it had a Malaysian stamp.

The return address showed it was from a solicitor's office in Penang. The next morning I went to Mr Leong's office with the letter and sought my lawyer's advice.

49

I flew into Penang. After checking into my hotel, I went straight to the solicitor's office. Mr Edmund Khoo greeted me like an affable headmaster of a boys' school.

'Welcome to Penang, Miss Chan! I'm very glad you could come as soon as you received my letter. Please make yourself comfortable. What would you like to drink? Tea? Coffee? A glass of sparkling white perhaps? Your inheritance is a substantial one. It does call for a little celebration.'

'Tea, please, Mr Khoo.'

An office assistant brought in a cup of Chinese tea, and I drank it hot while Mr Khoo took out a file from his cabinet.

'Besides the goldsmith shop, there's a substantial number of bonds and shares. You're a very beloved grandchild. Your grandmother left everything to you.'

He sat down, and took great pains to go over the details of my grandmother's will with me. But my mind floated away to that evening when a five-year-old had stuck her head through the stage curtains and stared at the woman in black who was smiling at her through her tears.

'Everything your grandmother had owned is yours now.'

I wished Meng were with me. I had been fighting against this neediness for the comfort of his presence ever since I received the solicitor's letter.

'Miss Chan. Miss Chan.'

'Sorry, Mr Khoo. I am overwhelmed.'

'It's very natural. Very natural. But don't worry. I've prepared everything. All you have to do is to sign some papers now.' He handed me a pen. 'Here. That's right. And here. And here. Well,' he gathered up the papers. 'That's all for the time being. I'll see to the rest.'

'Mr Khoo. I'd like to see… no, I'd like to visit my grandmother's goldsmith shop. I've never been there.'

'Not even once in your childhood?' He arched a brow.

'Not even once. I would like to see it. Today.'

'Well, by the by, Miss Chan. I'm sure you couldn't eat anything on the flight. I've made reservations for us for tea at the E&O Hotel. They serve the best English high tea in all of Malaysia. Can't claim you've been to Penang without going to the E&O,' he chuckled. 'Relax. Don't look so worried. I'll take care of all the legal nitty-gritties. Like what I did for your grandmother.'

The tearoom was quiet. Furnished in the English colonial style with a black and white tiled floor. Tables had starched white tablecloths, starched white linen napkins and silver tableware. A fan was whirring half-heartedly from the high ceiling, but it kept the room cool. There were few guests. We sat by the window.

A waiter brought the usual three silver tiers of delicate looking cream cakes, thin cucumber sandwiches of white bread, and small savouries of fried spring rolls and curry puffs, a pot of tea and a small jug of milk.

'I've been handling Madam's affairs for more than thirty years. She'd never had tea with me. Not even a drink. So I thought I should have tea with her granddaughter,' he chuckled again. 'Well! Here's to the new owner of Good Fortune Goldsmith!'

He raised his teacup.

'Thank you, Mr Khoo. I don't feel deserving of this. I don't even know my grandmother. In fact I've never met her at all.'

'Have you really never met her?' He was surprised.

'I may have caught a glimpse of her now and again. But I was very young.'

'Well, well,' then a long *Hmmmm*, and smile. 'Let's see. I don't know how you will feel when you visit the shop and meet her employees. They're very old, you know. And extremely loyal to your grandmother and the shop. But frankly, the shop has not been doing well for years.'

Ignoring the cream cakes, I selected a savoury curry puff.

'And, well, hmmm, Miss Chan, I might as well tell you now. A few developers have expressed an interest in buying over the shop.'

I bit into the curry puff.

'There's even talk of putting up the entire row of shops for sale.'

I nodded, drank my tea, not sure how I should handle this information.

For a while we ate in silence. Then I tried more savouries.

'Well then.' Mr Khoo was about to say something, but changed his mind when he glanced at his watch. He put down his fork.

'How time flies in good company.' Chuckling, he patted his paunch. 'I'd better take you to the shop to meet the employees. Mustn't keep the old folks waiting too long, else they will scold me,' he laughed. 'All of them are fierce true-blue Cantonese.'

'I'm Cantonese, Mr Khoo.' And smiled, probably for the first time since I touched down.

'I know, Miss Chan. The Chans are usually Cantonese. As you can surmise from my family name, I'm Peranakan. We Straits-born Chinese are said to be of softer ilk because of our rich life. Our forebears who had learnt English had clerked for the colonial masters and made a comfortable living.' Chortling, he patted his paunch. 'I used to play tennis. Must take it up again.'

We drove down Campbell Street in good humour and he pointed out various shops to me.

'Once they were very popular but had to close down or changed hands. It's sad. Very sad. The heyday of the Chinese goldsmith on this island is over.'

A mix of pride and resignation had crept into his tone. He drove slowly down the road. There weren't many cars, and few customers in the shops.

'Campbell Street was once the most important shopping street in Penang. People would come from all over to shop here for jewellery, high quality textiles and watches. The Chinese used to own all the shops here. Look at those faded Chinese signboards. Those shops have changed hands. Soon there will be pubs and coffee houses and shops selling tourist curios, Malay baju, sarong and kebaya. The younger generation have different ideas. Change, as they say, is inevitable,' he sighed for the first time since we met.

We drove on in silence till a majestic mosque came into view. Mr Khoo stopped our car outside a half-shuttered shop at the end of the row of two-storey shophouses. Two large white lanterns and a white banner covering the shop's signboard showed that the residents were in mourning.

'Well, here we are. The only remaining Chinese goldsmith and jewellery store on Campbell Street.'

I was taken aback. A line of dismal-looking old men and women were standing outside the shop. All sorts of thoughts rushed through my head – are these the old employees? For the life of me I couldn't see myself as their employer and owner of this goldsmith shop where my mother had bled to death on the kitchen floor. No, no! I didn't want to meet these old people. That was my first thought. My second was Meng. If he were here he would hold my hand. He would know what to do. I remained seated in the car while the memory of how Meng had held my hand when we visited Madam Mei Lai flashed past. I glanced again at the six old men and two women. One of the women was hunched.

'Mr Khoo, I would like to pay my respects to my grandmother first.'

'Yes, of course, of course.'

He got out of the car and came over to my side. As he opened the car door, he bent down slightly and said in a low voice, 'If you'd asked for my advice I would have advised you to wait till I've introduced you. These folks have been waiting all week to meet you. Ever since I told them you are coming.'

Still I made no move to get out of the car.

'What happens to them if I sell the shop?'

'Oh that. You needn't worry. You must have forgotten what was in the will. Everyone has been provided for. Your grandmother made sure of that. These people are her family. They've been with her all their life. Through all the ups and downs of the business. Looked after her throughout her troubles and illnesses. They are extremely loyal to her. You mustn't say a word against her. They joined the shop when they were just teenagers. Grew up with your grandmother and the goldsmith business. They're very skilled craftsmen too. Every one of them.'

I got out of the car and walked towards them.

'Welcome home, madam.' A tone of restraint in their greeting.

Mr Khoo introduced the oldest among them.

'This is Mr Chong, the manager.'

They were in their seventies, years older than me. Tradition and manners, their age and the fact that they were such faithful employees dictate a change in my greeting. I felt I had to address the men as Uncle and the two women as *Jieh* because they were unmarried.

'Uncle Chong,' I greeted him.

He smiled. At eighty-two with thinning silvery hair, still spry and wiry, and dignified, he acknowledged my greeting and introduced the others but kept his introductions brief.

'Our Madam had waited all her life for her granddaughter to come visit,' he said in Cantonese. 'I'll take you to her to pay your respects.'

He led me into the shop, ushered me into the hall behind the shop front and opened the door to a prayer room. The others including Mr Khoo crowded inside with me.

A red glow lit up the spartanly furnished wood-panelled room. The centrepiece was a rosewood altar lit by an electric red lamp. In front of the altar, a small table, a footstool and an armchair. On the wall behind the altar hung a large framed Chinese scroll. A prayer cushion, looking much used, lay on the floor. The room had the lonely air of a widow's solitude. No one spoke while I stood before the large black and white photograph propped up on the small table. My grandmother had such sad eyes. Such a sad, sorrowful face of lines and wrinkles. She wore no ornaments other than a pair of jade earrings. Her memorial tablet on the altar stood between two other memorial tablets of dark wood. On one side was my grandfather; on the other side was a tablet carved with two names. One of the names was my mother's; the other was my father's. Behind the altar hung a large framed scroll of Chinese calligraphy written in the cursive style.

'Written by your grandfather when he was a young man.' Uncle Chong broke the silence. 'Your grandmother said her prayers here every evening.'

'And cried here on many evenings. From five to six after the shop had closed. We were not allowed to come in.' Kan Jieh spoke fast. Adding what Uncle Chong left out. 'At six sharp, she came out. And dinner began. The men ate first. Women later. We had a lot of workers then. Ah Mooi here,' she pointed to the hunched woman, 'was our cook.'

'But I rarely cook now,' Mooi Jieh chimed in. 'The cooks before me had to cook three times a day. I used to set the table twice for each meal… breakfast, lunch, tea and dinner for more than twenty workers.'

'Enough, enough. Madam is waiting.' Uncle Chong shushed them.

No one said a word after that. Kan Jieh lit a joss stick and handed it to me. I bowed before the portrait and stuck the joss stick into the urn of ash. Then with the others standing behind me, I knelt and kowtowed to the grandmother, grandfather and parents I had never met. My eyes were a little damp. The result of instinct or reflex perhaps. But not grief. For I felt no sorrow. Just a dull ache in my heart. And regret that I had not met this grandmother. This kneeling and kowtowing was a ritual passed down the generations, a ritual I had to perform to comfort the living around me. These old, loyal employees sniffling behind me. I didn't know who to pity – I, the tearless descendant or the eight elderly employees. With a sigh, I stood up and turned around. They came forward, smiling through their tears. One by one, they took my hand in theirs.

'Welcome home, young madam.'

'Welcome home, young madam. It's good that you've come home at last.'

'Your grandmother in heaven is very happy now.'

'Yes, very happy. Her soul can rest in peace at last.'

We returned to the shop front, and as if the sense of restraint among the men seemed to have dissipated with the incense smoke everyone started to speak.

'We are still in mourning so the shop counter is still covered with a white sheet. We haven't opened for business yet, young madam.'

'And these six rosewood stools in front of the counter are for customers only. They sit while they look through the ornaments.'

'And young madam, here are the two leather armchairs Madam bought ten years ago. No other shop had them at the time. Very modern then. See this armchair? It's very worn now.'

'That's been Madam's seat for years. She sat here every day,' Kan Jieh said, stroking the worn leather with a loving hand.

'See this spittoon? It's for her after she recovered from her stroke,' Mooi Jieh added. 'Old Madam used to sit here to meet clients and conduct business. I would bring her a flask of pu'er tea mid-morning to remind her to stop working.'

'Ah Kan, Ah Mooi. You two are tiring our young madam.'

Laughing I said, 'Uncle Chong, this young madam here is no longer young. My daughter is already more than twenty-one.'

'Twenty-one! Is that so?'

Exclamations of delight lit up their old faces.

One of the men said, 'I remember our Madam's great granddaughter. She's just a toddler in that photo upstairs! How time flies!'

'Blink of an eye! And now she's more than twenty-one,' Uncle Lau laughed.

'And the toddler has gone overseas to university!' I added.

'Is that so? A smart girl! We have a scholar in the family!'

They were so proud and delighted at the news.

'How did all of you know about my daughter?'

'Old Madam told us. Whenever she came back from Singapore, she always brought back news of you.'

'And sometimes of your daughter,' Kan Jieh added. 'But first she would go into the prayer hall to tell your grandfather. Then she would come out and tell all of us over dinner.'

'Really? What's my grandmother like? I'd like to hear more about her.'

'*Aaah!* You'll have to stay for dinner then,' Mooi Jieh turned to me, beaming. 'Your grandmother's spirit will be very happy if you stay for dinner and the night. You've come all the way from Singapore. Why stay in a hotel? This shophouse is yours now.'

'That's right! Why stay in a hotel?'

There was such expectation in their old eyes. How could I say no? It was very difficult to refuse. Besides, I didn't relish the thought of eating hotel food alone, and I wanted to know about my grandmother, see the gold smithy, and get to know these elderly craftsmen who had made gold ornaments by hand for more than fifty years. Such Chinese goldsmiths were rare these days in Singapore and Malaysia. Most had already retired or passed away, their craftsmanship and skills dying with them. None of the young Chinese wanted to learn the goldsmith trade and perfect a craft that took years to master. Technology had replaced craftsmanship, and factory produced gold ornaments were much cheaper and in greater demand. Traditional Chinese goldsmith shops had declined. Many had been sold and pulled down by developers rushing to build shopping malls and hotels.

I turned to Uncle Chong.

'But I've left my bag in the hotel.'

'No problem. Chauffeur here!' Uncle Seng quipped. 'I can drive you to the hotel after dinner. After that, we'll all go *makan angin*.'

Everyone laughed for I must have looked very puzzled by the Malay phrase.

'Literally *makan* means eat, *angin* means wind. So *makan angin* is to eat wind,' Mr Khoo explained. 'Metaphorically, it means to go for a leisurely drive or spin. Enjoy the breeze, especially the sea breeze if you go down Gurney Drive in the evening to *makan angin*.'

'That's such a lovely expression. If it's not too much trouble, Uncle Seng.'

'What trouble? No trouble at all!'

'But in case our not-so-young madam changes her mind,' Uncle Lau grinned, 'let's fetch her bags now before dinner.'

'Well then, Miss Chan, I see you are in good hands.'

Mr Khoo took his leave, and I promised to call on him the next day.

After his departure, Uncle Seng and Uncle Lau drove me to the hotel while Mooi Jieh and Kan Jieh got dinner ready.

We ate alfresco under a square of night sky in the inner courtyard that was an air well, a common feature of old colonial shophouses. Two fluorescent tubes kept the dining area well lit and a standing fan kept the insects away.

'In the old days a fan was a great necessity. It was very hot inside the workroom. Ah Lau used to do the firing and melting of the gold in there before shaping them,' Uncle Seng explained.

On a sudden impulse, Uncle Lau got up from his seat. He took me into the workroom and switched on the overhead lights. The thick walls were blackened from years of fire and heat.

'For more than forty years I worked in here every day. See this machine? It's my gemstone grinder from Germany. And this here is my polisher.'

His wrinkled hand stroked the two machines like a man stroking his old faithful workhorses. Pride shone in his eyes.

'I was the first to train with goldsmiths in Hong Kong. When I came back I taught the others. In my time, we were the first goldsmith shop to modernise. Before that everything – from cutting, firing, shaping, polishing – everything was done by hand. Very laborious. This here is Ah Seng's desk.

And here is his wooden plane for intricate work. His set of goldsmith tools. See those?'

He pointed to the sets of small hammers, tweezers and pliers.

'His tools were always neatly arranged at the end of the day. These things sadly are retired. Like us.'

'Hey! You two in there! Ah Mooi's steamed fish is growing cold!'

A chorus of voices called out to us.

Dinner was a simple meal. Every dish was steamed. There was soft steamed rice. A steamed sea bream with sliced ginger, sesame oil and soy sauce. A large plate of minced pork steamed with salted fish and salted egg. And steamed *choy sum* vegetables.

'All the food your grandmother likes. We ate what she could eat. So we could eat together as one family. Every night we sat here together. Like this.'

Mooi Jieh's eyes started to redden. Kan Jieh and a few of the men coughed and tried to stifle their sniffling.

'Young madam.'

'Please call me Xiu Yin, Uncle Chong.'

'Don't mind us, Xiu Yin. We get a little teary at meal times. More than half a century together. How can we not miss her?'

'Like Madam, all of us came from the same village, Saam Hor,' Uncle Lau said. 'At fourteen, fifteen or sixteen, poor and starving, we came here to work. Madam fed us well. Very well. Gave us clothes. Bought us shoes. I wore my first pair of shoes here. And had to learn how to walk in leather shoes.'

We laughed, and started to eat.

'She was unlike any woman from Saam Hor. She knew how to read and write and count. Her accounting was like the men's. Quick and sharp. No one could cheat her. She told us your grandfather had taught her how to read and how to use the abacus. And… and she taught me,' Uncle Chong's voice was hoarse and whispery. 'Every night after dinner, she… she taught me how to… to do the accounts. For a village lad in those days, that was a big, big skill to learn.'

'And she told us, she was ignorant like us when she first came out to the Nanyang. Work hard, she always urged us. If you want to learn, I will make sure you get training. She sent me to Hong Kong. I was the first to go. And she… she paid to send me to learn from a master goldsmith. For a year.' Uncle Lau choked up.

'She scolded us but never caned us girls. Never deprived us of food. Unlike other employers.' Mooi Jieh blew her pink nose on a large white handkerchief. Her voice growing gentle and soft, she said, 'Madam, bless her soul, was like a mother to us.'

'She even acted as matchmaker,' Kan Jieh chipped in.

'*Aaah*, how she enjoyed that!' Uncle Lau said, chuckling as memories filled his eyes. 'She found spouses for those who wanted to marry. Many of the men and women who worked here were betrothed to each other here. In this very courtyard.'

'On their wedding day the lucky couple served tea to Old Madam as though she were their mother, and she gave them each a large *hong bao*. We were a very happy family then. Aye, it's fate truly. Fate that her own life was so dark and tragic.' Kan Jieh started to sob.

'Hey, hey!' Uncle Seng broke up the sombre cloud that threatened to descend on the table. 'Is our young madam to dine on sorrow on her first night in her grandmother's home? Old Madam is happy in heaven! Very happy that her granddaughter has come home at long last.'

'True! True! Let's drink and wash off the dust from your journey, Xiu Yin. *Yaam seng!*' Uncle Chong raised his cup.

'*Yaa…aaam seng!*' The others shouted and raised their cups of tea.

'Bring out the pu'er tea and stop sniffling, Kan Jieh! Let Xiu Yin try Old Madam's favourite brew.'

Red-eyed but smiling, they settled down again to eat.

'She had a good head for business, your grandmother,' Uncle Lau began again when we were drinking our tea after dinner. 'Our shop was the only shop on Campbell Street that made and sold jewellery that the Malay women liked. Let me tell you how clever she was. One day Madam looked at the mosque over there. She said to me, Ah Lau, many Malays go to the mosque near us. They should come to our shop to buy our jewellery then. Come. Let's go for a walk in the market. See what jewellery the Malay women wear. After those walks, we started to change our designs. And slowly, the Malay people came. After a good rice harvest, even Malay farmers on the mainland would bring their wives here to buy our gold chains for Hari Raya. We made and sold a lot of gold chains and gold pendants in those days.'

'*Aaah*, those were happy years. Every Chinese New Year, the married ones brought their wives and children back to serve Madam tea. Every year we had a big reunion dinner. Three or four tables at least. At night, we fired strings of red crackers. Young Master and the other children screamed and laughed. Sometimes Madam took all of us and Young Master to watch the opera. One year Madam bought a car. And Young Master, your father had a car...'

'Enough, enough! Let's go *makan angin*.' Uncle Chong rose from the table. 'I want to show Xiu Yin where Madam walked when she could still walk before her stroke. We'll go to Gurney Drive.'

50

I sat up in my grandmother's bed. I could not sleep. Not because of her bed. It was the photos. I couldn't take my eyes off the wall that was covered with framed photographs of me from the time I was a toddler to when I was married and had Janice. Many of the childhood photographs were black and white grainy images, taken with a camera from a distance. There were photos of me in school uniform outside my CHIJ primary school. Photos of me as a teenager in jeans and tees. Photos of me with my classmates near my CHIJ secondary school in Victoria Street, then some of me as a young woman in a frock, in a graduation gown standing next to my beaming grandfather, and in a wedding gown in a photo studio. Many of the newer photos were clear images in full colour. Some were publicity photos for opera performances when I was a youngster. There was a large framed photograph of Meng and I posing arm in arm as tortoises in *The Legend of Madam White Snake*. And several photos of the two of us attired in different costumes in other operas that I had forgotten. In others, I was posing with Por Por or Great Grandfather Wu and other opera actors. There was a grainy photograph of Robert and I coming out of the Holy Family Church on our wedding day. Obviously shot from a distance by a stranger. And then there was a blurry photograph of a very pregnant me walking into the National Archives. And another photo of me with Janice cradled in my arms at the doctor's. And a beautiful coloured photo of Janice, her chubby arms outstretched, toddling towards Robert and I in the Botanic Gardens.

The sight of these photographs shocked me when Kan Jieh brought me into the bedroom.

'How did these photos get here?' I raised my voice. I was so shocked.

'I... I don't know,' came her evasive reply.

I tried not to sound accusing when I asked her again.

'Some of these photographs are private, Kan Jieh. I didn't know my grandmother then. And I still don't know her. If she hasn't passed away I will ask her. How did she get hold of them? My Por Por and Grandfather would never have sent her these photos. Did she send someone to tail and photograph me? Throughout my life from the time I was a baby? Oh my god! What was she doing? Robbing my life like this. What did she think she was doing?'

By then I was very upset. And so was Kan Jieh.

'These photos saved your grandmother's life! Gave her a purpose to live!'

Kan Jieh's voice rose as high as mine.

'You have to understand, Xiu Yin! Your grandmother wanted to end her life! Many, many times! Her world had shattered after your father died! The night she lost her only son was the night she lost her purpose in living! It was also the night she hung herself. In this very room. From there. From that beam up there. Luckily Chong Suk found her and cut the rope. We were all traumatised. We never left her alone after that. She had lost the will to live. Months later, that photo of you arrived.'

She pointed to the black-and-white photo of a baby, eagerly crawling towards the photographer.

'That saved your grandmother's life,' she said, and left the room.

I studied the photo's background. It was my grandparents' attic in Great Grandfather Wu's shophouse in Keong Saik Road. A stranger would have had no access to their attic. This was a photo taken by someone who knew my grandparents. Who had sent the photo here? I thought of Madam Mei Lai, but dismissed the thought. She was in Hong Kong at the time. It couldn't have been Por Por or Grandfather either. They would never do such a thing.

I couldn't sleep. I kept thinking of the obsession behind the wall of photos. An obsession that drove an old woman to steal images. To steal and possess something of the grandchild she had disowned and could no longer have. Some of the grainy black-and-white photographs of me were taken in private domains. Taken without my grandparents' knowledge and permission. The later ones of me as an adult were taken without my knowledge. Most likely by a hired private eye. Or even by my grandmother herself. I thought of the woman in black. Seated in a corner of the theatre. She looked like a venomous black spider to me now. I felt both contempt and sorrow for her. I could not connect her with the picture of the old lady downstairs. The one with such sorrowful eyes. I could not sleep.

I left the bedroom and went down the stairs.

51

There was a streak of red glow from the prayer room. Its door was slightly ajar. I pushed the door and went in. Uncle Chong looked up from his chair. His face was wan and sad.

'Can't sleep?' he asked.

'Those photos on the wall...'

'I know. Kan Jieh told me.'

'How did my grandmother acquire them?'

I pulled the footstool towards me and sat next to him. I was not going to leave until he told me.

Uncle Chong let out a sigh. 'I got them for her.'

'You?'

'She tried to kill herself. Not once. But several times. You must understand your father was her life. Her only child. The apple of her eye. The core of her heart. After he died in that horrific car accident she had nothing to live for. No husband. No son. No daughter-in-law. No grandchild. Nothing. We didn't count at the time. We were just her employees. She tried to hang herself. Twice she drank poison. Tried to hang herself again two more times. Cut her wrists three or four times. I had to do something. I had to...' His voice trailing off, he fell silent.

'So you paid someone to take those photos?'

'I boarded the train for Singapore. It took me two days before I found Master Wu. I begged him. Literally went down on my knees to beg him for a photo of you. Then I made him an offer. An offer he could not refuse.'

He took out his handkerchief and mopped his brow. The room was so silent I could hear his breath.

'I asked around. Then I found out the Golden Phoenix Troupe was in financial trouble. Your Por Por was in no state to perform. Your grandfather was in deep grief. But their troupe had to eat. Musicians had to be paid. I offered Master Wu two thousand dollars.'

'Two thousand dollars was a lot of money in those days.'

'It was a fortune. That first photo of you,' his voice turning hoarse and whispery, 'that photo was worth every cent. Her son's flesh and blood. That photo of you brought a smile to her pale gaunt face. The first smile in many, many months.'

He looked at me. His eyes pleading.

'Xiu Yin, you've got to understand. Your grandmother was a stick by then. Just skin and bones. She had no appetite. She could not eat. But after seeing that photo of you, she started to eat. Started to take an interest in the goldsmith business again. I told her she had a granddaughter to think of. Her only son's flesh and blood. A grave responsibility.'

I took a deep breath but I said nothing. Above us, the old wooden floorboards creaked. Someone was going to the toilet. There was the sound of flushing water, then the creak of the wooden boards again. Then the house settled down, and quiet returned.

'You saved your grandmother's life.'

'Two thousand dollars was a princely sum in those days, Uncle Chong. How did you get so much money?'

A smile rippled across his wrinkles.

'I pulled the biscuit tin from under my bed. Counted up all my savings. And the others contributed the rest. Then I took the train back to Singapore, and five days later, I came back with your photograph.'

I looked at his eighty-two-year-old face and shook my head.

'All your life savings, Uncle Chong.'

'We couldn't bear to see her wither away before our eyes and not do anything. Couldn't bear to let her life's work go to greed. Her in-laws in China would have come and taken over the shop and the business that she had worked so hard to build when she was a widow.'

We looked at her photograph propped up on the table. The red glow of the altar lamp fell upon her sad eyes. I noticed that Uncle Chong had the same sad eyes. His face reflected the same sorrowful look, the same sorrowful lines etched on my grandmother's face. They could have been husband and wife, and he could be my grandfather. I patted his old wrinkled hand. I felt very close to this kind old man who, a few hours ago, was a stranger to me.

'My grandmother was very fortunate to have you take such good care of her.'

A wan smile flitted across his face. A hand brushed off my comment. I thought that was the end of our talk. But then his eyes lit up as he turned to me.

'You're wrong, Xiu Yin. I am the fortunate one. I had the good fortune to be by her side. I accompanied her everywhere. Once a year the two of us travelled together for two weeks to the mainland. To buy gold and precious stones from the native Orang Asli, people who live in the jungle. We had to travel by elephant for part of the journey. She wasn't afraid, your grandmother. She was very brave. She used to travel with your grandfather, she told me. After your grandfather passed away, one of his cousins used to go with her. When the cousin returned to China, she chose me to go with her. For more than fifty years, fifty years,' he repeated, 'we travelled together. Two weeks. Just the two of us. For more... than... five... decades we...'

He spread out his fingers on his knees, muttering more to himself than to me, his voice edged with pain and anger at what could have been if only, if only he had had the courage to reach for it. That was what I was thinking as I listened to him, but it was my interpretation so I said nothing.

He sat in the armchair, staring into the silence. His mind, I thought, his mind was probably seeing not the sad old woman with the wrinkled face in the photograph, but the young widow who sat swaying against him in the basket on the elephant. A young widow who wore a white flower in her hair. Just like the young widow Por Por had described in her journal.

'During one of our trips she twisted her ankle and couldn't walk,' he went on. 'Our two Orang Asli guides offered to carry her back to the village. But she refused to let the two men touch her. After a lot of persuasion, she finally allowed me, and only me, to piggyback her to the village, and I put her on the bed in her room. That night I washed her feet in warm water and massaged her foot with the oil provided by the guides. She was a very stubborn woman in those days,' he chuckled. 'We stayed three days in that house. And I massaged her foot every day and night. She had such small feet and smooth hands.'

Smiling to himself, he was silent for a long while.

'Why didn't you marry my grandmother, Uncle Chong?'

'Uh?' he awoke from his reverie. 'Marry her?' he asked, the two words rolling out of his mouth slowly as he smiled at my ignorance. 'Xiu Yin, don't you understand? We lived in a different time. There was strict protocol. She was my employer. She would have sacked me if I so much as whispered marriage.'

The wrinkles on his face cracked with pain. Then he caught himself and turned to me, his eyes twinkling.

'But just between the two of us, and in front of her good self here, I wouldn't say I didn't think of marriage all those years ago. Every night, in fact, I dreamt of it. Countless times a day, in fact, I thought of it as I stood next to her. I was already in my thirties. I did want to marry but the tides were against me. The times were different then. Tradition bound us like chains. The old ways circumscribed our lives. Imprisoned our minds. Hierarchy was so strong. The elders' law was unbreakable. The law of the village. We could not escape it. Even though we had left the old country, its laws followed us into the new. She had to remain a widow. She would lose her son, her shop and her business if she remarried. And worse, if she were to marry me, her servant. The business community here would shun her. And then, there was always Young Master, her son, your father, to think of. His lineage and his inheritance to protect. A very heavy responsibility for a young widow and mother. How could I a servant be Young Master's father?'

I shook my head. The hidden sorrows of the old among us would follow them to their graves.

'It would have been very nice if you were my grandpa.'

I placed a hand on his. His fingers grasped it tightly. So moved was he that he could not speak. The house had grown very quiet by now. Everyone except the two of us was asleep. I didn't move away my hand, but remained seated on the footstool close to him till he finally let go. I stood up and walked over to the altar. I lit a joss stick and bowed before my grandmother's memorial tablet. Sorry that I had thought of her as a venomous black spider earlier. Then I stuck the joss stick into the urn and stood watching its white wisps of smoke rise and curl before dissipating. Poor woman. She too must have suffered.

When I turned around, Uncle Chong's eyes were closed. Thinking he had fallen asleep, I walked towards the door.

'Don't go yet, Xiu Yin.' His hand stopped me. 'Please sit awhile more with me. We don't know if I'll be here to meet you again after this trip.'

I sat down back on the footstool. He took my hand in his again, his palm warm and dry as parchment.

'Before you leave Penang, Xiu Yin, before you leave us, I want you to know your grandmother was not a cruel woman. But a mother blinded by love, and rage, and disappointment with her son on the night he brought your mother here. In one single act of wrong doing that night, she lost all she treasured. And you, poor babe, were left an orphan. It was tragic. Most tragic. She couldn't forgive herself. All her life she regretted it. And tried, tried very hard to make amends. Tried to send money for the little orphan, her granddaughter. But the money was always returned.'

He squeezed my hand and held it.

'I was very well cared for,' I said. 'Por Por and Grandfather treasured me. They loved me very, very much.'

I tried to console him, and he squeezed my hand again. I got up and hugged him. He coughed! Coughing into his handkerchief several times. And wiped his face several times to hide his sudden tears.

'How... how like your father.'

He choked on his words and dabbed his eyes.

'No.'

'Yes,' he stopped my protest. 'When your father was this little, six or seven years old, he hugged me too. I've not been hugged like this since your father was a little boy. One evening I gave him a kite and taught him to fly it. He hugged me. After that he hugged me each time we flew the kite. Every evening the two of us would go out to the back lane to fly that kite. When he could fly it on his own, I bought myself another kite. Every kite season we flew our kites in the back lane. The neighbourhood boys joined us. And we competed to see whose kite could fly the highest. And your grandmother, a young mother then, would come out to watch us and bring us towels and drinks. Later when it was the top-spinning season, I got him a top. Taught him how to spin it faster and longer than the other boys' tops. Aye, he loved me then, your father. He followed me everywhere. There was one evening he refused to go with Madam to the opera unless I went along. That was how I started to accompany Madam to the opera,' he said, his voice growing soft and dreamy. 'The three of us sat in the third row. Your father seated between us. We looked like a family, I thought. I could see that Madam was pleased too. She didn't mind my presence. Even enjoyed my company. And... and we talked of other things, not the shop, not the business. But other matters. ... Aye, matters close to our hearts,' he sighed again. 'I was so happy then. I felt I had a family.'

I said nothing, listening to him quietly lest if I said the wrong thing it would spoil his dreams and memories, and make an old man unhappy. Poor Uncle Chong. What self-sacrifice, what self-restraint he had endured. Curbing his young man's desires. Restraining his flesh. What should not be felt, he tried not to feel. What should not be said he left unsaid, what could not be touched he left untouched. And my grandmother must have punished herself like this too. He for his beloved, my grandmother, and she for her only son, my father. What strange complexities of love and guilt between these two. Their lovemaking was reduced to the massage of a young widow's small delicate feet.

The joss stick had burned down to the halfway mark by now when Uncle Chong, who had fallen silent, spoke again, his voice soft and melancholic.

'Aye... happiness dies young; sorrow has a long life. In those happy years when Young Master was growing up and flying kites with me, Madam often spoke to me about him. She had so many plans for him. But, aye, life is a wild stallion. It always throws us off when we least expect it. In the book of *The Three Kingdoms*, it was said that planning belongs to man, success to Heaven. Nothing could change this; nothing ever will. I sit here every night and think of her. I no longer plan. If Destiny permits, I humbly request Heaven to let the two of us be man and wife in our next life. It's my only prayer till the day I die.'

The tears he was trying to hold back rolled down his wrinkled cheeks. And this time he did not take out his handkerchief to wipe them away. I stroked his hand, dry and papery to the touch. What could I say? What had cried out to be said he had finally said it with such restraint and grace. The young would not understand him. Most would think him a fool. But not I. Who was I to judge him? The old man had loved. And loved far more deeply than any man or woman I knew.

We were silent for a long time. I sat beside him on the footstool and waited till he fell asleep. Then I got up and went out to the hallway, and closed the door.

The old shophouse was in silence except for the occasional squeak of a bed when someone turned in his sleep. I walked out to the courtyard where we had had our dinner earlier. There was something I wanted to see before I leave the next morning.

A soft breeze came through the air well as I made my way into the kitchen. It was dark inside except for a bit of light coming in from a street lamp in the back lane. I saw the silhouette of an old-fashioned coal stove. A large wok, a pot and a pan sat on the cooking range. The floor was plain concrete. Down the two steps into the kitchen were two pairs of red wooden clogs. I wondered where she had lain down. Where they had placed the mat and rags for her to lie. Whether she had cried out aloud for assistance. And who had helped her. Did someone hold her hand out of pity? She was just seventeen when she gave birth to me. Was there a midwife with her? Or did they leave her alone to bleed to death? I blinked away my tears. I had never missed her or cried for her before.

'Ahem!'

A soft cough made me turn round. I saw the hunched shape.

'Mooi Jieh,' I greeted the former cook.

'I knew you'd come tonight, ' she said softly.

'I had to see where my mother died.'

'I understand. Every anniversary we set up a table here. And your grandmother made offerings. Prayed that she would rest in peace and be reborn to a good life. I'm sure after so many years of prayers your mother has been reborn.'

'A comforting thought. But it doesn't change anything, does it?'

'No, it doesn't,' she sighed. 'Nothing changes our past until compassion and forgiveness enter our heart.'

I remained silent.

'Please don't hate your grandmother. What's past is past. Let it go. Let it flow away like water in the river. Like water, life does not flow backwards. Your mother's spirit is no longer in my kitchen. I'm the cook here. I know. Go to bed. It's very late.'

I stooped down and my hand swept the concrete floor. Once. A sudden gesture. Done before I realised it. An instinctual respect. I straightened up.

'Good night, Mooi Jieh.'

'Good night, Xiu Yin.'

52

The next day I met Mr Khoo in his office, and arranged for the shop not to be sold for as long as one of the employees was living in it.

'Are you sure?' He met my eyes. 'Is this what you want to do? There are three very interested buyers willing to pay a high price for the shop.'

'Just follow my instructions, Mr Khoo. I've made up my mind.'

'How like your grandmother,' he chuckled as he shook my hand.

That same afternoon, he drove Uncle Chong and I, with Uncle Lau and the others following in another car, to view the home that my grandmother had chosen for them to spend their last years.

Set amidst lots of greenery halfway up Penang Hill, the home had a lovely view of the sea and the city below. I turned to Uncle Chong.

'It's entirely your decision. You and Uncle Lau, Uncle Seng, Kan Jieh, Mooi Jieh will decide whether you wish to move here or not. The decision is up to you. Not me. Not Mr Khoo. Not even my grandmother. The goldsmith shop remains your home. It will not be sold as long as one of you is living there. But any time you wish to move here, Mr Khoo will arrange it. You understand, Grandpa?'

Uncle Chong patted my hand.

'Mr Khoo,' he grinned, 'looks like I've just gained a granddaughter.'

'Looks like it, Old Chong!' the others laughed.

I stayed three more days with them. When I said goodbye, I felt I had gained a new family. Everyone came to the airport to see me off. We had lunch, took photos and shed a few tears.

'But happy tears, happy tears,' Kan Jieh laughed as she dabbed her eyes.

Uncle Seng grinned. 'You must come again and *makan angin*.'

'And I will cook for you again,' Mooi Jieh hugged me.

I hugged each of them in turn, and at the final call for boarding, I embarrassed Uncle Chong with a hug and a kiss on his cheek.

'Goodbye, Grandpa,' I whispered in his ear.

53

August. The hottest month of the year. Metallic sunlight scorched the skin. Diesel fumes from the city's buses and the stink of human sweat agitated sensitive noses. Passengers poured out of the buses and scrambled into the shaded walkways. A woman clutching her handbag pushed through the crowd, hurrying to catch up with a man who was likely to be her husband. Her face wore that anxious, harried look I knew so well. As I stood outside the coffeeshop watching her, the sudden realisation that I was no longer like her struck me. Hand on my breast, I thanked God as I watched the harried woman pushing and nudging through the crowd until she was out of sight.

Gone! I said to myself with great relief. The hounded anxious wife who had followed me out of Sea Cove along with my luggage when I moved out, had finally left me. Or was it I who had left her? I was the agent. I had shed her off, like an old skin, bit by bit, ever since I moved to Jin Swee. How many years was that? Time was immaterial. My new self had emerged, no longer a sapling but a strong tree, firmly rooted in my new environment. I had taken charge of my inheritance in Penang. Had instructed Mr Khoo to make the necessary legal arrangements for Uncle Chong and the others to continue the goldsmith business and live in the shop for as long as they wished. Looking back to my Penang trip, I was amazed at myself. Everything had happened so fast in the few days I spent in my grandmother's goldsmith shop with my new family. Everything had fallen into place. At last I felt I could claim with confidence to be the descendant of two strong grandmothers. Their strength was part of my lineage.

I walked into the coffeeshop and ordered an iced coffee. When it came, I sucked on a piece of ice, and my thoughts, which had been racing, calmed down. I ordered a bowl of fishball noodle soup, and when it arrived, started to eat. What I had done in Penang confirmed that I had discarded my timid self. My old self-confidence, the confidence I had before I married Robert, had returned. Hasn't it? I wanted to ask Meng. I ate slowly, slurping up the strands of white rice noodles as I thought. Such a change had not happened all of a sudden. Change took time. And intention. 'Intent guides our every action,' Meng always said whenever he tried to teach me the slow graceful movements of tai chi. I wished he were seated in front of me and I could discuss with him all the thoughts and memories flooding into my head now.

I ate another mouthful of noodles and bit into a fishball, my mind returning to the night I had walked into the dark sea intending to die. But when almost drowning, my limbs had fought against the surging waves and battled against strong currents, fighting ferociously to return to shore. Why? I longed to ask him. To hear what he would say. Was it because buried under the fog of pain and shame, unknown to my conscious mind then, my intent was to live? Not to die? To fight, not to submit to defeat?

Later when legal action had finally freed my body from abuse, fear had remained frozen in me. Unaware of the iceberg of fears buried deep inside my heart, I kept telling myself I was all right. I was fine. I was healed. Didn't I take charge of the renovation of the flat? Didn't I make all the decisions on my own?

'I've started to go out and shop now,' I told my counsellor. 'I'm healed. I don't think I need to see you anymore.'

'Your mom is all right now,' I told Janice. 'I'm no longer timid and afraid as before,' I assured her. 'Didn't I stand up to that arrogant eye doctor?' I crowed. And we laughed when I retold the story of my rudeness to the ophthalmologist.

But an iceberg takes a long time to melt. Years in fact.

I sucked another ice cube from my coffee. Felt the ice melting slowly in my mouth as my perception of that night changed. I could see how my sudden angry cry of 'No!' against Meng's proposal was the cry of fear. Fear of the future. If Meng were here in front of me in the coffeeshop, I would tell him so right now. Tell him I was still a prisoner of my fears. He would understand.

I pushed away my noodles, finished my iced coffee, took out my phone and rang Meng in Hong Kong. One, two, three… I counted the ringing tones as I left the shop and walked through the crowded walkway with the phone pressed against my ear. Too excited to sit down, I kept on walking. Pick it up, Meng, pick it up. Please answer the phone. At the umpteenth ring I had to admit defeat. He wasn't going to take my call. I switched off and kept walking. I couldn't stop. Couldn't bear to return to my empty apartment.

That blazing afternoon, I walked to all the places he and I had been. The community centre where he taught Cantonese opera. The Kreta Ayer People's Theatre where he and I had stood in the rain, recalling our performances in the old theatre before it was pulled down and rebuilt. Why didn't he answer the phone? Bitterly disappointed with him one minute, and the next with myself, I knew I was to blame. I had been blinded by my fears that night. Fear of the past repeating itself. Fear of the unknown future.

'*Mea culpa! Mea culpa! Mea culpa!* Through my fault, through my fault, through my most grievous fault!' I muttered softly the traditional Catholic prayer of contrition as I walked, and kept walking despite the afternoon's scorching heat and humidity. As I edged past crowds of people at the bus stop, their eyes seemed to mock me. I kept walking. I walked as far as Tiong Bahru where the temple of the Monkey God stood at the corner of the road, a grim reminder of a time when my heart was young and fearless, but in middle age, it was afraid. What was I afraid of? Of spending the rest of my life with Meng? Or not having him by my side? Or that he would slap me after we'd lived together a few years? Or was I afraid that I would need him too much? Grow too dependent on him? Was that it? What then? What? Why couldn't I make up my mind? Don't I love him? I felt foolish. I was no longer young. At my age I should know what I wanted.

I walked that day till the sun was setting, slipping behind the blocks of high rises and shophouses. Till exhausted and thirsty I walked back to Jin Swee through the shady park under the rain trees, and sat down on the stone bench, and watched the city's noisy crows flying in the rain trees, making a racket as they fought and argued before nestling down for the night. An exhausted emptiness filled me. I felt old and lonely. I got up and headed home.

In the lift lobby I stopped to check my letterbox. Inside, was a letter from Hong Kong.

54

Heart beating fast, I closed the door and locked it. Then I looked at the letter in my hand. Read my name on the envelope, written in Chinese characters in a neat straight style. How very old fashioned, how like him to write like one of his characters in opera. The letter had been sent by fast mail. Why didn't he phone or email me? It would have been faster. I turned the envelope over. His address in Hong Kong was printed on the back. On the front he had pasted several colourful Hong Kong stamps. The letter felt a little bulky. I took a small knife from the kitchen and slit open the envelope. There were six sheets of thin paper. I took them into the living room, sat down in the armchair, and read the vertical rows of his neatly written Chinese words.

Dearest Intimate.
I hope you will not think the greeting inappropriate.

Please accept my apologies for the long silence. When Ling told me that you had phoned to enquire my whereabouts, I knew you were concerned about me. I was comforted but I didn't want to worry you with events here in Hong Kong.

It has been a very chaotic, frightening, frantic time for me. My emotions were turned upside down. I thought I was going to lose my beloved Suk Mei. And one night we did come very close to losing her. Richard, my son-in-law, was so distressed. He felt so helpless at one stage, after talking to the specialist doctors. Everything was left to me. The baby's birth had been extremely difficult. Suk Mei had to have an operation immediately after the birth. She was placed in intensive care for two weeks. Two of the longest, worrisome weeks for Richard and me. After that, she had to stay two more weeks in the hospital before she and the baby were allowed to come home. You can imagine how I felt during those days. The doctors had found a hole in her heart. And that had led to other findings and complications too difficult for me to explain here.

No wonder my poor daughter was always pale and tired when she was a teenager. I blame myself. I should have been more careful. I was her father. But I had paid more attention to my opera than to my daughter. I had left her in the care of her maternal grandmother. My poor Mei. She lost a lot of blood. Had to have two blood transfusions. She was very pale and worn out when she came home, and needed a lot of care. I wanted to look after her myself. Richard is half Canadian half Chinese. He knows nothing about the kind of food Suk Mei needs after childbirth and a serious operation. I stayed with them to cook for her the special dishes and herbal soups that Cantonese women have to eat to grow strong again after giving birth. Richard's job was to see to Benny my older grandson who is three years old and goes to a nursery. The poor child. He missed his mother so. He refused to go to his nursery. Kept crying for his mommy. Everything was in a mess.

Thanks to the mercy of Heaven, the baby is a healthy boy. But he cries a lot in the night and keeps us awake. The doctor says he has colic. Nothing to worry about. What I worry about most is Suk Mei's health. I am very fortunate that I have good friends in the opera world. When Suk Mei came home, the women cooked special strengthening soups for her every day. And brought pots of pig trotters stew cooked in dark vinegar and old ginger to warm her blood. Suk Mei needed a lot of rest, so Richard took leave from the bank to help out. But he is a senior bank executive. He had to return to the office now and then for important meetings. Often I was the sole general holding the fort without an army.

By the time you receive my letter, I would have moved back to my own apartment. Richard's mother has flown in from Toronto to stay with them. I still go over to my daughter's apartment every day to take Benny to his nursery. And I still go to the market every morning, do the shopping, and cook the dishes my daughter likes to eat. Just like when she was a little girl.

After my wife passed away, it was just the two of us at first – father and daughter. That was when I learnt to cook for Suk Mei's sake. My earnings from my opera engagements could not afford employing someone to look after her. I stopped working. I cooked and washed and cared for my little girl myself until her maternal grandmother came to live with us so I could return to the opera stage. From that time onwards, my family in Hong Kong had been just the three of us until Suk Mei's granny passed away. And then we were two again until she met and married Richard. In a few months Suk Mei and Richard and my two grandsons would leave Hong Kong. Then I will be on my own. But don't worry. I am just stating a fact. Not eliciting sympathy. Such changes in a parent's life are normal. Like birds, our children must leave their parents' nest. The parent understands. Nevertheless the heart feels the pain of parting.

Things are smoother now that Richard's mother has arrived. The haphazardness and untidiness in a household run by two men and a toddler are over. She has engaged a helper who does the cleaning and laundry while she does the cooking. Now our meals are on time. The table and chairs are clean. Benny's books and toys are kept by bedtime. And clean clothes are taken out of the dryer, folded and put away. The baby is no longer crying as much as before. I am very grateful to Richard's mother. She is Cantonese and knows how to cook herbal soups. I know Suk Mei will be in good hands when she leaves to live in Canada. Richard's bank is transferring him to Vancouver. Richard's parents will move to Vancouver to live near them and help out with the children. I can see that Suk Mei is excited about going, and sad at the same time because she has to leave her father. I reminded her that departures are inevitable. I had left her when I returned to Singapore to take care of her Uncle Tony for two years. And Tony has left me. Her mother had left us. Her granny had left us. And we had learnt to let go. Letting go of those we love is part of living, isn't it? Life is full of departures and farewells. Sometimes, when sleep eludes me, I wonder how many farewells, departures and rejections can a man bear. I fear the day I have to bid my daughter, my only child, goodbye.

These past several weeks I have had some time to think. Many nights as I lie in bed unable to close my eyes, my thoughts have turned to you. To us, actually. To that night when I asked you to marry me. I admit I was angry and selfish that night. And I apologise deeply. I must confess it is not just the fear for my daughter's life and the chaos that ensued that had held me back from phoning you or writing to you. It is also the past and recent events that had hurt and swamp my head each time the phone rings and I know it is you. Then once again just as I am about to press Receive, I hear your voice and that emphatic angry 'No!'

The humiliation of being rejected twice. The second rejection had knifed my heart most deeply. Humiliation and anger had blocked out thoughts of you. Of how you might feel. Like a thick monstrous fog, anger and humiliation filled my entire head. I could not imagine another's pain.

When the fog finally cleared, I saw that your sufferings at the hand of another man had maimed your heart. Of him you have not spoken much, and I have not asked about him. Not because I do not wish to know. It's more because I do not wish to hurt you by probing your pain. Like a finger poking into a deep wound.

Memories hurt. The deeper the hurt, the deeper our silence. In silence, our hurts sink and secrete themselves in the crevices of the unconscious mind. And there in the dark they fester like pus and sores till one day they explode all of a sudden in NO! So emphatic, so forceful you ran out of the apartment. Away from the man who had loved you since you were seventeen.

I am very sorry I had hurt you. In your experience, marriage entails great suffering. The 'No!' was to preserve yourself and your freedom. I see it now. But I could not see it that night. Hurt and humiliated, I could not see what you were going through as I waited for you to come back. When you did not return to the flat I left to look for you. At the playground, the coffeeshop, and the supermarket where you often went to let the air-conditioning cool your anger after an argument with me. I walked up to the park certain you would be there. It was raining hard by then. Finding you not in the park, I returned to my flat, drenched, angry and tired. That was why I did not call you. Then Richard's sudden phone call threw me off course, and I took the first flight out of Singapore. Full of fears and worries, and guilt. I should have returned to Hong Kong sooner. I was furious with myself and you. You were the only reason I stayed on in Singapore after Tony's funeral. I shouldn't have left Suk Mei and Hong Kong for so long.

In a few months, it will be Suk Mei's turn to do the leaving. I am not sure if I have come full circle. But I have decided to stay on in Hong Kong after her departure. I doubt I will come back to Singapore. Not because I am angry with you. Not because I no longer love you. (For I do most dearly.) It is more because I love the stage. Cantonese opera is my life. It is not enough for me to teach a few classes in Singapore and put up one opera a year with government subsidy. That is not living my art. That is putting my art on the drip. My art and I have to live.

In Hong Kong I will have many more opportunities to perform than in Singapore. Almost every weekend, an opera is performed here often to full houses in the small theatres in Kowloon or Sha Tin outside the city centre. In Hong Kong there is a large audience base that supports this Intangible Cultural Treasure, this Cantonese operatic art. All the skills I have learnt from Master Wu and your Por Por flourish and grow here with or without government subsidies. I am not getting younger. I don't have another fifty-five years to hone my skills.

Dearest Intimate, do you understand? Will you try to understand?

I pray you will not only understand and forgive this opera artiste, but you will also finish the translation of your Por Por's journal and write. Like me, you do not have another fifty years.

I am not saying goodbye. We will see each other when we see each other.

As the saying goes: 有缘千里見 *Yau yueen cheen lei geen*
If there is affinity even a thousand li apart we will meet.

I folded the letter, and returned the six pages to the envelope. Then I closed all the windows, went into the bedroom and packed a suitcase.

While waiting for the taxi to take me to the airport, I reread his letter and changed my mind.

Focus, focus. I hear him say. Lift hands. Lean forward. White stork flashes its wings. Brush knee and twist step. Step forward and strike with fist. Tai-chi teases my concentration and impatience. The early morning breeze blows away my sweat. And scatters nocturnal longings.

There's no giving up. I meet with Liang *Lao Shi* in the park every morning to learn the slow fluid movements with a group of neighbours. Evenings, I go for walks. Daily I write and wait. I wait for the mail, and I write in the night.

After the monsoon rains the angsana trees are flowering again.
The red kerenga ants, addicted to the golden blooms, are out in
full force. Somehow another year has slipped past.

55

I am in the auditorium of the Kreta Ayer People's Theatre. It's full house again despite a week of bad weather. Meng and his troupe from Hong Kong are performing *Forty Years of Cherished Love,* the acclaimed opera based on the tragic love between the twelfth-century Southern Song poet, Lu Yu, and his wife, Tang Wan.

Meng is reprising his role as the poet Lu Yu who is forced by his mother to divorce his beloved wife Tang Wan because she is unable to bear him a child. Three years later, at a chance encounter in the Shen Garden, he meets Tang Wan and her second husband drinking wine in the pavilion. By then, Lu Yu has also remarried. Eyes brimming with tears, singing a long aria of how she came to be remarried, Tang Wan offers him a cup of wine, and leaves. Heartbroken, Lu Yu drinks the bitter cup and finishes the whole jug of wine. Drunk, he sings his aria of pain and regret, and calls for brush and ink. He takes up the brush and writes in his drunken state on the pavilion wall his famous poem "The Phoenix Hairpin".

红酥手，黄籘酒，
满城春色宫墙柳。
东风恶，欢情薄，
一怀愁绪，几年离索。
错，错，错！

Blushing soft hand, yellow cane wine,
Spring in the city, willows by the walls.
Cruel the east wind, happiness worn thin
A bosom of sorrows, years of loneliness apart.
Wrong! Wrong! Wrong!

In the darkened theatre, the audience's hearts go out to him, the captive of a despotic filial tradition. Heartbroken, Lu Yu leaves his family and home to fight in the war in the north.

In the next scene, Tang Wan returns to the pavilion. When she reads Lu Yu's poem on the wall, she is so moved she immediately writes the reply, a verse below his, written in the same form. She returns home, sick with longing and regret, and eventually dies of a broken heart.

In the final scene of the opera, forty years has passed. A defeated General Lu Yu with a grey beard returns to the same pavilion in Shen Garden. He comes upon Tang Wan's poem.

春如旧，人空瘦，
泪痕红浥鲛绡透。
桃花落，闲池阁。
山盟虽在，锦书难托。
莫，莫，莫！

Unchanged is spring, but her person has grown thin
Tears stain cheeks, soak silk handkerchief
Peach blossoms fall, pond and pavilion deserted
An oath firm as mountains never again to be uttered.
Never! Never! Never!

The auditorium is a sea of smiling teary faces when the lights come on. Wave after wave of applause resounds in the theatre as the troupe takes their final bows. When Meng comes out with the *fah dan*, who plays his beloved wife, Tang Wan, there is a standing ovation, and the applause is the loudest, the clapping going on and on and on.

The troupe has performed the opera for three nights, and tonight, their final performance, is the best. I was in the theatre for all the three nights, my attention focussed on Meng. And what the old lady in Hong Kong told Janice all those years ago has turned out to be true. Meng's performance each night is different. The variations in his singing and acting are distinct. The incredible precision and control of his voice, the restrained emotions, and the vocal power and emotional depth as he sang the last aria is so moving.

Forty years have gone by...
The willow in Shen Garden is so old it no longerrrrrr...

The air on stage quivers with grief. His vocal technique and emotional range are astonishing yet nuanced. An old poet, defeated in war and love, he stands on stage each night, stroking his grey beard, a master of grief and self-control. So different from the performer who sang the Abbot's role, leaping onto tables and chairs in *Madam White Snake*. In the three years since he left for Hong Kong, his art has matured like old wine. Rich in colour, emotional depth and range.

It's five in the morning. I'm lying in bed, listening to the steady sound of rain falling. It has been raining since last night. Towards morning there was a deafening crack during the thunderstorm. So deafening the sound had shot through the din and clamour of the storm, and woke me up. I knew at once it was the old rain tree. I had to get up. I had to see it before the National Park workers cordon off the park.

Outside, the sky is still dark, but the rain has petered to an insistent drizzle. I get out of bed quietly and pull on a sweater. Bringing an umbrella with me, I leave the flat and take the lift down. Splashing through the playground and puddles of rainwater and lamplight, I make my way carefully up the slope. After the week of wet weather, the moss covering the steps is treacherous. A hand holding on to the railing, and the other to my umbrella, I make my way slowly up the steps. Halfway up, I pause to listen to the sudden silence. The wind has stopped blowing.

When I reach the park, it's strangely exciting, and a shock to see the old majestic tree lying on its side, its leafy branches splayed and fractured like the limbs of the war wounded. I gaze into the dark space where the trunk should have been. Its stump with sharp broken edges stands before me in the lamplight and rain like the defeated General Lu Yu in last night's opera. And for some reason, Meng's words in one of his last letters return to me.

In old age, we fall and die. But before that, in the autumn of our
life, although sex no longer draws us, touch, that curious care
and exploration of the flesh, and the intimate heart to heart talk

in bed, the bond of companionship and care of friendship, these become most precious; and to me, that is love.

A rising wind is rustling the trees. I hold on to my umbrella. The drizzling is growing heavier. I take a last look at the majestic old tree lying on its side like a fallen emperor, and I bow my head and turn away. It has been a good forty years between us, the tree and I. I will miss its comforting shade and shadows, its outspread branches like the gnarled arms of an old grandmother welcoming her grandchild. I will miss the shushing of her leaves and the shelter she gave my grief. 'Goodbye, my friend,' I whisper. And walk back down the steps.

The sky has turned a dull slate grey. Rain is drizzling down steadily. I hold on to the railing carefully. It was installed a year ago after someone had slipped and fallen on the steps. Life in an HDB public housing estate is a series of mostly small occurrences like the fall of a man or a tree in a storm. Or like a man playing his erhu under a rain tree to accompany his wife's singing in the park. Her voice rises in the pale pink dawn spreading over the rooftops. Then one dark early morning there was a cry. Khim's husband had fallen to his death. A drug addict who stole from her, she had locked him out of their flat the previous night. No one had seen him climb over the parapet of the corridor on the twelfth floor. At the funeral, Khim did not cry. 'Heaven has eyes,' she kept murmuring during the wake. 'My children and I have suffered enough.'

However the year before when Madam Soh passed away suddenly at eighty-five, Khim had sobbed till her eyes were red and swollen. I was the one who had knocked on Auntie Soh's door. I hadn't seen her for three days. When there was no answer, I called Khim. With the help of some neighbours, we broke open the door and found Madam Soh dead on the floor. Rigor mortis had already set in. At the wake, Khim wailed.

'Four children. Two sons. Two daughters. Yet she died alone. She was like a mother to me. She looked after my children, you know, when I had to work two or three jobs to make ends meet.'

A few months later Auntie Soh's flat was put up for sale. A young couple and their toddler moved in. Seeing that I lived alone, the young couple invited me over for dinner one night. I made sure that I brought food that was halal. The young husband is a Malay Muslim, an engineer who works in the aerospace industry, and his wife is a lovely Chinese Muslim girl from Xian in northwest China.

Jin Swee's demography, like the rest of Singapore, is changing, and so is our street food, I wrote to Meng.

Let it change but I still want to eat my char kway tiao with lots of cockles and sweet red sausage, and prawn noodle soup when I return, he wrote back.

I shake off the raindrops from my umbrella before opening the gate and door softly. I don't want to wake Meng. After the opera last night, I had come home on my own instead of waiting for him like the other two nights. It being the last performance, many fans and sponsors were waiting to take group pictures and selfies with him and the troupe, and the sponsors had invited the whole troupe to a lavish supper as well.

I put away the umbrella and go into my study at the back of the kitchen. This study is a new addition to the flat, a small room that was built during Meng's absence under the government's Home Improvement Programme in Jin Swee Estate. I have been coming in here to write every morning. Some evenings I sit in this room to write to Meng before going out for a solitary supper and a walk. Often I would walk through Temple Street between its stalls and shops, and make my hurried way to the Sri Mariamman Temple to stand among the Hindu devotees and tourists, listening to the bells and chants of the Brahmin priests. How very alone and lonely I had felt then. How I had suffered during that time, yet no one, least of all, Meng, was aware of my anguish and loneliness during those three years he was away. The disappointment and anguished loneliness and longing had been unbearable at times. I pushed against it, fought it off by walking through crowded places to distract myself. But when I reached home, and shut my door, silence still fell upon me like a thick blanket. I made a cup of tea, but there was no one to drink with me. Drinking my tea alone, I often mulled over what Meng had written in his latest letter before I picked up my pen, and wrote to him.

When I received that first letter from him, my first impulse was to book a flight and fly to him. But then on rereading his long letter, reading it slowly and more carefully, my impulse died. He needed time to be alone, time to grow in his operatic art. If I were to fly over, although welcomed, I would be a distraction. So I cancelled my flight and wrote to him instead. He wrote back quickly. And I replied just as fast. And willy-nilly a correspondence grew between us over the months as if the telephone and email did not exist.

The sight of his pages of handwritten Chinese characters with their solid horizontal and vertical strokes and elegant lines and flourishes moved me in a way I could not explain. Like reading poetry, I suppose. His strokes of black ink on thin sheets of off-white paper moved me. His strokes had such grace and beauty. There was careful thought given to the content he penned. As I read, I imagined him sitting up after a night's rehearsal or performance at the theatre, a solitary figure at his desk writing like me late into the night in his apartment which, he told me, overlooked Hong Kong city.

I found myself looking forward to his letters. A feeling of anticipation would grip me on the day when his letter was due. If I found his letter in my letterbox, I would take it up to my flat, unopened, wondering in the lift what his reaction was to my last letter. When I reached home, I did not open his letter immediately. I left it on the kitchen table, my companion while I prepared dinner. As though he was in my kitchen, watching me. Like what he used to do, sitting at the table watching me cook. After I had eaten, I would make a cup of tea and take it and his letter into the living room. Then, and only then, would I open his letter carefully with a letter-opener, and pull out the three to five thin pages of off-white paper covered with his beautifully handwritten Chinese words.

I turn away from the falling rain outside the window. Open the drawer of my desk, and take out the box of Meng's letters, written in Chinese over our three years' separation. My letters to him written in English are with him. If I were to put my letters together with his, our combined pages will be a record of our three years of intense epistolary bilingual conversations and courtship. Such an old-fashioned word, courtship. But Meng is an old soul.

> ... and, dearest, if we do speak on the phone, our words no matter how intimate will dissipate once they are spoken. Our memory of them will change over time, and their meanings in our memory will be coloured by our current mood and sentiments. But the written word is permanent. Forever on the page. That is why in the history of the world, the wilful

destruction of books and official records is such a crime. And in the world of fiction, and opera, the burning of a lover's letters is a symbol of great pain and betrayal.

And my dearest intimate.

When I write to you, or read your letters, my mind is fully engaged with you and your words on the page. You are inside my head, more present to me in your handwritten words, and more known to me than when you were physically present. When we write in the quiet of our room, in the solitude of our mind, we reveal truths that are seldom uttered. When I write to you forming my words sometimes slowly, deep in thought, sometimes in a rush of eagerness to respond to something you have written, it is as if the feelings in my heart are flowing or rushing from my heart and mind through my arm and hand to my pen. The ink is like my blood. Just like in Cantonese opera, there are scenes in which the hero or heroine bites her finger and writes her letter with her blood. Writing by hand with a writing brush or pen is a very personal act.

When I hold your handwritten letter, it is as if I am holding your hand. As my eyes follow the curls and curves of the English words, I hear your voice trying to reassure me that you are well when in fact you are on the brink of an illness but you do not wish to worry me.

Darling, may I call you darling now? I hold your letter in my hand, and pray you are much better. The touch and fragrance of the thin blue paper you write on, the sight of your handwritten words stir multiple sensations and emotions in me. Our handwriting is like us, full of thought and will, like a green sapling pushing through, revealing truths and beauty and grace, and things we are often too shy, too ashamed, too afraid to utter in person to the other.

Tonight I hold your letter close to my chest. Then I fold it and place it in the drawer of my bedside table. Then I fall asleep knowing you are near. And you will understand what I am trying to say to you tonight.

On nights when your next letter has not yet arrived I take your latest letter out and read it again. The sight of your handwriting refreshes me. Especially on a night when my performance is disappointing and not up to standard. I don't think you will be surprised to know that my first teacher and mentor is still your great grandfather. Master Wu is still inside my head. Stern and exacting as ever. When I recall his critical eyes, hear his critical voice, self-doubts plague me. Each night before I go on stage, I say a prayer to the Patron Gods of Opera and to him. Will I remember my lyrics? Will my voice rise and fall at the right place as natural as water flowing smooth as a brook or forceful as a waterfall? I know not where the force and frenetic energy of performance come from. When the drums roll and cymbals sound, nothing else matters. I walk through the *Fu Doh Muen*, the actors' invisible gate, and out onto the stage, transformed. I turn and move and sing. Not as I, the Meng you know, not the Meng I know, but as another. Like waves my heart and voice rise and fall indifferent to my fate till the curtains fall at the end of the night. Then backstage, I take off my costume, remove the makeup from my face and drink some tea. Gradually I return to my normal self, bid goodnight to the other actors, wade through the crowds outside, get into the car and I come home to your latest letter.

And it is as though you are here in person at the door to welcome me home and take me into your arms, no matter how good or poor my performance has been. At that moment, nothing matters. But you and what you wrote. I take a hot bath, slurp up a warm bowl of porridge, and settle down in bed to read and reread your handwritten words. Then I take out my pen and write to you in bed, my love, and it is as if we are talking intimately in bed in each other's arms. The intimacy of a handwritten letter! Or is it our imagination that gives it this intimacy? You're the writer, please tell me. And darling, I know you will smile as you read these words.

Outside my window the rain has stopped. The light is changing as the sun comes out from behind the grey clouds. I put Meng's letter back into the box with the other letters and sit looking out at the changing clouds. In my mind his solitary figure writing in bed, overlooking the lights of Hong Kong city, his hand wielding his fountain pen like a Chinese brush, forming the curves and strokes with the irregular quirks that speak far more fluently than if he were to speak to me in person. He was sometimes tongue-tied, faltering when we were in bed and often economic to the point of incoherence in his speech. He would never have said, *Darling, may I call you darling now?*

Three years of reading each other's handwritten letters every night before we went to bed, an intimacy had sprouted between us. I have yet to tell him this. But it's hard to tell him in person what palpitations and great joy I had reading his letters, what the tactile feel of paper and its creases, the visual beauty of the cursive strokes of his Chinese words had had on me. And how in writing to him, I had slowly found my way to writing, *my dearest Intimate.*

But I believe he already knew. Two months before his return, my book based on Por Por's journal was published in English. And I had titled it *Dearest Intimate.*

Meng called me from Hong Kong. His first phone call in three years.

'I'm so proud of you, Yin! So very proud of you!'

Like Janice he could not fly back for the book's launch at the National Archives. Their absence however did not upset me. I had finished my book. Nothing else had mattered against the fact of this. I had accomplished what I had set out to do after my divorce. What surprised me most at the time was a congratulatory card from Robert. At the back of the card, he had scribbled, *'FYI, I have retired. Am attending AA now. Giving up drink.'*

I was happy for him, and sent him a card to wish him well.

Hmmm… I smell coffee.

I put back the box of Meng's letters into my drawer. The unexpected smell of fragrant toast and coffee from the kitchen makes me smile. It reminds me of old times. I call out.

'Are you making breakfast? You're up early.'

'You gave me a fright. Where were you earlier?'

I come out of the study and go into the kitchen.

'I was up in the park this morning.'

'So early and in the rain?'

I sit down at the kitchen table.

'I had to say goodbye to our rain tree.'

'Oh? What happened?'

'It fell during last night's storm.'

'*Ahh*. I must've slept through it.'

A long moment of silence. Our minds travelling back to that remote night when I had run out of the flat to the rain tree. A painful guilt still troubles my conscience. As if he knows what I'm thinking, he walks over and wraps his arms around me. I lean into him and put my hand up to stroke his unshaven chin.

'Shall we eat?'

We sit at the kitchen table facing each other just like before. As if he had never left. He places a piece of toast on a plate and pushes it towards me. And pours out two cups of coffee – a dash of milk and no sugar in mine, two spoons of sugar and no milk in his.

'Slept well?' I spread butter on my toast.

'Like a baby.'

'You were superb last night.'

'I had to work extra hard for that role. First I had to convince the producer and director to do *Forty Years of Cherished Love* in Singapore.'

'With its theme of regret. I know, I got the message.' I reach for his hand and squeeze it.

His mouth is full of toast. We eat in silence, and he finishes his coffee.

'The troupe is flying home at eleven this morning. I'll go over and have a cup of tea with them in the hotel before they leave. I'll be back soon. You won't run off this time, will you?'

I rise and go over to his side of the table, and kiss him on the lips.

℘—ℭ

THE AUTHOR

Suchen Christine Lim is an award-winning author of novels, short stories, children's stories and a non-fiction book. She was awarded the Southeast Asia Write Award in 2012 for her body of work.

Fistful of Colours, winner of the inaugural Singapore Literature Prize, is cited as a classic Singapore novel. Later *A Bit of Earth* and *The Lies That Build A Marriage* were short listed for the same prize. Her debut novel, *Rice Bowl*, is considered a landmark novel on post-independence Singapore. *The River's Song* was chosen as a "100 Best Books of 2015" Kirkus Reviews (USA) and Book of the Month in *The Sunday Times*, Singapore.

Awarded a Fulbright grant, she was a Fellow in the University of Iowa's International Writing Program, and later its Writer in Residence. She was a Fellow in Creative Writing at the Nanyang Technological University, Singapore, and has held writing residencies in the US, UK, Australia, South Korea, the Philippines, Vietnam and Myanmar.